Praise for *Travers Corners* (The Lyons Press, 1998):

"A debut collection that offers a brilliant image of small-town life in Montana."

—*Kirkus Reviews*

"...a charming debut collection of stories. Waldie builds his tales around character, creating a small community of homespun folk who are quintessentially American and just a bit eccentric."

—*Publishers Weekly*

"This wonderful collection of Montana short stories made me want to drop everything and light out for Big Sky Country and never look back. *Travers Corners* is a terrific debut by a gifted writer, who gets the contemporary American West just exactly right on every page."

—Howard Frank Mosher

"The book has a little of the feel of *The Last Picture Show*. Waldie also manages a paradox, demonstrating that the decent, more-or-less ordinary people in this pretty nice place live lives of consequence, knit one to another by community, history, affection or animus. They matter."

—*Fly Rod & Reel*

"Visit *Travers Corners* for a good read; it's a town full of people worth knowing."

—*EXPO Book Review*

". . . a lovely tongue-in-cheek look at make-believe small-town America."

—*Arizona Daily Star*

"Like the characters he writes about, Waldie's pace is slow and deliberate, and he demonstrates why the journey is the destination. He leads the way to a tiny corner of the world where we can refresh ourselves and still make it home for dinner. Travers Corners is just such a place."

—*Woodland Hills Daily News*

"With a shrewd eye for rural characters, the book may remind some readers of *Winesburg, Ohio*, *Lake Wobegon Days*, or *A River Runs Through It.*"

—Billings, Montana, *Gazette*

"Scott Waldie has captured the essence of a small Montana town and the characters who live there. Written with warmth and wit, these stories will make you long for a second home like Travers Corners."

—*Montana Outdoors*

"Best of all, the warmth isn't sappy and the wit isn't just tinsel. Both are generated from a generous understanding of human nature."

—*Montana Magazine*

Praise for *Return to Travers Corners* (The Lyons Press, 2002):

"Waldie's gentle stories are filled with love for Montana, and the people who live there because they love it, and the way that love spills over onto others who are just passing through. Travers Corners might not be especially realistic, but it gives readers a fine place to visit."

—*The Tribune* (Great Falls, Montana)

"Waldie creates a town with the depth that only richly talented storytellers can accomplish. Waldie's characters live life to the fullest. And so do we when we read this collection. It's a place where we can go—and return to again and again."

—*Big Sky Journal*

"The book is a thoroughly enjoyable journey to somewhere in Montana where everyone can be trusted and the fishing is legendary."

—*The Denver Post & Rocky Mountain News*

"Honesty and integrity are foundations of the West, and Waldie does a fine job in portraying these in all his stories The charm and wit of the writing carry us along and keep us chuckling to ourselves."

—*The Missoulian*

"Rhapsodic, resplendent reflections. . . . Immediately entertaining for those to whom fly fishing is synonymous with religion, Waldie's stories are equally appealing to anyone whose only fishing experience involves the Mrs. Paul's section of the grocery freezer."

—*Booklist*

"Waldie once again celebrates the simple pleasures of rural Montana, returning to the fictional town he depicted in his debut short story collection (*Travers Corners*) for another set of cozy tales. Waldie reprises the friendly, optimistic narration of his first collection. . . . This well-crafted sequel more than measures up to the standards set by its predecessor."

—*Publishers Weekly*

"The simplicity of the West beckons with every tale."

—*The Idaho Statesman*

Travers Corners: The Final Chapters

Scott Waldie

THE LYONS PRESS
Guilford, Connecticut
An imprint of The Globe Pequot Press

The Lyons Press is an imprint of The Globe Pequot Press.

10 9 8 7 6 5 4 3 2 1

Printed in the United States of America

ISBN 1-59228-574-0

Library of Congress Cataloging-in-Publication Data is available on file.

To my wife, Jane, for my grandsons, Cole and Dominico,
and dedicated to the memory of Bud Kanouse

~

Contents

~

Acknowledgments

Thanks to Cam Cooper, Greg Campbell, Rose Marye Boudreaux, Mike and Sherry Chandler, Jim and Jan Wallace, Frank and Kay Colwell, Jim and Pam Pappenfus, Terry Pearce, Tom and Doug Steding, John and Judy Brendel, Eddie Scott, Mandy Kennedy, Scott and Julia Russell, Jesse Carroll, Sharon Glick, Dale Forbes, Bob Kaufman, David Kolln, Carl Rimby, Bill Hight, Ridge and Marge Harlan, C. L. and Connie Clark, Richard and Linda Sutton, and a special thank you to Lilly Golden.

Travers Corners: The Final Chapters

~

Introduction

From The Journals of Traver C. Clark

August 4, 1873—

My train arrived in Denver yesterday. It was two days late. I telegraphed Father yesterday with that news and he was not pleased. Our train was held in Ogallala over the weekend because of a train derailment outside of Fort Morgan. Consequently, I missed the Monday meeting with the shareholders. Somehow a train's derailment two hundred miles away was my fault in Father's eyes. I am now instructed to stay in Denver for the next few days, to meet the investors individually.

But the day was not a total loss. Last night after dinner at the hotel I met this most extraordinary man, one D. Downey, a giant Scotsman and a fellow fisherman. This prompted me to run upstairs to my room and get my new Leonard fly rod. It is a beautiful thing and never has it been fished.

The rod looked positively tiny in D. Downey's hand, but the way he held the rod, delicately, and by the way he waved it around, appreciating its action and balance, I could sense he was a man who knew about fishing.

We were instant friends. He is such a grand character. The kind of man who's known and liked by all in downtown Denver. He talked about the salmon fishing at home in Scotland and about the fishing he'd heard about north of the Yellowstone. "Trout as long as the length of ya," he said, "and so plentiful, ya canna see the river's bottom for the profusion."

He makes it all sound so exciting. I would love to go.

We are going to have supper again tonight and we are to be joined by D. Downey's sister, Carrie. She sounds lovely.

Supper—1.25
Bar tab—19.00

P.S. Drinking with D. Downey proved to be very expensive. His capacity for whiskey is great while his funds are small.

That was the very first entry into *The Journals of Traver C. Clark*, a five-volume set, a daily diary Traver C. Clark kept until his death in 1926. Most all of you, this being the third book in the trilogy, *The Final Chapters*, already know much of the town's history having learned it in the first two volumes, *Travers Corners* and *Return to Travers Corners*. If you haven't read the first two books or at least one of them then you really don't have too much business in this one. But, if you are just new to Travers with this collection in your hand, or you have a memory like most of us, that history will be recounted in the first story.

Know that all is how you left it up and down the Elkheart Valley, the Elkheart River, and Carrie Creek flowing through town; the fly fishing is better than ever, and around Travers everyone is in place. Junior is behind his counter in the pharmacy over at McCracken's General Store. Dolores is at her beauty parlor. Doc is seeing patients down at the Elkheart Valley Clinic. Sal and Sarah are tending the Tin Cup Bar and Cafe. Henry is moving cattle.

And Jud is more than likely in the workshop up at the Boat Works unless the trout are on the rise.

August 4, 1873, wasn't just the first entry into Traver's journals, it also turned out to be the first day in the history of Travers Corners, Montana, a mountain town born from the love of fly fishing, a friendship, and a bamboo rod. A small, out-of-the-way town where nothing much has happened since, barring the day Herbert Hoover stopped for gas.

Introduction

From The Journals of Traver C. Clark

September 28, 1923—

There's to be a celebration in Travers Corners today and I am afraid Albie and I are at the center of it. Naturally, the whole thing was John Rossiter's idea. John, a man who could never let a sleeping dog do just that, and who is simultaneously burdened by having more dollars than sense, decided some months ago that what the town needed was a dedication of some sort, a ceremonial to the town's founding fathers. And what did he end up with? A damned monument! The great unveiling of which is this afternoon and it will stand down by the river. I find the whole thing embarrassing. The men who died fighting in Germany deserve a monument. Abraham Lincoln deserves a monument. But three guys on nothing more than a holiday, an exploratory lark centered around a little fishing, and who just happened to stumble into and thereby discover this small valley half a century back don't deserve a monument. But that's what Albie, D. Downey, God rest his soul, and I did—fifty years ago today.

We were quite a group—me, the East Coast delinquent traveling on trust fund money; Albie, part Indian and our guide; and Carrie's brother, the one and only D. Downey. Of course we weren't the Elkheart Valley's first discoverers. The Blackfoot and Shoshone have that distinction, beating our arrival by about five thousand years into this part of Montana. A dedication to them would make a fine monument. But we were the white men and the ones that stuck our names on a land the Indians couldn't imagine owning: Albie's Pass, Mount D. Downey, and Travers Corners. Carrie, in her absence, had a stream named after her. We didn't think at the time that any of the names would stick.

And now we're about to get honored *because we had the arrogance to name nature, a wildness that is far too grand to go by any man's name. And that's just exactly what I told John Rossiter when he came to me and proposed this cockeyed idea.*

But he and the town were dead set on this dedication and now they're going to get it. Carrie has just called me downstairs. It's time to go. Have to give a speech today on top of everything else. In my seventy-two years I have never given a speech. Had to do it I guess because it was a damn sure thing Albie wasn't going to give a speech. The man has never put more than nine words together in his life. It's a miracle that he's coming to town for all of this, but he promised he'd be there. I only wish D. Downey could be here as well.

September 29—It wasn't nearly as bad as I thought it would be. The whole town was there and the newspaper in Helena sent a man with a camera to take it all in. John Rossiter did waffle on about our place in American history, and according to him Albie and I are just behind Columbus and slightly ahead of Admiral Byrd on the list of discovery.

It was good to have the family there, Carrie most of all. Albie showed up and remained quiet through the entire ceremony, as is his custom, quiet except at the unveiling. When John removed the sheet to reveal the marker, which admittedly at first sight looked more like a tombstone, he leaned over and whispered to me, "Funny, I don't feel dead."

The marker, albeit a little funereal in tone, perhaps it's the marble, was only there to hold the bronze placard. The piece of sculpture, an embossed bronze, shows the three of us, our horses, and the river in the background at our original campsite fifty years ago. Looking at it brought back a rush of memories. We were just three young men out for an adventure, a lark on my father's money, and now half a century later we're an historical marker. The words on the placard were simply the date of our first arrival and our names. Under the heading of Founding Fathers it read, "These three braved the elements so that we might have a home." It was a nice sentiment, malarkey of course, but nice. We weren't in the valley looking for a home—we were looking for trout.

I look out from my window and see the ranch Carrie and I carved out of a wilderness, and I wonder if anyone should be allowed to carve into the wilderness. I remember the day we came into this valley, our supplies and time dwindling, how we swam the horses over to our campsite, and where we stayed for an extra day simply because it was just too beautiful to leave. Now I look down from the ranch house past the carriage house down to the General Store and Town Bridge and on to the river and where we camped fifty years ago. But here I am sitting, writing at the edge of a town bearing my name and now there's a monument to me—funny how things sometimes work out.

There was talk today about hard wire coming into the valley. The Elkheart electrified—things will change then. Too many changes. Sometimes I think the Earth is spinning faster than she was meant to go.

~

PBS, the Pentagon, and Neal's Spring Creek

Travers Corners was nothing more than a western outline, a ghost-towned shadow against a sky lit by nothing but the new moon half hidden in the storm. Not a trace of light anywhere. The Elkheart Valley had been without power for three hours.

Up on the hill above town at the Carrie Creek Boat Works and Guide Service, the winds, stronger than any Jud could remember in recent years, were causing the old timbers of the carriage house to groan and creak. It was nearing midnight and Jud was still awake, but not because he wanted to be. He, by himself, could have slept through the winds and all the thunder and lightning the night could offer, but Annie the Wonderlab, on the other hand, never could handle this electrical phenomenon. Eighty pounds of shivering, whimpering, yellow retriever lying the full length of him, howling with the rolling thunder, whining after every flash of lightning, understandably prevented him from nodding off.

"So this is how you guys came to be called yellow Labradors. Not for the color of your coat but the color of your spine." He rubbed Annie's ears hoping that the storm would soon pass so that she would calm down and he could get some sleep.

The winds ended and the rains came. His stomach began to growl, growling by way of hunger since tonight's dinner had been meager, and growling by way of complaint because this evening's fare, though it may have been meager, was thoroughly tasteless and evenly overcooked. Cooking was Jud's shortest suit. Forks of lightning surrounded the Boat Works, and for a second Jud's room was brighter than daylight. A deafening thunderclap came in an instant and Annie wiggled up his bed to tremble even harder and nervously lick his face. The summer storm had been a long time coming and it would be long time leaving. He was in for a night of it.

Then he remembered a quart of ice cream in the freezer, Rocky Road imperiled by the outage and in danger of melting. Needing something to eat, coinciding with something that needed to be eaten, it was looked upon by Jud as a midnight destiny of sorts, a chocolate destiny starting immediately. Blankets with Labradors were sent flying. Relighting the kerosene lamp that had guided him to his room, Jud headed down the steep and dark stairwell to the kitchen hindered greatly by Annie, who thought the safest place on the stairs would be between his legs.

Jud's kitchen, for the most part, was ornamental, a room in which to keep his beer cold. The pantry was as empty as it was dark. There was no need for a refrigerator light since there was nothing to see. But, in the dark recesses of the freezer, resting atop something wrapped in white paper dating from the Reagan administration was the brand new quart of Rocky Road. He filled a bowl full.

Sitting down at the kitchen table watching the storm put on its show he laughed at his bare cupboards, but cooking only for himself, with Sarah's cooking and the Tin Cup Cafe just a shortcut down the hill into town, would be silly not to mention nauseating.

The lights flickered on and off then on. The few lights that were normally lit in town at this hour were on once more. The clock radio, short-circuited and fooled by the outage, switched on. The digital dial flashed on and off as the late-night DJ from Helena gave the time and weather. ". . . this weather will be with us off and on through late tomorrow. It's five after twelve and here's an update on two stories we have been following: those recent bombings in . . ."

Jud switched off the news. While watching an electric storm, eating Rocky Road with his best friend nosing his plate, life was too good to hear of war. He reached behind him to his vest hanging on the back of the chair and pulled out his pocket watch. It read 10:14. "That's about right, Annie girl." His grandfather's Waltham, a pocket watch with a time all its own, lost about twenty minutes on the hour during the summer months and lost about fifteen minutes during the winter. The difference, Jud theorized, was the change in barometric pressures on the wheels, balances, and springs. But then there were those instances when the aged watch would become completely erratic, doing everything but run backward. When this happened Jud could do nothing but blame the timepiece's temperaments on a variety of hypothetical factors: the alignment of the planets, the tides, the stock market, the greenhouse effect, unemployment rates, and the prevailing winds. During a day's time he could never be sure if the Waltham had gained ten hours or lost two.

To Jud, exact time was commonplace. He was surrounded by the exact time: the digital clock radio, the clock on the stove, on the microwave, on the VCR, the alarm clock by his bed. He liked the way the pocket watch and its many errors made exact time as relevant as it deserved to be. He also liked the heft of it, the craftsmanship, the beauty of its silver case, the engravings, the tooled wind stem, and the lettering and the Roman numerals of its face. He liked looking at the time through its beveled crystal.

The old watch, precious like the time it carried and always at his side in his vest's pocket, was Jud's reminder that life was just a matter of time, that he was lucky to be able to spend his life and times in Montana. An amazing thing when compared to the people enduring their lives and times through "those recent bombings in . . ."

Trundling back up the stairs, Annie between his legs, Jud thought about tomorrow and a day off from boatbuilding, a well-deserved day off for fishing in the meadows of Carrie Creek with Doc Higgins. He deserved it. The last month had been a push, but four dories, finished this afternoon, brass shining and cedar varnished, and representing nearly a year's work, awaited their owners in the workshop. Four boats for one family, the Sextons, a father and his four sons. The Sextons were arriving Wednesday, paycheck in hand.

~

Jud went to bed smiling since he was soon to be fat, and he had delivered the boats on time as promised. Well, not exactly on time, they were ready a month later than promised, but a month late on a year's work was close enough. Time, it appeared, looked at Jud through a thick and beveled crystal.

On his way into sleep, Jud wondered how he would spend the money once his bills were paid. There were going to be some extras, extras being Jud's term for money to burn. Maybe he'd go to Bermuda, or buy that bamboo rod he'd been wanting for years. Maybe he'd give the Willys a new paint job, maybe take a few of the extras and look up that beautiful woman working at the bookstore in Helena, take her out to dinner or something, maybe . . .

He was dreaming before his mind ever got around to possibly investing the extras in bonds or stocks. Jud's lifestyle prescribed taking the "d" out of mutual funds. If he had a dollar he spent it or gave it away. The future? He'd cross that bridge when he got there at age fifty. The bridge was right around the bend and that curve would more than likely catch Jud leaning the wrong way.

The next morning, according to routine, he was on his way down the hill from the Boat Works, following his well-trodden shortcut. The sky was cloudless and the only traces of the storm's violence were branches strewn along his path, his usual path, to the alley behind town, and through the backdoor of the Tin Cup. When Sarah saw him coming she knew it was shortly after seven. She also knew to throw on his regular: two eggs, over easy; three pieces of bacon, crispy but not too crispy; and two portions of hashed browns. Jenny saw him come in and set his usual place at the end of the counter with his customary ketchup and Tabasco, and poured Jud's regular glass of orange juice. Jud poured his own coffee. He then walked to his traditional stool, the closest one to the grill, to have his morning conversation with Sarah and read the paper. While Jud was not a man interested in exact time, he was a man on a very certain schedule. Some people would view Jud's life as slow and monotonous, but Jud's daily groove had a pace that fit him just fine.

"Morning, Sarah," he said taking his stool, grabbing the morning paper, and setting his coffee down in one well-practiced motion.

Sarah could only wave. Up until Jud arrived it had been a slow morning, but three tables of four, all coming in at once, had just ordered. This, to Jud's way of thinking, was when Sarah was at her finest, certainly at her most amazing. Pots and pans twirled in her hands. and there were breakfasts being fried, baked, boiled, and toasted. Food was being mixed, diced, sliced, grated, and mashed in a high-speed ballet with three-minute-egg precision. He couldn't imagine moving that fast.

He opened the paper. Looking past the recent bombings to the National League standings, he found himself peering back over the pages to Sarah, the lovely Sarah, in her uniform behind the grill—Hawaiian shirt, apron, and New York Yankees hat. Wisps of hair, streaks of gray, hung from beneath her cap and balanced on her shoulder. She was beautiful at fifty but she was a vision when she and her Uncle Sal first came to Travers years ago and bought the Tin Cup Bar and Cafe, the New York urbanites moving to a rurality with nothing more in the way of luxuries than electricity—sometimes.

Thinking about Sarah at thirty became a most pleasant daydream, one that took him through breakfast, a second cup, but one suddenly disrupted by Junior McCracken slapping him on his back. "Man, have I got some news." Junior was out of breath. He'd run from the pharmacy, across Main Street, and into the café. It was only a fifty-yard dash but one Junior did full out. With a coordination level measuring well below normal, walking being difficult enough, Junior had just ran as fast as he could, and when Junior ran it wasn't pretty. All of his extremities seemed to fight one another, one arm flailed into the other. His legs, knock-kneed to begin with, were all wrong and one leg seemed to run at an independent speed from the other. He nearly fell five times and did fall once. So, by the time he had made it to the back of the Tin Cup, he was not only winded but slightly beaten.

Sitting down, gasping for air on the stool next to Jud, Junior panted, "Yo-you're not going to believe this. PBS just called the town. Wa-wanted to talk with the mayor. This lady named Marilyn Delmar tells me she was in Montana to make a special about Le-Lewis and Clark. She had just read Traver's journals and is interested in making a short film or something. Wants to come to town and talk to us. And when I told them about you and He-Henry, the founding fathers four generations later, the lady really got excited. They want you two to be the stars."

Jud was disappointed he had missed watching Junior run. It had entertained him since they were kids. "Oh, yeah," Jud said with disinterest and took a skip of his coffee. "And when do they want to do that?"

"This afternoon. It's her only time to see us."

"Can't do it, Junior. Going fishing with Doc up in the meadows."

"But, PBS coming to Travers Corners—now that would be something. It would be great for the town. More tourism. You could maybe sell a few more boats with that kind of exposure." Junior, being the mayor, was looking out for Travers.

"I don't want more tourists. I want less tourists. I don't want more boat orders. I can't keep up with the boat orders as it is. And I would go slow around Henry with this idea—being a movie star ain't exactly in his line. You know how he can get."

Junior nodded knowing just how Henry could get and that was why he had come to Jud first. Between the two Jud would be the one he could convince to do such a thing, and he would then leave it to Jud to convince Henry. Going straight to Henry with this would be a mistake. "This lady Delmar is waiting by the phone at the Missoula Airport and she needs an answer right now."

"You can tell her if she wants to talk to me she can come and talk to me tomorrow, Junior. Today, I'm fishing with Doc. I mean calling and giving you an hour's notice and you're supposed to drop everything and bend your day around to meet theirs—I don't think so. Sorry, Junior." He, without Henry, had done the dog and pony show about his great-grandfather's journals quite a few times over the years for local and statewide television, and most of their media experiences had been sour. PBS might be different because of its status—or it might be worse.

Junior walked back to McCracken's disappointed with Jud, but at the same time he understood the value of a day of fly fishing. PBS would have been good for business. But one thing Jud had right, Junior thought, was this Delmar lady was pretty pushy. She first wanted Jud and Henry to drive down to Missoula so that they could be interviewed there. He elected not to tell Jud that part.

Sarah, finally catching a break, stepped out from behind the grill and sat down beside Jud for a short breather and a cup of coffee. "What's going on with Junior?"

"PBS wants to film a documentary right here in Travers—about the journals—and Junior has it starring me and Henry. They called about fifteen minutes ago and want us to meet with them immediately. But not this time—I'm going fishing with Doc."

"Nice day for it," Sarah said wistfully. "Sure wish I could go with you."

"Well, twist that sign on the door to 'Closed' and come on."

"Can't. Somebody's gotta tote that barge and lift that bale." She took a sip and then sat there smiling into her coffee. "PBS and Henry. There's two ends of the spectrum—together—on film. Masterpiece Theatre meets Louis Lamour."

"Tonight," Jud lapsed into an announcer's voice, "Merle Haggard, Luciano Pavarotti, and the Boston Pops will be performing at the Grand Ole Opry. That's tonight at seven right after Jim Lehrer brings you the livestock report."

Sarah's laughter was cut short by two tables of three coming through the door at the same time. She stood putting both hands on Jud's shoulders and said as she headed for the grill, "A movie starring Henry, I mean that's rich. They must be making a silent movie." Jud nodded and grinned at the thought of Henry, who brought a new dimension to stoic and taciturn with the face of a paralyzed poker player, in front of the camera, and whose words when he talked came in a mumble through lips that seldom parted. Henry was unintelligible to the untrained ear. You would get more movement and sound if you held his photograph up to the lens. This and the fact that he had a blanket dislike for the media in any form made Henry the perfect candidate for a starring role in a documentary.

Jud waved good-bye to Sarah, who was once again awhirl in pots and pans, and headed out the back door of the café where Annie was waiting.

Up the hill he thought about Henry in front of the camera, and then his thoughts returned to Sarah and his daydream during breakfast—Sarah at age thirty.

When he first saw Sarah he remembered lust and love coming simultaneously. At thirty he was still at the stage of falling in lust first and asking questions later, but with Sarah it was different. Yes, she was beautiful and it was those big green eyes, the long dark brown hair, warm smile and sensuous mouth that first drew lust's full attention, but her wit, her brains, her warmth were so readily apparent that love came in an instant. He remembered marriage crossing his mind fifteen minutes into their first meeting. But Sarah made it clear at the beginning that she wasn't interested in marriage, men, love, or courtship, and when Jud found out why, he understood. Six months prior to her and Sal's moving to Travers, and the reason behind it, was that her husband, Bill, and son, Jeremy, were killed in a Brooklyn schoolyard, innocent victims of a drive-by shooting. No one alive could equal Bill's memory, so Jud instead of becoming Sarah's lover became her best friend. Though there are still those times when her warm green eyes laugh, when the light hits her hair, now streaked in gray, and that smile blossoms through those Italian lips, that he gets distracted—not quite to the point of lustful but close.

Doc pulled into the yard of the Boat Works and Jud loaded his essential fishing equipment into the back of Doc's truck: rod, reel, waders, vest, and, of course, Annie the Wonderlab. This afternoon it would be trout, and plenty of them. He could feel it. He lifted Annie into the bed, her old legs kept her from leaping in on her own, and said, "Morning, Doc," as he climbed into the cab.

"Good morning there, Judson," Doc smiled from behind his pipe, "What a day, huh? Can't think of a place I'd rather be going, can you?"

"Me either, but I almost didn't make it."

"Oh?"

"Yeah, me and Henry were needed down in Hollywood. Wanted us to be movie stars."

"Huh?"

PBS and the Pentagon

On the way out of town and into a perfect day, Jud explained about the documentary, Junior, and the possibilities of Henry appearing on PBS. "Sarah said it would be like Louis Lamour meeting Masterpiece Theatre." Doc laughed and went about lighting his pipe as Carrie Creek Road turned to gravel, and with a plume of dust behind him, and a day of trout and the rest life has to offer ahead of him, Jud felt full and easy.

It would turn out to be one of those afternoons of fishing—windless, cloudless, mayflies, and rainbows. Perfect. And on those rare parts of the afternoon when he wasn't being entertained by a trout, those times when he was tying on a new fly or fetching an errant one from a willow, and those times taken just to look around, his thoughts were entertained by Henry in front of the camera and Sarah aged thirty.

The following morning Jud was in the workshop putting on the very last of the finishing touches to all four boats, a small brass plate that read, "Carrie Creek Boat Works, Judson C. Clark Boat Builder, Dory No. 172." He'd done 173, 174, and 175.

Annie's bark sounded the arrival of someone coming up the drive. Jud looked up to see four pickups with trailers, the Sextons, on time and coming for their boats. A fifth car, a white Mercedes, followed them.

The four sons and father were soon surrounding their dories. "My name is Jonathan Sexton. These are my four sons and these could only be our boats. Are they not ready?"

Sexton made no attempt to shake Jud's hand. There was no *how ya doing*, no *nice morning*, no *these boats are beautiful,* not so much as a *kiss my ass.* Jud disliked this guy immediately. "Well, they will be shortly," he answered barely looking up.

"I wait two years and then an extra month and now I have to wait some more?" Sexton said. Jud looked up this time but not out of courtesy as much as out of curiosity. There before him was a man starched and pressed in a pleated shirt and ready for a day on the river. Not only was he fresh from the laundry, but his bandanna was fashioned just so, and while he was a handsome enough fellow on the outside, Jud knew in an instant that he was ugly under the skin. Jud prided himself on the accuracy of his first impressions and he found his first-time take was usually close if not spot on.

"Your boys can go ahead and load those three. This one will be done in about thirty seconds," Jud said. The Sexton Sons were all lined up to one side of their father and stiff as rails.

"All right boys, get on with it," Sexton ordered.

The boys broke ranks while Jud looked on as they began backing and loading the boats. This was enough to tell him that rowing was going to be new to them.

"Is my bill ready?"

Jud stood 175's brass plate in place. "Now this one is ready. I have your bill right here." He pulled the folded invoice from his shirt pocket. Sexton looked at the bill then leaned on the decking to fill out his check and then handed it to Jud.

Jud stuffed the check into his pocket without saying so much as a *thank you*, or a *your order was appreciated*, or a *kiss my ass*. Jud said only, "Your oars are stacked and ready on the side of the workshop. You can use some of that rope there if you need to—" Jud was interrupted by a small car coming up the drive.

"Looks as though you have another customer so before you get entangled, know that I have decided to stay in town for a few days. My boys are all leaving for the Madison, and I want you to tell me where the very best fishing is around here and, if it is private water, I expect you to make the appropriate call. I am an exceptional fisherman and I am ready for any kind of fishing, I even have a float tube if necessary though I favor spring creeks. I prefer casting to the rising fish."

This guy had torn it with Jud and he had done it in record time, *I want, I expect, I prefer, I-I-I . . .* But, he remembered he had told Sexton when he ordered the dories that he would be glad to send him out for a day or two fishing at some of the special places, Carrie Creek, the East Fork, the Braids. What he wanted to do, now that he had met the man, was to send him and his float tube to the sewer ponds south of town. Check in hand, he decided to split the difference. Stepping into the workshop and coming out with paper and pencil, Jud grinned, "Here, let me draw you a map." He set about drawing the map, explaining every turn as he drew them in detail. It was an intricate map, with lots of turns, lots of gates, three muddy fields, and small swamp to a stagnate backwater on the Elkheart, where there were lots of rising fish—carp. It was also a spot easily accessible from the other side of the river off a two-laned blacktop. He kept looking up from his drawing to see who it was who had just arrived. But, because of all the activity of four boats being loaded onto four trailers being driven by four guys who had never backed a trailer in their life, the mystery driver had found it necessary to park in the field behind the house.

". . . and then you wind down through one last field to the river and you're there," Jud said handing Sexton his map. It was then that he first spied the driver coming across his backyard, a long-legged woman in shorts who stopped so that she could properly greet Annie the Wonderlab with a few scratches behind her ear.

"Good," said Sexton. "I'll want another map for tomorrow's fishing." He turned and left and went over to his four sons who were now loading their second boat. Not a *thanks* or a *kiss my ass*. Jud hated this guy. He was now even happier with the map.

As the woman came closer Jud gained a much better appreciation for the legs, long legs made for striding, and the lady could cover ground. There was a lean body riding on those long legs. She wore glasses, intellectual, round, tortoiseshell glasses. Her hair was piled up on top of her head and held in place by combs. Her blouse was open to the second button. She was tan. She was beautiful. When she was close enough to speak Jud had seen all that a man needed to see and by the time the first words left her lips Jud was in love. *This is one sensuous female*. There was one problem of course, she was twenty years younger than he was, at least.

In a voice, part cream, part honey, and backed by a throaty purr, the woman asked, "Are you Jud Clark?"

Lady, even if I weren't Jud Clark I would say that I am, was what he was thinking, but Jud answered, "That's me."

"I'm Marilyn Delmar. I talked to your Mayor McCracken yesterday. I work with PBS as an independent film producer."

"Yeah, Junior told me that you called, but I couldn't meet with you yesterday. I needed to get these boats ready and I had little time for anything else," Jud lied. Only a stupid man would tell a woman like this that he would rather be out fishing than meeting with her.

"I'm sorry I couldn't give you more notice, but everything with PBS is tightly budgeted hence tightly scheduled." She then walked over to number 175 and stroked the teak decking. "I love your dories. They're beautiful. I love to fly-fish. I wish I had time for you to row me down the river. I've read and heard about the Elkheart, but I never fished here."

"Well, I would be more than happy to take you on the—" but Jud didn't finish his sentence though several possible endings crossed his mind: take you on the river, take you on the town, or take you on the stairs. He was interrupted by two things coming at once. The first thing was the sight of a man videotaping the old carriage house. The second was the internal dialogue. *What are you thinking about you gray-haired old fart? It isn't flirtation at your age, it's lechery.*

"Oh, that's my husband, Carl," Marilyn pointed. "We're pretty much a two-man crew. Listen Jud, I hate to be in a hurry or in any way rush you, but we have extended our stay in the hopes of talking with you.

"We were here in Montana to help with the filming of a documentary, which includes a small segment on Lewis and Clark, and while we were in Great Falls we met with a man who showed us a copy of Traver's journals.

"Starting this fall, PBS will begin a series called *Stories from the Homeland* and this story, your story, is absolutely tailor-made for this program. What we were hoping for was if you could please spare us a little of your time and show us around a bit while we shoot some video? We then have something to show the powers that be back in New York, give them some footage showing the beauty of your valley, plus an idea of the singularity of your story.

"If they like the story, and I am sure that they will, they will send us out probably some time in the fall, camera and crew, to do the actual shoot."

"Well, I . . ."

"We can't bother you long because we need to catch a flight back this afternoon," Marilyn added.

"Okay, I guess I could take some time to show you around." It was impossible to say no to this woman. She was at once so kind and so appealing.

"Oh, that is so wonderful of you." Marilyn was elated.

Videotaping his way across the lawn, Husband Carl joined them and Marilyn introduced him. Husband Carl was a long-haired, fit, handsome, and young man. Jud hated him, too. Well, not hate. It was hate with Sexton. He envied Husband Carl.

"Do you think we might be able to meet with Henry Albie as well?" she asked.

"Now that I don't know. Henry will be the rub in your documentary. Not exactly camera friendly is our boy Henry, and he's not altogether keen on strangers, especially strangers involved in the media. Henry believes that the media is responsible for everything that's wrong with the world. He'll be a tough sale, but I think, if we go about it carefully, we can do it," Jud smiled and gave Marilyn a wink.

"Could you give him a call?"

"I could but I can tell you now he is nowhere near a phone and even if he was he's probably not going to answer it. Henry's a rancher. His place is just outside of town. So let's do this—I'll take you down and show you the journals and then I'll show you where they camped. Then we'll deal with Henry."

"I haven't—" she was interrupted by the sound of all the Sextons' trailers and boats rumbling out the drive, all of them leaving, including old man Sexton in his Mercedes, without so much as a wave. Marilyn continued, "I haven't had a chance to read the complete journals yet. Only snippets from the edited version. If you wouldn't mind could you tell me about your great-grandfather, just an abridged version—a very short history—the five-hundred-words-or-less approach. And Jud, if you could, tell it as though you were telling it to someone who knows nothing about it."

"Sure, I guess, let's see, mmm . . ." Jud felt uneasy with the camera on him, but he was comfortable in the telling of the story since it was one he had told hundreds of times.

"Well, my great-grandfather, Traver Burns, was a very wealthy young man and a bit of a rounder at heart. In his early twenties, under the guise of a business trip, Traver went west to do a little adventuring, a little fishing. In Denver he chanced to meet up with D. Downey, a Scotsman, and together they hired a guide, a man known only as Albie, to guide them up into the Yellowstone and into Montana. That was in September of 1873.

"They stumbled into this valley, the Elkheart Valley, and camped at the confluence of Carrie Creek and the Elkheart River. Not much in the valley really had names so they named a few things: Mount D. Downey, the tallest mountain in the Elkheart Range; Carrie Creek, that's the creek you crossed coming in here, was named after D. Downey's sister, my great-grandmother, who Traver had fallen in love with back in Denver. And you came into the Elkheart over Albie Pass.

"The town came to be known as Travers Corners because the ranch became the crossroad for the Yellowstone and Missoula stages.

"Traver went back to Boston, sold all of his holdings, and returned to Denver and married Carrie. They came to the Elkheart a year later and pioneered this valley and owned pretty much as far as you could see. The Carrie Creek Cattle Company. The winter of '88 killed his herd. They kept things together by selling land and working a much smaller ranch. Carrie died in 1925 and Traver a year later.

"Years later the original homestead burned to the ground and all that is left of the Carrie Creek Cattle Company is the old carriage house," Jud said and pointed to his home.

"That was perfect. Just perfect, Jud. Carl, what do you think?" Carl nodded. She then explained the need for brevity wasn't only because they had so little time. "When PBS or some one like them announces a new series that will feature independent filmmakers well, you can imagine. We've worked off and on for PBS for years so we have an inside track but still—" and her eyes went skyward and her head tilted from one side as though her thoughts drained from the right to the left side of her brain. "We'll use Jud as the intro and fill in as we go." She was either talking to Carl or herself, Jud couldn't tell. Talking to Jud, "We have to tell our story in a two-minute treatment."

Marilyn nodded to Carl and then stepped in front of the camera moving until she had the Carrie Creek Boat Works sign behind her. "And now four generations later here in Travers Corners lives the great-grandson of Traver, Jud Clark, a builder of extraordinary river dories: and the great-grandson of the man called Albie, Henry Albie, a rancher. They are best friends and they fish together." She motioned to Carl and he dropped the camera. "I think that is the most appealing part of the story." Carl nodded. "Did you get a shot of the boats against the carriage house?" Carl nodded.

"So, I guess it's time to go look at the journals," Marilyn suggested, grabbing a bag of video equipment, "and hopefully meet up with Henry. Damn, I wish we had more time." Then she gave Jud a soft-eyed look of admiration that Jud thought might have had some flirtation behind it. "I envy you your craft. I could spend a month here, fly-fishing, floating down the river in one of your boats."

"Thanks," *Oh, lady. There is nothing on this world that would please me more than floating your boat and envying your craft, screw the fishing. Relax, you old pervert.* Jud wanted to wave his hand and send Husband Carl on an assignment—Antarctica. Then snapping back to the reality of his old graying self, "Uh, there is one other thing that you don't know concerning that fourth-generation thing," Jud added, "and this is pretty amazing." Carl hoisted his camera once more. "A few years ago, now get this, the great-grandnephew of D. Downey, one Sir Gordon Pendleton from Scotland, shows up here in Travers. Seems as though Penny, that's Sir Gordon, was rummaging around in his castle one day and found, hidden away for a hundred plus years, the bamboo rod given to D. Downey by Traver right after they left here. It's all in the journals. I mean that's a great story all by itself. Penny's a great guy, spent a few days fishing with us."

"You're kidding!" Marilyn jumped up and twisted in midair, "That's it! That's the hook—the clincher. Oh, this is going to be a slam dunk. We perhaps could get Kentfield Studios up there to shoot Sir Gordon and then tie it all together for BBC and PBS. With both involved—more funding."

Carl entered the world of verbal communication albeit just one word, "Yeah."

They walked down the hill to town with Jud talking about the valley, talking about the history, and when prompted by Marilyn, Jud talked about himself. "Oh I've lived here most of my life—went away to college, did some kicking around in the sixties. It's home." Jud stopped for a moment on the path, "See over the theater, the house with the red-topped roof? That's where I grew up."

At the library, Jud showed them photographs and articles about his great-grandfather, and Carl videoed random pages from the original journals. Then he took them over the bridge to the town's Little League diamond and the monument marking where the three adventurers had camped. And before Marilyn and Husband Carl packed up their cameras and headed back for Missoula, Marilyn taking with her a small piece of Jud's heart, he took them out to meet Henry.

That evening, over the crack and roar of another storm, much to Annie's dismay, Jud reported this episode from his day and all other events to Sarah on their nightly call. "So anyway, on the way to Henry's I tell Husband Carl not to get out and start poking his camera about. Henry might get a bit touchy about that sort of thing. I mean Marilyn was the ticket to winning over Henry 'cause this woman was seriously beautiful *and* there was no doubt about who was the brains. Husband Carl was pulseless."

"Yes, Jud, I know about the beauty this being the third time you've told me. I usually get most things after twice," Sarah said tiredly. Jud and his flirtations, his romances, always rankled Sarah slightly. It felt almost like a jealousy but Sarah knew better. She knew Jud too well and wrote her feelings off to impatience.

"Well, you know how Henry can get about a pretty woman. Anyway, we drive out to Henry's and he's out in the barn cleaning stalls. Straw and horseshit flying everywhere and Henry's in the kind of mood that only cleaning stalls can bring to a man. He comes out of the barn and the first thing he sees is Husband Carl jumping from the car and putting the camera on him. I don't think Husband Carl really quite understood the danger he was in at that moment.

"Marilyn gets teed off and tells him to drop his camera. There was a fairly tense moment between the two of them. I mean if looks could kill neither of them would still be standing. Anyway, I introduce her to Henry and within minutes she had taken Henry from ornery to eating out of her hand. This woman can actually purr."

"Oh, please," Sarah moaned. Jud laughed.

"No, she can, honestly. Kind of an Eartha Kitt thing. Did I mention that this woman is beautiful?"

"All right, already."

"Anyway, I had told her to take it slow and easy with Henry and that's just how she did it. She played him perfectly. Turns out that she knows something about horses so she talks about quarter horses for a while then gently moves into the documentary and PBS. But as soon as Henry heard his name connected in the same sentence to a camera, Henry vapor-locks and gives her the no-can-do. She then comes at Henry from another angle. She appeals to his civic duty, to his cultural responsibility that the film needed to be made, it had to be made, to ensure the true legacy of the town and its heritage.

"Well, that worked. Henry even agreed to a bit part. She asked Henry the same thing she asked me—to give a short account of Albie and his life. Henry goes—'My great-grandfather was a trapper. Not too much is really known about him. He helped pioneer this valley. My grandfather and my dad ranched. I live here now and ranch.' He then turns to Marilyn and in vintage Henry he says, 'Hope I didn't go on fer too long.'"

Sarah started laughing and could barely stop. "Oh, man, hey, it's getting late. I'm going to bed."

"Need any help?" pointing directly at the lack of romance, though he never would have minded, in their friendship.

This kind of flirtation was usually met with a wave of her hand, tonight it was met with a, "Yeah, Yeah." Then she added, "Oh, Johnny Sexton, the guy who bought all those dories from you, came in for lunch today, said he didn't have much luck fishing where you sent him, but what a nice man."

"*Nice* man—" Jud was about to launch into the creep, but the lights went out in a crack of thunder. The phone went dead. Jud lit the candle and grumbled up the stairs with Annie trying to hide under his every step.

The next morning Jud headed down the path to the Tin Cup with more than breakfast on his mind. He was going to straighten Sarah out on this Sexton bozo—*Jo-o-ohnny.* But when he came through the café's backdoor, there sliding onto his stool, the last stool at the end of the counter, closest to the grill, known by all to be Jud's stool, was *Jo-o-ohnny. To me he was Jonathan, but with Sarah he's Jo-o-ohnny. I'm nauseated.* Jenny, his regular waitress, already had Jud's usual Tabasco, ketchup, and orange juice in place; Sexton shoved it all to one side. *And Sarah? She's just smiling at him and actually letting him sit there.*

Jud had no intention of sitting down next to him, instead he ducked through the bar and took a seat at the first stool by the window at the opposite end of the counter. He sat down next to Bo Jones. "Good morning, there Bo," Jud said sitting down next to him.

"Mornin'. How's fishing?" He and Bo chatted about the fishing and the weather while Jud could only look on as the wretched Sexton flirted with his Sarah. Even from the opposite end of the restaurant you could see that Sarah was buying it.

Bo had finished his breakfast and was gone by the time Jenny brought his usual order. "Sorry this took so long, Jud, but just about every order this morning is taking a little longer than normal. He was in here the better part of the afternoon yesterday and they sat in the back booth through dinner. There's enough sparks flyin' between 'em."

Sal appeared from the bar side of the café to ask, "Hey, who is dis guy, Sexton? He was here half the night. I talked to 'im maybe t'ree minutes and I don't like 'im."

Jud laughed and then saw the look of concern in Sal's eyes, an uncle's eyes, and realized how serious the Sexton situation was. "Affects me the same way," Jud answered while Sal grabbed a rack of glasses and headed back into the bar.

Jud was nearly winded from his disbelief. *How could there be sparks flying between them? How could she like this creep? How could anyone like him? He's been sweet-talking her and she's been buying it. Sarah, you can be so gullible sometimes. But, hey, Saint Sarah falls for everything*. It felt almost like jealousy but Jud knew better. He knew Sarah too well and he wrote his feelings off to impatience.

There was one good thing about being relocated from his usual stool because this time Jud could see all of it. In full sprint, not that anyone would recognize it as running, came the anatomically impossible Junior McCracken; windmilling, all limbs juxtaposed, defying all the laws of motion, and heading for the Tin Cup.

Out of breath, Junior was through the front door and headed automatically for Jud's usual stool and was halfway there before he saw a stranger sitting in the spot. Looking around he was quickly back to Jud, "You're not going to believe this. This guy just called from PBS. A programming honcho. A guy named Smith. He saw Marilyn's video. He loved the idea. They want to go ahead with the documentary. BBC in Scotland is contacting Penny. I gotta go. Busy day. I just had to run over and tell you. It's so exciting." Then Junior was gone, and as a bonus Jud got to watch him run back to his store.

Sarah had just finished burning Nancy Sillaphant's French toast when she finally looked Jud's way and waved him down. He had to go because it was Sarah who was asking. Nobody else could have gotten Jud any closer than miles from this guy, Sexton.

"Hi ya, Sarah," Jud said and in one look managed to convey to her the following: why is this guy in my seat, why did you let him sit here, and why are you talking to this jerk?

"Hello, Clark, interesting water you put me on yesterday," Sexton said through a mean smile and with ice-cold, G. Gordon Liddy eyes that gave Jud the creeps. "I now hesitate to ask for your *second* choice in quality trout water on this my last day." Then he turned to Sarah, and in a completely different manner and tone he explained, "You see, Sarah, my dear, Jud and I made a deal: in exchange for me buying forty thousand dollars worth of drift boats, he would tell me about a few of the best places to fish around here."

Sensing the tension between them, "Why don't you take Johnny out to Neal's Spring Creek?" Saint Sarah suggested trying to make the important peace with her best friend and the guy who was making her think about things she hadn't thought about for years, romance, needs, and urges. She thought about Jud that way now and then, but better judgment always managed to quell such ridiculous notions. Being involved with Jud romantically, after knowing him all these years, would be like dating a man thirty years her junior though they were born in the same year.

"Can't do 'er today," Jud lied looking at Sarah in complete disbelief that she would suggest such a thing. He wouldn't take *Jo-o-ohnny* anywhere, but to the spring creek—never. But Jud had forgotten that he'd told Sarah during last night's call that he was toying with the idea of doing a little fishing himself out at Neal's this afternoon. Sarah looked at him with a look that summed it all up for him. It told him that she wanted him to do this, that this was what best friends are for, that he owed her more than a few favors, and that this was payback time, bucko, and he better not let her down.

"Yeah, I guess I can draw you a map," Jud said delighted by the prospect of sending this yo-yo on another adventure into frog water. This drew a nasty glance from Sexton, which Jud returned with a smile.

"No more maps," Sexton said, "the last one, though I could have misread it, took me to a backwater."

"Hey, I've got an idea. I'll get Penny or Diane to come in and cook lunch and I'll come with you guys. I'll make some sandwiches."

"Sarah, that sounds lovely. I'll get to spend more time with you," Sexton said looking into Sarah's eyes, which held his gaze.

"I wish you could stay a few more days. There are so many things to see here and Jud knows all the best fishing spots."

"Can't do it. Have to be back in Washington. Flight leaves early in the morning."

"Well, we'll have today."

"And tonight," he added. Jud's entire body went rigid and he felt a snarl forming on his upper lip.

And with that it was settled. The plans for the day quickly fell into place: Jud would head home, gather up his fishing gear and Annie the Wonderlab and drive back, Sexton would walk down to the Take 'r

Easy and gather his gear, and they would meet back at the Tin Cup in a half hour.

Jud hit the path home with long strides. He was fuming. *How could Sarah come up with such a bullshit plan? How could she even mention the existence of Neal's Spring Creek to that creep? But that was Saint Sarah all over again, trying as always to make everybody happy.*

Annie barked as they neared the Boat Works snapping Jud from his thoughts, but Sexton wasn't out of his mind for long. *That guy doesn't want me around to spoil his play on Sarah, and he is going to make a play, and I don't want that guy around out at the spring creek. But here I am taking Jo-o-ohnny fishing. The guy who wrote me yesterday's check for four of the most beautiful dories I've ever built like he was paying for groceries and without so much as a thanks or a kiss my ass.*

The drive out to the Neal ranch is a short one from town, about two miles, something Jud was grateful for since Sarah had jumped into the backseat of his Willys with Annie. Now the man he was hoping never to see again was sitting two feet away from him and riding shotgun on the way to an otherwise perfect afternoon. Thankfully, he didn't have to say much because Sarah was leaning forward and telling Sexton about the valley, the history, but Jud was paying no attention. He was still steaming and when he had the first chance to get Sarah alone he was going to straighten her out on a few things like what a complete jerk this *Jo-o-ohnny* was, and he was going to explain to her, slowly and without raising his voice, the first rule of angling—someone simply does not invite anyone, let alone a near stranger and an asshole at that, into another man's day of fishing.

Jud turned into the Neal ranch, wound his way through a series of open gates and parked the Willys in the shade of a calving shed. The spring creek flowed beside them. Sarah and Annie were instantly out of the car, Sarah wanting to breath in every minute of her day, Annie wanting to take a jump in the creek, but this was Neal's and she knew better. Jud never let her swim in this creek.

"This is a short spring creek," Jud explained, "flows maybe a quarter of a mile before it joins the river. The fish here are real spooky so you have to be careful."

"I have fished spring creeks all around the world, Clark, I think I can handle anything you or Montana has to show me, and I would like to thank you again for that wonderful spot you sent me to yesterday." Then Sexton opened his door and confident that Sarah was out of earshot added, "That mutt of yours, is he along to fuck up my day of fishing?"

"Annie knows not to—" Jud then found himself talking to a man who wasn't there. Sexton was out of the Jeep and walking down to the creek to join Sarah near the creek.

I hate this guy. This is hate. I know hate when I feel it. "Did you hear what he had to say about you, Annie girl? Wanted to know if you were going to screw up his day," Jud kneeled down. "You wouldn't do that would you?" Annie replied with a lick to his face. "But would you do it if I gave you a bone?"

Jud threaded his rod and told Sexton to fish upstream. He headed downstream. No need for waders, the spring creek required the stealthy, on-bended-knee, long-leader, from-behind-the-bush, and covert tactics. He looked back to see Sexton putting his arm around Sarah's shoulders. *Jesus, what is she thinking about?*

Nothing was happening on the spring creek. Not an insect in sight. Not a nose.

But back in town plenty was happening. The buzz was out—Travers Corners was going to be in the movies. Up and down Main Street it was the topic of conversation, except at Dolores's Beauty Parlor where PBS and stardom was already page two news. Page one was just now being reported by Jenny. With her morning shift over at the Tin Cup she was thumbing a magazine, her hair awash in unnatural colors and matted against her head under cellophane, clips, curlers, and pins. Jenny reported in detail the latest, all the things she knew and didn't know about Sarah and her new beau.

In Travers there is no better place to gather the gossip than Dolores's. Here, from under the hairdryer and beneath the curlers, rumors have been known to escalate into reality and beyond. This morning, with embellishments and conjecture, the true and false facts, such are the composites of hearsay, Jenny's account would be no exception. "So, I mean this guy is all over Sarah, I mean not physically or nothin' but he's really comin' on. And Sarah's blushin' like a school girl. I mean he seems okay and nice enough and everything. Works for the government. At the Pentagon. I heard him tell Sarah about having lunch with Henry Kissinger."

"Whoa." The Pentagon and Kissinger aside Dolores needed to get to the more important matters, and being in a business devoted to outward appearances, her first question was of course, "Is he good looking? In short, Jenny darlin' is he doable?" She asked this in the interest of gossip, to find out what kind of a threat this Pentagon man was and she asked it with Sarah's best interests in mind. Sarah was Dolores's best friend and she knew that while Sarah might be capable beyond measure she was also vulnerable beyond belief. No man had turned her head this way in a very long time.

"Well, yeah. I guess he's kinda good lookin'," Jenny answered from her twenty-year-old vantage point, her nose slightly wrinkled at the thought of *doable.* "I mean he's gotta be fifty.

"But ya oughta seen old Jud. He was beside himself 'cause this guy was doin' all of his flirtin' from Jud's stool. Jud had to sit down by the window and wasn't real happy about it. And now, and here's the best part, Sarah talks Jud into taking her and the Pentagon guy out to Neal's Spring Creek for some fishin' and that's where they are at right now."

Dolores was a month and a week away from turning fifty and Jenny's remark struck a dissonant chord. A shiver ran the length of her. Fifty fingernails on her chalkboard. But even on the eve of fifty, Dolores was looking better than the best of the forty-year-olds up and down the Elkheart. She had the cheekbones, she had the eyes, and she still had the body, which she knew how to accessorize with the man in mind. Today she had on something from each of her favorite fashion houses, from the bowling alley, roadside café, and truck stop collections. Today, it was very tight-fitting purple toreador pants, a green blouse, unbuttoned just so, and large orange earrings to accent the true redness of her hair. Men of all ages travel from as far away as Reynolds to have their hair cut at her parlor, and there wasn't one twenty-year-old cowpoke the length of the valley who wouldn't want to spend some time alone with Dolores.

But spending time alone with Dolores was Henry's job and had been for years. They live together, but in separate houses, and it's an arrangement that works well. They even married one another once when they were nineteen and that didn't work out at all.

By the time Jenny had her cellophane removed and she was rinsed, blow-dried, combed, teased, and sprayed, Susan Cardinet, Bonnie Cotton, and Julie Smith had all stopped by the parlor as they do every day, to hear the news, any news. And while PBS news was the big news, certainly the biggest thing to happen in Travers since Herbert Hoover stopped for gas, there was more interesting news, juicier news—Sarah and the new beau. Susan, Bonnie, and Julie took the news and spread it and before lunch, up and down the Elkheart, it was known that Sarah was either in love, engaged, or had eloped depending on how soon the rumor reached you. What made the news front page and all the more wonderful was that something good was happening for Sarah.

Henry was at McCracken's picking up metal fence posts when he heard about PBS from a very excited Junior. Henry was hoping for the opposite outcome, but he said he would do the documentary. Now he had to do it and damn. But he didn't get the news about Sarah until he stopped by Dolores's to find her sweeping up between appointments.

Dolores instantly reported everything she knew about Saint Sarah and Pentagon Man, which took Henry, not in the best of moods since the PBS news, by surprise, "Well, I'll be." Henry was more amazed than anything. Sarah had turned a shoulder to every advance he'd ever seen come her way.

"And now here's the best part," Dolores said snapping her gum, "this guy was sitting on Jud's stool this morning while he's flirting with Sarah. Oh, and this is the same guy who bought all those boats Jud's been working on."

"Ahhh," Henry nodded as the connection was made.

"Then Sarah talks Jud into taking this guy fishin' out at Neal's Spring Creek for the day. And Sarah took the afternoon off and went with 'em."

Henry grinned and couldn't help but laugh at the thought of his best friend out on one of his most cherished waters with some guy he doesn't like, who would be spending the afternoon putting his moves on Sarah. "Oh, somethin' is gonna break loose there."

"Jeez, I'm telling ya, those two," Dolores said, and she and Henry exchanged the look, the look they now used instead of speech whenever the subject of Sarah and Jud was broached. It was the subject of hundreds of conversations, those had by Henry and Dolores, and those had by the rest of the town. It was a look of puzzlement and wonder and if printed the look would read, "Why can't Jud and Sarah figure it out—it's each other they're in love with." They shook their heads, shrugged their shoulders, then Henry headed back to the ranch as Cheryl Block's pickup, Dolores's ten o'clock, rolled up in front of the parlor.

"Let's eat at my place tonight. I got some nice steaks," Dolores kissed his neck and gave him a tiny bite. She had plans for tonight and the bite was just the first in a series of teases.

"Okay by me," Henry said. Tipping his hat toward Cheryl he headed up Main Street trying to imagine the situation on the spring creek, but having a hard time. He could see Sarah and some guy but couldn't put Jud in the picture at all.

Annie the Wonderlab knew her place on the spring creek and stuck close to Jud's heel. If she was on the river she'd be in the river, but at Neal's where she'd been fishing since she was a pup, she knew through a series of scoldings that this was crouch-and-stalk fishing. No swimming allowed. She hated fishing here except at the end of the day when Jud would throw the stick for her down at the river. There were now several rises. She and Jud were creeping into position.

Jud took his mind off Sarah and he took time to look around. It was a day for the taking. Secreted behind rosehips he watched the spring water flow smoothly past, rolling glass, creased slightly, randomly, by the sway of weed beds and watercress. Here, a hundred feet above where it joins the Elkheart, the creek is wide, it's shallow, and it was where the rainbows dined. Partially shaded by the cottonwoods, a ring appearing now and then, a few mayflies in the light, this bend held the largest fish on the creek. Jud thought of it as the best single bend in the valley and, naturally, he took it for himself. He wasn't about to give it to *Jo-o-ohnny.*

Ordinarily Neal's was Jud's ideal for heaven on earth, but today the beauty of the spring creek had been defiled by the presence of Sexton, and he looked back to see Sarah and him standing very close. *Oh, shit.* It was too far away to tell for sure but it looked like they were kissing.

They weren't kissing, Sexton was only tying on a fly and Sarah was looking on. But she was close enough to be kissed and the thought was crossing her mind. What Sexton had on his mind included kissing. "There is something I need to know: is there something going on between you and Jud? I feel he might be jealous and it is very apparent he doesn't like me."

"No, nothing between us though I can sure see that he's not too pleased to be here. Jud is my best friend but sometimes he can be a real pain. It's just that he's always looking out for me, like a brother I guess. You go ahead and fish. I'll walk down and talk to him."

Leaving Sexton's side, he reached down and grabbed her hand and held it until her fingertips fell free as she moved away. "Don't be too long."

Gathering a few wildflowers, Sarah wandered along the creek, aiming for Jud but thinking about Johnny. There was no doubt about the fact that this fellow was winning her heart, and she hadn't felt this strongly about a man since her husband, though there had been momentary weaknesses with Jud over the years, but nothing rational thinking hadn't been able to cure. Johnny was kind, considerate, he loved classical music. He loved all music. They shared the same tastes in everything. It was incredible. He was well traveled, rich and successful, an analyst with the Pentagon, a year away from an early retirement. Last night they even talked about going to Italy together and his coming back for a longer visit in a few months. Her mind was reeling from the romance.

The rising trout, quite a number of them now, had all of Jud's attention. Especially one large rainbow, larger than any trout Jud could remember in quite a while, that was coming up on a very regular basis, and contrary to normal fishing governed by the laws made by Murphy himself, the fish was the easiest one of them to reach with a fairly short cast. He'd already made several casts and thought, *If I don't make any sloppy attempts. I am just going to take this fish. A better than four pound rainbow . . . any time now . . . Oooo, that was a pretty cast. Floating down to him. Should be over him in another foot or two.*

The sudden appearance of Sarah at his side startled and distracted him just as the trout took his fly. He tried lifting his rod tip but he was too late. Jud looked to see just an empty hole in the creek where his fish used to be. Still kneeling he looked up to see a smiling Sarah and her path, and as he stood he could then see her footsteps in the still wet grass, paralleling the water a couple of feet from the bank. There would be no point in fishing the water for the rest of the day.

"How are you doing, Judson? Catch any yet?"

"Well, let's just say I was on the verge," he answered in his usual slow manner. He was upset with her, there was no doubt, but it had nothing to do with the rainbow. "Ya see, at the exact moment you were walking up here, the fish I was trying for, a real nice fat rainbow, a big one, took my fly. But I mis-s-sed it. And judging from the path you created coming down here, there won't be any point in fishing this-s-s water for the res-s-st of the day." Jud said it all calmly but some of the hissing sound betrayed his deeper feelings.

"Oh, sorry," Sarah apologized, dismissing the trout and its importance in the brevity and lack of sincerity in her apology. It was time, as was her custom, to come to the point. "Jud, did I . . . we . . . Johnny and I do something wrong? You've been awful short-tempered this morning."

"Should I start from the beginning?"

"A good place to start."

"Well, I'm not as enamored of Jo-o-ohnny as you are." *I hate this guy—that's hate.*

"Obviously," Sarah said as the Italian blood in her started to stir. When angered she was excitable, excitable and Italian being interchangeable. "And why not? He is a very nice man."

"Okay, first thing yesterday he shows up with his four sons, crew-cut clones of the old man, and they pick up their boats. Not him, not one of the sons, said a word about the boats, not a thank-you, not a good job, a well done, a way to go, or a kiss my ass."

~

"So, that's it. And that's why you sent him to some horrible fishing place yesterday."

"I couldn't help myself," Jud grinned. "He had it coming. The guy doesn't ask, he expects." *He's a rude and arrogant asshole.* "So I sent him out to Platt's slough but I sent him there through the Eslinger ranch."

"Jud, the man wrote you a check for thousands and thousands of dollars and you sent him out to Platt's? Well, then it's no wonder. Johnny said he went through a hundred gates to get to this bog and when he got there he could hear the sound of the highway."

"Yeah," Jud sighed from the satisfaction of it all.

"Well, that's vindictive and childish not to mention a damn stupid way to run a business."

"And then," Jud wasn't finished, "you invite the guy out here. You invite this stranger into my fishing day, you invite this yo-yo to the most secret and private of waters without asking me first. I mean that just isn't done."

At this point the Italian came to the surface. "Well, you didn't have to bring him out here, did you?"

"I tried not to, remember? But you shot me one of those Saint Sarah looks and I knew that I had to."

"Well, you could do a lot worse for company. John Sexton is a fascinating man. He's traveled and well read. We have so much in common. Books. Music. He lost his wife to an accident, a plane crash. He raised those four boys himself and sent them all to West Point. He's successful. He's . . . he's . . .," Sarah was exasperated once again with Jud.

"He's a phony. I'll be glad to see him go. And I'll be glad not to have any more of his business. I wouldn't give a damn if he wanted fifty drift boats."

"Yeah, well know this—he's coming back in three weeks and we're talking about going to Glacier."

Stunned, saddened, hurt, he wanted to say something but couldn't. He'd been silenced. Sexton had now left his distant position, that of the capricious stranger, a man traveling through, and entered the world that is protected, the no-win quagmire world of bad-mouthing the loved ones of loved ones, especially the new loved ones of loved ones.

When Jud snapped back from the paralyzing news that Sarah had just dealt, it was to see her purposefully returning to Sexton and using the path he had just scolded her for using, only this time she was walking along and waving her arms to ensure any trout that went without being spooked on her walk down would surely be spooked on her return.

Jud could only do one of two things. One, he could run after Sarah and apologize. *Apologize for what? Calling that asshole an asshole? How can she be so damn blind?* And two, he could just walk over to the Jeep, drop off his fly rod, and he and Annie could walk home. Leave the lovebirds alone. It was only a little more than a mile as the crow flies to town. He decided on option two. *They can use the Willys to get back to town.*

Dropping his rod off at the Jeep, he could clearly see the two of them. Sarah sitting on the shore and Sexton fishing. Closing the tailgate he looked back again and this time Sexton had a fish on. A big rainbow leaped from the creek and Jud felt slightly sick to his stomach. It had been a bad couple of days.

He grumbled all the way back on his walk to the Boat Works and grumbled into the night. At nine o'clock that evening and the time for his nightly call to Sarah he grumbled his way to the phone. He was going to apologize. Having Sarah mad at him for any reason wasn't worth it. But her phone was busy at nine, at nine fifteen, and busy at every ten-minute interval until ten thirty when he finally gave up and went to bed, his mind still grumbling. *Her phone is off the hook. Sexton is still in town. They were kissing this afternoon so who knows what they were doing by now. Damn, will I be glad to see that guy go.*

The following morning according to the dictates of his routine, Jud wound his way down the trail to the Tin Cup Cafe to find the Willys parked in the alley. He started through the backdoor and there sitting on his stool was *Sexton*. He couldn't see Sarah behind the grill. Deciding not to have the Sexton experience yet again he went back to the Jeep. He started to climb in just as Sarah appeared from the storage shed across the alley, rolls of paper towels in her arms. "Hey, where are you going?"

Jud turned and trying to be polite, "Oh, I decided I wasn't that hungry today," he lied.

"Johnny's sitting at your stool again. I know. But it's only for today. He changed his flight. He's leaving tomorrow."

Great goddamned news. Another day with that jerk. Third day in a row ruined because of this creep. This overbearing, self-satisfied, supercilious, schmuck. They say bad luck comes in threes. Well, that's a fact. The first piece of bum luck came when Sexton showed up. The second came when Sexton began bird-dogging Sarah on my private trout water, and now the third—Sexton staying an extra day, an extra night. The very thought of him touching Sarah made Jud ache. He decided to say nothing about it. "Tried to call you last night."

"Yeah, I had the phone off the hook."

"I kind of figured. I was calling to apologize."

Sarah only smiled. "Thanks," she reached out and touched his arm. "I gotta go. I'll call you later." Sarah then headed back to a grill full of bacon and eggs.

Why couldn't she fall for some nice guy, just some guy, a regular guy, someone like . . . like . . . like me. And with that thought he and Annie drove back to the Boat Works.

Once in the workshop, Jud began looking to his next order, a dory for a steelheader from Idaho, but his mind couldn't let go of Sexton and Sarah. *What if they got married? What if he moved here? What if I have to see this guy sitting on my stool for the rest of my life? What if—*

The phone rang and interrupted the daytime nightmare. "Hello."

"Hello, is this Judson C. Clark the boatbuilder person?" asked a female voice.

"Yes, it is," Jud answered.

"This is Mary Sexton, John's wife, and I was hoping you might be able to tell me where he is? I seemed to have lost track of him."

"Yeah, I just left him. He's down at the café having breakfast." *And hitting on another woman. Married?*

"Could I ask you to do me a small favor? Could you have him call me at home? He just became a grandfather for the first time and in a big way. Our daughter-in-law Linda just had twin girls. And tell him that everything went well."

"You bet, I could do that for you," Jud said grinning ear to ear, the kind of grinning that can only come from being right. *Man, did I have this guy pegged.*

"Oh, thank you very much. I have to run. So many people to call, you know. Good-bye, Mr. Clark."

"Yeah, you bet. Good-bye." Hanging up the phone he shouted, "MARRIED!" It took a while for it all to sink in, but when it did, "That son of a bitch." The first thought was to go down and thump the guy for lying to the kindest woman around. *That's what I'll do, I am going to go down there and thump him.* Then Jud remembered his eyes, the G. Gordon Liddy eyes, the eyes of a sniper. *I'll call Henry. I'll have Henry thump him. No can't do that. No percentages in thumping a Pentagon man. I should go down and tell her myself. Nah, that won't work. I won't be able to tell her that this guy is about to break her heart and do it without some hint of I-told-you-so even if I try to control it. But, I did tell her so.*

I'll call Dolores. Dolores could run over and tell her. No, Dolores will tell Sarah and then tell the town. No, I'll call Sal. No, I'll call her myself.

That was it. He made the call. But while his fingers dialed his mind and heart softened as he thought about Sarah. He loved her in all ways and big brother would be one of them. He felt the pain he was going to cause, but it had to be done.

"Morning, Tin Cup Cafe."

"Jenny, I need to talk to Sarah."

"Well, she's kind of busy right now, Jud."

"It's real important."

"Okay."

Sarah came on the line, "Hello."

"Listen, this is a bad-news phone call. I'm sorry. I really am. Anyway, so here it is. You know Sexton's wife, the one that went down in the plane crash?"

"Yeah?"

"Well, she just called. She wants him to call home. Seems as though his daughter-in-law just had twins." There was nothing but silence at Sarah's end, but Jud could feel her rage coming down the wires. Then came the click. Now, a phone slammed down and one returned to its cradle gently both make the same click to the listener. He'd seen Sarah really mad, full-on Italian mad, and it was impressive. He was willing to bet that her phone was slammed down if it wasn't in pieces against the wall. *Sexton might be in for breakfast but he's about to be handed his lunch.* At that moment Jud would have liked to have been a fly on the café wall.

He would find out late that afternoon at Little League practice from Sal, who had missed what had happened next but had heard about it from Jenny. Dolores heard about it, and it had been the talk of the town for hours. According to Sal it was over in seconds. "Sarah gets off da phone with youse, grabs the biggest spoon in the kitchen, walks over to the guy, and whacko, she cracks the creep right where he parts his hair. Jenny says you could hear the sound of it all the way up to the cash register. Da guy sees stars and Sarah says, 'Get outa my restaurant, you slimy bastard.' Which he does and without a word. And dat was dat. Sarah goes back to the grill and finishes a few omelets without missing a beat."

That evening he made his nine o'clock call. Sarah was home but not answering. But his call would accomplish one thing—she would know that he was thinking about her and that would be enough for right now. Knowing Sarah the way he did, and no one knew her better, she would be her old self in a few days. He would help her out of the doldrums by making her laugh. He could always make her laugh.

The next morning, as Jud expected, Sarah didn't come to work. He had his usual breakfast then retrieved his uneventful mail at McCracken's and headed home. Setting the mail down on the kitchen table he realized that there stuck between two catalogues was a letter from London, England.

It was a short note from PBS Marilyn:

~

Dear Jud,

Too tired to write. I will be back in New York in three weeks.

I hope to be back in the Elkheart to start working on the Traver Clark PBS script the following week.

Things are insane in my life. Carl and I are getting a divorce. I am sure it will be fairly amicable but stressful all the same. So when I reach Montana I am going to be looking for some R and R mixed in with the work and I want you to take me fishing. I'll need some help with the script so maybe we can combine the two with a few glasses of wine in between?

I'll call when I get back—Marilyn

That woman, that younger woman, that much younger, bright, and beautiful woman wants to have a glass of wine with me? Jud had to sit down, the joy of it made his knees buckle. Husband Carl was down the road. The thoughts and possibilities of having such a young and beautiful woman wanting to drink wine, needing some R and R, wanting to go fishing, were mixed with other fantasies centering around her long legs. *Wait until Henry hears about this. He's gonna pass right out.*

Jud, upon such wonderful news, decided to put the new dory, number 176, on a one-day hold. Instead he packed up the Willys with rod, reel, and Wonderlab and headed out to Neal's Spring Creek hoping that good things, like bad things, come in threes. He had two goods down. The first, and he was in full gloat about this one, was that really good feeling that comes with being right, right about Sexton. The second came in a good-news letter from long-legged Marilyn. So, he really had no choice but to try and parlay this two-in-a-row streak into a third with a good day of dry-fly fishing over pure and precious water.

From The Journals of Traver C. Clark

June 29, 1885—

The Elkheart School is about two weeks away from completion, and education will come to Travers Corners this fall. Our new teacher, a Miss Axtell, arrived yesterday. The timing could not be better since Ethan and John are now both old enough to attend. Carrie is thrilled and so am I, because an educated man will succeed, at least that is what she tells our sons over and over again.

I ran into Rick Nobles this morning in town. He said fishing on the river last night was the best he'd ever seen. I'd like to go out there this evening, but I can't. Carrie is having the new teacher, who from all reports is a very nice lady, over for dinner to meet our boys. I'd much rather be fishing—so would the boys.

Spoil the Rod and Spare the Child

There are times in everyone's life when you have to pull back and take a breather, an unscheduled but necessary respite, an intermission, a time-out, a brief vacation, a time, as Taj Mahal puts it, to *take a giant step outside your mind.* Now this break can come in the form of a fleeting daydream for some, while for others it cannot and will not be satisfied without physically leaving the someplace loathsome and traveling to the somewhere chosen: board meetings shined on for a round of eighteen, the long lunch taking you through the weekend, and the ever-favorite taking a deserved sick day when the truth is that you are just too damn well to go to work.

Today when a student needs a reprieve from the everyday scholastics, the repetition that is school, it's called ditching. In 1963 for Jud, Henry, and Donny this voluntary expulsion from reality, this all-day carte blanche hall pass, was called hooky.

Playing hooky from Travers Corners High School for these three compatriots in very small crimes was particularly brave because it was a dead certainty that in their junior class of nineteen students their absence would not go unmissed. This was made even more certain since Jud's mother was their teacher for English Three.

It was also just as certain that their punishment would come, but only in the form of detention and not suspension since Henry and Donny were the two best athletes at Travers High. Jud's protection was a given because of his mother being a teacher. He was also the best student in school.

Now detention to this trio was a small price to pay for taking a cloudless and warm day off. It was the fourth day in a row of July weather in mid-May, and from the high school parking lot, from the front seat of Henry's '51 Ford, the three conspirators could see clouds of mayflies lifting above the willows, the sun hitting their collective wings turning the clouds into waves of rolling light.

There were decisions that needed to be made.

To their left it was school, homework, books, and bells signaling you when and where to go. They watched the other students filing through the front doors and into their daily curriculum. Behind those doors awaited American Government and a lecture from Mr. Busby, a painful way to start the day, and, of course there was Mr. Schmidt, the principal, known to all students as the Messerschmidt with his strafing runs down the corridors looking, hoping, praying for any signs of trouble; a horrible little man detested by the students and by the town but tenured and entrenched. He ran Travers High with an iron fist, an iron fist on every infraction. Jud's own mother called him a Nazi, but never to his face.

To their right it was the river, and though they couldn't see the Elkheart, save for the occasional glint coming through the willows, they knew without looking that trout were rising and would be all day.

The five-minute bell rang. It was a narrow window on a Friday morning . . .

"Well, what's it gonna be, fellers, seven periods of bullshit, or a little dry-fly fishing up in the meadows, maybe bring along some salami and a couple of cold beers?" Henry asked. He purposefully let his Ford idle its glass-pack rumble, giving a rap of his pipes at the tail end of his question to let the other two know that his mind was made up.

"I don't know," Donny answered, "I think the Messerschmidt would really go nuts on us this time." But he said it with hooky in his eye. There was no place he would rather be than up in the meadows and fishing. "Plus, there's only a week left of school. Maybe we should wait to go fishing then."

"In another week the river will be running mud and when it clears everybody's gonna be up to their neck in irrigatin' and hayin'. When you give it some thought this might be the last good day of fishin' for quite a spell," Henry countered.

There was a moment of shared appreciation as Dolores Del Vecchio walked past in her summer dress, *the* summer dress, the dress the boys had been waiting for since fall. The pink one, whose neckline was cut low and in such a fashion that when she carried her books against her chest it would force her right breast to bulge from her top like a half-moon rising. The three boys silently howled for the other half. She gave the three a wink and a wave.

Jud, who had been silent from the backseat, watched as his girlfriend, Jeanne, joined Dolores on the steps to the gym. He and Jeanne had a fight the night before, and she was purposefully not looking their way. Not seeing her for the day would be worth detention alone. Facing his mother tonight was his biggest concern.

"C'mon, you two," Henry pleaded at the wheel. "I mean, the only good reason I can come up with for goin' into that school today is a closer look down Dolores's dress. I mean this is the best day of the year so far and we all know what the fishing in the meadows is gonna be like. You're only young once."

Jud leaned forward and slapped him on the back, "Henry, more truant words have never been spoken." A vote was taken. Would it be school or the meadows? Through shrugs, nods, and a laugh or two, with nothing being said, the vote was taken, and the winner by mandate was the meadows. Henry wheeled the convertible around and with a squeal of the tires left the slavery of high school for the joys of fly fishing. A rational abandonment given the beauty of the day.

They had made the necessary stops, the stops required for their parents to unwittingly subsidize their independence: at Jud's to gather the needed fishing gear, a couple of dozen cookies, and a half gallon of milk; at Donny's older sister's to borrow some gas; and at Henry's to purloin the beer and salami. Their freedom was ensured, the next ten hours autonomous, Henry's glass packs rapping out their anthem.

Then it was the roar of the Ford, top down and flying out of town down Carrie Creek Road for the meadows. Dust billowing behind them, giddy, and buoyant, radio blasting, riding the high of cutting school, the three escapees (truants to be sure) were bending time in their favor. If tried in the courts, the charge against them would be truancy, but because fly fishing was the only motive to their day, a dry-fly day to be filled with the barbed forgeries such as adams, cahills, and humpies, they could only be convicted of hooky.

"I gotta tell ya, this beats the hell out of what's ever happenin' in school," Henry yelled over his pipes while glancing at the clock on his dash. "Hey, it's eight thirty and, for a fella on vacation, that's soon enough to have a beer."

"Ya know, every once in a while, and it's a mighty long time between whiles, you come up with a good idea," Donny grinned, and with the long arm that dunked the winning bucket at the state championship he lifted two beers from the cooler in the backseat.

Jud, leaning over the front seat, said, "Now Donny, I've known Henry his whole life, and I am pretty sure that *this is* his very first good idea."

"Hey, you peckerheads, this here day has been brought to you by me. And if I get one more ration of shit from you two, I'm pullin' over and kickin' some ass." To emphasize his point he reached across and punched Donny solidly in the arm.

"Here's a good spot to pull over," Donny suggested smiling his boyish smile, the one that makes Dolores swoon.

Henry began to brake, but Jud intervened, "All right, you two, you can just wait until we get up to the meadows. Then you can kick each other's butts all day for all I care, but I'm not going to miss any fishing while you guys bash each other around. And if you don't believe me then pull over and I'll kick both your butts, simultaneously or one at a time." He then took a few imaginary jabs toward the rearview mirror. All of the threats were in jest, of course, and most of all Jud's because both Henry, the muscled running back, and Donny, tall and uncommonly strong, could maim him.

"But Henry, when you're right, you're right. I mean if it hadn't been for your daring and forethought we'd be in Mr. Hawk's geometry class, bored out of our minds, and talking about hypotenuses, triangles, and shit."

"Well, the only geometry I'm interested in today is that straight line that's gonna be the shortest distance between me and a five-pounder," Henry said.

"The only geometry that interests me is that perfect half circle that pops out of Dolores's dress. I guess geometry books are good for something," Donny said laughing. "I wonder how one would go about finding the square area, the mass, the weight of a perfect cone?"

"Actually, I know that, you make the cone into a cylinder and using the radius, base, and height, you form another—," Jud was answering from his 4.0 average, but was interrupted.

"Well, I say that geometry might be fine but I think a man, a man with a delicate pair of hands, could heft one of those beauties and come within an ounce or two. A-h-h-hw-o-o-o-o," Henry howled at the very thought of such a prospect while the other two, sharing his daydream, howled in unison as the Ford rolled along the back road, five miles from the meadows, past the old mill, past the Irwin ranch, the Johnson place, several summer cabins, then onto forest service land at the edge of the Elkheart Wilderness. But a mile from their favored waters, the stretch of water above Nielson's Bridge, the left rear tire blew.

"Sh-i-it," Henry yelled as the car shuddered and thudded to a stop. He couldn't believe the luck. The three went around to the rear of the Ford to see the hub resting on the remains of the tire. Donny opened the trunk and started moving cooler and tackle and to one side, clearing a way to the spare.

"I've got some bad news, boys," Henry said sheepishly.

"You don't have a spare?" Jud asked.

"Nope, I got a spare all right, but my dad needed my jack on the stock truck last week and I kinda forgot to git it back."

"Judson C., you know you and me were talkin', and just a few miles back, about Henry and the regularity of his good ideas?"

"Yeah."

"Well, don't it seem like having a jack with ya, especially when you're in the middle of nowhere, is a *good* idea?"

"Yeah," Jud agreed once more.

"Then don't it seem like that this is the kind of dumb-shit move that deserves a good thumpin'?" With that Donny grabbed Henry around the waist, lifted him off the ground, and deposited him in the weeds. Henry threw down his hat and dove at Donny's feet and the two tumbled to the ground.

Jud, thinking that the tire problem was one best addressed at the end of the day than at the beginning of a hatch, gathered his rod, hip boots, filled his creel with salami, bread, and beer, and started up the road shouting back at the combatants, "I am not going to come all this way not to fish. I mean the best fishing of the year is a mile down the road. Anyway, after we fish we can walk back to Johnson's and borrow a jack." He tried not to think of the future but only of the moment, because at the end of this day and for the week coming, his mother would be inventing chores as punishment while the Messerschmidt was sure to make his life a living hell. And Jeanne, already mad at him for what reason he hadn't a clue, was going to be even madder because today at a special school assembly she would be receiving the annual Governor's Award for Citizenship. Jud's not being there was not going to please her.

No doubt about it, things were going to be tough on all fronts for a while, but today was going to be worth it. Right now it was blue skies, windless, and warm and the trout were going to be everywhere. He was feeling wild, as wild as anyone could feel afoot, and every bit the outlaw.

Donny and Henry ended their daily battle, ran to the trunk, grabbed their fishing gear, the remaining beer and salami, and on a dead run caught up with Jud. Then it was the three, the same three as it had always been since they could remember, shirts off and tied around their waists, laughing, and walking up the road for Nielson's Bridge and rainbow trout. There was Henry under his straw hat, short, muscled, dark-skinned, quiet until riled, sixteen but looking twenty; Donny, tall, boyish and fair-haired, a gentle giant, easy going, the heartthrob of the Elkheart; and Jud, freckled, slender, still growing, and slightly clumsy because of it.

With rods in their hands, creels over their shoulder, trout in their eyes, they walked the dirt road, a sunlit study in truancy.

They naturally talked about women and the unattainable: Ann-Margret, Sophia Loren, Natalie Wood. They talked about the nearly attainable: Dolores, Jeanne, and they talked about a girl who was supposed to be easily attainable, a girl from Helena called Roxanne, who, according to gossips and rumors, would do it with anyone who picked her up after school. A trip to Helena became part of their plans. But, as they closed in on the bridge, and they could see the river, all the dialogue concerning girls stopped and the talk turned to trout.

The fishing the first hour was, as predicted, tremendous and it was surely the beginning of a day filled with record catches, laughter, and sun, but at the end of that first hour came catastrophe, on the heels of mishap, followed by the unforeseeable arrival of a cold wind and the leading edge of a spring storm. The mishap was Jud's. Chasing after a large rainbow he tripped in the shallows and soaked himself thoroughly. But the catastrophe struck all three when Donny, the only fly tier in the group and holding most of the day's flies, dropped his fly box, two months of tying, at the top of a riffle only to watch it float a few yards before sinking beneath a logjam.

The wind gusted and the clouds were coming fast. In minutes the peak of Mount D. Downey was covered in clouds. "Hey, you guys we gotta get out of here," Donny said trying to smile above the adversity and his recent loss but failing miserably. They all agreed—they were in for it and they started running for the car. Dressed only in flannel shirts, Henry and Donny were cold but Jud, soaking wet from his swim, was shivering, painfully cold, so he ran a little faster than the other two.

The sun was still out as the three reached Henry's crippled Ford and though the tire was flat the heater was working fine. In a short time Henry and Donny had warmed up but it was going to take a while longer for Jud to unthaw even though he was now in dry clothes, a pair of bib overalls Henry had under the seat, and he was beneath a blanket that Henry kept in the trunk in case some Saturday night Dolores wanted him to show her the stars.

Donny was slicing up pieces of salami and handed them around, "Well, Henry, ya did it again—promised us a great day and then served up this crud. I mean, geometry is looking good compared to your ideas. Right now we'd be sitting warm in class, about ten minutes away from a hot lunch, but no, we're stuck up on Carrie Creek Road, cold to the bone and miserable."

"Yeah, b-b-but at least we have a flat tire," Jud quipped through chattering teeth. He tried to smile but couldn't.

"This is positively the last time I am listenin' to any of your fool notions," Donny added, warm enough now to open a beer.

"Okay, okay. Now yer blamin' the weather on me? I mean jest imagine if'n we woulda hit it right, the whole day coulda easily been like that first hour. We woulda been up to our eyeballs in trout. Then I'd be a goddamned hero. I try my best to show you guys a good time—lead ya outa purgatory to paradise and what do I git for my efforts—a full ration. You know for ten cents I'd take you both outside and kick the shit outa ya."

Donny smiled, "I got a dime."

Henry laughed, "Yeah, well when we git back to someplace warm I'll be glad to work your gums."

"You and whose backbone?"

"Yeah . . . well . . ."

"Okay, okay," Jud intervened managing to laugh now that he could once again feel his extremities. "We have to get back down to Johnson's because it's gonna pour." They all turned to see the storm coming up the Elkheart. It was black over Travers. They sat in the car for another fifteen minutes until Jud had fully recovered, then all three took off for the Johnson ranch.

A quarter mile into their hike they came to the first of the summer cabins that dot the first meadow. The cabin was set back from the road fifty yards and surrounded by evergreens. It was still boarded up for the winter. "Hey," Henry puffed, "why don't we run up to the old Morris place—see if there's a jack somewhere?"

"That's worth a try," Jud agreed and the three veered off and ran up the drive. They only knew the cabin as the Morris place, but none of them knew who owned it these days. A barn and garage sat just below the house. The side door to the barn was open and sure enough, inside the barn there was a car, the keys were in the ignition, the jack was in the trunk. Done deal.

"Well, that small detour sure saved us a couple of miles of runnin' through the mud," Henry said quite pleased with himself and posturing in such a way to remind the others that coming up here was his idea.

"Yeah, we'll add that to the list of the other brainstorms you've had today," Donny said leading the others out the door.

"Remind me right after we change my tire to kick yer—"

Donny jerked back from the doorway in disbelief and held his finger to his lips to signal silence. "What's wrong?" Henry asked.

"It's the Messerschmidt," Donny said in a loud and surprised whisper.

"He's followed us up here. Man, he must really be pissed off this time. He's gonna—" Henry was interrupted by the sound of a female voice.

The three lined up at the crack of the door to see a woman following the Messerschmidt down the stairs. "It's Mrs. Pembroke," Jud recognized her first having been an award recipient in eighth grade. Seeing her gave him a pang of guilt because Jeanne was this year's junior class recipient at this afternoon's assembly, an afternoon he had traded for flat tires, freezing in the wind, and very few fish.

"Who?" Henry didn't know her.

"Mrs. Pembroke. Yeah, that's her. You know the lady from Helena who comes down to Travers every year to give the Governor's Award."

"I don't remember her," Henry shook his head, but then looking out from behind the crack in a door and fifty feet away from the lady that gives the award would be the closest Henry would ever get to a prize for citizenship. He was a rebel, tried and truant.

One above the other, like a totem behind the crack in the door, it was Donny who asked, "What're they doin' up here?"

"Whaddaya mean what are they doing up here? They're up here doin' a little hosin'. Look they're holding hands." Henry, who had worked up a genuine hatred for the principal over the years, was loving this.

"Holy shit. Principal Messerschmidt and Pembroke the Good Citizenship Lady from Helena," Jud would have laughed but the two were coming their way and there was nowhere to hide.

But the Messerschmidt stopped on the steps, turned, and dove directly into the ample bosom of Mrs. Pembroke while proclaiming his lust, "Margaret, I must have you once more." The collective mouths on the totem dropped.

Then it was Mrs. Pembroke who took the controls. Grabbing the Messerschmidt by his stick, she flew him back up the stairs and into the wall where she thrust against him, "Do we have time, my darling?" she asked.

"Yes, yes, my love. We have plenty of time."

Then came an interchange of tongues, grinds, and gropes, "Then take me, have me, oh Edwin, ride me like an Arabian." And with that Mrs. Pembroke and the Messerschmidt disappeared back into the cabin.

The three boys looked at one another in complete disbelief and then took off on a dead run into the trees and didn't stop until they were a safe distance from the cabin. They were winded, but it was impossible to catch their breath because of the laughter. Every time any of them would recover, Jud would imitate Mrs. Pembroke once more, "*Take me, have me, oh Edwin, ride me like an Arabian.*" Then it would be tears of laughter once again, the kind of laughter that feeds itself and that only the pain of oxygen deprivation, the side ache, can stop—that and being outside in the snow and wind.

They ran back to Henry's Ford, changed the tire, and were soon motoring back to Travers, luxuriating in the warmth of the Ford's heater, cold beer, salami, and what they had just witnessed. "I couldn't believe the way the Messerschmidt was frenchin' on her." Henry said, his mouth twisted in disgust, a revulsion shared by the other two and young people everywhere when they see older people getting lusty. "Licking on each another, gettin' all lathered up. Ahhhhhhh, I just might puke." Of course, they were doing exactly what Henry wanted to be doing with Dolores, but on them it would look good.

"God, wait until Dolores hears this one," Henry said. Dolores dined on gossip. The Messerschmidt and Pembroke would be a feast. He would tell her in the hopes of getting into her good books—the ones she carried at chest level. This and the fact that telling Dolores was the best way to spread things around town.

"Yeah, I think the Messerschmidt is about to make a crash landin'," Donny agreed. "And jest think how Mrs. Messerschmidt and his daughters are gonna take the news."

"Maybe there's a better way to handle this," Jud said slowly, his speech precise, his words delayed by the thoughts that were forming. He motioned for Henry to slow the car, not wanting his ideas to compete with Henry's glass packs, making sure they would hear what he had to say. "Remember . . . remember what we learned in humanities last year, about how knowledge is power? I don't remember who said it, Plato, Aristotle, Yogi Berra—one of those guys. Anyway, about how knowledge is power and the more people who share your knowledge, the less power you have?"

"Yeah, okay," Donny nodded like he remembered but didn't. Henry shrugged his shoulders, completely blank. He was probably fishing that day.

"Don't you see? This knowledge is worth something—a lot. It's the kind of knowledge that could give us a year's worth of . . .," Jud's mind searched for the right words and finally settled on "a senior year's worth of possibilities and privileges."

"Ye-a-a-a-ah," Henry's eyes shined as the bulb lit above his head. He instantly had visions of a senior year filled with fishing and hunting and earning nothing but As.

"Yeah, and we'll be needing to play that hole card come Monday mornin'. You can bet we're gonna be the first thing on the Messerschmidt's mind. But, we got that sorry bastard right by the oysters." All three of them howled and the Ford roared for Travers.

But at the turnoff it was decided to take full advantage of their truancy and they headed for Reynolds, the A&W, and a few games of pool at the Mint, eight ball being the logical way to round out a day of nonattendance, pool being to truancy what fishing is to hooky. Every few miles they would chant through their laughter, *take me, have me, oh Edwin, ride me like an Arabian.*

They were worry-free. They had the goods on the Messerschmidt, and he was in their sights. It was a blackmail of the finest and highest order.

Their secret, their knowledge, this newly found power would have to be handled carefully. They had a weekend to get their ducks in a row.

Saturday morning found the truant trio as follows:

Donny was working with a foal. He was relatively safe from any parental reprimands, the Boyer ranch being twenty miles from town, and his parents rarely knew about their son's minor delinquencies. This was fortunate because Donny's father was strict, abusive, and ruled the Boyer family with an iron Baptist fist.

Henry lived on an outlying ranch as well, but he was never worried about any form of punishment at home for his truant transgressions and it had nothing to do with his distance from school. Henry had his mother wrapped around his little finger, and his father always reacted in pretty much the same way when Henry ran into trouble. "Well, son, I was young once myself." Everett Albie didn't much care what Henry did at school as long as he was a good boy and did his chores.

But for Jud, as predicted, punishment was as certain as it was swift. His mother had him up at six o'clock Saturday morning for a day of meaningless, invented, and repetitive tasks. Yard work would be an integral part of his weekend. Dora Clark was mad, but she never got too mad because Jud was an A student and a good and dutiful son who, since his father's death four years before, hadn't been anything but a pleasure to raise. However, hooky, especially a hooky perpetrated by her own son from her own class, well, this would not be treated with impunity.

Of course, his mother, in her own inimitable way, never let the punishment end with chores. Lessons needed to be learned. So, when Sunday night rolled around, Jud trundled up the stairs not tired from his day as much as bored by it, only to find the butt end of his fly rod with its tip missing and a note. "I have taken half of your fly rod and I will return it on the last day of school so that you might be spared any more punishments. You know what they say, 'Spoil the rod and spare the child.'"

But as monotonous as his weekend might have been it was not without some laughter. The first bit of unbridled hilarity came by phone on Saturday morning. Henry couldn't stop from laughing as he filled Jud in on the latest developments he'd just learned from Dolores, that yesterday's citizenship assembly, scheduled for the last period, was all but canceled because the Messerschmidt and the Pembroke were no-shows, finally arriving an hour late and about five minutes after the final bell. The only ones to see Jeanne win her award were her parents, Dolores, and the two janitors. "And now here comes the clincher, Judson C.," Henry said after regaining his breath, "You wanna know why they were late?"

"Yeah."

Then Henry, who normally wasn't a big laugher, more of a quiet chuckler behind a stoic smile, as dictated by the cowboy code, again burst into laughter. Jud, holding the receiver away from his ear and waiting, thought that Henry sounded as if he might be doubled over, "They . . . they . . . had a flat tire."

Jud then joined him, laughing so hard he dropped the phone garnering a suspicious look from his mother. He finally answered, "Well, that's good."

Henry regained his breath realizing by Jud's reaction that his mother must be in the kitchen with him. "There's somethin' else you gotta know. Yer not bein' at the assembly has really set Jeanne's jaw. Dolores says she's madder than a wet hen.

"I'm pickin' Donny up in a couple of hours. Goin' to the horse sale in Ovando. We'll swing by. Meet you in the alley in an hour."

Between the side streets of Travers lies a grid of alleyways, and the one running behind the Clark's house had always been their in-town meeting place. It was an alley laid out with clandestine behavior in mind, full of shadows, blind spots, trees and alcoves, and it had been the hatching place for the trio's nefarious plans since kindergarten, but due to the brevity of today's meeting, Henry just let his Ford idle at the end of the alley in plain sight of Main Street. Donny was riding shotgun and Jud was leaning on the convertible's door.

They had to finalize the plan needed for tomorrow's confrontation with the Messerschmidt, collectively the biggest plan ever formulated in the alley. As it turned out, it was a plan that took less time to hatch than it did for the water-ballooning of the neighbor's cats.

"Look, you guys, there's nothing we can do here except wait. The Messerschmidt is going to be on our butts as soon we hit first period and he's gonna be pissed off. All we can do is wait for the right time," Jud explained, "then we spring it on him."

Henry fired up the Ford, shifted into first, glass packs arumble, then they all looked at one another knowing from each other's glances what was coming next, and ended their meeting with the chant, "*Take me, have me, oh Edwin, ride me like an Arabian.*"

Henry backed out of the alley and headed up to Main. Jud headed back to the house just as Jeanne and Dolores drove past once more and for the sixth time. Dolores waved each time, Jeanne, behind the wheel of her Daddy's Caddy, looked straight ahead. Jud had tried to call Jeanne several times, but all her mother would say was that she was away from the phone.

He couldn't drive over and see her, or even walk over since Jeanne only lived a mile out of town. His mother was furious with him and there was no sign of her letting up. He was tethered to the yard, grounded for a week with no television. No Red Skelton. Life, if looked at by the aforementioned, would have been painful. But the prospect of tomorrow morning kept Jud, as well as his cohorts, buzzing. There was nothing on their mind but Monday morning and the Messerschmidt's office.

Monday morning at 7:59 the three gathered on the school's steps and simply nodded to one another. There was nothing left to say, nothing left to do. All they could do was wait. They went to their eight o'clock class. They didn't have to wait long. At 8:01 their summons came by way of a hall pass. The moment was here. They left government and headed for the principal's office, only this time they were going in armed.

They all could envision the Messerschmidt, the sniveling little weasel, sitting at his desk with his slits for eyes coming to you through Coke-bottle glasses, with a thin mustache crossing his nonexistent lips, with his constipated scowl, his thinning hair slicked back, and his clipped way of speaking. But he was the Messerschmidt and nothing escaped him—you lit a cigarette in the boy's bathroom, and he would have you by the collar and suspended before you could exhale. He was still the all powerful, and the three were now as frightened by the secret that they held as they were exhilarated by it.

Mrs. Gillespie, the school secretary, let them into his office, whispering to Donny as he walked past her. "He's talking about suspension but what he would really like to do is expel you. What he would *really* like to do is nail your hides to the wall. Good luck. You're gonna need it 'cause he is *re-e-eal* mad."

But to their surprise the Messerschmidt wasn't in his office. They looked at each other and sat down in the familiar chairs of reprimand facing his desk. "Remember, you guys, wait until the time is right." They sat there fidgeting for a few moments. The door swung open.

"So, if it's not my little juvenile delinquents." Principal Schmidt went to his desk and assumed his usual inquisitional posture, leaning on the back of his chair, leering at them like a perched vulture looking at fresh roadkill. "What do you think you three were up to? All three of you mis-s-sing school on the same day," he hissed from his pursed mouth, which twisted to one side of his face. "Did you think it would go unnotic-c-ced?" The three sat there saying nothing, as they had agreed, expressionless save Henry who had a smile on his face. "Don't you know I have thoughts of suspending the three of you? Truancy is a lie. Are you all liars?" he asked, walking behind to the back of his office to stand beneath the photograph of him shaking hands with Nixon.

"Mr. Boyer, I will start with you. I should call your parents. No, I will just call your father. I am very sure he will know just what to do with you," the Messerschmidt threatened, smiling and knowing, as did Henry, Jud, and the rest of the town, that for such an offence Donny would surely get a beating and that seemed to please the principal. His mustache twitched from side to side.

He then moved along the wall and turned his attention to Jud. "I know that you have good grades, Mr. Clark. I also know that you are depending on a scholarship. But do you think any university would take you if you received an F in citizenship? Let me tell you the answer—not a chance.

"Then comes Mr. Henry Albie. Oh, the model student. I am giving you detention until the day school is out. I know that you are the instigator, you're the one who is always behind such plans. I should suspend you and make you repeat your junior year, but then I'd have you around for another year. I can see your resentment for me in that stupid grin of yours. You take away being a football star and you ain't worth spit." Coincidentally but unintentionally, a visible drop of spit launched from his mouth and landed on Henry's shoulder. At that moment, watching the spittle arc over the Messerschmidt's desk to hit Henry, Jud and Donny knew that Henry would no longer be waiting for the right time.

"Well, bein' a liar has gotta be better than bein' a cheatin' little prick," Henry said calmly. Jud and Donny were both taken aback. In all their years of schooling they had never heard a student swear at a teacher, let alone the principal. Even though they were protected by a shared secret, a secret, if known, that would cripple Principal Schmidt, the two thought *liar* and *prick* was taking it way too far.

It took a few moments for Henry's words to register, but when they did, the Messerschmidt's face turned red then purple, veins began to bulge from his temples, his head was palsied with rage, his eyes were manic and magnified behind the Coke-bottle eyeglasses. "What did you say?" His words came in a hoarse whisper, his windpipe constricted by anger.

"I said you're a cheatin' little prick," Henry repeated himself as easily as he might repeat a phone number, then lifted one of his boots and rested it on the corner of the principal's desk, his smile growing wider. Following the prescribed dictates of the cowboy way, he tried never to show any emotion, but, even though one wouldn't know it by looking at him, Henry was in a rage. To have this sniveling wimp of a man say that he wasn't worth spit would enrage anyone, but this was an anger based on a four-year hatred because ever since eighth grade he'd been the Messerschmidt's whipping boy, some of the discipline deserved, a great deal of it not. The ranch was a much better way to spend his day than attending classes, and Henry, at that moment, had nothing to lose.

"That's it, Mister Albie. You are not just suspended, you are expelled." The Messerschmidt took off from the far corner of the room, banked at the windows, and swooped down until he was an inch from Henry's face. "Now, leave this school at once."

"Sit down, pip-squeak, you ain't expellin' nobody," Henry said. Donny burst out laughing.

The Messerschmidt peeled off Henry's face to land in Donny's. "That's it, Mr. Boyer, you are suspended for three days. I will call your father."

If Donny wanted to he could pick the principal up just to see how he might glide, but he didn't budge. "Call my old man, Messerschmidt, and you and me are gonna have words." There was a standing rule in the halls of Travers High that if anyone was ever heard referring to Principal Schmidt as the Messerschmidt it would be two weeks of detention, though, in truth, he secretly loved the title.

Being called by his prohibited name while being threatened sent the Messerschmidt flying all over his office. "Suspended for ten days . . . no . . . no . . . suspended for the rest of the year," he screamed.

"Ten days is all the school we got left, you dim bulb," Henry quipped.

Jud didn't say a word. He just sat there frozen. Everything was different for him, a teacher's son, and that teacher being just three doors down the hall made him fraudulently respectful of the principal's words. This wasn't going exactly as planned. He envisioned this as more of a quiet negotiation. He looked straight ahead. He was petrified. But, when Henry stood, walked over to a hot plate in the corner of the room, and poured himself a cup of the principal's coffee, it hit him as singularly the funniest thing he had seen in his life to date, and he lost it with laughter.

"Well, Mr. Clark, since you think that this is so funny, you will now earn that F in citizenship. And that will be it for your scholarship." He then wheeled on Henry, who was calmly adding a little sugar to his cup. "I told you to leave this campus at once, mister. Now move." Then he was back on Donny, "I'm starting with you, Mr. Boyer," and he flipped the switch to the intercom. "Mary, call Mr. Boyer's father for me."

Sweat pouring from his forehead, the collar of his shirt damp, the Messerschmidt pointed at the three screaming, "You will live to regret this morning all of you. You will—"

The three boys exchanged glances. It was time to put the Messerschmidt in their crosshairs, and in unison they fired their chant "*take me, have me, ohhhh Edwin, ride me like an Arabian.*"

It was a direct hit. Edwin stalled, sputtered, then black smoke streamed from the Messerschmidt, and he began to pitch and roll around the room. He was going down. He clutched at his chest, and for a moment Jud thought he was going to explode in midair. It was a crash landing. Bouncing first off a filing cabinet, he flew directly into the wall, then spiraled down into his chair where, metaphorically, he burst into a ball of fire. Shell-shocked he just sat there in his seat, dazed, his glasses twisted on his face in the wreck.

Mrs. Gillespie, sitting at her desk outside the principal's door, couldn't hear everything that was being said, but words like expel, suspension, regret, and leave could be heard. She did hear the crash. She hit the intercom and buzzed into the principal's office, "Mr. Schmidt, I have Mr. Boyer on the line."

"Eh . . . eh . . . cancel that call, I mean I can't take the call right now . . . I uh . . . tell him I'll call him back." Edwin wasn't thinking very well. He was knocked nearly unconscious from their chant, and was slightly concussed by his in-flight collision with the filing cabinet.

"Is everything all right in there?" she asked.

"Oh, everything's, uh . . . mmm . . . fine . . . ummm . . . hold all my calls." The Messerschmidt just sat there smoldering in his own wreckage. He had gone down and he was unarmed and in enemy territory. Every part of his countenance said surrender.

"Yeah. We were all up there at the old Morris place, and we saw you two pawin' each other on the porch," Henry explained. The Messerschmidt gasped and turned pea green, for a moment he looked as thought he might throw up.

"Now, here's the deal, Edwin, and it's real simple so even you will git it," Henry said, lighting a cigarette, which sent Donny into spasms of laughter.

"Only the three of us know about you and yer deal with Pembroke, and we won't tell nobody in return for a few favors, starting with—we want you off our back—we want you off everybody's back." Henry had taken charge, which seemed only fair since he held the most hatred for this man. Normally he was a boy of very few words, but at that moment Henry was a young man on a roll. "On the other side of this coin, you try and do anything to us and we'll tell the town. And, of course, these favors yer gonna do for us, yer gonna do for us next year, too."

"And, sometimes," Henry paused and winked at his cohorts, "sometimes these favors jest might be extended to the entire student body, like a surprise field trip to Johnson's Hot Springs—or something along them lines. And, Edwin, you ol' Arabian riding stud, you, that's about it. Is it a deal?" Edwin nodded. He was a beaten man.

Then Jud, who had been waiting to see how everything was going to play out, joined the fray. "You know, you guys, I think this morning, this warm-with-mayflies-everywhere morning, would be the perfect morning for the Messerschmidt to hand down our punishment for cutting school." Jud was now out of his seat and pacing back and forth before the principal, who could do nothing more than sit in his chair paralyzed, helpless to do anything against them. He couldn't even stop Henry from smoking. "And I know just what that sentence should be," Jud continued, looking the principal in the eye, "you are going to send us home, where we have to write a thousand-word essay on honor and ethics—'course we ain't gonna write 'em."

"This is blackmail . . . extortion . . ." the Messerschmidt said.

"Nah, let's jest call it gettin' even," Henry said flipping his cigarette out the window, "'cause you are the worst thing to ever happen to this school. Sneakin' around like the weasel that ya are. Always tormentin' some poor student. Well, that's all over. In short, Edwin, I'd say yer Schmidt out of luck."

"Just like Schmidt on a stick," Jud smiled.

Then Donny stood from his chair and unfolding his long frame he leaned down over the Messerschmidt, "And, when you call my dad, the reason for your call is just to tell him what a great kid I am. And if you say anything else you'll be in some deep Schmidt."

Following Donny's lead, the three left the Messerschmidt's office, leaving just a burned-out shell of a man. "Jud, are you boys all right?" Mrs. Gillespie asked.

"Yeah, we're fine," Jud answered faking a hangdog expression. "We just played hooky and now we're paying for it. We've all been sent home to write a thousand-word essay on ethics." He shrugged his shoulders like a man resolved to his fate, an essay-filled afternoon, but then turned and left the office with a smile so wide he barely made it through the door.

Then it was top down, glass packs, salami, a few cold beers, and dry-fly fishing, and even now, forty years later, Jud and Henry can't hear the words truancy, hooky, principal, or Arabian without their minds taking off to that day. The day the Messerschmidt went down in flames.

Their junior year was a week from being over; there was no time to exercise this free license to commit hooky, but the following year, their senior year, Donny and Henry had plans for wholesale hooky. Jud's hooky would be far more limited—teacher's son. But none of that came to be. A month later Mrs. Schmidt caught the principal with Mrs. Pembroke. Scandal. Divorce. The Messerschmidt was transferred to Cutbank.

That Monday was a helium-filled afternoon and near the top in their lifetime of memories—shirts off, wading wet, windless, hot, smoking Lucky Strikes, knee deep in their delinquency, and large trout rising to their flies all day. Donny, sharing his rod with Jud, caught a rainbow over seven pounds, his best fish ever, and he would carry the memory of that day with him as well, but not for as long. He would be killed in Vietnam four years later.

However, for that one day, that trio of best friends were free-floating yahoos, good-time bandits, thieves in the afternoon, at no one's beck and call, victorious over authority, fishing dry flies, with enough beer to break the fun barrier, and lost to that warm and watery world of legalized truancy, and truancy at its best—hooky.

From The Journals of Traver C. Clark

August 4, 1923—

There was a tragedy in Travers Corners last night. A lumberjack, a man by the name of John Whiting, beat his wife to death.

How could a man beat a woman? The very thought of it sickens me.

~

A Day Given to Luck

There are all types of fishermen ranging from the intrepid to the lackadaisical, from the masterful to the pitiable, the seasoned angler to the beginner. But no matter what type of fisherman you are, you will fall into one of two groups—the unlucky or the lucky. Of course, lucky comes on a sliding scale, changing daily, some days luckier than others, but overall if you are a lucky fisherman you will consistently outfish an angler with similar talents, but who fishes from a place farther down on that scale. Jud, Henry, and Doc were all skillful fishermen and surely considered themselves to be lucky fishermen, but not lucky by their successes at landing trout, just lucky to be fisherman, lucky to be out there knee-deep in the local waters and fishing.

Nearing the top of that scale would be, for a lack of a better title, the *extremely* lucky fisherman. Everyone knows one or has heard about one. The fellow who sets his fly down once on the same water another's been fishing unsuccessfully for hours and, with a cast no different than the first fellow's, pulls in the catch of the year. This kind of fisherman will beat another angler's most auspicious day and will usually have it beaten before noon.

Then there is Tommy Harlan, the Gladstone Gander of Angling, and easily the luckiest fisherman alive. Tommy was in a luck league of his own. Not only is he the fisherman who will be successful while others fail over the same water, the fisherman who goes around the bend catching every trout in sight and some that are not, but Tommy took luck to another level. He would be catching those fish, which others could not, on a brand new fly rod and reel given to him, the millionth customer, with flies from someone's forgotten box he found streamside, while fishing an all-expenses-paid vacation he'd won in a raffle. The kind of fisherman who could catch trout from a bucket of sand, the kind of fisherman with no real necessity for a hook and line, whose charm alone would lead the trout out of the creek to feed from his hand. The kind of fisherman who could wade around the next bend and come upon two nineteen-year-old Swedish girls who had always wondered what it would be like to have sex with a man in waders. That kind of lucky.

Of course, luck was not only with him streamside, luck had been Tommy's fraternal twin. He was born to wealth. He was handsome, bright, father of two sons, both at Harvard, with a beautiful and gracious wife who traveled with him for most of his fishing. But for this trip into the Elkheart, Tommy was traveling alone, and he was due at the Boat Works tomorrow for two days of guided trips. Henry and Jud had been guiding him for years.

"Now, I've fished and guided on the Elkheart all my life and of all those folks I've taken nobody holds a candle to that guy," Henry said staring out the window.

"The guy's timing is impeccable," Jud said looking up as he gathered the tools he'd been using for the day and returned them to their places about the workshop, calipers on their hook, hand plans back to their shelf, saws in their cradle.

"You and me been guidin' that guy for years and always, and I don't mean most of the time now, I'm talkin' about *always*, Tommy arrives and the waters part, the heavens clear, and the trout swim right up his line. I don't think the man has suffered through a bad day of fishin' in his life."

Jud laughed, "I know—luckiest man I've ever met. Hand me that router will ya?"

Henry bent down and pulled the outline of a router from its thick sawdust covering, shook it off, and handed it to Jud, "You wanna know what's the most bothersome thing about Tommy?"

"What's that?" Jud asked.

"That he's such a nice guy," Henry answered.

"I know, lucky along with handsome, rich, and nice is a hard combination to like, especially from your station in life, you know—ugly, poor, and hard to get along with," Jud said with a laugh. "You wanna cold one?" Henry nodded and Jud retrieved two beers from the fridge in the corner of the workshop and then joined Henry who had gone back to staring out the windows, windows that had been closed for months, that were now wide open and welcoming a change in the weather. "Looks like Tommy is going to time it right again," Jud said handing Henry a beer.

Below them the town of Travers was in and out of the shadows as the last of the clouds moved along the Elkheart Valley. To the east—blue skies that would be here within the hour. The sun dipped below the clouds and the warmth hit them like a wave of water on a Caribbean tide. "My guess is, by that band of blue sky," Henry smiled, "Tommy's plane has just touched down in Helena."

A blue station wagon crested the driveway into the Boat Works. It was Junior McCracken just returning from a weekend of fishing. Henry, realizing their predicament, said through clinched teeth, "We're trapped."

"No getting out of it this time," Jud said. He instantly understood what Henry was talking about because now they were about to hear in detail, and in details so finite as to bore even the most avid angler, about Junior's last few days of fishing in stories so tiresome as to bring on premature narcolepsy. If sung, Junior's stories could serve as lullabies.

The complete opposite of Tommy, Junior was the Joe Btfsplk of angling and easily the unluckiest fisherman alive. Not only is he the fisherman who will be unsuccessful while others around him are reeling in the fish, the fisherman who goes around the bend frightening every fish in sight and some that are not on a fly rod he bought brand new but had recently stepped on, with flies he stayed up late tying, while fishing a rare weekend off and paid for with money borrowed from petty cash. The kind of fisherman who can't catch a fish in an aquarium, the kind of graceless fisherman who stumbles and spooks his way up the creek while slapping his fly repeatedly on the water with untimely, unproductive, and heavy-handed casts. The kind of fisherman who will wade around the next bend to come upon twins of his own in the form of twin calves belonging to a startled and angry cow moose. That kind of unlucky.

Fortunately, Junior limited his misfortunes to streamside. The rest of his life was good with his wonderful wife, Pam, and two sons of his own both at Montana State. But the wonderful wife and the two sons are where any similarities between Tommy and Junior came to a stop. Junior was not handsome, but rather short, balding, with glasses, and a little overweight. He was not born rich, nor would he ever be rich.

"I can't believe it." Junior ignored any greeting as he came through the workshop door and went right into his lament. "I get one weekend off in the last five months and it turns out to be cold and windy." Jud handed Junior a cold beer reading in the pharmacist's eyes that two fingers of Jack would be the better prescription. Both Henry and Jud knew how dear a weekend off was to Junior. Being the town's only connection to needed medicine he was forever at work and always on call. "Of course the fish weren't biting. Water temperature was forty-five degrees. I mean I did catch a couple. I had this weekend so built up in my mind. I just can't believe it."

This is what Jud loved so much about Junior—there he was, the world's most optimistic angler and at the same time its most inauspicious one. Having bad luck fishing somehow came as a surprise to Junior and he looked at an unsuccessful day streamside as an abnormality instead of the constant, like every failure he ever had had been forgotten except for his last one, like this most recent defeat at the hands of the wily trout was an uncommon occurrence and that he will surely catch them the next time. "But I gotta tell you about this one fish I caught. Now, I never saw a rise all weekend. Anyway, I tied on a nymph pattern, a modified hare's ear with silver ribbing, rubber legs, peacock head. I tie it on a twelve, the old Mustad hook, the 3906B, sproat bend—they don't make them anymore, but I can still get them from this place I know about in Seattle. I use four wraps of .017 lead. I was using seventeen feet of leader. Anyway, when I get there nothing, like I said, nothing was rising on in the creek, so I drove over to the lake. At first I tried one of my emerger patterns, you know the ones that . . ."

Henry, knowing what they were in for and painfully aware that the fly pattern used was always a brief preamble to the body of one of Junior's fishing stories, went over to the fridge and pulled out two more beers and handed one to Jud. They were going to be there awhile. Normally he would have fabricated an excuse to leave, but he couldn't this time. After fishing with Junior for a lifetime Henry knew just how miserable Junior really was—one weekend off in five months to do the one thing he loves the most. He stayed and listened.

Jud, on the other hand, stayed but didn't listen. Over the years he had perfected a method for coping with Junior's stories. He simply nodded now and then, shook his head, smiled at the proper time, trying, without listening, to match his facial expressions to Junior's inflections. In the meantime his mind went ahead with his daily business. He looked past Junior to the river dory, its bare cedar turning yellow in the light, and made a mental note that he needed a new blade for the band saw. A quick inventory of tools needed for the dory's upcoming trim work also told him to order more mahogany; he thought about tomorrow's fishing as he briefly tuned into where Junior was in his tale. ". . . my first seventeen casts were made with 6X but then I added nineteen and a half inches of 7X, but I still wasn't having any luck so I . . ." Then Jud went back to Friday's plan and its options—the river, Carrie Creek, the East Fork, everything should be fishing fine. Finally he decided to save any decisions until tomorrow when he would meet Tommy, as was their routine, at the Tin Cup for breakfast.

Jud returned to Junior's tale once again having no idea how long he had been gone. His timing was perfect. ". . . and I know it was only ten inches long," Junior rationalized, "but it was feisty."

Jud and Henry quickly exchanged glances. Junior had landed the fish, in a chronicle lasting roughly fifteen minutes longer than the actual event, and they both knew it was time to break it up or Junior would be off on another tale. It was Henry who made the first exit, "Well, I gotta get goin'," he said pulling down on his hat. Henry had been fidgeting in place ever since Junior's first emerger pattern.

"Yeah, I better get this place cleaned up as well," Jud said yawning.

"I better go, too," Junior said. "Pam will have a stack of work waiting for me. I'll see you guys later." With that Junior walked to his car and not, as they both noted, with his usual ducklike steps but rather stoop-shouldered and defeated.

"Henry, I'm gonna say something right now that I am going to live to regret," Jud said and called after Junior. "Hey, if there is any way you can get off on Tuesday, I'll row you down the river."

"Hey, all right. I'll figure something out. You got a deal." And with that the duck, his feet at ten and two, was up again and waddling.

"I'll call you tomorrow." Jud waved and then moaned like a man who had just invited a curse to a crap game.

"I have to admit to thinkin' the same thing, there old buddy," Henry said, "but I jest couldn't bring myself to doin' it. I've done it. God knows I've done it, but nowadays I find that I need about two years between fishing trips with Junior."

Jud laughed and they both looked at one another realizing what Jud had signed on for—one day of fishing with Junior or the floating eight-hour narrative from hell, because in a boat there is no escaping Junior and his detailed accounts on every aspect of the angle.

The following morning Jud met Tommy at the Tin Cup and after breakfast their usual day of fishing ensued, Jud at the oars and Tommy in the bow catching every trout in his path. He caught rainbows in their riffles. He caught browns from the pools. He caught trout behind logs, beneath the willows, in the eddies, in the backwaters, out in the middle, and under the banks, and on one backcast, just as his fly was suspended a foot above the water in that split second when the line lingers at the end of a long, perfectly timed backcast while waiting on the rod's bend to send it forward, his fly was taken in midair.

Jud held a private theory that when Tommy was fishing, trout would leave their home states and native drainages and swim to the Elkheart just to impale themselves on Tommy's hook. But, while his luck in numbers of fish was with him, as it always seemed to be, the luck in their size eluded him all day—the largest fish brought to hand being fifteen inches.

Even by Tommy's standards, the fishing was wonderful and nearing day's end, Jud at the oars of the SS *Lucky Me*, Tommy turned and said, "Jud, I want to thank you so much for this day of fishing. It might be the best day of fishing I've had on the Elkheart in quite a few years." In the bow of the boat he sat still and not because the fishing had gone sour, if anything it had picked up, but his arm was tired from the incessant casting and sore from the constant catching. He looked as though he just stepped from the shower, every hair was in place, the creases still held in his shirt.

"Oh, I called Henry last night and asked if he and Dolores, of course, would be my guests for dinner tonight."

"And Henry's answer to a free meal was . . .?" Jud asked with a smirk.

"They'll be there. I hope Sarah is cooking."

Looking like a man in need of a bath, in a stained T-shirt, his hair lying on his head in a sweaty mat beneath his hat, Jud answered through a pair of twisted incisors set against his skin, blotchy and red from his first day in the hot sun since November, Jud answered, "I'm pretty sure she is."

Then it happened. Something that wasn't supposed to happen for at least another three weeks even in its earliest years. But, perhaps in all the annals of fishing there is nothing more unpredictable than the most fickle of all the flies—the mythical and mystical salmon fly. The three-inch pterodactyls of the insect world were climbing from the shallows, a few were hatching, but when one of them flew into Jud's face, that told them the much heralded, incredibly elusive, salmon fly hatch was about to begin. Hitting the hatch is as easy as hitting a perfecta during a blue moon.

"I don't believe it." Even in all of his years of trying, Tommy, the world's most fortunate fisherman, had never been on the Elkheart during *the* hatch. But the day was ending just as the hatch began, and as they floated under Town Bridge, Jud shipped his oars thinking out loud, "If the weather holds, which it's supposed to, tomorrow's fishing is going to be nuts. You and Henry should have a real time."

And Jud was sure to have an interesting day ahead of him as well. On what very well could be the definitive angling day of the year, he would be at the oars with Junior fishing from the bow of the *Lucky Me* turning his dory's name into a contradiction.

Tommy, naturally, was a town favorite. After years of fishing the Elkheart most everyone in Travers knew him or had heard of him. The men heard about him from Jud and Henry, hearing mostly about the guy's phenomenal luck and timing. The women heard about him from Dolores, hearing mostly about his charm and good looks. Women, unsurprisingly, were attracted to Tommy, and Dolores was no exception.

That same morning, around the time Jud and Tommy were getting on to the river, Henry, in town for general supplies from the general store, poked his head in long enough at the beauty shop to tell Dolores about the dinner plans for that night. "Yeah, they're on the river today and we're supposed to meet up with 'em at the Tin Cup around seven."

"I'll be there with bells on," Dolores purred and winked at her man. "You know how I like to see Tommy." She pushed out her butt, batted her eyes, and blew Henry a kiss, then went back to working on Vicki Whitehead's hair. Vicki looked at it all as a silly flirtation, but there was much more to it than that—Tommy had long been a standing joke between Henry and Dolores. Dolores, in her own way, flirted with every man, but with Tommy he knew it was a little different. While Dolores was a flirt to the world and was certainly the kind of woman who drew flirtation and had all her life, flirtation was where she drew the line. Though she would never dream about cheating on Henry, there were times she wanted to grab that cleaned and pressed, educated and refined, wealthy and charming polar opposite of Henry by the hand and drag the world's luckiest fisherman out into the woods and show him what lucky was really all about.

Henry just smiled. He wasn't worried. "Tell me why it is you gals call them things ya git done to your hair *permanents*? You're always back in here a week later gettin' it twisted again." Henry didn't wait for an answer and headed for McCracken's.

A Day Given to Luck

That evening Tommy, Jud, Henry, and Dolores, who was dressed more for a cocktail party uptown than for a ditch at the Tin Cup, took the back table of the café. She was wearing a low-cut, thin-strapped, tight-fitting, short, red number that caught everybody's eye and turned every head in the café. The dress was pretty over the top, even by Dolores's standards. She had her makeup on and her red hair stacked up on her head and she was enjoying herself. But, perhaps no one in the restaurant was enjoying her more than Ol' Dan Connor who dropped his coffee cup into his soup as Dolores wiggled past.

The Tin Cup was Saturday-night busy and Sarah had steaks flaming, chickens broiling, fries sizzling, and could only wave to the four as they seated themselves. She was dressed in her usual Hawaiian shirt with her Yankees' hat cocked back on her head, and she had only the briefest glimpse of Tommy, but it was enough for her to retie her apron and tuck her hair back under her hat. First chance she was going to put on a little lipstick—such was the effect Tommy had on women. The two waitresses, Linda and Sandy, were on a dead run and catering to a full restaurant, tables, booths, and counter. Country music filtered in from the bar side. Linda took their drink orders. But it was Sal who delivered them.

"So Tommy, how ya doing?" Sal greeted him, setting a tray of drinks on their table and then passing the orders around. Sal always remembered Tommy but it wasn't because of his luck, charm, or good looks. It was because Tommy always ordered from the top shelf of the back bar and made sure everyone at the table joined him.

"I'm doing well, Sal. How did our Yankees do today?"

"Dropped a game to Boston this afternoon," Sal answered sadly, "my boy Clemens pitches the distance, t'rowing the good stuff. We're up two-zip in the ninth. Then he walks two and serves up the grapefruit to Martinez, of all people, who sends it into the cheap seats."

"Then by all means, as a way of expressing my condolences, let me buy you a drink, Sal," Tommy offered.

"Thanks, I think I will," and with that Sal turned and headed back into the bar and the top shelf.

~

Linda came to take their dinner order—rib-eyes all around. "And can I git some horseradish with that?" Henry added.

"You bet," Linda said.

"Linda, you feeling all right, honey? You look a mite puny," Dolores asked.

"Just a bit tired is all," Linda answered.

The evening fell into a wonderful rhythm of steaks, laughter, stories, and wine from Tommy's vineyard. Tommy told of his travels, his life a total fascination with Dolores dangling on his every word. This was a man whose parents played with the Kennedys, a man who had attended state dinners, whose father was an ambassador. Jud listened to his tales and wondered how one guy gets to be so powerful, so rich, so wealthy, good looking, and so damn lucky on the river to boot? Was he just born lucky? Were his parents lucky? With people like Tommy, was it some kind of unexplainable fusion of good fortune and genetics? Jud wondered how something as ephemeral, so unpredictable, and elusive as luck could form any union whatsoever, with something so finite, and unambiguously scientific as the predestined permutations within the human genome. Contradictions within unanswerable problems is where Jud spent much of his time.

Linda delivered coffees all around and Jud came back to the conversation as Tommy was at the end of another story. ". . . so, when my father was no longer in public service, the family left Paris, and we moved back to Vermont. That was in 1964."

Dolores, glowing slightly from the wine, a redhead in a red dress, embarrassed about her life when compared to the things Tommy had done, laughed, "Can you imagine such a thing? Being born in Paris, France—seeing ballets, goin' to all them famous art museums? Can you imagine spendin' the weekends with the de Gaulles, dancin' at the Winter Ball with Picasso's daughter? I mean that there is a childhood.

"In 1965 I'd spend a weekend now and then at my Aunt Agnes's and went to hoedowns with this yahoo," said Dolores. That vision in red, approaching infrared, laughed and put her head in Henry's shoulder.

"An excellent choice, Dolores," Tommy said and toasted her with his coffee cup.

"Hey, it's getting kinda late and if we're gonna wanna be on the river at first light tomorrow—" Henry said.

"Right you are, Henry," Tommy said, pushing his chair from the table, but as he began to stand there came a great crash of dishes. He turned around to see Linda lying on the floor, her orders splayed out in front of her. Sarah came out from the kitchen. Patty ran to her from the cash register, but it was Tommy who got to her first. Appearing dazed Linda was immediately struggling to her feet.

"Are you all right?" Sarah asked as she and Tommy helped her into a chair.

"Yeah, I think so," she answered through deep breaths. The color was already returning to her face. "I just got a little dizzy for a second and tripped over my own damn-fool feet. I'm okay, really."

"You better go lie down in the back for a while. Patty and I can handle this," Sarah said.

"No, no. I'm all right, really I'm fine." Linda stood to prove it. "I just didn't eat very much today, I guess. And the baby kept me awake most of the night." Sarah then insisted that she lie down and Tommy and Henry helped Linda to the couch in Sarah's office. As Tommy eased her down on the couch, he was amazed at how small she felt, birdlike in his arms.

"Really, I'm okay now. I still have to—" Linda protested.

"No, you are staying right here," Sarah ordered. "I'm going to bring you some soup."

Dolores and Jud appeared at the door. Of all the people in Travers, it was Dolores who probably knew Linda the best and that was hardly at all. Linda was new to town. She had come into the beauty parlor to have her hair done the same day she went to the Tin Cup looking for waitress work, and this was only her first week at the café. All anyone knew about her was that she was from Texas, she had two children, her husband was out of work, and that they were living down at the trailers, a string of run-down single-wides south of town. It was a certainty that things could not be easy for Linda, because people didn't live down in the trailers unless they absolutely had to.

Dolores took over. "Now, honey, you take it easy now. You jest need some food in your tummy," she said putting a cool cloth on Linda's head.

Sarah came back with a cup of soup. "Dolores, can you keep an eye on her for a while?"

"I'm fine, really, you guys. I am," Linda implored. "I'll eat this soup and then I'll be right out and help you."

"You boys go on ahead. I'm gonna sit with her for a spell," Dolores said.

The three men stepped out into the back alley of the café. Jukebox music from the bar side drifted out to join them. The skies were cloudless, the night was warm, and tomorrow was almost sure to be hot and windless. Perfect. Salmon flies would be hatching by the millions. All the stars were out and shining and every one of them seemed to be lucky. The light of a half-moon lit the Elkheart. It was agreed that the three would meet at the Boat Works at five thirty. They would be on the river at six.

Not one dare say it, to avoid any possible jinxes, but tomorrow held all the probabilities of being *one of those days*. One of those all-magical angling days, perhaps *the* day, that floats high above all other remembered days streamside. All anglers have one. Well, all anglers except Junior, who was still down in the basement and tying salmon flies. His house sits on the Elkheart, and while missing trout was his pastime, Junior didn't miss seeing the hatch.

Jud walked back to the Boat Works laughing about the fact that on what was almost sure to be one of the best days of fishing ever imagined, he would be guiding the world's worst fisherman.

Henry crossed the street to Dolores's knowing that Dolores would be home shortly and that she would be in the mood. Wine always put Dolores in the mood. Wine or anything else liquid.

And Tommy walked down to the Take 'r Easy, enjoying his evening, enjoying the prospects of tomorrow's fishing, but troubled by, and not able to shake the image of, that little waitress struggling to her feet.

At five thirty Jud stumbled down the stairs of the Boat Works to see Junior, who had been there since five, wandering around on the drive.

Henry and Tommy drove up the hill just as he was pouring his first cup. Once dressed he was ready and out the door at 5:34, coffee in hand. At 6:13 both boats had been launched, Jud and Henry at their oars guiding Junior and Tommy. At 6:15, owing to a slow start, Tommy landed his first fish, while Junior had irretrievably sent his fly into the bank and was tying on another one.

By the time they had floated down to the Channels, where the river unravels into a series of braids, a few salmon flies had been seen. The hatch would come with the heat of the day. Jud took one channel, Henry another. From here on, depending on their timing and the channel chosen, they would either see each other off and on all day or not at all.

Taking a pull on his left oar, Jud spun the SS *Lucky Me* toward the rest of the day and watched Henry's dory disappear from view with Tommy's rod bent to a fish. He would use his right oar again as soon as Junior was done unwinding his line from its oarlock. Jud made a promise to himself—he was not going to get frustrated with Junior.

Henry moved the dory around through a small rapid, then paused in the tailwater, treading his oars, so that Tommy could pause to tie on a new fly, the last one being shredded in the jaws of a very large brown trout. Holding his new fly up to the light and threading the leader, he asked aloud, "I wonder how our little friend Linda is doing?"

Henry knew, and in some detail, exactly how Linda was doing though he would have never talked about it until asked. Such is the cowboy way. All his information came late last night right before Dolores had her way with him. "Seems like Linda's husband has taken to beatin' on her. The drunker he gets the meaner the beatin'. Last night after we left the Cup, Dolores said that when she started to talk about it all she could do is cry. She showed Dolores her bruises." Henry's mouth went straight and his lips disappeared. The last emotion Henry wanted to feel on a day like this was rage, but at that moment, rage was what he was feeling. "And now here's the best part—there's Linda no bigger 'n a minute and her husband is a two-hundred-pounder."

"Oh God," was all that Tommy said.

"Yeah, I think I jest might have to go over there soon and have a little talk with that guy, show 'im how it feels to be the hittee instead of the hittor for a while." Henry smiled at the prospect. He was a true believer in the vigilante law of the Old West, and in years passed, he had dispensed this form of justice on more than a few occasions. There were several steadfast rules in the Elkheart Valley—you don't sell your calves before the first of July, you don't infringe on another man's water rights, and you don't mess with Henry Albie, a two-hundred-pounder himself, short, mean when riled, and all muscle.

One might have dreamed of such a day, but now they were fishing it. By midmorning it was warm and sure to be hot. Cloudless. Windless. Lucky. Salmon flies were on the river by the tens of thousands, on the river, on their dories, in their hair, under their sunglasses; landing, flying, and crawling, a million wings catching the light. Henry was at the oars and Tommy in the bow catching every trout in his path. Just as the day before, Tommy caught rainbows in their riffles. He caught browns from the pools. He caught fish behind logs, beneath the willows, in the eddies, in the backwaters, out in the middle, and under the banks. Nothing in midair. But the difference held by today's fishing was that today's trout were much longer. All the big trout were up, tempted by the pterodactyls, a meal in themselves.

The fishing throughout the afternoon would turn out to be better than any day either Henry or Jud had ever seen. A broad statement considering their collective years of guiding and two lifetimes of fishing the Elkheart. But it was a fact that they would agree on come day's end and for the rest of their lives. Even Junior was catching a few, though the fish on average would be considerably smaller than Tommy's. With Jud at the oars and Junior stumbling about in the bow, Junior frightened every trout in their path. He spooked browns from the pools, he terrified the rainbows from the riffles. He caught his fly behind the logs, beneath the willows, in the eddies, out in the middle, and under the banks, and on one short and erratic backcast when his line wavered just before it hit the river behind them, while waiting on his rod's bend to bullwhip it forward, Junior caught Jud in the neck with a size six fly, sending Jud into midair.

"Ow-w-w," Jud yelped.

"Geez, I'm sorry, Jud." Junior apologized turning quickly in his swivel chair, rocking the boat, and in doing so knocked his Coke into his lap. "Lucky for you I was using the BL-127. It's a 3X long, thin wire, barbless hook. It's an upturned eye. When I'm fishing dries, especially large dries, I think an upturned eye, as opposed to a ring eye, is better because . . ."

Junior's esoteric ramblings forced Jud to escape once again into the recesses of his mind, wondering as he did so how anyone could talk about the arcane intricacies of fly fishing, intricacies best suited for nighttime fireside angling, when there were trout actively feeding everywhere around him. But then it was Junior, and after knowing him for a lifetime, Jud also knew there really wasn't an explanation for Junior. Not hearing a word of what Junior was saying, but nodding and smiling just the same, he looked upstream into the late afternoon light, scattered and dancing across the water, between the shadows. It was warm and it was sunny and Jud was feeling lucky—because there he was, drifting on a river through a paradise, sitting at the oars of the *Lucky Me,* floating and fishing on the luckiest of all fishing days. There was only one thing that could make this day even luckier, that being if he were in the bow and fishing for himself. But, that would put Junior at the oars and this was something he was unwilling to risk. He had just caused damage with a nearly weightless fly because of his abundant lack of motor skills, and Jud's neck was still stinging. The kind of damage Junior could issue trying to row a three-hundred-pound drift boat, with two lives in the balance, was painful to imagine.

The water tower above Travers appeared over the trees as the Channels began weaving themselves back into one river, deep, heavy, and slow moving. A quarter mile behind them Henry's dory emerged from the trees and the far channel, "I wonder how those guys did today?" Junior said, ecstatic with his catch of fish, an even dozen.

"I don't know, but knowing Tommy I imagine he caught a hundred or two," Jud answered.

Junior smiled from past tales told by Jud and Henry over the years about Tommy and his fishing. "Ya know, I don't envy that guy for his good looks, and I don't envy him 'cause he's rich, I just envy that luck of his," Junior, paraphrasing Walton, said wistfully.

"Yep, the guy's lucky and that's for certain. But you caught some fine fish today, Junior." Which brought Junior right back to beaming.

They had no way of knowing that Tommy had landed fifty-seven fish, Henry had been counting, and had just finished landing his largest trout of the day—a twenty-six-inch, eight-pound rainbow.

Lazy, sunburned, and happy, Junior retied his fly and put the hook in the keeper, missing it completely. Not noticing his line, now trailing out and under the boat, he pulled his second cold beer from the cooler. They floated into town, past the first of the riverfront homes, the Smiths and the Corys.

They floated past the fairgrounds and under Town Bridge. While Jud positioned the dory for the takeout, Junior's loose fly caught on a pylon and quite a bit of line was stripped from his reel before he could drop his beer and gain control. When the line straightened, his fly came loose and was sucked under. "Hey, I got lucky," Junior said smiling and had no idea just how lucky he was about to get.

There from the deep hole below the bridge, where the tourists drown their worms, where the children and their dogs come to swim, below the deafening echoes of the rumblings as car and tractor trailer roll past, down in the dark water, it was coming for Junior's fly.

His fly rod lying loosely across his lap, Junior took another long pull on his beer, finishing it with a smack of his lips and an "Ahhhhhhh." Not a big drinker, Junior sat in his seat and gave a giggle, self-satisfied from his twelve-fish day, not to mention slightly high from back-to-back beers. "Man, what a day it's been." He had no idea that the day it had been was going to pale to the day it was about to be.

The fly rod slowly began pulling from his lap and Junior lackadaisically grabbed the butt. He lifted the tip of the rod, "Oh, I've caught a snag." Jud laughed thinking how wonderful it was that Junior was actually somehow surprised that his line had caught on something, like it hadn't been happening *all day long*. But then Junior could snag his fly on a dance floor. The rod jerked and leaped from his hands. It slid along the gunwale and would have been pulled overboard if the reel hadn't wedged long enough against the oarlock for Jud to grab it.

There in the curling deep water flowing from the pylons, not twenty feet from the boat, it rose. "Grab the rod," Jud yelled. At first Junior froze at the sight of such a trout at the end of his line. Then he snapped into action. Lunging past his seat he grabbed the rod with a miraculous two-handed snatch, but there was a part of his response that Junior should have never attempted and that was—the lunge.

Lunges are for professional stuntmen and trained acrobats and not anything that should be attempted by the world's clumsiest pharmacist. Lunges on dry land are risky, lunges in boats can be titanic. In a Chaplinesque whirl, Junior, the rod still in his hands, attempted to stand but slipped, landed on an oar bouncing it from its lock. All of his weight came falling on the upstream gunwale tipping the *Lucky Me* over far enough for water to rush in amidships. The only thing that saved the dory from capsizing was Junior's falling overboard, well not completely overboard. Somehow he managed to hook himself on the oarlock by the back of his suspenders. With one oar out of its lock the dory was impossible to row. Jud couldn't put it back in place because Junior's head was in the way. He couldn't cut his suspenders because they were floating in deep water. He knew Junior's swimming skills were equal to his fishing skills and Junior, swimming in full waders, would be one drowned druggist. Jud wasn't panicked because they were in slow current, but they were now floating past the takeout. "Hand me the rod and I'll pull you back in the boat."

"Not on your tin type," Junior shouted. His rod had never left his death grip. He was still straight with his fish and seemingly oblivious to his surroundings: fifty-degree water a foot higher than his waders. He watched the large brown surface again this time ten feet away and from river level. This was the biggest fish he had ever hooked, ever seen, ever dreamed about, this was a trout to drown for.

Jud did what he could with the one oar, but with the weight of Junior tipping the boat to port and the water in the boat sloshing to that side, it wasn't very much. He might have done a little more if he hadn't been weak from laughter. The sight of Junior, strung up to the oarlock, hanging like a marionette, bobbing along in the current, his bobbing doubly funny because of the elasticity of the suspenders, was a scene straight out of Mack Sennett.

"What in the Sam Hell?" Henry said slowly as his mind tried to make sense of what was going on downriver. Jud was still at some distance but Henry could see something was amiss. Junior looked to be out of the boat and the *Lucky Me* was definitely listing to one side. Henry turned his dory around and began rowing to the rescue.

"This is a big fish!" Junior shouted.

There was no doubt about it—Junior had on a very, very, large trout, an old wide-as-he-was-long brown trout that had been living under the pylons for many years, fat from the tourists' worms. At first there came a series of heavy tugs, which Junior thought might break his line. But fat old brown trout fight like fat old men, furious for a few moments, their sheer weight their only defense, but they don't fight for very long before they tire. The fish boiled not two feet from the boat, its brown and red spots turning an inch below the surface, and trout being a music all their own, each spot played in the sunlight like the notes on a piano roll.

It was the single most glorious moment of Junior's fishing career. "God, would ya look at that fish!"

Jud was ready at the net. Steadying himself over the gunwale of an already listing drift boat, he warned, "Now, Junior you just keep your rod right there. Don't move." But when he went to scoop the trout from the river he soon found the old brown hadn't spent years picking worms from the tourists' hooks while dodging the spoons and lures not to know something about human nature. The fish knew it had to time its last effort perfectly—when the human was at his most confident. When it felt the net coming the brown threw all it had left into one last run and made a dive beneath the boat, but got no farther than the other side. Jud moved carefully to the other side of the dory to see the fish spent and easily brought it to net.

"Got him, Junior. What a beast!" Jud yelled and held the net up high. Still a hundred yards upstream but closing, Henry could see, even at such a distance, that it was a very large fish.

Junior, in the meantime, had thrown his rod into the boat and managed to unfasten one side of his suspenders enabling him to turn, grasp the gunwale, and pull himself up for a look at his fish. For Junior, the turn, grasp, and pull falls into the same degree of difficulty as the lunge. Under his full weight the water in the dory shifted once more and rushed to his side. It was then Junior proved to Jud, through demonstration, the theory of the catapult and at the same time created a new meaning to boat launch. Now Jud was overboard and when he came up sputtering for air he was still holding the net, but the net was no longer holding the trout.

Jud swam for shore as Henry and Tommy rowed up to Junior. "You all right, Junior?" Henry asked as he nosed his dory up against the *Lucky Me.*

With the trout on his line Junior had hardly noticed the cold water, but with the loss of his fish he was now freezing. "Yeah, b-b-but I'm r-r-real ch-ch-chilly." Tommy leaned out and unfastened Junior's suspenders from the oarlock and pulled Junior aboard while Henry tied a rope to Jud's boat and started to tow it to shore. "D-d-did you s-s-see my f-f-fish?" Junior asked.

"Just saw it in the net from a ways off but I could see she was a dandy," Henry answered as Tommy threw Jud the bow rope. "But, I gotta tell you, guys," Henry said smiling, "I've been down this river a thousand times and every time I go I end up seein' somethin' different, some new thing, but seeing this here rodeo falls into that category of things I ain't never gonna see again. How'd you git yerself out of the boat like that, Junior?"

Junior didn't hear him. He was staring down into the river. "I had on the b-b-biggest fish of my l-l-life. I l-l-landed it. Jud had it in the n-n-net," Junior chattered his lamentation, "but I n-n-never really g-g-got to see him."

"Yeah, but I did. It was twenty-five inches long—guaranteed," Jud said dripping wet and pulling the two boats to shore. "But it was the fattest fish I have ever seen. Looked like a puffer fish. Had to have been ten pounds." A smile crossed Junior's shivering cheeks knowing that while he hadn't seen his fish someone else had, which in many ways, given a fisherman's bend toward fabrication, was even better.

"How'd you guys do?" Jud asked knowing full well how it must have been.

"Well, it was *pretty* good but I never caught anything the size of Junior's fish."

"I got twelve other nice ones, t-t-too. Hey, that m-m-akes the one I lost the thirteenth—f-f-figures." Junior ached from not seeing that fish, to look at it, lift it in the net. Smile for the camera. How wonderful it would have been to cradle such a trout in his hands when he let it go. The pain of his loss, the loss of such a moment, was far more serious than the hypothermia and it showed in his face. The hot sun would quickly cure his hypothermia, but it was Tommy who would cure Junior's blues.

"Well, I think that's about all we caught, wasn't it?" Tommy asked, looking at Henry, eyebrows raised, signaling for accord.

"Uh, yeah, uh . . . that's about right." Henry agreed not knowing at first what he could have been talking about. Tommy had boated fifty-seven, counted, and one twenty-six-incher, measured, and most important, Tommy's trout was purposefully caught compared to Junior's accidental brown. Anyway, Henry ruminated, weight counts for something sure, but in fishing, length is *the* measurement.

And then it came to him. To his amazement Tommy had given the day to Junior—something Henry had never heard of and doubted that it had ever been done. Fishermen can give one another excuses, they can give one another lies, and they can give one another endless advice, but no angler in history, Henry imagined, had ever given a better day to a lesser fisherman. "Yep, I guess it was about twelve. And we did have that big one but it was nowhere near as big as yours, Junior."

Junior beamed. Jud stared at Henry in amazement and wondered how, on a day where Blind Lemon Jefferson could have caught twelve trout, did the world's luckiest fisherman catch a dozen and the world's unluckiest fisherman catch thirteen—well, thirteen with an asterisk. Then he caught the look in Henry's eye and knew there was more to the story and that he would hear about it later, but right now he had to bail the water from his drift boat.

And hear about it he did that evening when Henry phoned with the truth about the day's incredible fishing, and about Tommy giving the day away. But that wasn't his only phone call. Sarah had some good news.

"Hello."

"Hey, Jud. It's me. Listen to this. Tommy came into the café on his way out of town and he gave Linda a check for five *thousand* dollars. He told her to take the money and get out of town. Leave her husband and find a new life. And by God you know what—she and her kids are going to be on the midnight bus out of Reynolds. Sal's driving her up right now. She doesn't know where she's going but someplace that creep of a husband can't find her. Isn't that amazing? She'll make a go of it, that one. Hey, I gotta go. We're busy. That Tommy is such a good guy. I just had to call you. Bye."

Jud hung up the phone and went outside into the warm night feeling lucky. Annie the Wonderlab, asleep on the back porch, wagged her tail and got up to greet him as he came out the screen door. He rubbed her ear and stared straight up into the evening sky and its endless stars thinking about luck, wondering why Lady Luck either taps you on the shoulder or passes you by, that sliding scale on which everyone weighs in from Park Avenue to Mogadishu; wondering if people like Tommy somehow create their own luck by sharing theirs with others—given days, thousand-dollar checks.

He thought about the day's cast and crew: Tommy would be almost home and flying first class, Henry would be asleep—he'd be up at five. (If Dolores had her way he'd be up at five, again at six, and up once more at seven fifteen.) Junior, asleep yet or not, would be at home and smiling. As for himself, he was feeling good, feeling tired, but most of all he was feeling lucky.

And that fat old brown trout, the luckiest one of them all, is back under Town Bridge, down deep behind the pylons, and waiting for the morning, the tourists, and their worms.

From The Journals of Traver C. Clark

April 9, 1911—

This evening the light on the mountains was magnificent. I have made sketches in my life, none of them very good. But to be able to paint, something other than the barn, to be an artist—this is a gift I would love to own.

~

Float Trip the Light Fantastic or Where the Judson Meets the Hudson

He was Hudson Kenneth House, nicknamed Hud as a child until the movie by the same name came to the big screen while he was in medical school. Round faced and round bodied, Hudson House was far from the chiseled Paul Newman character, and the film caused him to change his name to Ken for defensive reasons right after medical school. His earlier works were signed Ken House, but now he was Hudson House, *the* Hudson House. His oldest friends and family still called him Hud.

Sarah, Doc Higgins, and Junior McCracken all knew, in varying degrees, the art of Hudson House. They knew his name as well as his paintings. Sarah had even attended art shows and museums displaying his work in New York before moving to Montana.

Jud would recognize some of Hudson's more famous pieces, but coming up with Hudson's name would be a stretch, though he had certainly heard his name.

Henry had neither heard of Hudson or seen any of his work, but it wasn't because Henry didn't appreciate art, and out at his ranch the prints of Remington and Russell hung on nearly every wall.

Sal's view of the art world was nonexistent. His knowledge of Hudson House would be "I'm not sure on dis, but I think a guy by dat name played second base for the Cards in da late thirties. Now dere was a team. When they had Ripper Collins, Frankie Fritch, the Diz . . ." It would never take long for Sal to bring a subject like art around to baseball, but it was only fitting since to Sal baseball was art.

Dolores was in an art world all her own. Like Dolores's wardrobe, her display of artwork fit in well with her decor of what might be called K-Mart decoupage: lava-lamp orange with lime green trimmings, gold filigree, and highlighted by two original black-velvet portraits, one of Elvis, the other of a mariachi player.

The rest of Travers Corners, the other three hundred and eleven residents, had a knowledge of Hudson House that fell in line with one of the aforementioned seven. But one thing was a certainty, no one, not even Sarah, would have known Hudson if he tripped over him and his easel. A point being proven right now because signing the guest card down at the Take 'r Easy Motel was one Ken House. He signed Hudson House on little else but his artwork.

To Florence Alpen, tending the reception desk, he was just another fisherman coming to stay, for two nights, and another one asking directions. "Young lady," Hudson inquired as she handed him the key to room nine, the best room, the one with the kitchen, "could you tell me how I might find the Boat Works?"

"First right out of town," she said pointing north, "go across the bridge and up the hill."

Following Hudson out the door Florence pointed to the Boat Works, "See that big old log house up there? That's the Boat Works."

"Oh yes, thanks again."

Things were as usual at the Carrie Creek Boat Works and Guide Service. Judson C. Clark, proprietor, boatbuilder, and guide, was in the workshop working over a dory, lacing rope through the oarsman's seat, and waiting for glue to dry. It was a warm and perfect day in July, a perfect day for a lot of things, but waiting for glue to dry wasn't one of them. It was a perfect day for fishing. Annie the Wonderlab barked at a car, a nondescript four-door rental, coming up the drive. A short, pudgy man got out and walked toward the workshop while looking at the large, old log structure, a building whose progress could be measured in thirds, one-third nearly renovated, one-third under serious construction, and one-third crumbling. "Hello, are you Jud?" he asked.

"Yep," Jud answered and turned down the radio just as a paid political advertisement for Reagan's reelection began to play.

"My name is Ken House," he said shaking Jud's hand. "Your name was given to me by a man in Helena who said that you build beautiful river dories." Looking into Jud's workshop where a completed dory awaited its final touches, he added "And I see that you do indeed. This fellow, and I can't remember his name right now, also said that you were a fine fisherman. Well, anyway, cut to the chase, I was wondering if you could take me down the river tomorrow?"

"Well, I'd like to but I've already got a trip booked for tomorrow. I could take you down the river the day after," Jud answered.

"Oh, that's no good. I have to leave day after tomorrow."

"Well, let me make a call," Jud said. He went to the phone and made a call but the line was busy. "I was just trying to call Henry but he's on the phone. He might be able to guide you tomorrow. The fishing has been pretty good."

"Oh, I can imagine. But tomorrow," Hudson explained in a raspy and high-pitched voice reminiscent of Andy Devine, "I won't be fishing. Tomorrow I will only be doing some drawing, watercolors, take a few photographs. It is *you* that I want to do the fishing while I sketch.

"I know this is a bit unusual, and I know that this is very short notice so if there is any inconvenience caused by either know that I am willing to pay a little more."

Jud looked out the window for a moment and smiled as if there were a second camera instead of a reflection to catch his aside. He went to the phone and tried Henry again while he watched Hudson walk over to the nearly completed dory for a closer inspection. Hudson was round, almost perfectly round, not fat by any means, just round. Jud, a long-legged stick of a man, brought to vertical what Hudson brought to circular.

Henry's line was free. "Hey, Henry, can you take a trip for me tomorrow . . . yeah . . . okay . . . a couple a folks from New Mexico, the Boyles . . . yeah . . . I was going to take them but another trip just came in . . . yeah . . . sure . . . No way . . . I wouldn't do that, and just so you know these guys I'm taking are huge. The guy is two hundred and fifty pounds easy and his wife is slightly heavier, a whiner, hates to fish, hates to be here, wants to be back at the mall." He nodded and grinned to Hudson and continued, "Yeah . . . well . . . but I know how much your back has been bothering you lat—yeah . . . it's going to be a bitch . . . yeah . . . but hey, what are friends for . . . okay . . . I'll call you later." Jud hung up the phone and looked back to the window for his second aside.

"I have a buddy like that," Hudson laughed. "Our whole friendship, starting at birth, has been spent trying to pull one over on the other guy."

"That would be me and Henry to the tee, right down to the starting at birth part. But hey, here I am confronted with a choice between two trips, one trip is rowing two people, only one of whom is an avid fishermen expecting a pound of your flesh at the oars for his dollar spent, or the other trip, one of rowing one person, who wants *me* to fish, and who is willing to pay extra if there are any inconveniences. I can see no inconveniences. In fact I should be paying you a little something."

"Well, there is going to be one inconvenience," Hudson clarified, leading Jud to think that the clinker was coming. "It's just that I need to be in a place, one of the places that you think to be the most beautiful, a place you can easily float to, and a place that would be good to fish."

"That would be down in a stretch of the river everyone calls the Bends—the river horseshoes there a couple of times just before you enter the canyon," Jud said without hesitation, the Bends being a magical place.

"Tell me about it."

"It's a place where rock walls come straight up out of the river, and the mountains behind that are mostly aspen. Guaranteed good views no matter which way you look."

"Perfect. It sounds perfect. What time will we have to leave to be there for the first morning light?"

"Well, uh . . . first light comes around . . . so in order to float down to . . . we'd have to put in at Second Bridge . . . it's about two . . . doesn't get light down in the Bends until late . . . and . . .," Jud said doing the math, his voice trailing off at each computation of river speed and distance. "So, we'd need to be *on* the river at four." The hour of four stuck in his throat. On the river at four meant up at three.

"Great," Hudson agreed. "And I will bring the lunch."

"Or another place we could go to that's a lot closer," Jud suggested, closer in this case meaning later and out of bed at six. "We could—"

"Nope. The first choice is always the best choice." There was nothing about the hour of three that made Hudson even flinch, but it made Jud cringe.

The details were quickly hammered out, and the following morning the SS *Lucky Me*, with Jud at her oars, was floating under a clear sky, a full moon, and into first light. Hudson was in the bow, high in the bow since the stern was laden down with too much stuff. There was barely room for Jud's fly rod. Annie the Wonderlab, usually at his feet for float trips, was sent home from the motel, her seat taken as was every cubic foot of the dory. Jud had never seen so much stuff. The man had cameras, canvases, easels, palettes, paints, brushes, rags, films, tripods, and more cameras, and one very large umbrella.

Hudson was a one-man hive ahead of him. There were photographs being taken, videos being made, and line drawings leaving his sketch pad at an impressive rate. Hopping from one side of the boat to the other, the round, little man, shaped like a hive himself, never stopped moving, and talked rarely, only asking politely for Jud to pull to the bank every so often. The float was slowed even further by Jud constantly having to leave the oars to hand Hudson one piece of equipment or the other, and though they had only been on the river for two hours with Jud rowing hard and fast when he could, they were running behind. If they were going to make the Bends for sunrise something needed to be said, "Ken, you know if we're going to get to the place we talked about, we had better put my back into it."

"Oh, I am so sorry. Okay. Let's hurry. Can't be late. Please hurry. I'll make it well worth your while."

The float trip, Jud was thinking as he turned the bow of the *Lucky Me* downstream, was not turning out as he had first thought. If he wanted to be in the Bends at dawn it would have to be rowing at ramming speed and with stamina, but the words *worth your while* to a man forever in need of money gave him the needed encouragement. The boat was sluggish because of all the cargo and the flat water, but Jud had brought Hudson to perhaps the best view on the first horseshoe just as the sunlight was inching down the rock walls and hitting the tips of the tallest aspens.

The *Lucky Me* eddied up in the shallows and Hudson bounced out on to the bank. He scrambled around over the rocks looking for the best place, the best light. Then he was back with orders, "I will need the gray bag. I'll need the easel, that book, no, the big blue one, that brown box there, and the umbrella." Jud was handing him the items in turn as more instructions came his way. "Could you move the boat upstream to just above that log? Then get ready to cast, fishing just past the bow of your boat. Thank you."

Jud had just rowed two miles in record time and now he was hauling the *Lucky Me* a hundred yards upstream, against the current, while sinking up to his calves along the muddy shore. All of a sudden, the first trip, the Boyles, was looking a little better through hindsight. He pulled the dory up on the rocks past the log, set up his rod, and walked over to where Hudson was signaling him to stand. When he was in position, Hudson shouted out over the rush of water, "Go ahead and cast like there were fish involved, but don't move from that spot."

Casting from his assigned spot was as close to fishing as Jud would get that morning. To make things worse, just out of casting distance, there were fish rising. Hudson painted and Jud faked his fishing, but even at his distance, even from his side of the easel, Jud could appreciate the intensity and speed at which the man worked. The painting done, Jud continued his false casting as the photography began. There was a short break from the modeling between the mediums in which Jud unloaded the rest of the bags, boxes, cases, tripods, and alike from the drift boat. Then Jud was back to being a subject and was captured in several different formats.

Suddenly with a wave of his hand Hudson shouted, "That's it. The light is gone. Jud, I am going to sketch for a while. Why don't you fish for a couple of hours then we will have lunch?" Jud agreed. Lunch sounded very good right now since the three o'clock alarm had left no room for food. Grabbing his fly rod, he walked downstream, but the fish were gone or at least they had stopped rising. There wasn't a mayfly in sight. There wasn't a nose to be seen. He didn't catch a thing. He fished his way back to Hudson and a lunch he had been looking forward to since he loaded the cooler into the dory. The ice chest was crammed with stuff wrapped in white paper, which, to Jud's mind, meant fresh and expensive.

When Jud had retuned, all of Hudson's supplies had been stowed away in the *Lucky Me* and the ice chest was open and stuff was spread out everywhere. "How was the fishing?" he greeted Jud, handing him a glass of wine.

"Didn't catch a thing," Jud answered while he looked over the food. Unwrapped it wasn't recognizable and it was far from appetizing. In fact it looked better wrapped. "So, Ken," he asked nervously, "what do we got here for lunch?"

"Oh, some wonderful things I brought in Missoula from a specialty food store. It was a great little shop. They had aubergine, foie gras, and this came as quite a shock, they even had some of my favorite Stilton," Hudson explained while picking up each of the dishes for Jud's closer inspection. Everything looked ugly and smelled worse. At that moment Jud's hunger pangs turned to waves of nausea and he ached for one of Sarah's roast beef sandwiches.

"How'd your painting go today?" Jud asked and gulped down his glass of wine. He'd need some wine, perhaps all he could get his hands on, if he was going to stick anything displayed on the cooler into his mouth.

"Oh, it went well. It really did, thank you, and thank you for this place. It's just as beautiful as you said. The light this morning. Fantastic.

Well, here I can show you." Hudson bounced over the river rock down to the dory. His movements were surprisingly nimble Jud thought, for a short, round man, and he was back quickly with his painting rolled up in a tube. He unfurled it to show the work, the drift boat, the river, and Jud's casting.

Not knowing much about art, but knowing enough to know that this was very good art, Jud said, "Hey, that is really great. I mean I really like that a lot."

"That's very special, nothing means more to the artist than praise from the subject. This piece," Hudson went on to explain, "is a commission for an old friend of mine who fly-fishes." The old friend being Jimmy Carter, but he had left that part out. Hudson was that way.

"Well, I can sure see why someone would want to buy one of your paintings."

"I do sell some of it. I give some away. It's nothing more than a hobby really. I—" Hudson's humility was interrupted by the sight of a boat floating into view, Henry at the oars. He rowed ashore and Jud walked down to greet him. They met halfway and out of earshot of either client. In the bow of Henry's dory sat an older, petite lady, in the back sat a young girl, who looked to be about ten. "What's going on?" Jud greeted.

"Well, it's like this, J. C. I go to pick these folks up at the motel, and Mr. Boyle ain't feelin' up to speed and begs off. But his wife and the grandkid wanna go. They don't fish; jest wanted to take a float down the Elkheart. Now here's the part I like the best. They tell me to bring along my fly rod because the grandkid's never seen 'er done before. Now I don't know what it was like for you, but the fishin' this morning was insane, damn it was fine. How'd you do?"

"Seems like it's a day for sightseers and nonfisherman."

Henry looked up the hill to see Hudson sketching away. "Hey, I thought you were rowin' some serious tonnage today. Who's that guy?"

"An artist. Ken House. And he is some kind of artist. We've been on the river since four. He's been painting, photographing, and sketching me since daybreak. Nice fellow. He had me casting all morning and he put me in the best light for painting, but the fishing was a hundred feet away. He's got more gear than you can imagine."

"Yeah, I can see yer boat is kinda ridin' low in the water."

"Very nice man. He brought lunch. Stuff you wouldn't want to eat. You got any of your lunches left?"

"Ahhh," Henry realized as he caught the guilt in Jud's eyes. "Ain't you the prankster, though. I git it now. You were goin' for the hoodwink. You figured on takin' the easy trip for yer ownself. That's why *I* got the Boyles. Makin' me think you were thinkin' about my bad back and all. That was an extra touch. Well, look's like it all mighta backfired some.

"Lunches? Let's see. Oh, Sarah really outdid herself, too. Fried chicken, potato salad, cookies. Nope, there ain't a crumb left. Damn. I don't know when you are going to learn, son. You can't beat me. I am too lucky and too good lookin'," Henry said grinning from ear to ear. Normally stoic to the point of inanimate, an ear-to-ear grin was Henry's equivalent to doubled up in laughter. "And here I am winnin' again."

"Well, you know what they say?" Jud laughed.

"What's that?"

"To the victor go the Boyles."

"I gotta git goin'. They want to be off the river at two. My kind of fishing trip. On late, off early, and I do all the fishin'."

Jud watched Henry row away and just before he swung his drift boat into the current he saw Henry lean down to come back up with a drumstick of Sarah's chicken in his mouth, held firmly in place by the grin. Then he walked back up to where Hudson was sitting in the shade.

"I've had a great idea. I would like to stay here for the afternoon and paint here again in the evening light."

"Stay here and paint this all again tonight?" Jud asked slightly staggered. "We wouldn't be off the river until after midnight."

"It's a full moon," Hudson pointed out. "I know that is a long day and I would insist, of course, on paying you whatever extra you think is fair."

"Well, I guess. But—"

"You see, Jud, it's all about the light. Morning brings us that dazzling electric, vibrant light, evening brings the light with the rich, deep colors, two different lights, two different paintings. To an artist, the flat floodlight that illuminates the rest of the day has no other purpose than showing us where to go, lighting our way. When the light is gone the art is gone." Hudson poured Judson another glass of wine. "I have always said . . ."

The afternoon passed with surprising speed where Jud had thought it might painfully crawl along. Ken was easy, polite. Back at the Boat Works he had been a man of few words, and up to lunch Ken had said very little, concentrating on his art. But over lunch and a bottle of wine the conversation flowed freely, brief biographies were exchanged before the stories began. Jud was amazed to learn that before turning to painting Ken had been a doctor, but Jud was always amazed when a man is able to work from both sides of his brain. Usually a doctor and an artist are two different guys.

Hudson led an unbelievable life, flying all over the world to catch the light, traveling normally with his wife. This year, and it was only July, he'd been to Polynesia, Scotland, and Italy. In that same time Jud had made it as far as Billings. But when Hudson told his tales it wasn't to flaunt his fabulous travels and obvious wealth. It was all about the art, all about the light. He paused in the middle of talking about the light of Tuscany to remove his glasses and rub his eyes. Jud, up to that moment, had thought his large blue eyes were made that way by the lenses, like optics are wont to do, but Ken's eyes *were* that big and round and they fit in with the rest of him perfectly.

"You know," he continued, leaving Tuscany for a completely different tack, "when I was a boy in Michigan I loved to fish, and I am sure given the time I would enjoy it again."

"Why don't you?"

"Well, as you know, the best times for fishing and the best times for painting are the same times and I am afraid my painting wins out."

They talked on until Hudson said, "Jud, if you wouldn't mind I would like to rest a while, take a nap under that tree there." And with that he stood and headed for a grassy spot in the shade.

"Don't mind a bit," Jud said, and grabbing his fly rod he headed downstream, hungry beyond measure. He had even forced down some of the cheese. It was awful. He fished for an hour or more until the heat of the July sun forced him under a tree. Then following Hudson's lead he fell easily into a wine-induced sleep.

Jud awoke, fished leisurely back, and returned to see Hudson the hive buzzing all over the banks, cameras, easels, bags, cases, boxes, and umbrella all in place. And when the colors, shadows, and light began to entwine to just right, Hudson began to paint. It was a light artists dream about, to capture and yet never capture, a light changing constantly by thin clouds sailing across the sun. Shadows folded and rolled over the river, the aspens, the canyon walls, across the sage, and to the mountains. Jud was once again sent to his place where he spent the evening air casting from his compositionally correct spot, out of reach of any trout.

But this time Hudson gave no attention to his cameras. This time he never left his easel. Jud looked over to see Hudson, stationed under his umbrella, painting like a man possessed, racing against the light. And in the time it took for the perfect light to fade, for the sun to leave the canyon walls, Hudson had finished three paintings. All of which, to Jud's untrained eye, were truly beautiful. Broad simple strokes, nothing defined but everything represented, the painting can take you there faster than a photograph. Hudson was noticeably pleased and excited by his work.

"These are really great," Jud said looking at the paintings.

"Thank you so much. Tonight the light was magical."

Once things were stored aboard the *Lucky Me* the two drifted into the twilight, and a full moon. Hudson and the Judson chatting away. With every mile floated, Jud realized more and more that he was rowing a great man, and still totally unaware of Ken's artistic station. "Your casting tonight, the light hitting your line, back and forth like a brush stroke—it's an artistry all it own."

It was twelve thirty by the time the two were off the river and rolling into Travers Corners. "Listen, Jud, it's late, would it be all right if I paid you tomorrow morning?"

"Sure, no problem," Jud answered and with that pulled into the Take 'r Easy Motel, room nine, and unloaded.

Jud crawled into bed that evening, dog tired from the marathon float trip, twenty-two hours start to finish. He fell asleep dreaming about a large tip.

In the morning Jud awoke to a hunger he had never imagined. He showered with nothing but one of Sarah's breakfasts on his mind. However, he would have to wait until Ken showed up to pay his bill. But when he reached the bottom of the stairs he found that Ken had been there and gone. There on the kitchen table was a check for yesterday's trip, a check for the exact amount, and sandwiched between a folded piece of paper was a small watercolor, a painting of the *Lucky Me*, no bigger than a postcard. There was no tip. It was a nice watercolor, a nice gift, but fifty bucks would have been a whole lot better and more relevant to his financial condition, which forever was teetering at the edge.

"Sh-i-i-t," he said loudly. Jud couldn't believe it, and while he wasn't raving mad because it was a nice gift, he was disappointed. "All day long he had said that he would make it *worth my while* and *compensate me for trouble*, and I get this postage stamp of a painting." For what he went through yesterday Jud thought fifty dollars to be at the low end of the tip scale.

With Annie the Wonderlab at his heel he walked quickly down the hill to the Tin Cup, his Ken House watercolor in hand. Inside the café he joined Henry and Dolores at the back table and then ordered most of the items on the menu. He waved to Sarah behind the grill.

"Whaddaya got there?" Henry asked.

"My tip from yesterday," Jud said a little tight-lipped and opened the envelope to show the watercolor. "I was on that river with that man, nice guy, a real gentleman, for *twenty-two* hours. I pulled off the river at midnight. No damn tip."

"What?"

"Yeah, after you left Ken tells me that he wants to paint one more painting but we needed to wait just where you left us for the evening light. I mean the guy can paint but . . ."

Sal walked past with a stack of bar napkins and leaned over Jud's shoulder. "Hey, nice picture. You see da game last night? Yankees stunk up da place." Then Sal continued to the bar side to the café.

"It's a re-e-eal nice picture, Judson. The Boyles were kind enough to tip me a fifty," Henry said through a grin, the same smile that was last seen holding a chicken leg.

Dressed more for Carnival than Travers Corners, Dolores, the Carmen Miranda of the Elkheart, agreed. "Yeah, that's a pretty good picture," she said rolling her eyes while wondering how any one could put a picture of a boat on their walls. *Some people's taste,* she said to herself. Elvis on velvet was the only art worthy of a wall.

Dolores and Henry finished their breakfast and were gone by the time Jud's food was brought to him. He read the paper, ate his breakfast, visited with a couple of cowboys from the Morris ranch, and quietly groused to himself about the parsimonious painter, Ken House. He was amazed at how badly he had been deceived; House appeared as one of the kindest men he had met and visited with in a long time.

Sarah took a break from the kitchen and came out for a cup of coffee. She flopped down next to Jud, "Busy morning. Were you hungry today or what? When Betty turned up your order I thought I was cooking for a table of four."

"Yeah, I was hungry. Now I'm just tired and slightly pissed off." He slid the watercolor out of its sleeve and handing it to Sarah proceeded to tell her of his yesterday, his no-lunch or dinner, nonfishing, twenty-two-hour float trip, artist with the zero tip yesterday. She looked at the painting. Her mouth dropped. She turned to Jud in total disbelief.

"What's wrong?"

If she wasn't momentarily speechless she would have been yelling, but she gathered herself and then explained to Jud, "You . . . you . . . know that . . ." her voice cracked and she started over. "You know that print in my hall? The street scene in the French Quarter? The one you like so well?" Her words were slow and deliberate, speaking in the tone used when trying to get through to someone who doesn't quite get it.

"Yeah."

"You remember who painted it?"

"Well, no, but I really like that painting."

"Hudson House."

"Yeah, okay, but this guy's name was Ken House."

Sarah pointed to the name signed in light pencil at the bottom of the watercolor. Jud had to squint almost to see it, "Hudson House, hmmm, I saw that but I guess I just read the House part." She turned the painting over and found a note, again in light pencil. "'This could go a long way toward a new roof my friend, Hudson. Thank you for the light.'"

"You are the luckiest son of a . . . damn. I mean . . . I can't believe . . . I couldn't—" Betty rang the bell calling Sarah back to the grill and a new order. "I can't . . ." She headed for the kitchen and then turned back to say, "I don't . . . and you were complaining about a fifty-dollar tip. Hudson House. I . . . I'll bet that painting is worth five thousand dollars."

"*WHAT!* This tiny picture? C'mon."

"Hudson House is one of the preeminent artists in America, of the twentieth century. I just can't—" Sarah's hands were whirling above her head. Jud sat there frozen for quite sometime. Then, carefully, he gathered his Hudson House and headed back to the Boat Works where he sat down on the porch and tried to get everything in perspective. Annie did what she could to help by licking his face.

Jud spent that morning and afternoon wondering and theorizing as to how things happen and how this had happened to him. "Light," he instructed Annie "that's what it all boils down to, it being the absurdity and glory of being alive. It's nothing but light, light, and a bit of luck. Light, squared, divided by Luck equals Life." His mind went to work on his theory.

Light. First, he established that it must be understood: there are two different kinds of light. That's why it needed to be squared. There is God's light, God's or whoever is in charge, which is indiscriminate. It's up and shining everyday, like clockwork, shining on everything and everybody. You can depend on precious little else in life, but you can depend on His light being there in the morning; has to be—it's in the Genesis clause of His contract. Morning light, evening light, artist's light, are all His doing.

Then there is the light of another gender, the one only Lady Luck can make shine. Light speed being a constant, Her light must travel at the same speed as God's light, but Hers would pinball around the world, flying low to catch all crap games, striking here then there, shining on people by chance. But one thing was for certain, Lady Luck had shined on him yesterday and she hadn't spared a watt.

Soon he would call Henry about the watercolor tip and *the* Hudson House. Then who'll be grinning through the chicken leg?

From The Journals of Traver C. Clark

June 9, 1922—

A new man by the name of Jim Foley moved to town this week. He bought a section of bottom ground from the Hanfords and is in the process of building both house and barn. He was in the book business back in New York. Fed up with the city and everything that goes with it he came out here to become a rancher.

Carrie baked him some bread and we drove out to welcome him to the Elkheart. A nicer fellow you could never meet and greener than new grass. But I've seen what he's already done on his place and I can tell you he is going to make it. It takes a certain kind to stand up to Montana.

~

Rose's Ragtop

The High Road, as it is referred to by the locals, once the old highway from Travers to Missoula, is now a two-laned and lonesome stretch of neglected asphalt, which takes the traveler the old way over Albie Pass. But to those who know where to turn, and fortunately very few do, there is a dirt road, an old logging route as High Road nears its summit, a logging road that hasn't been maintained in forty years, the Burnt Fork Road. The word "road" is misleading. It makes the path less traveled by look like a turnpike. Burnt Fork Road is now nothing more than two washed-out tracks crawling over a boulder-infested trail. Not for the weak at heart, but allowing the kind of privacy and hopefully the kind of fishing John was needing.

He guided the Jeep, a rental, down into the canyon. No stranger to the out of doors, a whitewater rafter and backpacker in his younger years, John knew how to drive back roads, but he wasn't taking the Burnt Fork lightly. He was still a thousand feet above his goal, and it would be nothing short of certain death to drop a tire over its edge. But facing this danger was worth it if the fishing on the Burnt Fork lived up to the stories he was told back in Travers Corners—stories and ensuing directions coming to him from a pharmacist at the general store.

Now and again he would stop, get out, and walk out ahead to scout the best possible route over a particularly nasty bit, one that he could get through without depositing his oil pan.

Setting the hand brake, he was once again out of the Jeep to see that this piece of road could be navigated even though one of his tires was perched on a boulder, two tires were in the mud, and the fourth tire was unaccounted for, buried somewhere behind the sage. The same sage that had just scratched the length of the passenger side. "Oh, Mr. Hertz if you could see us now. I'll bet somewhere in your contract you forbid exploration." John was talking to himself as he often did. Lately talking to himself was the only time he heard what he liked hearing and could agree with everything that was being said.

The last few weeks had been full of things he didn't want to hear—mostly things from his boss, Harry. And, though he was standing in the Montana wilderness, the place he had come to forget such things, he was hearing them clearly once again. Things like *your stuff has stunk lately*, and *if you don't start bringing in some fresh ideas soon*, followed shortly by *if you don't have the outline for something on my desk by Friday.*

And when Friday came, when he was called down to Harry's office for his imminent firing, he had already left Chicago and was somewhere over the Dakotas, flying for Missoula.

Getting back into the Jeep, the familiar theme of failure ran over and over in his mind—John Worthing, the writer with such promise, Guggenheim recipient, now a contributing editor for a right-wing rag.

Driving down the face of a large bowl, John could look ahead to see where he was going and he could look behind him to see where he'd been. The road on which he ventured came to him as nothing more than a long crease in a landscape of forest and scree. Below him where it silvered in the sun, he could see glints of the Burnt Fork—the stream promised to him by the pharmacist to hold the best fishing to be found with the least amount of company. Now that he had seen the road he could well imagine why very few travelers would want to take their vehicles to the bottom of the mountain—Mr. Hertz at the top of his list. He thought about the drive back out and it gave him a shudder even though it was a week away.

He carried on down the switchbacks, bumping his way until the road finally leveled out and the stream could be heard. The very last bit of road was completely impassable resulting in John carrying all the camping gear, tent, stove, ice chest, et cetera, about one hundred yards to a place that had been a camp many times, a fire ring still in place. And, of course, he unpacked his novel, the paper anvil carried in a burlap sack that hadn't seen the light of day for four years. Moving quickly he unloaded the Jeep, stacking the gear in the shade of the surrounding pines. Then he rigged his fishing rod, shaking his head as he threaded the line through the guides while realizing it had also been four years since his line had seen the light of day. Then he headed into the moment he'd been dreaming about for too long.

The day was exactly as he had imagined it, blue skies, no wind, warm, and quiet. He headed upstream as the druggist had told him to do and began fishing the flies the druggist had sold him, but when the afternoon and the fishing were over he walked back to his camp wondering if the druggist knew what he was talking about. There were the fish as he was promised, but he never saw a trout over nine inches in water he had been guaranteed to hold three-pounders. "Maybe the druggist has been sampling his wares."

Tired from travel and the fishing he stumbled back into camp, downed three cold beers, cooked up a burger with onions, and fell asleep.

The next day he fished even farther upstream hoping it was only distance that separated him from the long trout. He tried every riffle and piece of pocket water until the creek narrowed and began tumbling over giant boulders forming the large pools coveted by angler and trout alike. Here the Burnt Fork was a thing of beauty as he wandered under the tamarack and birch in the warmth of another perfect afternoon. But in the end, the fishing was as it had been—some fish, not many, and small.

The following morning he decided to take a different tack and headed downstream, fishing as he went. The Fork flattened out into meadow stretches, deep bends, tempting sweeps, and undercut banks; sensual and flowing, feminine in form. But with the morning long gone and the afternoon waning, his fishing had been poorer than his first two days. With the cocktail hour about to begin, Chicago time, he decided to fish one more bend and then head back to camp. While the fishing might not have met expectations, it had worked its magic as fly fishing is wont to do. He had forgotten about downtown Chicago, he had forgotten about work as he imagined it had forgotten about him, he had forgotten about Harry. Trying different patterns until it seemed he had tried them all, he went back to a small dry fly, one of the flies the druggist had recommended.

Breaking through a stand of willows he looked up and saw a car and not just any car but a Cadillac, one of the behemoth long-finned Caddies from the early 60s; a one-wheel drive, low-riding, well-worn, once-red Cadillac ragtop, trunk and doors wide open, top down. At first John imagined it to be a junker left here from the last days of the old highway, but the Caddy was surrounded by signs of recent habitation. Several fishing rods were leaned up against a tree along with a portable camp table and cooler, but there was no one around.

"How in the hell," he started to say aloud and then thought the rest, *did someone get that thing down here when I barely made it here in the Jeep*? He shook his head in amazement and laughed. Though curious, he ventured no farther, respecting the privacy of his fellow angler, who had to be equal parts mechanic and magician to get that luxury liner down the nearly impassable road. He waded back into the creek in complete disbelief and the impossibility of a road car coming down into this terrain. Soon another creek of decent size came in from the east nearly doubling the Burnt Fork. Checking his topographical map, the creek wasn't shown.

Moving along from one bend to the next he couldn't stop wondering who in the hell was fishing with him. His answer came in a few more hours. There, just ahead of him, and casting a very respectable line, in fact an enviable line, was that fellow angler. Standing in the middle of the stream the fisherman was hunched over, looking quite old, white hair hanging down from under his hat, and a wading staff trailing out behind him as if it were a tail. He threw out another cast. The miracle driver throwing another perfect loop over slow moving water. John knew a good line when he saw one, threw one himself. The difference, however, in their skills became immediately apparent—when the old angler's fly hit the water a very large rainbow took it. The trout was airborne for three leaps and then provided a lengthy fight before coming to the net.

"Damn," John muttered under his breath and looked on as the old man released his fish.

The angler then shouted out without turning his head, "Well, come on out here and show yourself. Quit skulking about in the willows." John then realized his old man was an old lady.

In the time John had worked his way along the bank until he was opposite her, the old lady had thrown another perfect cast and caught another rainbow, smaller than her first one but easily twice as long as anything he had caught since he started. "Havin' any luck?" the old lady asked, quickly reeling in her trout.

"Nowhere near as much as you've just had, and I've been fishing for three days."

"Well, you must have been fishing above Gin Creek. Nothin' but dinkers above Gin Creek," she cackled and let her fish go with a flip of her wrist.

"Is that the creek that comes in about a half mile back?"

"Yep," she answered then slogged her way out of the creek, leaping the high bank as if it were barely there.

"Well, it doesn't make the map."

"That's 'cause it ain't there after the middle of July—she nearly dries up. Then the fishing here gets mighty delicate."

The woman, who had just taken the bank as easily as Edwin Moses takes a hurdle, was now in front of him. She was all the things that made someone old—wrinkled to the bone, white hair, liver spots, an old voice—but the way she moved told him that there was a much younger person within. Taller than she first appeared, she was an unattractive lady, looking like Charles Laughton. The woman removed her glasses to reveal keen and youthful eyes. Her fishing vest filled to overflowing and her waders patched beyond description told John that she was no stranger to streamside, but her casting had explained this already. "You throw a beautiful line," John said.

But there was no reaction to his compliment, as if she hadn't heard it. "If that's what you been fishin' with," she laughed, "it's no wonder your luck's been runnin' against you. You need big flies on the Fork, big as you can tie them. I tie 'em on eights. Don't much matter what pattern you use as long as it's big. You got any big ones in your box?"

"Nope."

She reached into a vest pocket and produced a bulging fly box filled to overflowing, popped open its lid, plucked several flies from hundreds, and dropped them into John's open palm. "Here, use these. And fish 'em at the head of the riffle. Now let's get ahead—only have an hour left on the Fork—shuts down like clockwork at four."

They proceeded downstream and stationed themselves above sequential riffles. On his fourth cast John took a fish over two pounds. Fish were feeding, rises appeared everywhere, and in that next hour he took three more, and the woman, solidly in her seventies, took eleven. At four o'clock all risers ceased and she waved him over. "Time to call 'er a day, Sonny." Having had perhaps the best fishing hour of his lifetime, John was reluctant to leave the creek. But who could argue? This was the lady who told him to fish with eights and where to fish them. She had also driven a Caddy where no Caddy had gone before. He would have been a fool not to listen.

"Tell me something, Sonny, how did you find out about the Fork?"

"The pharmacist back in Travers Corners told me."

The old lady cackled, "Then that explains who sold you the flies and told you where to fish 'em. That's Junior McCracken. Without question the worst fisherman in the Elkheart Valley. The man could be up to his top lip in trout and he wouldn't catch a thing. He's famous for it.

"You better come and have a drink, Sonny." Then she turned around abruptly and set such a pace through the woods that it nearly had John running. She kept calling him Sonny, but she couldn't have called him anything else since they had yet to introduce themselves to one another. That would come over drinks, in the shade and in the back seat of the Caddy.

Sitting on a leather seat, over glasses of gin and tonic, with the luxury of lime, they finally got around to it. "I'm John Worthing by the way," he said holding out his hand.

"Well, it's nice to meet ya, Sonny." It was evident that his introduction had meant nothing just as it was clear that his name was going to be Sonny. "Just call me Rose," she said leaving her last name out of it as if it didn't really belong, its absence seemingly intentional like a surname at streamside wasn't necessary.

Top down, from the backseat of the Caddy, gin at the wheel, the conversation roared down a hundred different avenues. Rose was a fascinating old gal. She'd done everything and been everywhere when she was young, and now she was operating on her pension left to her by one of her late husbands who numbered four. She spent her winters in Arizona and her summers in Montana and the rest of the time anywhere in between, anywhere temperate enough to hold rising trout. "Great cars these Cadillacs, you can run 'em 'til they're down to their hubs and they just keep on going. This is the seventh one I've owned. And I never buy 'em new. Buy 'em with about a hundred thousand miles on the odometer and you get another hundred thousand on 'em without spending a nickel."

"I have to say I could not believe that someone had driven down here in a car like this when I had trouble getting here in a Jeep."

"It's like everything else you attempt in your time. It all depends on how you're aimed." She winked, then shifted around in her seat and brought the conversation back on around to fishing. "You're not a bad fisherman, Sonny, but you look like you're a mite rusty."

"It's been four years since I've been fishing."

"Sonny, you got your priorities all screwed up. How is it that you're fishing now?" she asked with her feet up on the front seat, stretched out in a fashion that told him the gin and tonics from the backseat were a nightly activity.

"Well, I got fired."

"Hot damn, Sonny. That's great news. So, you gonna spend the rest of the summer in Montana?"

"I'd like to, believe me, but I'm going to have to get back to Chicago—leaving on Tuesday."

"What the hell for?"

"Gotta get back. Have to find another job."

"What the hell for?"

"Well, I gotta live."

"This life you were leading in Chicago, would you call it living or just breathing in or out?"

"Barely breathing."

"Then I guess I'll have to ask you again, what the hell for?" John looked at her blankly. Blankly because he had no answer. "I mean ain't there something else you'd rather be doing, something that needs doing because ya haven't done it, something out there that's just begging to be done?"

"Well, I've been kicking around my novel for the last few years, or maybe I should say my novel has been kicking me. I take it with me everywhere I go but I haven't added a page in four years. Most of the time it boils down to the fact that writing for magazines is perhaps what I should be doing and a novel isn't in me."

"There ya go, Sonny. Maybe this is the time for you to write a book, but ya might look at it from a different angle. Maybe you shouldn't look at it as *your* book. Write it like you're writing it for all those who want to read it. Write it like it's a gift. Ya gotta remember, Sonny," she winked and reached for the gin, "half the people in this world would rather take a sound beating than write a letter. You're offering them a book. They depend on people like you to give 'em something to read at night after another numbing day at work." She looked over at him in a wise way—wise way past his years.

"Are you ready for another drink?"

"No, but I can get ready," John said with a smile, and Rose laughed.

They drank until dark and both agreed to meet where Gin Creek met the Burnt Fork at daybreak. Rose had plans to show him some real fishing.

John was far from his freshest at five the following morning, a time he hadn't seen in a long time, made doubly difficult from too many gin and tonics. Rose was out ahead of him on the trail, leading his way, taking the path, sprightly and whistling. Even chatting now and then. "Now I'm taking you to this place only under the condition that you never tell anyone about it. Ya promise?"

"I pro-pro-m-m-mise," John panted his answer. His legs were burning. Rose was skipping.

"I believe ya," Rose said and then talked a steady stream all the way to the top of the ridge telling him about how she and her fourth husband had come here for years. She also told him about her prior three marriages, "One of 'em died, one of 'em I wore out, and one of 'em I had to get rid of. But Billy, now he was a keeper. We were married twenty years. How he loved this place, bless his soul."

John could hardly hear her at times over the sound of his pounding heart but he could hear her well enough to hear the sadness in her voice as she talked about Billy. "Now there was a fisherman. Catch a fish from a bucket of sand." They crested the hill to look down on the genesis of Gin Creek where it flattened into a narrow meadow and then disappeared into the trees.

"Down there, Sonny, lies the fishing found only in dreams." The creek, even from five hundred feet above it, looked too small to hold much in the way of trout, no wider than a needle, threading its way through the grasses. Rose had barely paused at the summit long enough for John to catch his breath then it was down the back side of the hill and into the meadow. John arrived covered in sweat, Rose smiled looking as fresh, if not fresher than she did when they first hit the trail.

They followed the meadow, no more than a lush corridor of green against the bare escarpments that had crumbled into giant boulders. He still couldn't understand why they had come to such a place, Gin Creek was no more than two feet wide and half that deep, and he would have asked her why if he could have caught up with her. The last several hundred yards of the nonexistent trail deteriorated into deadfall, large pines littered the forest floor. Rose seemingly floated over the fallen timber like a leaf caught on the wind, while John crawled over, but mostly under, the deadfall with the same fluidity one could expect from a sack of wheat caught on the wind. Angry and excited at the same time, angry because he had let himself get so far out of shape, and excited about fish only found in dreams, he struggled on. Twenty years ago he would have taken the terrain like a deer, which really didn't help explain the seventy-year-old woman who was now out of sight and already fishing.

Breaking out of the forest, he saw the reason for coming. A large pool, almost a pond, lay in front of him and, dissected by a falls, a thin transparent lace of water spilled over a ledge, the first watery whispers of Gin Creek. The pool was rimmed in cottonwoods and aspen, and above them was a cornice with winter's snow still clinging to its face. And standing just to the right of the falls, there was Rose sending her third cast. A second after her fly landed, a very large fish was on. Scrambling along the shore toward her he watched as she fought the fish, the extreme bend of her rod, and the waves made by a dream trout, the size of which was bigger than he had ever seen, bigger than any dream.

But once he reached her he realized the fish was even bigger than he first imagined, maybe two feet in length. "My God, Rose. What a fish."

"This is the average length you'll find in here," she explained, letting her fish go. But the fish didn't move. It sat in the shallows regaining its strength. "Here," she said digging into her vest. "Put one of these on the end of a long leader and see what happens." She dropped several small flies into John's cupped hand. "It would be best if ya worked yer way around the pool so that you were standin' about where I'm standin' but on the other side of the falls."

Unable to take his eyes off the rainbow, which was now slowly swimming back into the depths, he asked, "What kind of flies are these?"

"Them are freshwater shrimp. Billy and me planted 'em in here in the fall of sixty-one. Ain't that a kicker? On his last trip in here Billy landed a trout ten pounds or better."

Working his way around the pond he watched large trout feeding just beneath the surface. On his very first cast, and after a few twitches of his shrimp, he had a fish on. Another trout the size of Rose's was out of the water, then steaming through it. It was Gin Creek, and this was his tonic.

In the first few hours he landed nine fish, seven of which were huge, two of which were trophies. So, when Rose whistled him over and motioned it was time to leave, John couldn't understand it. He hadn't seen much of her during the morning since she stood on his exact opposite and behind the veil of water, but he had been able to see her line doing its work well enough to know that she had landed at least double his catch.

"Time for us to go," she said to him after he had rounded the pond.

"Time to go?" he questioned her decision while sounding at the same time as if he were questioning her sanity.

"Sure. There won't be another fish caught here. As soon as the sun is full on the water you won't be able to buy a fish in here. But, if we hurry, we can be back on the creek just in time for a hatch of small stone flies." The pace Rose set on their way in to the pond was a cakewalk compared to the pace she set going back to camp. There was no way he could keep up with her so he didn't try. Arriving at the Cadillac he saw Rose downstream, naturally with a fish on. They fished the day away and when evening came they were once again found in the backseat of the Caddy, top down, gin and tonics in their hands.

"I have never seen such fishing in my life. I loved it. I could have stayed there a week."

"Not too bad, Sonny, not too bad," Rose laughed, then added, "but I'm leaving soon."

"Leaving?"

"Felt the beginnings of a south wind this afternoon, south wind is the kiss of death around here. Going to rain tonight," she said and he looked up at a cloudless sky.

The old Izaac Walton rhyme came to his mind. But he couldn't remember it exactly and drew a blank about the wind from the south. "Rose, do you remember the old Izaac Walton poem about the winds?"

"Izaac who?"

"You know, Izaac Walton, the guy who wrote, *wind from the north angler does not go forth, wind from the east fishing the least, wind from the west, fishing the best*, but I can't remember what he said about the wind from the south?"

"Wind from the south put a gin and tonic in your mouth."

Which is exactly what they did and continued to do until the stars found their way through the dusk, until a campfire lit their conversation, and until the gin bottle was gone. There is no better loosening agent for a man's tongue than gin, and John, prompted by Rose's stream of questions, rambled over his life talking about what seemed to be a litany of failures mixed with a smattering of successes. Rose never let up with her questions until the coals had died, but she had one more.

"You know how I made you promise about not telling anyone about the Burnt Fork?"

"Yeah."

"And how I made you promise not to tell anyone about the pond?"

"Yeah."

"So, if I ask you to promise something right now, but I won't tell you what you're promising to until tomorrow morning, would you do it?"

"Sure." John agreed with a shrug of his shoulders knowing that every secret Rose had sworn him to secrecy, had worked out for the best.

"Promise?"

"Promise."

"I'll be down to ask you in the morning, Sonny, but right now I'm turning in," and with that and not another word she walked over to the Caddy, put the top up, and curled up in the backseat.

Walking and stumbling, tired and sore, John found the way back to his camp wondering what he had promised. But most of the time his mind was dominated in thoughts of the pond and the beautiful rainbow trout.

Long past dawn he crawled from his tent and into the rain. Pinned to the mosquito netting was an envelope containing more shrimp patterns and the following—

Sonny,

I'm guessing I'll be somewhere in Idaho by the time you read this.

I gotta say it's been a pleasure knowing you, maybe we'll meet again, maybe right here back on the Burnt Fork. The question I'm going to ask you is this—you can fish the pond again but you have to promise that you won't fish it again until Wednesday.

Your fishing is pretty good but it needs some work. No better way to perfect your casts than fishing them.

And it might be a good time to get after that novel.

Rose

She wrote this knowing he was flying out of Missoula on the Tuesday night flight.

It was a day of decision. The first decision was easy coming between his first and second cup of coffee. It was a decision made smiling though it ran contrary to his usual rationale—if he left on Thursday plane tickets would be sacrificed, his rent would be even more past due. All things weighed and measured, there was nothing on God's green Earth that could keep him from a return trip to the pond. He would keep his promise and wait until Wednesday.

But Rose's suggestion about how it might be the time to try his novel again was a decision he found daunting. Around three, John, still in his sleeping bag, had spent most of the day devoted to three activities: staring at his novel, which lay only a few feet from his grasp, catnapping, and watching the rain bucket down. Around five he finally reached for his book, a work abandoned for years. Much to his surprise, what he found as he read was encouraging and after reading what he had written, two hundred pages and change, the ending, the roadblock for years, came to him and came clearly. Though his book was still rough around the edges, it now had direction. Wishing he had a gin and tonic, he toasted Rose with a cold beer.

The following two days he fished in the afternoon and wrote in the morning, but on Wednesday he was up at first light and scrambling up the trail, over the ridge, and down along the meadow to the falls and the pond. Constantly moving, constantly feeding, giant rainbows with their fins and breeched backs cutting through dawn's reflections made the pond so alive it looked as though wind was working the surface. Within moments he was standing where he had stood before, slightly behind the falls, casting to and catching three-to five-pound trout. But when the sun was full on the pond, just as Rose had promised the first time, the fishing came to a halt.

But this time he didn't leave after the fishing was over. This time he lay down in the grass, dug one elbow into the dirt, and spent the next few hours making notes in his novel's margins, growing more confident that he could, if left alone, have the book finished in four or five months. Elation would then be nullified by reality and its ugly head, and he knew he had to return to Chicago. He even toyed with sucking back up to Harry for another chance. He could see the familiar hall on his way to Harry's office. Everyday he had walked past the magazine's masthead, painted in gold leaf, on the wall, *Leaders in Industry*—if ever there was a euphemism. John had other titles in mind: *Studies in Avarice*, *Profiles of the Hideously Rich*, *Lifestyles of the Truly Rapacious.* He felt relief when he realized that he couldn't do that ever. He'd be eating out of garbage cans before he did that. He had other contacts, something would work out, maybe.

Packing up his book, he started back with what he knew to be the first step toward Illinois. Tomorrow he would have to leave. God, how he didn't want to go. He made a wager with himself—if he threw his fly into the pond and caught a fish on the very first cast then he wouldn't go back to Chicago. He would get a job at a sawmill somewhere, write at night, borrow some money from his sister if need be. Of course, John was in no danger of catching a fish since this was a pool where, for an entire afternoon, he had not seen a rise, he had not seen a swirl. But due to the severity and value of this wager he needed to make this one cast count. The only place in the shade was the shadow cast by the lip of the falls, a small, dark place in an otherwise mirror-bright pond.

Judging the proper distance wasn't the problem. It wasn't that far a cast. But to get his fly in behind the falls, that was the tricky part. If he could get his fly through the narrow window allowed by the falls and the rocks, his fly would have a space to land in roughly about the size of the Caddy's backseat. However, when he made the cast, the fly was two inches to the right of where it should have been and it was caught by the cascading water. The line tumbled down to the bottom of the pond, and hopelessly out into the light.

Disappointed, though not really, he had known it was a futile attempt. He started to laugh at the folly of his internal wager. He was going to Chicago. He knew it and had known it all along. He shrugged his shoulders and gave the accompanying sigh, the visible signs of sorrow for the resolute.

Reeling in, his fingers guiding the line on to the reel, his line pulled, his reel spun, and the rod nearly jumped from his hands. The line tore through the water and from the middle of the pond there first came a wave, and then a jump. The trout flashed like a sword might flash, a silver scimitar poised for an instant high in the air. But when the trout landed, John's fly line came fluttering back to look like a mindless scribble lying limp on the pond. Even in that wink of an eye, even at such a distance, the trout was easily ten pounds. *This* was a sign. To prove it he fished for another hour without a strike.

On the hike back to camp he engaged in internal arguments about going home, in addition to the standard argument concerning being rational and being foolish—Chicago and the sweatshop versus the valleys of Montana where he would write his novel. But there was no doubt about it, he would have to go back to Chicago.

Now listen, his mind was telling him, *you still owe on the furniture, you'll forfeit your last month's rent, you've got bills, man. Anyway it's all a moot point. The wager, you might recall, was if you* caught *the fish you wouldn't go to Chicago, and you didn't catch the fish.*

"I caught the fish," John puffed aloud as he hiked up the ridge.

Caught means in hand and landed.

"Hey, caught is fairly nebulous. How can I be caught on film, caught in the act, caught in the light, caught with my back turned, caught with my guard down, but my trout can't be caught unless captured? Caught doesn't *have* to mean landed."

No, you hooked the trout. What you had was a glorified strike before you bumbled the fight.

~

"Okay, okay, I'm going to Chicago."

The next morning he packed the Jeep and made the climb out of the Burnt Fork following the red slashes left on the rocks by Rose's Caddy. When he met the highway, Chicago was a right turn. Another valley, its fishing, and who-knows-what was a left turn. The Jeep sat in its tracks for more than an hour, before it wheeled south, toward Travers Corners, a destination achieved only by turning left.

From The Journals of Traver C. Clark

December 3, 1924—

Ron and Margie Smith split up yesterday for good. It had been a long time coming. Those two have been at war with each other for years. She was on the morning train.

I can't imagine being unhappily married. Carrie and I have had our battles, bound to be a few skirmishes in fifty years, but she is the very best thing that ever happened to me.

You can't always get what you want but if you try sometimes you just might find . . .

Ya Git What Ya Need

There are days when the soul wants to go fishing. There are days when the soul needs to go fishing. This afternoon Henry owned that soul in need of a day of fishing. He wanted to be away from the cattle, away from the ranch, away from the drought, the irrigating, the feeding, the horses, the fencing, the broken machinery, and the mosquitoes. But, above all else, he needed to be away from Dolores.

It was the first day of September after the hottest and driest August in the history of the Elkheart Valley. Dick Dobbins, at age ninety-nine and the oldest of the old-timers around town, said that during his century in Travers Corners he had never seen anything to even tie it. "Hotter than a June bride," were his exact words.

Drought, sweltering days, and hot nights, and adding a degree or two to Henry's temperature was Dolores who was supplying a heat all her own. She was mad for her usual reasons: "We never go anywhere . . . we never do anything . . . work, work, work . . . that's all you ever do." She was also more than a little furious about having turned forty in July. But the true flame below Dolores's anger, far outweighing but exacerbating all her other complaints, was that the Widow Wilson would be back on her ranch for the fall.

The Widow Wilson, as Jud and Henry referred to her, is a nickname most misleading. She was Susie Wilson to those who knew her way back when, and Henry knew her then as well as a man can know a woman. But that was twenty years ago. Nowadays she was known to all who traveled in her circles as Susanne. A native of the Elkheart, Susie married well and widowed even better. Susanne Wilson Smith was a very wealthy woman with a house in Palm Springs, Atlanta, the Bahamas, and the Bar 9, a two-thousand-acre ranch on the East Fork with four miles of the prettiest trout water Montana or any other paradise has to offer. She was also Dolores's arch enemy, and not a recent arch enemy but one dating from grade school. Dolores's hatred was reactivated ten years ago when Susie and her husband bought the old Whitcomb ranch, the Bar 9.

For the next month, Henry would have to contend with a very jealous Dolores. Around Travers it was understood that she belonged to Henry just as it was understood that Henry was a man who belonged to no one. The two had tried marriage once, but it ended because of his philandering. Their relationship was on again and off again for most of the eighties. But for the past four years the two have been living together but in separate houses and for those four years, according to all reports, Henry has toed the mark. Dolores would know if he hadn't. Owning the town's one and only beauty parlor, she is on top of anything and everything happening in Travers Corners, and all reports must pass through her.

"I hear your old friend Susie is due back in town tomorrow," crackled Sally Law with her smirk swimming across her fish lips. She handed Dolores the check for her haircut.

"That's what I hear," Dolores said coolly, and then went about tidying the area around her chair. With Sally safely out the door, Dolores turned to the others, "I hate that carp-faced old bitch." Everyone laughed. Now the parlor was the way she liked it. Her closest compatriots, her best friends, Margie, Bonnie, and Pam—the hen house was full and gossip was back in session. They were not there because they had an appointment. It was how Dolores scheduled her day. They were there to gather and deliver the news. It was a slow news day barring Susie being back in town.

"She isn't coming tomorrow," Bonnie said confidently. "She's already here. Got in late last night." Bonnie had the absolute inside track on this scoop since her sister was married to the foreman of the Bar 9. "Going to be here through October this year."

"Oh, great." Dolores rolled her eyes. "That witch will be out trollin' for Henry. She's never here for more than a day without somehow looking up my man. Sometimes I'd like to rip the hair right out of her head." Dolores was mad. The Del Vecchio blood had been stirred.

"Oh, come on now, Dolores, you don't have anything to worry about with Henry anymore. He's pretty domesticated these days," offered Margie.

"Yeah, Margie's right, Henry has been true blue for a long time," Pam piped in. "Anyway, Henry ain't interested. Oh, sure he loves it when Susie gives him the big eyes, all men do. I mean she is a looker. But Henry's not gonna fall for her line."

"The thing I can't quite get a hold of," puzzled Bonnie, is how she comes back here every year, parades herself through town in her diamonds and high fashions, and expects all of us who have known her her whole life, to somehow forget who she *really* is. The way I remember it is that Susie was born and raised here just like the rest of us. Oh, excuse me. I mean Susanne Wilson Smith." With that all four of them in unison raised their pinky finger, pursed their lips, raised their eyebrows.

"Yeah, I mean who does she think she's kidding. We all remember the way she used to get what she wanted," said Pam.

"The same way she got old Bill Smith's money—straight through the Fruit of His Looms," Dolores cracked, but if you listened closely you could hear a subtle spitting noise. Dolores didn't really hate Sally Law even though she said she did. But Susie she truly loathed.

In town twelve hours and, as Dolores had predicted, Susanne called Henry, but he was far from the phone. He was in a ditch up to his ass in mud, digging out a fouled headgate, fouled by an old cottonwood that died in the night to fall across his new fencing. His need for a day of fishing was just set back two days. Today it would be the headgate. Tomorrow it would be mending the fence. Henry was not in the best of moods.

So what happened that evening while Dolores cooked Henry his supper was as much in the cards as the queen of diamonds. There was Henry through the back porch door fresh from standing in three feet of mud running a shovel in record-setting heat with his lungs full, his nose clogged, and his mouth packed with mosquitoes. He was greeted with his customary cold beer. He gave her his routine peck on the cheek, too sweaty and dirty for anything more, and his evening, "How ya doin'?"

"Fine." It was the female *fine*, that clipped, terse, while-looking-at-the-ceiling *fine*, telling the male that everything was not fine, in fact it was as far from fine as one could get.

"Okay, what's wrong?" Henry wanted to cut to the chase then climb in the shower.

"Susie's back in town. Goin' to be here six weeks this year. Now that should make you happy. I suppose she'll be looking you up soon." There's jealousy and then there is redheaded Italian jealousy.

Henry was in no mood to go over this again, "Dammit, Dolores. I been dreading this for weeks. Let's just git to it. I hate going over this every year, on and on, and I jest ain't listenin' to it this year. She and me are just old friends and you know how much I like to fish Susie's stretch of the Fork." Henry came by his love for the East Fork because his Uncle Dean was ranch foreman for the Bar 9 for twenty years and Henry grew up learning to fly-fish on its waters. By merits of memories alone, the Bar 9, no matter what the fishing was like, would be his favorite place on Earth.

"You 'like to fish her stretch of the Fork.' I remember the days when you liked to *fish* her stretch of the *Fork*." Her inflections turned his statement into something one would not find on page nine of *Outdoor Life*, but on page forty-one of the *Kama Sutra*. "You got a whole river right out yer backdoor and you gotta go fish Susie's, and it's always real convenient that you only seem to fish it when she's in town." Dolores now was crying.

"I've told you a thousand times September is the best time and maybe the only time when that part of the Fork fishes good on a dry fly. And besides, like I've told you a million times, Susie and me are old friends and that's all there is to it. I mean jest cause you don't like her don't mean I gotta hate her, too."

"Oh, it damn well does, Henry Albie," Dolores yelled, and with that Henry's steak went sailing past his head slapping the kitchen wall with a thud seconds before the slam of Dolores going out the door.

Henry picked up his steak, brushed off the dog hair and threw it in the skillet saying only, "Women." Then shedding his work clothes at various locations around the kitchen floor, Henry took his cold beer into the shower with him.

Dolores spent the evening sobbing at Sarah's, her best friend and confidante, while Henry spent the evening installing a new fuel pump on his tractor. In bed at nine thirty, drained from a day of hard work and drained by Dolores. Now he had a month, no six weeks this year, to contend with her jealousy. The phone rang. It was Susie.

The Tin Cup Cafe was busy the following morning. Jud and Henry were at their usual stools, and although they had barely finished their first few sips of coffee, Henry with his usual economy of words, had already filled Jud in on most of his yesterday. "Big cottonwood fell on one of my gates. Spent the day up to my ass in mud. Naturally, it fell down across some new fencin'. And on top of all that Dolores is on the fight." But before Jud could find out why Dolores was on the fight, Mark Sillaphant came up behind them and had some questions about his horse for Henry. At which point Jud busied himself with the sports page.

Mark gone, their breakfasts were ready and it was Sarah herself who delivered them. She broke away from the grill long enough to set down their plates just so she could say, "You are down in Dolores's bad books, Henry Albie." She said with a mocking scold. She knew Henry's philandering reputation, just as well as she knew all of Dolores's dramas and her reputation for overreacting especially when it came to Henry.

"How are you doing this morning, Jud?" Sarah asked on her way back to the kitchen.

"Better than Henry," Jud answered, then turned back to Henry and asked, "So, what's Dolores mad about?"

"Susie." That's all Jud needed to know since he's seen this drama many times before. In fact, he should have known without asking.

"Every damn year. I gotta go through this." Then Henry looked up with a wry smile, discernable only to those who had known him for a lifetime, and added, "Susie called me last night. Said she was just back from the river. Said it was near boilin' over with trout. Invited me up for some fishin'. She invited you, and Junior, and Doc to come up anytime, too."

"Doc, Junior, and me are subterfuge. What Susie wants is the same thing that she's wanted for twenty years—that being you."

This time even those who had never seen Henry before in their lives would have caught his wry smile. "Very few things finer in the world than fishin' the Fork."

Dolores and Henry did not speak to one another for the next three days. She filled her days down at the parlor. His days were filled with fencing, wrangling, vaccinations, and irrigating. The temperatures dropped from the high nineties to the low nineties, and Henry's need for a day of fishing reached its peak. He wanted to go to Susie's, but he didn't need to go to Susie's since the Elkheart River was no more than a hundred feet away from this backdoor. So, at five o'clock, Henry quit work like the rest of the world, and ducked down to the river with his fly rod to get in an evening of fishing, and fishing was all that he got. Catching, as he knew it would, didn't enter into his evening. If he wanted to catch trout during the dog days of summer, the Elkheart River would be his last choice. But it was all he had time for and just standing in the cool water at day's end, throwing his line into futile waters, took his mind off irrigating and fencing, but it didn't take his mind off the Bar 9 and the cool headwaters of the Fork. But going to fish the Bar 9 was a far cry from ducking down to the river to throw a line. Fishing the Fork was a day's adventure; it was thirty miles of bad road just to get there.

The next afternoon Henry stuck his head through the parlor door and was glad to see Dolores was in between appointments. He didn't need anything to be thrown at him in front of witnesses. "Hi ya, Dolores," he said taking off his hat. She looked over at him like she had just heard something unimportant coming from his direction and then went back to preparing her bank deposit. Ostensibly, she was mad, but Henry could see right off that she was nowhere near as angry as the other night. "Listen, I've been givin' 'er some thought and I think I've come up with an answer about this fishin' up at Susie's thing. So here it is: every time I go up there, I'll just go up with Junior, or Doc, or Judson C. And we'll fish all day. We'll give our thanks to Susie for lettin' us come up and then I'll come straight back to your place for supper and some lovin'."

Dolores thought the plan through. If he went up with Doc that would be fine. Doc would keep an eye on him for her. If he went up with Junior, Henry would never get away from him. Junior loved fishing with Henry and was the only angler who actually talked about fishing while he was fishing and, as much as he would be hating it, Henry would never stray any farther than earshot with Junior. And Jud, well, Jud was no problem. He might not be able to be trusted when sworn to secrecy by his best friend, but Jud couldn't lie. His face contorts into unnatural expressions. His mouth goes into a stupid smile, his eyes glass over, and his voice breaks—the world's worst liar, not a fitting attribute for a fisherman. She looked over to her man who had gained ground by just standing there, hat in hand, with a face longer than well rope. "Well, that might work."

"It's like havin' a chaperone. And anyways, I don't need a chaperone. What happened between me and Susie was almost twenty years ago." He put his hand on her shoulder. "C'mon, that's a fair deal. You know how much I love fishin' up there."

"Well, all right," Dolores acquiesced, "but don't think I won't be checking up on you."

Bonnie came through the parlor door, bursting with recent news of Susie, but stopped short when she saw Henry. "Oh, hello, Henry," she greeted him, with a reserved coolness in deference to her good friend's recent depressions—Henry being their cause.

"Listen, I gotta go," Henry said leaning in to kiss her, "I'll call you tonight. See ya later, Bonnie."

"See ya, Henry . . . and you take care now," Bonnie called out after him. The kiss indicated that all had been forgiven and she could once again be nice to Henry, which was a relief because Bonnie loved Henry. With Henry out the door, the Susie news was the first thing out of her mouth. "Talked to my sister Lindsey last night. Are you ready? Susie had a boyfriend come in yesterday. Lindsey says they are real lovey-dovey and he's staying for the month." Dolores's shoulders sank with the added relief of Susie, the low-lying slut, having a true love of her own and of the fact that when someone is freshly in love she has little time for anything or anyone else. With the chaperone promise and Susie in love, Dolores felt that the Susie threat was over.

As promised, Henry was going to the Bar 9 with Doc and Jud, but his first trip into the headwaters of the Fork was to be with Junior. With Dolores in agreement with his plan, Henry went about scheduling his chaperones. Doc, being on call every day save one, could only go on Wednesdays, and Junior, the town's pharmacist, could only go on Sundays. Abhorrent of schedules of any kind, even Henry was careful with his time. Being a one-man hand on a two-hand ranch he had more than he could do, and the fencing and headgate had put him days behind schedule. He would be going into the hills to gather his cows on the first of October and there was much to ready. Jud could go whenever.

So it was down on the calendar, Henry would be making his first trip with Junior on Sunday, September 10. This was purposeful since the best fishing always came later in the month, the last week, the last ten days of September. So, when Junior ruins the fishing for him, it would be best for him to ruin a day with the lowest potential. But fishing the Fork even on a slow day in September is still better fishing than anywhere else.

It would then be Doc on the twentieth, and Jud on a day that suited him. On that Sunday morning, Junior, excited about his day with Henry and the Bar 9 rainbows, was pacing back and forth. Henry was up and had fed the horses and was just loading his fly rod when he heard the fire siren in town. Henry and Junior, both members of the Travers Corners Volunteer Fire Department, were on their way to the firehouse, both of them hoping it was a false alarm or some easy emergency that could be handled by a few men. But it wasn't to be. It was a grass fire at the Siefker ranch, and by the time the fire trucks arrived it had become a barn fire as well. Instead of fishing the cool canyons of the East Fork, Henry fought a hot fire on a hot day.

~

Missing his day of fishing, fried and tired, Henry made it home only to collapse. For a moment he felt sorry for himself—not fishing. But that moment passed quickly when he compared his day to the Siefkers, who lost their barn and their corrals.

Wednesday, September 20, and winter arrived on the same day. Only in Montana could forty days of record heat be followed by blowing snow. Henry and Doc awoke early to the sound of wind, a Canadian howler, that blew all chances of fly-fishing out of the water.

Naturally, on the twenty-first it was beautiful again, warm during the day but cool at night. The Fork would be fishing like a dream. Jud and Henry chose September 24 for their day at the Bar 9, and early morning found them fifteen miles in on the East Fork Road, probably the worst road in the Elkheart Valley, with fifteen miles to go.

"You know that old saying about gettin' there being half the fun, well that don't apply to gettin up to Susie's," Henry said.

Jud, having the advantage of being able to stabilize himself by gripping the wheel of his old Willys, wasn't being jostled about as badly as the Jeep found its way through the ruts, but was equally shaken over the long stretches of washboard. "It's worth the trip, though," Jud replied, "'cause when the Fork is fishing right, and it will be today, I can feel it, the fishing is about as good as it gets."

"That's the truth," Henry's mouth watered at the thought. He'd be fishing the Fork in an hour's time after thinking about very little else for a month and this time he would not be denied. No fire sirens out here. No chance of a storm today. There wasn't even a chance for a cloud. Things were perfect. "But you'd think with Susie's money she would hire a grader to come in here and at least blade the worst parts. Man it must be somethin' to have that kind of dough."

"Well, according to Dolores, all you'd have to do is drive up to the Bar 9 any time, sweep the Widow off her feet, and you could be fishing the Fork whenever you felt like it."

"Shit."

"You know that Dolores called me last night. Wanted me to make sure I didn't let you out of my sight."

"You're kiddin'?"

"Nope," Jud grinned, and then stepped on the gas because here the East Fork Road leveled out for the next three miles. With clouds of dust building as the Willys gained speed, Henry watched the river winding along with the road, and his thoughts turned to large rainbows dancing at the end of his line under cloudless skies. He was freewheeling on a fall day. The air cooled as they gained in elevation. They crossed the Bar 9 entrance with five miles to go.

Back at the beauty parlor the coffee klatch was just starting the morning cackle—Pam, Margie, Bonnie, and Dolores, who was in amazingly good spirits considering her man was up at Susie's ranch. But this year Susie had a man of her own, Henry had a chaperone, and just for added insurance Dolores had her way with Henry last night—to take away his legs so to speak. It was Bonnie who headed the news, "Just talked to my sister. Hadn't talked to her for a few days. They've been moving cattle. Anyway Susie and the new beau had a big fight. They broke up. He's gone. Left the ranch a coupl'a days back."

All eyes turned to Dolores. They could see the knowing mistrust, the suspicion, and the same old hatred she had held for Susie. "If that woman so much as goes near my Henry, I'll . . . I'll . . . Oh, I don't know what I would do."

Being privy to one another's lives, to the chaperone solution, Pam asked, "But Henry's up there today with Jud, isn't he?"

"Yeah, but that's like asking one rounder to keep an eye on another one."

The Willys crested one last hill and the Bar 9 came into view, outbuildings, barns, corrals, and finally the ranch house. Their plans were to fish first then extend their thank-yous at afternoon's end. Jud's thank-you was a jar of his aunt's huckleberry jam. Henry's gift was a pound of chocolates in remembrance of her sweet tooth dating back to high school. They would visit with Susie for a polite period of time, have a drink, then head home. But that would come later. Right now there were trout to attend to, and there was no shortage of rainbows already rising.

They parked the Jeep in the shade and pulled out their rods and started threading the line through their guides when Nick, one of the hired hands, came driving up. "Hey, Jud," Nick called out from his pickup window, "Junior McCracken just called. Said there's a guy in town to see you. Said he had made an appointment to meet with you today. Junior says you better give him a call at the pharmacy. Said it was important. He just called a few minutes ago."

"Shit!" Jud's eyes rolled back and his shoulders gave way. A date that needed to be remembered hadn't been. "What's today?" he asked Henry.

"The twenty-fourth."

"You sure?"

"All day long, Judson C." Henry looked at him in disbelief. The handwriting was on the wall. "Whoa, I thought it was around the nineteenth or so. Shit."

"There's a phone up at the barn," Nick shouted. "Hop in and I'll run ya up there."

Leaning his fly rod against the Willys, Jud only said, "I think I might have just really screwed up." He ran to Nick's pickup and then left for the barn.

Henry watched the truck head down the road, disappearing into its own dust. He knew he was watching his day disappear with it. Jud would be back in five minutes saying that he had to get back to town. No doubt. At first he was angry at Jud and his uncommitted approach to the calendar. His whole life had been based on approximations, except when building his boats where everything was perfection. This nonchalant attitude toward schedules of any kind was best exemplified by the old pocket watch Jud carried with him at all times whose hour hand and second hand had nothing whatsoever to do with the time. But his anger quickly dissipated because this was Jud he was dealing with, and after a lifetime of being best friends, he should have known.

"I knew it was too good to be true," Henry mumbled, and then caught the roll of heavy rings carrying across the pond. Large trout rings. All set up ready to fish with five minutes to spare before heading back into town. Henry decided to try for it and waded into the slow-moving current. In four casts he caught a trout of as many pounds. Then the pickup was back just as he released the rainbow.

Jud was out of the truck and it was just as Henry had expected. "I gotta get back to town." Henry started to reel in. "But it's okay because Nick is going to town. I'm gonna go in with him. Put my stuff in the Jeep, will ya? I'll get it tomorrow." Jud waved and Henry was alone with his day.

Henry thought of it before he made his next case. Jud thought of it as he neared town. Dolores thought of it as Pam reported it, as only a close friend, a correspondent, and a gossip at large could, that she'd just seen Jud roll through town with Nick. Their common thought being: Henry was up at the Widow's and without a chaperone. But after that large rainbow on his fourth cast, fly-fishing on a perfect autumn day, and with more rainbows on the rise, the thought of going back home was ludicrous.

Susie, now with the knowledge that Henry was on the Bar 9 and alone, had thoughts of her own.

Another large trout rose.

So there was Henry all alone on the day he had imagined and *just* as he had imagined it, *just* as wanted it, *just* as he needed it. There is no perfection like the imagination. Here the Fork tumbles and pools with meadow stretches in a narrow canyon. Here the cottonwoods were turning and the aspens had turned. Here was his boyhood—the barn, the fences, the trout, all just as it was thirty years ago. He had stood where he was standing now for as long as he could remember, and the feelings were as strong as the day he took the six-pound trout on worms at age nine. These were his home waters, the genesis of his fishing. His body was getting ready to cast a fly on the East Fork's lazy water, but his soul wanted to skip across her like a stone.

Another rainbow took his fly and with that all of the guilt concerning his unchaperoned self sailed away. He was here fishing alone because of unforeseeable circumstances, happenstance. No one to blame, no one to fault. A man can't fight happenstance, and the fishing was going to be fine. A murder of crows circled and landed then circled once again before vanishing over the trees in a wind of wing beats while calling out in their usual racket. Deer grazed with the cattle. Trout were everywhere. Thoughts of fencing, irrigation, and Dolores had flown away with the crows.

Henry's day was spent under cloudless skies, warm, and without mosquitoes. It was a day filled with rainbow trout, big ones, small ones, and at day's end he had fished his fill. A day beginning and ending in paradise. At four o'clock the sun left the water and the fishing slowed and then stopped. He would now drive up to Susie's, have his annual cocktail, give her the chocolates and jam, and then head back to Dolores's for a late supper.

Dolores's day was spent in worry. Her man was alone on the Bar 9 and that she-wolf would be after him like she always was. If he would have been true to his word, the way Dolores looked at things, he would have come home with Jud. At four o'clock, after canceling her last two appointments, after three shots of tequila, Dolores was flat out down the East Fork Road. Tears and anger in her eyes, Dolores was a click or two away from cocked and one shot of tequila away from being loaded. The road turned bad but it didn't slow her.

Back at the Willys after a day of fishing he could have only had on the Bar 9, Henry was feeling better than he had in months, feeling like that nine-year-old with a six-pounder on worms. He put Jud's tackle into the Jeep then began to break down his rod when a fish rose, something he hadn't seen for the last half hour. Then it rose again. It was another good-sized rainbow. He decided to try for it.

And try for it was all he did. Henry tried for that trout with different flies, different leaders, with different and not so different methods. But nothing he could do would send the trout down or keep it from feeding. There's a time when angling becomes a game.

But nothing worked and after a while he had given up hope, but hadn't given up fishing. Standing in the Fork, casting his fly, he was enjoying this trout as much as any he had landed. Sailing his line out over the reflections, the muted fall colors, and his boyhood. He settled the fly above the fish, which was shouldering its way around the Fork, eating late, dining alone, in an otherwise empty café.

The sound of a horn rattled him from his reflections and caused him to turn his attentions to the truck pulling into park near the Willys. It was Susie. It was then that he felt the fish and the fish felt the barb. Susie's distraction had cost him the moment of the strike, too much slack in his line. In order to free itself of the hook all the fish needed to do was shake its head, but the rainbow took it one better and jumped once, bright silver in the low light, and landed free.

"Will that be the one that got away?" she yelled from her window. "Are you coming up for a drink?"

"Right now. I was just about to reel 'er in," Henry shouted then mumbled under his breath, "and if you would have laid off the horn my reelin' mighta come in with a fish."

"I'll see you up at the house," she yelled again.

He then loaded his gear in the back of Jud's Jeep and drove to the ranch house where he had spent his summers with his Aunt Betty and his Uncle Roy. The old log homestead, then the foreman's quarters, had been remodeled and now it was Susie's home. Strong memories still lived there, not the blended watercolor memories of fly fishing, but the specific memories, the best chapters from his life.

He entered through what was once his aunt's summer kitchen, now windowed, decorated, and matching. Of course, the whole house, other than the logs, had been completely redone, and now it looked like some place seen in a magazine. Art work, furniture, imported artifacts, everything tasteful, but a bit much for Henry's preference. He liked it better as a memory when it was screened in, when pots and skillets hung on the walls, when bread was in the cookstove. "Hello," he shouted out through an open door.

"Come in. Come in. Oh, Henry it is so good to see you," Susie said crossing the floor. She was stylish and sophisticated, and dressed more for a day at an upscale resort instead of a working ranch. Seeing her now and listening to her talk, one would never know she was raised in Travers Corners. She was a far cry from how she looked and acted back on those afternoons they spent rolling in the hay, the nights in the backseat of his Ford. But he knew her for who she was and Susie, while poised, could be poison. There was something about her, however, that always got Henry's attention. An attractive woman without any doubt, the Widow Wilson, with her hair slicked back, and fancy earrings, and even though he knew she could spell trouble, Henry was a man. "How ya doing, Susie Q?" Henry asked using her nickname from high school.

She gave him a hug and a kiss to the cheek, then asked, "What can I get for you, cowboy? Your usual? J. D. on the rocks?"

"You bet."

"How was the fishing?"

"It was a long time gettin' here but it just couldn't have been any better. Well, leastwise," Henry grinned while adding, "until a certain party who'll remain nameless, came in and honked her horn jest as I was about to come up on the rainbow of the day."

"Here I am, up at the Bar 9 for nearly one month, and you don't come and visit me?" she asked.

Deciding it best to skip revealing the chaperone plan, Henry went with a different excuse. "The ranch has been kind of a nightmare lately, one disaster on top of another one. Sure wanted to come up though."

"You know what I was thinking about the other day?"

"Hard tellin'."

"In fact I think about it quite often. I was with you and Jud when we heard about Kennedy being shot, remember? You were so sweet that day. You drove me home and I couldn't stop crying. You stayed with me until my mother came home. I will never forget that kindness." Susie then delivered the J. D. with another kiss on the cheek.

"Sure I remember. But do you recollect that time me, you, and Jud went . . ."

The reminiscing began and they threaded their way back through the shared moments from years ago; through the specific memories, the big-time moments that shaped them all from their first-grade teacher to the Senior Ball, the party at the cabin, Donny's death in Vietnam. Back and forth with Dolores only being referred to once by Susie as "what's 'er name." Henry thought it best not to bring up her name up at all. The long-time hatred that Dolores still held for Susie was mutual.

At that moment what's 'er name was afoot, crossing the cattle guard with the lights from the Bar 9 still in the distance. She was angrier than even she thought possible, a little drunker, a whole lot colder, and on foot because the Datsun was dead. Having been pushed way past its limitations, it was a quarter mile back and spewing steam. Dolores had murder in her eyes and Susie in her sights.

The one drink led to two, two led to three, and during the third one when Susie had brought up the subject of sex through innuendo for the fifth time Henry started aiming for the door. The way Henry figured it was that his life had been complicated enough lately and he didn't want to complicate it anymore. It had been a great day of fishing, a day long wanted, a day most needed. Not that the Widow Wilson's attentions, especially after a great day and three whiskeys, weren't good for the mind, ego, and soul, and it wasn't that he wasn't interested himself. Letting the Widow have her way with him would put the capper to his angling, but the repercussions with Dolores would be catastrophic. No woman alive would be worth that sacrifice. "Well, I could go on talkin' about the old days all night but I gotta get goin'," he said. "Thanks for lettin' me fish, and thanks for the whiskey."

"Then why don't you?" Susie, who hadn't been more than four feet from him all evening, closed in.

"Why don't I what?"

"Spend the night talking or whatever." But the normally nebulous whatever was spoken in a tone that left no doubt as to what the what in whatever was.

"C'mon," he nervously laughed and waved his hand in dismissal as if Susie was kidding but he knew her well enough to know that she wasn't.

"Oh, all right, I know you have to go and *who* you have to go back to, which of course makes it all the more confusing. It's just that I've been up here nearly a month with a man who was far less than unexciting. Then I remember the times we used to have. Oh, what the hell. It was worth a try, huh, Henry?

"Oh, but before you go I want to show you something. I'll be right back."

Refusing Susie was tougher than he thought because he *did* remember the times they used to have, but he had to stay true. He gathered his hat and coat and then looked around the room, seeing it not as the renovated, upscale, country retreat, but as the ranch house it once was, comfortable and real. He saw his aunt's Singer sewing machine at the window, instead of the sculpture. He saw the piano against the wall where a television now sat. Everywhere he looked held a memory or an event. And standing in the hallway where his cousin broke his wrist, where his uncle kept his rifles, where he played on the stairs, stood Susie. "Sweet Jesus Marie," was Henry's natural response as she brought him back from boyhood to manhood in one stirring rush of womanhood because she was standing before him in a full-length white negligee, her hair was down, and she was beautiful.

"C'mon, Henry, just once for old times' sake?" Susie cooed. "We can have a time. You can leave. No one will know."

"I can't do 'er," Henry said, "Dolores and me been together a long time and I ain't goin' to tangle that all up by goin' to bed with you—as much as I would like to. I mean you're a fine lookin' woman," he added, more to soothe her feelings than anything else.

Now Susie suffered from a two-fold embarrassment: one, she was not used to being turned down by men, and two, she was now standing in the middle of the room in a see-through negligee which would have been just right if things had turned sexual, but after being refused she felt the fool. It was then she turned on the poison and Henry could see it coming. "All right, Mr. Albie, if you don't take me to bed and I mean right now, you will never be allowed to fish here anymore." She poured a drink, went to the closet, pulled out a full-length mink and put it on. "And that goes for Doc, Junior, and Jud as well."

The smile on her face would have told a stranger that she was kidding, but Henry, having known her his whole life, knew that she was not. The Widow was a temptation all on her own, and one that he thought he had navigated clear of by talking of Dolores. But now she had weighed in. She had threatened the sanctuary of his fishing, and not just any fishing, Henry's favorite fishing, and not only had she threatened to end *his* fishing, she threatened to end the fishing for his friends, Jud, Doc, and Junior.

He had maneuvered his way out of her first seduction, or so he thought, with the mention of Dolores. But she had outflanked him with the Fork. Now it was a matter of honor. There was the cowboy code of honor to consider, to be a man of his word, to keep the promise of fidelity to Dolores; and there was another code, the unwritten angler's allegiance. A loyalty as sure as a blood oath, sworn to without ever saying it, to protect at all costs the fishing privileges for himself as well as his three closest friends. One for all, all for one.

It was a dilemma. Decisions needed to be made. Sacrifices had to be taken. He loved Dolores. He loved fishing the Fork. He had to think of his friends. Fidelity, Fork, friends. Fidelity, Fork, friends. There was no compromise. The weight of this resolve didn't run through his mind as much as it ran over it, taking the buzz off the Jack Daniels and replacing it with a sudden headache. It was a decision where there could be no compromise. It was either do or don't. Sitting and staring out into the night, moonless and pitch black, he could see every fence post, every rifle on the water. Doc, Junior, and Jud would lose their fishing rights if he chose fidelity, but Henry would lose this and his favorite place on Earth.

Though the room was silent as Henry debated matters, no one heard Dolores sneaking through the porch door. She stood in the kitchen next to the stove, and remained silent except for the chattering of her teeth. She could hear Henry's voice clearly in the other room. "How would it be," he proposed, "if I ran in Jud as a kinda substitute?" He thought if that worked he would be off the hook with Dolores, the Widow Wilson's needs would be sated, and everyone gets to fish. Plus Jud would owe him one.

"Oh, I like Jud. But he's not my type."

"I suppose Doc is out of the question?" Henry smiled. Susie shook her head.

"Junior?" They both laughed.

Henry walked over to the bottle and poured a large J. D. and tossed it down. He poured another one and tossed it. Then he sat at the window and waited for the whiskey to do its work, knowing that he has done some of his best and worst thinking on whiskey. He turned to notice the mink had fallen open and that Susie was see-through once more.

"Well, I tell you Susie, I just can't do 'er. I mean you are mighty pretty and an old friend, and I would love to be in your bed and all, but me and Dolores, well, we've been together a long time. Now, I better be gettin' along before I change my mind." This piece of dialogue caused Dolores to crane her head down the hall. All she could see was Susie's back reflected in a window.

"Fine," Susie screamed. Her poisonous side, triggered by rejection and too much alcohol, had just joined the dialogue, "All right, cowboy, you go on home to Miss Trailer Trash."

Dolores nails lengthened. She was about to come down the hall and do some damage, but she stopped short when Henry made his reply, "Let me tell you somethin' about Dolores. She might not have all yer education, and yer style, and she sure as hell don't have yer money, but she has more heart than you'll ever know and more soul than you could ever buy." The whiskey had landed and the sexual favors for fishing rights, though they had been presented lightly, were registering now as nothing more than blackmail and he had been the bribe. It didn't set well. Henry grabbed his hat, said nothing, and headed for the door.

"Well, I was sure as hell good enough for you back when," she shouted after him and headed for the kitchen.

Dolores watched Henry going past the window, loving him at that moment more than she had ever loved him after hating him more than she had ever hated him moments before. She desperately wanted to settle the twenty-year score with the Widow Wilson, but overriding her anger with the Widow was the love for her man. All she wanted now was to be with him. Dolores came out of the kitchen. She met Susie in the hall.

Too cool and too drunk to be surprised, Susie stopped short, "Well, well, well, what do we have here?" She looked Dolores up and down. "What happened Dolores, bowling alley close early tonight?"

Still dressed in her beauty parlor garb of orange smock, red pants, purple shoes, and lime green earrings, her red hair all over her head, Dolores did look like someone who had just skated up to your window to take the order. Wrapped in her mink, her hair and makeup just so, Susie, though fairly drunk, looked like she just stepped from an ad. Her mink fell open to reveal the negligee so thin even Victoria couldn't hide a secret, and Dolores reacted by landing a beautiful overhand right to the bridge of the Widow's nose. The Widow went down.

On the run after her man, Dolores was out the door catching up to the Willys only after it started to pull away. "What the Sam Hell are you doing up here?" Henry asked as she got into the Jeep.

Dolores didn't answer that question. She just grabbed him and kissed him, "Oh, Henry, I love you so much."

Puzzled, Henry asked, "How did you git here? Where's the Datsun?"

"Go on ahead. I'll show you."

On their way out of the Bar 9, Dolores told the story about seeing Jud back in town, about Henry being alone up here with the Widow, about her jealous rage, the tequila, the death of the Datsun, about the two-mile walk, in the cold, about being in the kitchen through the attempted seduction scene, and about running into the Widow in the hallway, "and so I was so mad I . . . I . . . I . . . just ran after you." She mentioned nothing of the overhand right.

"Ahhh," Henry said knowing by her tone there had just been an omission.

Henry then proceeded to tell her about Jud screwing up a date with a customer, about how he caught a ride with Nick, about the phenomenal fishing, about the big ones, about the last one, about the Widow's innuendos, the negligee, and Dolores knew the rest except for the sexual-favors-for-fishing-rights clause in the Widow's contract.

"That bitch. I'm glad I . . . I . . ."

"Glad you did what?"

"Nothin'."

"C'mon Dolores."

"Well, I socked her one."

"You *what*?"

"I slugged her and it was a punch I've wanted to throw for twenty years. I know it was wrong, but damn it made me feel better."

Henry put his arm around Dolores, "You know, I think it's startin' to make me feel a mite better about things as well."

It was agreed that they could tell no one in Travers, other than the girls at the parlor, Bonnie, Pam, and Margie, her closest confidantes. The four of them might well have been the biggest gossips in town, but the shared secrets from the inner circle were sacrosanct and the gossip stopped there.

Susan Wilson Smith told everyone in her social circle that she had been kicked by a horse.

Henry had to inform Doc, Junior, and Jud what he had done and why he had done it. Junior, a deacon at the D. Downey Baptist Church, stood firmly behind Henry's moral stance and congratulated Henry on his choice.

Doc Higgins had to hear the story several times just to make sure that he was hearing it correctly. Finally he told Henry that he had made a wise personal decision. While he was sorry to hear about losing their fishing privileges on such privileged waters, Doc understood. He then smiled, slapped Henry on the back, and walked away mumbling something and shaking his head. There was a hint of a tear welling up in his eye. Doc loved fishing the Fork that much.

Jud, having grown up as Henry's best friend and fishing companion, and who had spent many an afternoon on the Bar 9 as well, had to ask, "Let me see if I got this right, a beautiful woman wants to have sex with you, nothing more than a roll in the hay, no strings, and if you don't have sex with the beautiful woman she will take away all your fishing rights, and those of your friends?"

"That's about it Judson C.," Henry answered.

"I mean all you had to do was put in twenty minutes worth of slap-and-tickle, sacrifice yourself so that you, Doc, Junior, and myself could continue fly-fishing the Fork, this is the Fork I am talking about, and you couldn't come through?" Jud, single and unattached, was dumbstruck by Henry's decision. Jud looked at such an act as a treason.

"Well, now it wasn't the easiest decision," said Henry, who had lost not only a fishery, the Bar 9 water, and in some ways a large part of his boyhood, "but the way I was lookin' at it was while I *wanted* to keep fishin' the Fork, I didn't *need* to fish the Fork. I've got the Elkheart River out my backdoor. I *wanted* to take the Widow up on her kind offer, but I didn't *need* to. I got Dolores."

From The Journals of Traver C. Clark

August 4, 1919—

A new dressmaker arrived in Travers today and did the men around town ever fall to their feet. She is young and beautiful and there is nothing I know of on God's green Earth that can make a grown man act more foolish than a beautiful woman.

~

Felicity

It was late and the road over Albie Pass was empty as Jud neared the summit. The Willys was full of shopping from a day in Missoula. He hated shopping. He hated spending money.

Because of the load there was no room for Annie the Wonderlab who would be patiently awaiting his return back at the Boat Works. Without Annie he had no one to talk to and was running the dial in the hopes of a radio station, any radio station. On some nights, very few, when the clouds were stacked just right, when the positive and negative ions had reached an alliance with the barometric pressure, and if the jet stream was at his back, he could pick up distant radio stations, and tonight was no exception as a Seattle station suddenly came into the clear. The host of some show was in the middle of an interview with Jack Nicholson and was asking, "If you had to, and I know this might be a question too difficult and too specific to answer, if you had to name a moment, a life changer, in your long screen career, a memory that stands clearly above the rest, what would it be?"

"That's an easy question," answered Nicholson with a laugh, and even over the radio Jud could see Jack working his eyebrows and smile, "that came when I got the call to do . . . "

Loud and clear for ten seconds, the station died away into static. Jud turned off the radio. With his tape player on the fritz he was alone with his thoughts as he followed his headlights through the curves. If an interviewer were to ask him to name his most career-changing memory, as a boatbuilder and guide, like Jack, his first choice came easy.

It was going to be a day like any other day but it led to a day unlike no other, twenty-some-odd years ago . . .

All that was left of the storm was a long, thin band of gray cloud running the length of the Elkheart Range. The morning light silvered the blacktop of Main Street, wet from last night's rain, and the usual puddle had formed in front of McCracken's as it had for as long as Jud could remember. The valley was in full sun and for the first time in more than a week there was promise of a better day around Travers Corners. Tucked into the hill above town, the Carrie Creek Boat Works and Guide Service still lay in shadow.

In the darkness of his workshop, a skeletal silhouette, the bare bones of a river dory, the ribs, stood awaiting their hull. Today's project. Such was his every day—breakfast at the Tin Cup Cafe, pick up the mail, switch on the lights, start the coffee, open the windows or fire up the stove, slip on his apron, turn on the tape player, and return to the drift boat at hand with whatever tool needed for the day. This was the facet weighing the heaviest this morning—the repetition of life, and there was little doubt Jud was not in the best of moods.

Not even the sun after a week of rain was going to improve his spirits, because his life, which at this juncture was being conducted by rote, now had the added worry of money. Neither the Boat Works nor the Guide Service was looking very good—financially. For the first time in five years Jud was about to catch up with his work, and there were no standing orders though there were a few on the fence. To make things worse there was nothing going on at the Guide Service branch of his one-man show either and there wouldn't be until the river cleared. Added to all of this was a new band saw, just delivered from Sears, a band saw he hadn't the money for, but without which no money could be made.

Grumbling, Jud went back to the workbench and grabbed a plane and the whet stone to sharpen its blade when he heard the sound of a car on the drive. A man and a woman got out of a Mercedes. She was young, blonde, bronzed, and beautiful beyond measure, and looked to be half the man's age.

"Good morning," the man greeted Jud who had stepped from the workshop and into the yard.

The introductions were made. They were the Masons, Harold and Felicity from Palm Beach, and though they could have easily passed as grandfather and granddaughter, they were husband and wife. Naturally, they wanted to go fishing. "Well, I'd like to take you, but there isn't any water in the valley that isn't running mud and even if we don't get any more rain, the river won't clear for another three or four days," Jud explained.

"Perhaps, we might see you on the back side of our trip," Harold suggested, lighting one cigarette from the one he was smoking. The color of his skin and the gravel in his gullet said four packs a day, and not just normal cigarettes but Pall Malls Longs, unfiltered. On closer inspection, Harold obviously was leading an abusive life, and had been for many years. Veins road-mapped his cheeks and all the roads lead to his nose, which was bulbous and swollen. He had on thick glasses that made his eyes appear tiny and strange. "I mean if that's all right with you, baby?"

"That's okay with me, sweetie," she answered in a baby's voice. In her outfit of short shorts and short blouse, Jud could see, as any man living or dead could see, that Felicity was the kind of beauty rarely seen. She was blue-eyed, gorgeous. He was bone ugly.

He and Jud talked some more about what kind of fishing they could expect if the river did clear, the fishing in general, a little about Travers, the weather lately, and other generalities. Harold was about sixty but looking eighty. There was nothing wrong with his mind and it sounded like he owned most of Florida.

"Do you have a card?" Harold asked.

"Sure do," Jud answered. He then ran back into the workshop and was back with his card. Then it was settled. They might call Jud in four or five days, and with that Harold and Felicity left for Jackson Hole.

But right before Felicity drove away, she rubbed the gunwales of one of the dories parked outside then looked at Jud, "I sure think your little dinghy is cute." She pushed her butt out and pouted her lips then climbed into the Mercedes. She was driving.

Felicity was *Playboy* material, and Jud, being a single man in his thirties, was attracted to her body. He would have liked to have been attracted to her mind as well but a burned bulb gathers no moths. In truth, Felicity might have been the most beautiful woman he'd ever seen in real life. But there was no there there. That didn't matter. The way she stroked the gunwale, pushed out her butt, and pouted her lips had gained his attention. The film of the stroke, push, and pout would play in his mind for the rest of the day.

Shaking his head in an effort to clear his libido, Jud returned to the workshop only to find that Sears had forgotten to include the saw for the band saw. He called Sears and after a full morning of calls and callbacks, the blade would be delivered sometime that day by an employee. Another day lost. "Okay, then I'm going fishing," he said aloud even though he was alone. Saying it out loud gave the decision more conviction to Jud's mind. He would go to Neal's Spring Creek, his private sanctuary and always his first fall-back solution when the water everywhere else was muddy. Then a strong gust of wind rattled the workshop windows. He looked out to see storm clouds forming. It would rain before noon.

Frustrated and madder than ever, Jud threw down his apron and decided to have a very early lunch, a deluxe hamburger, French fries, and a malted shake, followed by a piece of Carolyn Cory's apple pie. He headed down the hill to the Tin Cup Cafe. Sweets can be a great leveler and Carolyn made the best apple pie in Montana, maybe the world. Apple pie and a hamburger, Jud theorized as he walked down the hill into town, were the two barometers by which all restaurants could be judged.

At the back table of the café, empty and awaiting the lunch hour, sat the Corys. Carolyn and her husband, Jeff, were drinking champagne. "C'mon down and grab a glass," shouted Jeff. He poured a glass for Jud before Jud could refuse.

"What's the occasion?"

"We sold the Tin Cup," Carolyn answered.

"You did *what?*" Jud said nearly shouting.

"Signed the final papers not ten minutes ago and so you are the first in town to know it."

Jud was crushed. The Corys had owned the Cup since he was born. "Who bought it? I mean, I didn't even know you wanted to sell it."

"A lady named Sarah Easterly and her uncle. They're from New York City. They wanted to keep the sale under wraps until everything went through. They're gonna make some changes around here. They're gonna be here in a month or so."

"New York *City*? Well, I guess congratulations are in order," Jud said, lifting his glass. Congratulations was what he said, but his mind was asking what will anybody from New York *City* know about baking apple pies? The Tin Cup in the hands of New Yorkers. Jud hated the whole thing. Locals started filtering in, the regular lunch crowd, and as the word of the sale spread, more champagne was opened. Everyone was excited for the Corys, solidly in their sixties, thirty years running the bar and café, they deserved to retire. That is everyone but Jud. He was suspicious of any change.

He took his champagne to the counter and ordered lunch. The crowd grew. The party was on and Meagan, normally a waitress, was subbing for Carolyn behind the grill. Sally, who had never waited tables before, was his waitress. "Sorry, Jud, with all the excitement and signing the papers, Carolyn didn't get around to baking any pies this morning. You want any coffee?"

The change had begun.

Grumbling up the hill after lunch, no pie, Jud said to himself, "How can anyone from New York own the Tin Cup? And what about them not wanting anyone to know about the sale? Sneaky, that's what that is. Typical New Yorkers." The fact that Jud had never known a New Yorker in his life didn't slow him from forming a judgment. It was the anomalous vision of the future Tin Cup, remodeled with new menus, new cook, new bartender, new hours, New Yorkers, that unnerved him the most. He saw fancy dishes, diet plates, and fruit cups, and on the bar side he could just see the dishes being served with paper umbrellas and a twist of lemon. Chez Cup. Entrée at your own risk.

Nearing the top of the hill and the Boat Works Jud could see it all clearly—soon he would never have another good hamburger or another good piece of apple pie as long as he lived. As he stepped through the trees behind the workshop he saw a car heading down the drive. A box, the blade to his band saw, was sitting on the porch. The good news being that the blade had arrived early. The bad news being it was the wrong blade.

This day was just the beginning of a bad week for Judson C. Clark. During the next five days the phone did not ring for either the Guide Service or the Boat Works; the Willys died, a new engine was needed and installed; the hot water heater in the house went out; and he broke the middle finger of his right hand while moving the old band saw into the back shed. Doc Higgins had put it in a splint and now his finger, in a rude manner, was telling the world to do just what the world had been doing to him all week.

Things had gotten to such a point that on Friday morning he thought it might be best just to stay in bed, which was what he did until nine. Sleeping in was made much easier by his hangover—Henry had stopped by the night before with a bottle of tequila. "Nothin' eases the pain like a little pulque," Henry prescribed.

Having a broken finger was a good excuse not to go down to the workshop because the handling of tools would prove impossible. Around ten, feeling guilty for doing nothing, Jud began to clean the workshop. He was clumsy, but he could handle a broom and a vacuum, and he could handle the phone when it rang—the telephone company wanting to know where its money was. That he couldn't handle.

There was no way around it, he would have to go to the Elkheart Valley Bank and ask for a loan. He hadn't had a loan since he started the Boat Works, but things were lean and there was no hope in sight.

Stepping out the door, he was a man in need of a loan—clean shirt, fresh pants, boots polished, and bank ready. Jud took one more measure to ensure his best foot would be forward when he entered the bank—he took a pull on the pulque. He again needed to ease the pain, a pain that made his broken finger pale in comparison. It was the pain of entering a bank in need. He hated banks. He hated Hendrickson. Going for the loan was fitting in nicely with the rest of the week.

The Elkheart Valley Bank was owned and managed by Jim Hendrickson and had been for the last four years. Jud could not stand this guy. Hendrickson had bought it from the Eslinger family, who were known to be fair, understanding, and ventured out onto the limb with their customers and neighbors. Sometimes the limb broke. Now the bank was run like the company store. But the bank was the only game in town, and while some people from Travers and the surrounding ranches took their banking to Reynolds, it was generally understood that the banker there was even worse. Driving two hundred plus miles round trip to Missoula to make a deposit was too much.

Hendrickson was shrewd enough to recognize talent and enterprise and he knew those who would be good investments from those who would not. The bank's interest rates were higher, but only by a tenth.

The bank wasn't crowded. Julie Alves was the lone teller and was just finishing up with Pete Whitehouse. Pete gone, Jud stepped to the window, "Hey, Julie. How are you doing?"

"Good, how's Judson Clark today?"

"Broke or damn close to it. Need to see Hendrickson. Gotta take out a loan and man am I hating it."

"I'll buzz him when he gets off the line, Jud," Julie said.

"Thanks." Jud left the line, making room for two young cowboys, and went over to wait at a table and chair there for that purpose. The table was filled with financial magazines, the *Wall Street Journal*, and one three-year-old *Sports Afield*. He watched the two young cowboys cash their week's wages. Judging by the grins on their faces they were about to get a jump on the weekend and there was little hope that Monday would find them with a nickel. Jud sat there for ten minutes watching half-of-Hendrickson with the phone to his head, only half, and Jud found this the most telling thing about Jim Hendrickson, because the banker's office was arranged in such a way that while he was half hidden in a blind corner, the loan customers could be viewed by tellers and patrons through a wall-sized window, their lives a financial fishbowl for all to see.

Julie, who referred to her boss nonaffectionately as *The Henprickson,* was Jud's longtime friend since grade school. She had made a study of *Henprickson's* loan proceedings and had found that once you had been seated in the fishbowl, if the loan was going to be granted, Hendrickson would leave the curtains open during the application process so the world could watch you squirm, and then draw the curtains when the loan was about to be given. If the loan was going to be turned down he would leave the curtains open. Julie had to watch her aunt and uncle lose their ranch through that window.

Jud looked up to see Hendrickson motioning for him to come in, and the thought of asking the guy for anything made his skin creep. Sitting there in his corner chair the banker, a beady little man with beady little eyes in his suit shiny from wear, asked, "And what can I do for you, Mr. Clark?" He asked in such a way that put him in power, which he was. The smarmy little puke held Jud's destiny and the future of the Boat Works in his sweaty little palms. It made Jud's guts twist.

"I've come to see about getting a loan . . ." Jud began, and after a few minutes Julie was happy to see the curtains draw to a close. Thirty minutes later Jud stepped out of the bank to see black clouds showing themselves and a strong gust of wind kicking dust down Main Street.

Alone that evening at the Boat Works, Jud was in a blue mood. The loan, Hendrickson and everything else—his finger, the Willys—were getting to him, that and it been raining hard for six hours, enough to muddy the river once more. The next morning, after a night of fierce winds, he awoke to see that a cottonwood had blown down, missing the workshop but hitting the storage shed dead center. The only thing left standing was the old band saw.

The rest of the month things smoothed out a little and Jud suffered no more disasters. But while Jud's luck might have stabilized, his financial woes continued. The phone at the Boat Works had not rung at all and his bank loan was running low.

Felicity

On a warm July morning, Henry with his chain saw came to help Jud dismantle what was left of the shed and the cottonwood that hit it. "Damn, wasn't that a wind? Blew the bit right out of my horse's mouth," Henry said. Jud laughed then the two went back to work; Jud, towing branches to the burn pile, and Henry working the saw. Hidden behind the workshop with the chain saw roaring, the two of them were unaware of the fact that they had company. Looking up, Jud could see Felicity standing at the edge of the workshop jumping up and down and trying to gain his attention. Henry, seeing the look on Jud's face, turned to catch the last couple of Felicity's bounces. Harold appeared behind her. Felicity's jumping up and down, in the eyes of two young and single men, was certainly going to be the best part of the Masons' arrival and would probably be the best part of July.

"Hello," Jud shouted. Henry turned off the saw. Felicity, wearing a thin T-shirt and no other means of visible support, bobbed and swayed her way through the branches. Felicity was what Jud and Henry referred to as healthy. Jud made the introductions.

"Well, can you row us down the river?" Harold asked from a cloud of cigarette smoke in his immediate and matter-of-fact way. Jud had pretty much forgotten about the Masons. They said they would call in a day or two, and a month had gone by.

"When?"

"Right now."

Jud had been staking limbs for most of the morning, mostly with his good hand. His finger was only out of its splint by one day, and it was now in a light cast; pulling on an oar all day was going to be a challenge. Henry saw an opportunity. "Hey, Judson C., with yer finger and all, I'd be more than happy to take these two down the river for ya."

Jud had little doubt that the two Henry was talking about belonged to Felicity. He thought about his hand. He thought about the bills piled up by the phone, the bank loan. He had no choice. "No, I can do it."

Henry tried once more. "You know ya do somethin' wrong with that hand, and it'll end up back in the splint," Henry said shaking his head and trying for the voice of reason.

"Thanks, Henry, but I'll be fine." Then Jud looked at Henry through his veil of sudden concern and with a grin told him that he was going to take this trip even if his hand was missing. Henry wasn't the only one fevered by Felicity.

Lunches were ordered from the Tin Cup while Harold and Felicity transferred tackle and belongings from the Mercedes to the Willys. Jud hitched up the SS *Lucky Me* and in ten minutes the fishing trip was under way, but first they needed to pick up the ordered sandwiches from the Cup. Henry went back to work on the fallen cottonwood, sawing it up and stacking its limbs in record time. He went at that tree body and soul but he had Felicity and her T-shirt in his mind.

"Hey Carolyn, you got those sandwiches for me?"

"You bet. Well, Jim just talked to the new owners. We turn the keys to the Cup over to them tonight."

Jud winced at the news. "Carolyn?"

"Yeah."

"Can I come over to your house for a piece of apple pie now and then?"

"You bet."

"Damn, I am hating this. New Yorkers," Jud mumbled on his way back to the Willys. He would try, he vowed crossing Main Street, that from this date forward he would never complain again about his pedestrian life and the same old everyday routine. You do that, Jud reasoned, and you are inviting trouble. There are things much worse than the normal daily grind—blown engines, new band saws, broken fingers, fallen trees, to name a few. He ached for the dullness that was once his life. He needed something positive to counteract all the recent disasters. Felicity, living up to her name, was helping.

"Getting a late start like this," Jud explained, "we're going to have to take a shorter float, one that takes us down in a stretch of the river we call the Channels. It's about the only stretch of river you can run in a short time. And, I feel I can only charge you for a half day."

"No, you go ahead and charge us for the full day," Felicity smiled and wiggled in the backseat. Jud was liking Felicity more and more.

Once on the river, the fishing was good and by the time they had floated down into the Channels it was even better. As it turned out, Harold was a skillful fisherman, holding a saltwater record for tarpon for seven years. Felicity was his fifth wife. He did own most of Florida. He wasn't funny. He wasn't dull. He wasn't warm nor was he unpleasant or rude, and he was not at all arrogant about his wealth and success. He talked like a ticker tape in short, direct bursts. One thing was for certain, Harold had to be precancerous because by the time they had floated into the Channels, where the Elkheart river braids, Harold had put away a pack of Pall Malls.

Felicity didn't say much. But if she did talk it was to say something like, "Oh, that's a pretty fish, sweetie. What kinda fish is that again?"

"That's a rainbow trout, baby, and a nice one."

While Jud was maneuvering the *Lucky Me* into position for the netting of the trout, Felicity slipped from her T-shirt into a very small, nearly invisible, bikini top, and he turned in time to see her tying the strings at the back, the strings being the widest part of the outfit. She then rubbed ample amounts of baby oil on her brown body. With Felicity all bronzed and oily in the stern of his dory, Jud found himself looking over his shoulder, but he did so professionally and in such a manner that told her this is what the well-informed, prescient, all-around river guide has to do; treat the river upstream with the same importance as the river downstream. If Felicity happened to be in the way then she was part of the job and that's how it had to be. She was standing behind him and adjusting the towel covering her seat when the *Lucky Me* slammed into a rock nearly throwing Harold over the bow and bringing Felicity out of the stern. Oiled and bronzed she bounced off Jud's arms and his oars and she landed in his lap just as her top twisted free of its purpose.

"Jeez, I'm sorry," Jud said as he spun the dory free of the boulder. He was sorry for the inconvenience and he was sorry he'd put his dory into that rock, but he wasn't sorry nor would he ever be about the nearly naked Felicity sitting on his lap.

"You all right, sweetie?" she asked while she stood and immodestly attended to her top.

"Yeah, I'm fine, baby."

"You all right, Jud?" she asked, adjusting her breasts.

Jud, other than being a little oily from the encounter, answered, "Yeah. Hey, I apologize. I just didn't see that rock."

"Well, that was kind of exciting," Felicity said, climbing past and brushing up against Jud on her way back to her seat. "Okay, catch a big one, sweetie. It is so pretty out here." She sat back in her chair, put her feet on the gunwale, and slipped into her sunglasses with a shake of her hair.

It's so pretty out here. It must have been the hundredth time she said it, but Jud didn't mind. She meant it. He was getting a little tired of the *baby-sweetie* thing.

There she was, this long-legged goddess, not a mental giant perhaps, but a goddess all the same, sitting in the back of his dory and just moments ago she was nearly naked in his lap. He'd had some great and lucky days on the river, but this was going to be hard to top. Hitting the rock might have been *kind of exciting* for Felicity, but for Jud it was downright erotic.

"I'll bet there are some brown trout along there under those willows," Harold said who was back up and fishing, pausing only to light a cigarette to replace the one lost overboard.

"Downstream another quarter mile we're going to get out and fish one of the channels," Jud explained, trying to wipe the oil from his hands. "Hidden Channel. Hidden because the river looks as though it . . . well, you'll see. It's long lines and fine-tippet kind of fishing if that's all right with you?"

"Sounds very fine." Harold turned and looked at Jud when he gave him his answer. Jud felt uneasy as he had just had his wife nearly naked on his lap and many husbands might find that disturbing, but from all apparent tones, expressions, and gestures, Harold didn't seem to mind—he didn't even seem to notice. He was a hard man to read behind those Coke-bottle glasses, glasses so thick that it made it hard to believe that anything could be seen out of them, but Harold had missed very few strikes. "Are you getting hungry, baby?" he asked.

"Anything that suits you, sweetie, is fine by me."

"She's a beauty isn't she, Jud?" There was love in Harold's voice.

"Yeah, well . . . em . . . yes, sir, she is."

The beginning of Hidden Channel, the name Henry gave to it when they were kids, looks like nothing more than a large eddy disappearing into a swamp and into the trees, but the water flows again when it is joined by another braid eventually forming a narrow, heavily shaded, bayoulike channel filled with stumps and deadfall, alive with slow-water mayflies and some very large brown trout.

It was the two-minute lunch. Harold ate his sandwich in four bites, only pausing between mouthfuls for a drag from his Pall Mall. Then he was standing up and ready to fish. "Well, Jud, let's you and me go teach those trout a lesson." With that the two were off downstream; Jud would start his sandwich over on Hidden Channel. Just as he and Harold entered the willows, Jud looked back to see Felicity, who elected to stay behind and eat her lunch at a normal pace, throwing her towel down on the grass and lathering herself with oil. She was no longer nearly naked. Now she wasn't wearing a thing. "Sun worshipper," Harold explained.

All things were perfect on Hidden Channel as Jud and Harold came out of the brush and onto its water. It hardly looked a channel at all, but more like a long, narrow pond with a barely discernable current. "Some very large fish live here," Jud explained, "large browns." Two rings appeared almost simultaneously in the middle of the channel, and judging by their swells both rises belonged in the size group just mentioned.

"Jud, my boy this is exciting. That is a very big fish," Harold said from inside a cloud of smoke.

"Yessir, right now they're feeding on mayflies, but at night they dine on crayfish and this pond is full of them. My friend Henry caught one in here a few years ago around seven pounds. I can't bring but the best fishermen in here because the casts needed are long." Jud continued while pointing, "The water's deep, no way to wade in it, and backcasts are impossible because of all the willows. But down there in that kind of cove the bottom is rocky and you can walk out a long way. You have to make your cast to the middle where we just saw those two browns. Or you can make a cast and let your fly just set there and wait for a cruiser. Kinda like you're tarpon fishing."

"You ever fished for tarpon, Jud?"

"Nope, never have. Looks like fun."

"You come down and visit us in Florida. We'll take you out."

Harold made his way his way down the channel and began fishing while Jud pulled out his lunch. He pulled out his sandwich from its bag, a roast beef, sliced thin and rare, on fresh-baked sourdough, lots of onions, and at the bottom of the bag was a very large piece of apple pie with a note from Carolyn that read, "We're going to miss that smiling face of yours every morning." He ate his apple pie knowing it to be his last. Starting tomorrow *New Yorkers* would be in charge of his lunch. From here on out he'd be getting weight-watchers quiche followed by some form of holistic cookie made from tofu and wheat grass.

On Jud's last bite of pie, that saving moment to any fishing guide's day happened—the big one. The take was followed by a leap and a splash, but what got Jud's attention was Harold going, "Hooo-weee!"

"Need any help there, Harold?" Jud shouted.

"I'm doing fine," he answered.

Jud sat back and watched the fight, which Harold eventually won, and the brown trout was brought to net. He watched him land two more. For a man of his age and as frail and sickly as he appeared, Harold could lay out some line. His strength was gone, his movements were rusted by age, but the essential timing, the key to the cast, was there. The other reason for his angling success was that even through the Coke bottles and the clouds of smoke, Harold didn't miss a rise. He could drop his fly, bull's-eye right on the bubbles.

"Do me a favor, Jud?" Harold called.

"Sure."

"Go check on Felicity—she's a city kid. Just see if she needs anything. Tell her to come and join us?"

Jud waved and headed back to the boat thinking of his last view of Felicity, an image that hadn't left the back of his mind since, that of her buck naked, and he knew for a fact that Felicity wasn't in need of a thing. He felt uncomfortable. The whole thing was pretty weird—an old man asking a young man to go check on his naked wife. This was the strangest day he had ever had at the oars. But as uneasy as he was feeling he had no trouble complying.

Jud came through the woods whistling, not wanted to startle her, city kid and all, and he just didn't want to be suddenly upon her in her nude condition. Well, maybe he did. As he came out of the brush he could see his anxiety was for naught, Felicity was sitting in the shade, her hair wet from a swim, and once again dressed in her T-shirt and shorts. "Hey, Jud. What's up? Where's Harold?"

"He wanted me to come and see if you needed anything, to see if you wanted to come on over and join us."

"Oh, okay, is he catching some fish?"

"Yeah, some nice ones."

"Oh, good. Harold loves to fish." And with that Felicity was up and heading down the trail with Jud following behind. It was then he noticed a nasty looking bruise on the back of her leg. "That's quite a bruise. That happened when I hit that rock, didn't it?"

"Yeah, and it hurts like the dickens. I sat in the river for as long as I could stand it and the cold water helped a lot. Oh, it's so pretty down in here."

Jud was amazed. She had taken a shot that would make a grown man moan and she hadn't said a thing.

"Hi, sweetie," she waved as she and Jud stepped out onto Hidden Channel. She found a place to sit where she could watch him fish in comfort while Jud worked his way down way to where Harold was fishing.

"How are things going?" Jud asked.

"Couldn't be better. This is some place you have taken me to today Jud and I appreciate it. Caught one while you were gone and I just missed one. I saw one swim by here, I don't know how big it was but I've never seen a bigger one that is for sure. Damn, this is exciting."

"You need any flies or anything?" Jud asked.

"Nope, I'm all set."

Jud walked back up to where Felicity was sitting. "You know that was some of the best apple pie I have ever had in our lunch today," she said, brushing her hair.

"Don't I know it," Jud lamented and then went on to explain about the sale of the Tin Cup and the New Yorkers, which led into a stream of nonstop conversation lasting for the next two and a half hours while they watched Harold pull in another twelve trout. Jud had never met anyone so honest and immediate, and the story of her life unfolded in between her asking Jud about his, and not just asking but caring.

Felicity was from Baton Rouge. Her father was abusive, her mother a drunk. "So, when I was sixteen I went to where my mother hid her booze money and I took it. I left home with one hundred and forty-seven dollars and I've never looked back. I went to Miami. I took waitress jobs. I was a kid, gangly, and pretty ugly. One night I was working graveyard and Harold came in and wanted a cup of coffee. He came in every night for the next two years. We became friends. I was a late bloomer and then almost overnight I looked like this," she gestured at her body, "and then we became more than friends.

"We've been together for nine years and we'll be together until the end. I lo-o-ove that man. I know we must seem silly to the rest of the world cause of our ages and all, but I'll tell you something—our marriage works a hundred times better than most.

"Harold makes the money and I help him spend it, but we spend it on good things, helping people, and a lot of causes. Do you know that Harold is a billion—that's with a B—billionaire?"

All Jud could do was shake his head and smile. Way to go Harold, he thought, worth a billion, and married to an incredibly kind and at the same time beautiful woman. Jud hadn't had a date, kind or beautiful, in two months and was broke on his ass. Where was the equity?

"Hooo-weee!" Harold had another one on.

"He sure is enjoying himself. It makes me so happy when I see him like that." Felicity sighed.

The fish was landed and then Jud drew everyone's attention to the time, "If you want to be back in Missoula by eight o'clock we had better get downriver."

"That's fine," Harold agreed, "I'm tuckered out from catching fish and that's the kind of tired a man longs for." The kind of tired Jud longed for was a level of fatigue that could only be brought on by Felicity.

They floated the rest of the way. Hidden Channel being only two miles from town and with the river moving quickly they were in Travers in no time. Then, after the customary good-byes, the Masons were gone. Felicity kissed him on the cheek—something he would dine on for months to come. They paid Jud for the full day and had given him a one hundred percent tip, his biggest tip ever.

Back at the Boat Works the first thing Jud did was to try and reach Henry to tell of him of his hundred percent tip and Felicity's wonderfully oiled nakedness, but Henry wasn't home.

It was getting dark and he thought about going down to the Tin Cup for supper, but settled for a TV dinner that had been in his freezer for an indeterminate time. It was then his finger started to ache and within an hour it was swollen and hurting more than when he broke it. He took a few turns at the pulque but there was no relief. He called Doc Higgins and told him about the pain from rowing the river.

"What in the hell did you do that for? I told you to take it easy with that hand." Doc was surprised, having known Jud since he was a boy and knowing him to have a rational mind concerning most things.

"Mainly because I'm broke."

"All right, Meet me at the clinic in fifteen minutes."

An hour later Jud was in a fresh splint, his middle finger was once again speaking his mind, and that evening Jud went about as low as he could go. Now there would be no money from guiding because there wouldn't be any guiding, under Doc's very firm orders, for another two to three weeks. He would be broke again and in short order. There would be no choice but to go back to the bank and he ached from the thought of it. He left the clinic and came home to a dark and empty Boat Works.

The morning found him on his bed and still dressed. He had lain there for most of the night worrying. One conclusion he had drawn from the night—it would probably be best, given the string of misfortunes he was enduring, not to get out of bed; wait it out under the covers until his bad luck blew over. There was no point in getting up and going to the Tin Cup like he'd done every morning. Carolyn wouldn't be there, New Yorkers would. Jud was only drawn out of bed by the phone. In fact he had three phone calls within an hour all from people wanting him as a guide. "How much bad luck can a man have? I mean this has got to come to an end soon, doesn't it?" he mumbled as he started to make some coffee.

He was about to find out.

Wandering around still in the fog of a sleepless night, he was slow to notice a note pinned beneath the salt shaker in the middle of the kitchen table. It read:

> *Jud—*
>
> *Well, I've waited here for an hour. You must have a girlfriend you didn't tell me about. Hope you do. We decided to turn around and spend the night here. I came up here to see if you would like to make love to me. Don't worry Harold knows why we turned around and he's fine with that. He used to be a great lover but old age has taken that away. We have an understanding. We're down the street at the motel. I'll be in room 2. If you get back before six in the morning come down. We have to be on the road by seven to make the plane.*
>
> *I really enjoyed my day. So did Harold.*
>
> *Love,*
> *Felicity*

Jud calmly dropped the letter back on the table and walked out the porch door to stand in the open. His head drifted back and he looked to the heavens and he screamed, "Aaaaaa-hhhhhhh!" Raising both hands above his head, one hand with its middle finger in a splint, he expressed his disdain for the powers that may be, while his other hand beseeched those very same powers to explain what he had done to deserve this. The hot water heater going out, going broke, the new engine for the Willys, Henprickson and the loan—that was one thing, but missing that chance, what was sure to be his only chance, the chance of a lifetime, every man's fantasy to make love to a woman like Felicity—that was another thing.

Henry's truck came up the drive and pulled up to where Jud was waiting for an answer from an empty blue sky. "Jeez, what's the matter there Judson C.?" Henry asked. "You don't look so good."

Jud handed him the letter as he stepped down from his pickup. Henry read it and then asked, "That's the healthy Felicity that was here with her T-shirt when we were slicin' up your tree?"

"Yeah."

"Aaaaaa-hhhhhhh! Where in the hell were you last night?"

"I was down at Doc's, getting my new splint. Didn't see this note til just now." Jud said holding up his right hand and then started to laugh, "I cannot believe my luck lately. I—"

Jud was cut short by the phone ringing. "That's the fourth phone call this morning. Now *everybody* wants to go fishing." His middle finger said it all.

"Boat Works," Jud answered.

"Jud, its Harold Mason." Jud froze. This call was sure to be about last night and Felicity's attempted infidelity, but he was an innocent man. His virtue secured by a broken finger with Doc Higgins as his witness. "Listen, Felicity has come up with a great idea. I know you build dories but could you build a rowboat, a small two-man boat?"

"Well, sure I could build a rowboat."

"How much would it cost?"

"Oh, I don't know, exactly," Jud answered.

"Approximately—a horseback guess."

"Oh, somewhere between fifteen hundred and two thousand dollars, I suppose, depending on the woods you choose."

"Top of the line."

"About two thousand dollars then."

"Okay. Here's the deal. I'm building a resort and golf course with custom multimillion-dollar homes on a lake near Atlanta. Every home will have a dock, and Felicity thought an empty dock was sad. So what we need are twenty-three rowboats. Can you do it?"

"Uh . . . mmm . . . well, when do you need them by?" Jud was completely taken aback.

"In three years. We've got to build the lake first."

"Yeah, I can do that," Jud said, relieved that Harold's conversation had centered around boats and not his wife.

"Okay, I'll send you a deposit of one half and you'll get the remainder upon completion. Fair enough?"

"Yeah, you bet."

"I'll have one of my people get in touch with you to iron out the details and know that your check will be in the mail by the end of the week. Twenty-three thousand dollars or thereabouts."

"Well, thanks I really—"

"No, thank you. I have to go. Got another call. Good-bye, Jud." In a minute of conversation Jud had gone from broke and facing Hendrickson to debt-free if not a little bit rich.

Jud came back into the yard. "You're not going to believe this. That was Harold Mason."

"He wants to kill ya?" Henry said with assurance.

"No, he wants me to build twenty-three rowboats. He's sending me twenty grand for a deposit and it'll be here by the end of the week. He's building million-dollar homes on a lake in Georgia. He's also building the lake. Every home has a dock and he wanted a rowboat for each one. And it was all Felicity's idea." The idea had come to her the night before as she wrote her note. She couldn't help but notice the mound of Jud's unpaid bills.

Through his wry smile Henry said, "Damn, Judson, if you woulda been at home last night who knows how many boats she mighta bought."

"I have nothing but shit coming my way for a month and then this happens. This month has been a wild ride."

"I gotta get goin'," said Henry. "I only came up here in the first place to tell ya that I was just down at the Tin Cup for breakfast. Had maybe the best breakfast of my life and I gave the new cook the acid test—I had a piece of her apple pie. Judson C., it's not as good as Carolyn makes, it's better.

"And this new gal, Sarah, the new owner from New York? Well, I don't mind tellin' ya, she's highly attractive and single."

"Maybe I'm getting back to being lucky," Jud wondered, having no idea just how much luck Sarah would bring into his life. "But Henry before you go I gotta tell ya what happened to me out on Hidden Channel yesterday."

"I'll hear about it later, J. C. I got a meeting of the grange association in an hour."

"This is a story about Felicity, all oiled up and naked."

"Well, I guess I could find time for one more story."

The lights of Travers Corners brought Jud back to being fifty. He never saw the Masons again. But every time he thinks of that day he laughs, and not a week has gone by, even twentysome-odd years later, that he doesn't think about Felicity. During the winter months he thinks about it a little more, as that broken finger is now arthritic and it hurts like hell when it drops below freezing.

By the time he pulled into the Boat Works it was late, around midnight. Stepping from the Willys, Annie the Wonderlab was there to meet him, nosing his leg, reminding him with some urgency that her supper should have happened six hours ago. He looked up into the star-filled night and thought about Felicity, sweet Felicity once again, the bronzed, benevolent, and beautiful Felicity. It was a certainty that it was she and she alone who saved the Boat Works. Jud would have never made it through the next year because the boat business never materialized and the guiding remained slow. She gave him the life he was living today and for that he would be forever thankful.

Of course, that memory always drags the other memory with it. That coming from that following Monday when Jud went down to square things away with Hendrickson and the bank. He was first in line that morning with a check for twenty-three thousand. There were two guys in suits talking to Hendrickson, so Julie took Jud to the front desk to handle the paperwork. "Jeez, J. C., talk about a short-term loan." He explained about the Masons and rowboats while Julie filled the numbers and punched the calculator. There was a handling fee, a prepayment fee, a set-up fee, the interest fee, and one intrabank fee for something that was explained only by the initials, IBF, whatever that was, which cost twenty cents. Jud couldn't stand it. He repays the loan ahead of schedule. He deposits another twenty thousand into his savings and the bank wants to nickel-and-dime.

A week later the bank was suddenly and dramatically closed for an audit. Bank examiners were in town, and it didn't take long for the word to leak that Hendrickson, through his nickel-and-dime IBF fees, and some creative accounting, had managed to embezzle over twenty thousand dollars. He went on to do more accounting, accounting for his fraud, and while he should have gotten five to ten, or as they say in stir, *nickel-dime*, at fun-filled Leavenworth, Hendrickson only had to pay back the bank. His only punishment was five years probation, but the memory of his going down would serve Jud for life.

From The Journals of Traver C. Clark

April 9, 1881—

Carrie gave birth to Ethan this morning just after daybreak. Thank God for Laurie Berger, the midwife down from Reynolds. She's been down here staying with us for the last two weeks and waiting for this baby to appear. All went well. Ethan is a strong healthy-looking son, around seven pounds, Laurie estimated.

I know I have never been as excited as I was at the moment I could hear the baby's cry from up the stairs. Life is good and we are blessed.

Laurie's wages for two weeks *12.50*
New Cradle *3.25*
Shipping .... *.35*

~

THERE

It wasn't the kind of day that made you think about going for a bike ride, but there, heading down Main, pedaled a small boy. He was dressed for the sleet in nothing but a T-shirt. His legs poked through at the tattered knees of his pants with every pump he made against a bitter north wind. Behind him he towed two red Radio Flyers loaded with laundry.

Out in front of McCracken's, Junior was helping Etta May Harper out with her groceries as the boy pedaled by. Junior, wearing a sweater, was cold just coming outside. The thought of being on a bicycle made him shiver.

"Why that kid will catch his death," Etta May said. "Who is that boy?"

"I don't know," Junior answered, surprised that he didn't, for Junior knew everyone in Travers. With three kids of his own in school he knew all the children in town as most of them come through his living room on weekends, or so it seemed. But he'd never seen this boy.

He watched the kid pedal past Dolores's, then angle across the street to the Take 'r Easy Motel and its Laundromat.

Back inside, Junior returned to a small remodeling job he'd started near the front of the general store. He was running behind, as usual, so he only puzzled over the anomalous sight of the boy and his bike for a moment. Then it was back to the carpentry at hand.

In the charge of an accomplished woodworker, the job, new shelving around the front windows, would have taken one or two days. In the hands of a mediocre handyman, it would take maybe five days. Junior had been on the job for over two weeks, and given what he had been able to accomplish so far, he was confident he'd be finished sometime—maybe even soon. Tools didn't exactly leap into Junior's hands. They even looked odd there, as if they didn't belong, and this was because they didn't.

Consulting his plans, which were letter perfect, and his measurements, which were precise, Junior reached for the power saw. This is where things generally start to go wrong for him. Hand tools were a concern in his hands, power tools were frightening. While his plans and measurements might be perfect, Junior is always strong on the slide-rule end of construction. It is the application part of building that throws him. Sure, he could triangulate the most difficult miter and cut it to the exact degree, but it's the actual mechanics of the cut that confuses him. Tool coordination—he'd none. Coordination in general is not one of his strong suits. Wood in his hands becomes lumber and that's lumber the verb not the noun. An observer watching him work would hardly think the man was a qualified pharmacist, but a man afflicted with hopeless dyslexia. This inability to translate from the theoretical to the dimensional reality of spatial relationships was hampered even further by Junior's chronic absentmindedness. He made a grab for the saw. It was an air-grab. The saw wasn't there.

In all fairness to Junior, it should be mentioned that every time someone needed a prescription filled he would have to leave his shelving project, usually carrying whatever tool or material he happened to have in his hand with him. Somewhere between the front door and the pharmacy, he would lay whatever he had down, never in the same spot, hence initiating his next search.

A few hours later Jud came into McCracken's. Junior, just minutes before, had drilled some holes in the walls. So right now he was looking for the drill. The drill was the least of his worries. It was fairly large and brightly colored, but he couldn't find his drill bits, or the key for the chuck, for that matter.

THERE

"Hey, Junior."

Looking up from under a counter, "Oh, hello there, Jud."

Having seen Junior down on his knees before, Jud asked, "What are you looking for?"

"Um, some drill bits and a chuck key."

"Ah." The amazing thing about Junior, Jud thought, was that he had to spend 30 percent of his waking hours looking for things he had just lost, and it never upset him. He treated looking for tools as part of the process, part of the cost of construction. He was like that as a kid. He got straight As, but he never had on matching socks. He had a telescope in his room and he could identify all the constellations, but he would get lost on the way to his homeroom. In today's vernacular he would be a nerd. Back then he was a bookworm.

"Have you been fishing lately?" Junior asked, standing up and brushing off his knees.

"Got out last night."

"Did you do any good?" Junior asked.

"It was okay." Jud knew he needed to change the subject, and quickly, for once Junior got wound up about fishing he would be trapped. "I need some number ten two-inch brass screws. I need thirty of them."

He didn't dare ask Junior how his fishing was. He knew better than that. It was well understood among the fishermen in Travers, that you *never* ask Junior how his fishing was unless you have plenty of time. Ask Doc or Henry how their fishing was, and you get something like it was good, it was fair, it was lousy. But Junior tells you in detail. Starting with the fly he used and how it was tied, when he tied it and why, through all his fishing sequences, fish by fish, jump by jump, strike by miss, cast by false cast, riffle by pool, Junior wants to tell it all. Doc says that he comes away from one of Junior's fishing stories as tired as if he had spent the day on the river himself.

Passing by the corner window, heading for the screw department, Junior saw the young boy from this morning pedaling back from the Laundromat. This time he got a good look. "Hey, Jud, have you ever seen this kid before?"

The boy's face was pale, save for the reddened cheeks. His lips were bluish white. A pair of oversized eyes watered against the wind. He was still in his T-shirt. His bare arms were thin and mottled by the cold. He looked understandably miserable as he pedaled past. His face was sad—a look that anyone who had spent two hours in a Laundromat would understand.

"No." Jud hadn't seen him before. "Damned cold to be without a coat."

"I'd guess."

The boy pedaled beneath the window where they stood, and the two wagons wobbled in tow. Even though they were standing behind glass they could hear their rattles and squeaks. Wobbled past because they hardly rolled, there wasn't a matching tire in the eight. What few parts there are to a Radio Flyer were held together by baling wire. The laundry, done and sort of folded, shifted back and forth from the uneven ride. The loads were secured to the beds under the weight of several bricks.

His bike was a combination of bikes, a fusion of nonmatching parts, and though it was far from symmetrical, he seemed to pedal it quite well. A piece of cardboard, taped to and extending down the back fender, kept the spray of his rear tire from hitting the clean clothes. This wasn't his first trip to the Laundromat.

"Wonder what that kid's mother is thinking about?" Jud said as he watched Junior count out his screws.

"I don't know. Weatherman says it's going to start getting warmer. It was great last week. I got out on the river twice. Did I tell you about the day I had last Sunday?"

"Uh, no you didn't. But listen, Junior, I really have to get going. I'm expecting a phone call. Tell me about it later, will ya?"

On his way out the door, Jud called back, "Hey, Junior, your drill bits and chuck key are up here by the magazines."

"Thanks."

Walking back to the Boat Works he thought about the boy once more. Then he didn't think about him again until May.

Jud only thought about him then because bicycling up the hill came the boy. It was a far different day from the last time he saw him on his bike. It was a warm, almost summer morning. The door was open to the workshop, and Jud watched him pedal closer as he went about fastening cedar strips in place along the ribs of a river dory.

"Hello," Jud greeted him.

The boy greeted Jud back by coming straight to the point, "You need any help around here, mister?" The look in his eye was that of determination, but his voice was so shy it lacked only the hiss to be a whisper. He asked this not as a boy who was out trying to earn a little spending money, but as a boy who needed a job.

Jud was getting a good look at the boy who was thin, too thin. His color wasn't good. His face wasn't the face you would expect to see on a young boy. It was a troubled face, a face that was in dire need of some laughter.

"Well, I don't know. I might need some help," Jud answered as he took two Pepsis out of the fridge, then handed one to the boy. He took it, but he didn't smile. "How old are you?"

"Ten."

"What's your name?"

"Michael."

"Michael what?"

"Chase."

Grabbing his glasses, Jud picked up a piece of paper and a pencil from the tool bench and acting very formal he asked, "Well, Michael Chase, I have a few questions I'll need to ask before I can consider you for employment," then pretended to read off the paper. "Do you own your own car?"

"No," Michael's face puzzled.

"Do you have your Social Security number?"

"No."

"Have you ever been married?"

"No," he answered, growing a little impatient with questions that were only intended to make him laugh.

"Have you ever been arrested?"

"No!" He was missing the humor and growing visibly frustrated.

~

It appeared that nothing was going to make Michael laugh, but Jud wasn't going to give up and gave it one more attempt. He tried his combination of Jabberwocky and Jerry Lewis—a sure laugh getter with ten-year-olds.

"Okay, I do have a job. I need someone to spanner a winnelpeg on my credesvance so my mahalioprope will once again be able to transmogulate." He reached for his hat hanging behind the door, put it on backward while turning his glasses upside down and added, "Do you coginify my soliference?"

That worked. He got a laugh, but it was a short laugh. Then the boy returned to the business at hand. "Really, mister, I need to find a job."

"All right, I have a job. How are you at mowing a lawn?"

"I don't know. I've never done it." Annie the Wonderlab wandered in through the open door. Delighted to see a short human, the only size range in the species that really knew how to play, she ran to pick up her stick and then nosed it into the boy's hand.

Pulling his pocket watch from his vest, Jud asked, "It's almost eleven thirty. Why don't you join me for lunch? We'll go down and have a couple of hamburgers at the Tin Cup. If it's all right with your mom."

"She won't care."

Jud looked at Michael's shirt, ragged and outgrown some time ago. He looked at his hair, face, and elbows, which hadn't seen much in the way of soap and water lately. He looked into a pair of young and unhealthy eyes. He found his mother's not caring easy to believe.

On their walk down to the Tin Cup, then over a cheeseburger, Jud was finding out more about Michael. His mother was ill—a bad back from an automobile accident. No father. Mom was taking a lot of pain medication. She couldn't work. No money. A sister who was eight. They were living in one of the trailers across the tracks. At his house, it was Michael who took care of the laundry, the shopping, the cooking, his sister.

Michael ate from hunger. He wolfed down his fries, downed his shake, and had a helping of pie. But he divided his hamburger, wrapping one half in a napkin.

"Was your mouth bigger than your stomach?" asked Jud.

"I'm gonna give this half to my sister."

"Well, you'll need all of that hamburger if you are going to mow a lawn. Takes a lot of energy to mow a lawn. So, you go ahead and eat that one and I'll ask Sarah to make another burger for your sister."

Elated, Michael tore open the napkin, while Jud caught Sarah's eye and waved her over to the table. The prep work was done and she was poised and ready behind the grill, psyching herself up for the lunch crowd, shifting from one foot to the other like a shortstop. In her Yankee's cap it made for an easy analogy.

"Michael this is Sarah. Sarah owns the Tin Cup." This garnered the same amount of awe from Michael as if she owned Trump Tower. "Michael has a sister at home and he'd like to have a hamburger to take home to her, and a piece of apple pie, too."

"You got it, Jud. Do you live here in town, Michael?"

Michael with a face full of burger just nodded. All Sarah could see above the bun were Michael's eyes. They were beautiful and rimmed with red. He was too pale.

"He and his family just moved to Travers a while ago. They're living out in one of the trailers." At that point Jud raised his eyebrows, and he and Sarah traded questionable expressions, both knowing that if you were living out in the trailers, you were automatically impoverished. Michael's being way too slender and in need of a good scrubbing told her everything else she needed to know.

"Well, you come back and see me, Michael," and she gave him one of her soft Sarah smiles. She went back to the kitchen and they heard the sizzle of the burger hit the grill.

The lunch crowd came with the noonday whistle, but by that time Jud and Michael were gone. Michael delivered the hamburger to his sister at the trailer. Jud went back to the Boat Works to make a call.

"Sarah."

"Yeah?"

"Do me a favor? Ask around, see if you can find out anything about Michael's mother. There is big trouble in that boy's life."

"Will do. Gotta go. Got a grill full. Sure seems like a good kid." Sarah had a hair appointment at Dolores's after work. Dolores would know something about Michael and his family if anybody would.

Though Jud had only been around Michael a short while, he could sense a quality about him. He *was* a good kid. He was polite. His table manners needed work, but it could have been the hunger. He was smart and well spoken for ten. The eyes, though troubled, were bright.

Michael was quickly back at the Boat Works and trying to catch his breath from the bike ride. He followed Jud out to the backyard. "So, you've never mowed a lawn before?" Jud asked pulling the mower from a corner of the workshop.

"Nope."

"Well, grab a hold of it. See how it feels."

Then picking up a length of doweling from a wood bin, he motioned for Michael to follow him and to bring the mower. "Well, yard work, my b-o-oy," Jud said in his best W. C. Fields, "is the very b-a-ane of my existence. I'd rather take a sound beating than do yard w-o-ork. I have the lawn mower, mind you, but I lack the inclin-a-a-tion." Then he rested the doweling on his shoulder, as Fields rested his cane, and with his hat he mimicked W. C.'s patented schtick where he tries to put on his skimmer, but misses his head, and instead balances his straw hat on the end of his cane. Then he would look all around for his hat. Finally realizing where it really was, he would recoil surprised, fingers splayed, and say something akin to "Godfrey Daniel." Jud did the bit to a tee.

This time Jud got a belly laugh. A belly laugh when an hour ago he couldn't even make Michael smile. Now that was progress. Amazing what a little attention and a full stomach can do for kids.

"Now, you told your mother where you are?"

"No."

"Why not?"

"She was asleep. She always sleeps in the afternoon after she takes her medicine."

"What about your sister? Who's watching her?"

"She's over at Sissy Henderson's playing dolls. I gotta pick her up and take her home when I get done mowing the lawn," Michael answered, grimacing at the thought of playing dolls and having to put up with his kid sister.

Once he had checked Michael out on the lawn mower, gas, oil, throttle, and safety instructions, Jud returned to his workshop. From the window he could look out now and then to see how Michael was doing, and he was mowing that lawn as though his life depended on it. Back and forth he went, never stopping for a breather or to wipe his brow, only stopping a few times for a drink from the hose. He wasn't treating the lawn like a summertime chore, but as a pivotal point in his work record—his first job. He didn't want to look bad. He wanted more jobs.

Mowing the lawn wasn't easy as it was the first cutting of the season, and Jud had let it get a little longer than he should have. Yard work was way down an already long list of Jud's procrastinations. It took Michael over two hours, but he got it done. The lawn looked good, especially for a first-time mower, and a ten-year-old at that.

"You did a great job there, Michael," Jud said handing him a cold soda.

"Thanks, can I get paid now? I gotta get home."

"Well, uh, sure." Jud dug out his wallet then looked at his pocket watch. He put his glasses on and fingered through the bills while calculating what a fair price for the gardening might be. He realized from the urgency in the boy's voice that he was asking for the money, not for candy and comics, but for staples and rent.

He handed the bill to Michael, who was no longer there. He was now standing looking inside a just-finished river dory. His eyes were wide and Jud was really seeing them for the first time. He rubbed the gunwale and twirled the oarlocks. "You make these?"

"Yep."

"They're really cool."

"Well, maybe one day this summer I'll take you and your sister for a ride down the river. If it's all right with your mom."

"Yeah! That would be great." For a moment Michael looked like the child he was. Then he noticed the money in Jud's hand and started to reach for it, but then pulled back, unsure how one was to accept wages, these being his first.

"Listen, Michael, I don't want to pry into another man's business, but would you say that things were good or bad around your house right now?"

"Bad," he answered with no hesitation.

Jud pulled another bill from his wallet. "Now, I'm about to pay you roughly five times the price of an average lawn-mowing job. When a guy needs money five bucks isn't going to cut it. So, for a while, it will be you who owes me. You can work off the balance. I'll pay you three dollars and twenty-five cents an hour. I know that is well below the minimum wage, but that works out fine because you are well below the minimum age. So I am going to give you twenty-five dollars, you've worked for two hours and forty-five minutes at three dollars and twenty-five cents, off six, that means you own me . . . ummm . . . let's see, two and a half—"

"I earned eight dollars and ninety-three cents," Michael said. "That leaves . . . mmm . . . sixteen dollars and seven cents. So that would be . . . mmm . . . that would be 4.3 hours of work that I still owe you."

Jud gave him a double take.

"I like math."

"See, like that woodpile over there needs straightening, and the workshop needs a good sweeping, and there's weeding, et cetera. When you've worked off this advancement, this loan, we'll start afresh and I'll pay you as you go. But you have to check it out with your mother first. Okay?"

"Okay."

"You tell your mom to call me."

"We don't have a phone."

"Well, I'll come down sometime when it's convenient and meet your mom, and—"

"No. It's all right, my mom won't care. I gotta go." He was on his bike and down the hill. Jud went back to work, and for the rest of the afternoon things were quiet around the Boat Works. But he couldn't stop thinking about Michael.

Things are never quiet around Dolores's, and the beauty parlor was its usual jumble of noise. Margie Morris was under the dryer, while Dolores was curling Emily Hanford's hair in the next chair. The country radio station was playing, as it was always playing. Sarah was waiting her turn. She'd come a little early for her haircut just so she could share in a bit of the gab with Dolores, who with the phone to her ear, was making an appointment. If you want to know what's going on in Travers Corners, Dolores's is Command Central.

"Yeah, sure we can do it for you, Mary . . . okay, sweetie, see you, Tuesday . . . huh? . . . oh yeah, I heard. It's awful . . . how long have they been married? . . . no kidding . . . okay . . . gotta go."

Dolores put down the phone, scribbled the appointment in the book, and went back to curling Emily's hair, "Mark and Joleen are gettin' divorced. Been married a whole three months. Three months, that sorta sounds more like a timed event than a marriage. I've had head colds last longer than three months," Dolores laughed at her own joke.

Dolores was looking fine today, looking like only Dolores could look. She called it her early truck-stop look, bowling-alley colors. Her orange pants and yellow blouse were fitting tight. Dolores has, and always has had, a figure that favored the tighter fit. She had on red shoes and her hair was redder today than it was last week. Her face was lineless and beautiful.

She and Sarah have been best friends since Sarah moved to town, even though their backgrounds, other than sharing an Italian ancestry, lie on either ends of the spectrum. Sarah, the ex-schoolteacher from Brooklyn. Dolores born and raised in the Elkheart. You would never put these two together by fashion or looks. For Sarah was in her Yankee's hat, Hawaiian shirt, baggy pants, Reeboks, and her hair was the same color brown as it always was. When Sarah smiled, crow's-feet fanned from the corners of her eyes, and that smile has been known to turn a few heads as well.

Following the news of Mark and Joleen, the natural course for discussion was divorce. Who was thinking about it. Who had done it lately. Of course, they covered their favorite divorce topic: those who would do it if given half a chance and why. Sarah wasn't much for spreading gossip. She never repeated anything she heard, but she loved listening in. Loved it. A voyeur gossip.

Waiting until Dolores had finished helping Margie out from under the hair dryer, Sarah asked, "Do any of you know anything about a new family living out in the trailers? A young boy named Michael, his mother, and his sister?"

Dolores, Margie, and Emily all shook their heads. Then Dolores spotted Betty Dorsey heading for the library. "There's someone who oughta know somethin' about 'em." As principal of Elkheart Elementary, Betty Dorsey did indeed know something about the Chase family. In fact, she knew almost everything as a report concerning the Chases had been sent to her from the county offices only yesterday. Dolores flagged her down, and the principal crossed Main where Sarah met her in front of the parlor.

"It's a terrible situation, the Chases," Betty explained in her nervous and speedy manner, "They have no money. The father is gone. The mother is a former junkie who is right now in a lawsuit against the state over a phony insurance claim. The children are neglected and mistreated. The little girl, Marcie, is such a sweet little girl, but timid. The boy is having real problems. Temper tantrums in class. Fights, brought on mostly by other students teasing him. They come to school dressed in rags. She transferred those kids out of their school in Billings with only a few months left in the year. That's so hard on children.

"She's on heavy-duty pain medication for her supposed bad back and is in bed most of the time. She is reported to have late-night gentlemen callers. Very shady. The boy takes care of himself, the mother, and his sister. I just hate situations like this," Betty continued, shifting a stack of books in her arms. "As a school, we are helpless to interfere, as are any of the people at the county, because there are certain minimums a mother must drop below before the county can step in, and Mrs. Chase is raising those kids right at those minimums. Those kids would be better off in foster homes. How'd you come to know about them, Sarah?"

"Actually, I was asked by Jud if I wouldn't check it out for him. He seems to have taken a real interest in the boy. He says this kid is special."

"Oh, he is very special. I've watched him look after his sister. For an older brother he is very attentive and caring. He is also *very* bright. Mark Webster says he is without exception the best math student he has ever taught. Gifted. The little girl, however, is horribly shy and overly dependent on her brother. She isn't doing well in school at all."

"Thanks, Betty," Sarah said. "I'll relay what you've said on to Jud."

"It would be great if Jud could take an interest in that Chase boy. There is so much anger and frustration there. He just needs someone who will listen and pay attention to him." Then Betty turned for the library and Sarah went back inside the parlor.

During her haircut, since Margie was now gone and Emily was under the dryer, Sarah filled Dolores in on what she had learned from Betty.

"Why that's plumb awful," Dolores said. "After work, I'll go talk to the Reverend Allen and see if anyone in our church can help with clothes, or food, or anything for them kids." Then she swung Sarah around in her chair and handed her a mirror. "Is that short enough for ya, girl?"

"That's just fine," Sarah answered, as Dolores pulled away the apron. "Listen, when you find anything out about the church helping out, give Jud a call, will you?"

"Sure will," Dolores nodded.

"See ya later. Of course, saying see you later in a town the size of Travers is superfluous."

Dolores laughed, making a mental note to look up superfluous and popped another piece of gum in her mouth. Sweeping up the cuttings beneath the chair, she felt her mood change. She became frustrated and angry. Her sweeping and gum popping picked up tempo as her emotions gathered momentum. The Del Vecchio blood stirred. She was angry, because she couldn't imagine child abuse. All of her life she had wanted to have children, but was unable to with either of her husbands, or any of her lovers for that matter. If she had children she would smother them with love, while this witch of a woman down at the trailers had two children only to neglect them.

She looked at herself in the mirror. Everything that was female Dolores had done well. She was attractive and seductive enough to summon any suitor she wished. She had the build for motherhood and the pheromones to seduce any potential father she chose. But the ovaries had let her down. Barren.

She was also a little frustrated because Henry hadn't been around since last Friday night, and she really *needed* to see him. How she loved that man. Too bad she couldn't stand living with him.

Past the library, past the Roxy, up the hill, and for the rest of her walk home, the words neglected, mistreated, and minimum care echoed again and again in Sarah's thoughts. Minimum care, just the words you would expect from a bureaucracy. Social services would devise a two-word criteria for child care, and in those two words create an oxymoron. Minimum care—what is that?

The thoughts of her own boy flooded her memory, then her eyes. Being part Italian for times such as these is a plus. First, because Italians are in no danger of harboring any emotions, and second, God was kind enough to give the Italians wine, without which the race would surely be extinct by way of combustion. Once in her kitchen, she opened the good Chianti. Though she had been at the grill all afternoon, she suddenly had the urge to cook. She had the need to feed someone. She called Jud, inviting him to dinner. She made sauces, and she made pastas. Every pot in the house was being stirred. Linguine, cannelloni, tortellini. In a couple of hours, after a frenzy of cooking, slicing, dicing, sautéing, and drinking wine from a measuring cup, Sarah stepped back from the stove. Though she didn't really remember doing it, she had made enough food to feed twelve. She went to the phone and invited Henry and Dolores as well. Then she invited Sal—knowing how much her uncle loved her cannelloni.

Throughout dinner most of the conversation centered on Michael and his sister, Marcie. "So, the bottom line here is abuse," Sarah concluded as she walked around the table offering anyone more cannelloni. All refused. Everyone was stuffed. She was well into her cups, five and one half, well-measured cups. She'd eaten more than anyone else, yet she had room for one more large bit of cannelloni. She ate it with the serving spoon right from the dish, as she comically plopped herself back down in the chair next to Henry. Everyone laughed. Then she promptly burst into tears to no one's surprise.

Friends this long, they knew what was the matter. In fact, when she called for this impromptu dinner, they knew it was coming. It happened about three or four times a year. They knew a breakdown was imminent, because she was cooking Italian, and because of those she had invited. Her three best friends, and Sal, who was the only family she had left. It was a pattern her guests had come to recognize. After a lot of wine, the memory of her son and her husband would swell until she burst. "That great beast of a woman down there with those two children, not caring about them. I would give everything to have my family back," then she fell against her uncle's open arms and freely wept.

Dolores, being Italian herself, a woman, and deprived of children because of a tricky ovaries, began to sob. She knew the pain Sarah suffered at times, the pain of not having a child of her own. But what she suffered could not compare to Sarah's tragedy of having a child, only to lose that child and your husband in one senseless moment—killed while walking back from a playground, caught in the cross fire of gang members. The horror of that was unimaginable, and Dolores moved over to hug Sarah as well.

Henry started to clear the dishes. He felt uncomfortable being so close to this much emotion. Sal, with a few tears in his own eyes, shared in her sorrow as Sarah's loss was his nephew and grand-nephew. "Well, look what you do got, sweetheart—you got friends that love ya. I love ya."

"Oh, I know," Sarah blubbered.

"And, we want ya to know," Henry added as he picked up another handful of plates, "that we'll continue to love ya just as long as ya keep feedin' us."

Humor was about the only thing that helped, the only way Jud and Henry had ever found to snap Sarah from these bad moments. They also knew the laughter needed to come immediately, otherwise they could lose her to an all-night depression. She was a sucker for humor. If they could get her laughing, they could turn her blues around.

"There's one thing I would like to know," Jud asked, his tone and face as somber as he could make them, as if he were going to continue along the same serious vein as Sarah's tears.

"What's that?" Henry asked.

"What's for dessert?"

It had worked. They had caught her in time. Sarah's smile came through the tears, such understandable tears. She was content just to be held for a while. Then she sat up, slowly. Her eyes were red from crying and round from the notion that was formulating. "The county can't do anything, the mother won't do anything, and so the kids are all set for a future of never having anything. We can't let it happen and we're not going to."

"Well, what are we going to do?" Jud asked.

"I don't know, but the five of us are going to do something to help those kids out." They all knew the look. Her jaw was set. There was no stopping her now. Saint Sarah was on the case. "Give me a day or two to get some ideas."

"How old is this little guy, again?" Sal asked.

"Ten."

"Little League starts practice in just a coupl'a weeks. I need ballplayers—ballplayers I got. What I need here is some pitchin'." Sal shook his head as he thought about the returning lineup from last year taking the field again this summer. "I mean, if I don't find myself a pitcher this year, well, to be honest, we'll end the season in the cellar just like last year."

"Michael's going to be at my house in the morning," Jud said, "so I'll run the baseball idea by him."

"Yeah, tell him not to worry about buyin' the uniform. Tell him I'll spring for it. Tell him if he turns out to be a southpaw with a curveball, I'll buy him a new car."

The conversation then turned to baseball and lighter subjects until it was time for everyone to head home. Jud left for the Boat Works and a good book. Sal went home to ESPN. Henry and Dolores went back to Dolores's so that Henry, who was bone tired from a long day, could do something about her frustrations.

~

Sarah just went to bed. She stayed awake until after midnight, tossing, turning, and thinking about ways to help those kids. Bright and early the next morning, her morning off, she was up and on a mission. She drove to Reynolds and the county offices. Social services.

That afternoon, just a few minutes after the final school bell, there came Michael pedaling up the hill. There were tears in his eyes, and Jud could see his troubled face from the workshop and came out to meet him. "Are you all right, Michael?"

"Ye-eeh-eeh-Yeah," he answered between sobs. "But I-I-I can't work for you today, 'cause my mom says I have to stay ho-h-home and take care of my sister."

"So, you're crying because you are going to miss work?"

"Yeah."

"Someday, and somewhere, Michael, you will be named employee of the month."

"Huh?"

"Never mind. Well, that's okay, Michael, the yard work can wait until tomorrow or the next day. Day after tomorrow is Saturday, maybe you can get in a few hours on the weekend."

"Yo-you're not gonna fire me?" he continued to sob.

"No. I'm not going to fire you," Jud laughed.

"Marcie's going to a birthday party on Saturday. I won't have to babysit. I can work then."

"All right then, Saturday it is."

"I'd better get home, or my mom will kill me."

"Hold on. Let me grab my bike and I'll pedal down as far as McCracken's with you."

There is something so joyous to a child about watching an adult engaging in a childlike activity, such as the riding of a bicycle, and Michael was no exception. Pedaling in place, coasting in figure eights, turning in circles, and laughing for no apparent reason, Michael looked on as Jud quickly pumped a little air into the tires. The bike hadn't been ridden since sometime last summer. Together they pedaled down the hill.

Jud took in a deep breath, "Sure is a great day. Fishing will be good today. You like to fish, Michael?"

"I don't know. I never been fishin'."

"You've *never* been fishing? Why that's positively un-American."

They pedaled over Carrie Creek, stopping briefly so Jud could show him the trout swimming under the bridge. But Michael was edgy about getting home, and there was something about the way he said his mother would kill him that was backed by fear.

"You know, Michael, you are going through some tough times right now, but I think your luck is about to change."

"How come?"

"I don't know—just a feeling." He said nothing about the pact that was formed the night before; nothing about Saint Sarah and her appointed band of angels. Jud coasted up to McCracken's and Michael pedaled away, his bike rattling and squeaking. "See ya Saturday." Michael waved back.

Junior was out in front of McCracken's sweeping up and talking with Doc Higgins who had just ducked out of his office and over to the general store for a bar of candy.

"Who's your buddy?" asked Doc.

"His name is Michael Chase. Lives down at the trailers," Jud answered putting down his kickstand.

Doc rubbed his chin, "The Chases, mmm, the little girl was just in my office last week. The school sent her over. They were worried about her color and below-normal temperature. Turned out the child's malnourished. Evidently the mother is a no-good-nik. I had Kim call social services. They are aware of the situation, but their hands are tied."

"That boy does all the shopping. Food stamps. He comes in, buys what he needs. Never says a word," Junior added.

"Well, the kids are heading into a lucky streak," Jud said, "Saint Sarah has been re-canonized."

"Oh, I know," Junior laughed knowingly, "she was already in today explaining the situation. Talked me into giving the family a discount. I wouldn't have done that for the mother. I fill her prescriptions. That woman's a junkie. But for Sarah and those kids . . ."

Doc just nodded his head. No explanation was necessary, for it wasn't the first family Sarah had helped in Travers.

"Henry was in this morning. Bought a brand new bicycle, mountain bike with all the gears," Junior winked. "When I asked him who it was for, he just said that he knew someone who needed one. If ever there was a kid who needed a bicycle," Junior looked over to Jud. "Wonder if there's a coincidence somewhere?"

"More than likely," Jud smiled.

"Well, the fishing should be coming around on Carrie Creek. I'm going out on Sunday. Either one of you guys want to go?" Junior asked.

"Can't do it on Sunday," Doc answered. "We have guests coming. I'd better get back. See you two later," and he headed back to the clinic.

"How about you, Jud?"

"Yeah, sounds good. But I'll have to meet you out there, because I have someone coming in from Great Falls to talk about boats." He hated lying to him. No one was coming from Great Falls. But if Junior went with him, he would want to fish right alongside him all day. This would be Jud's first day of fishing for the season, his personal opener, and by tradition, a tradition observed only by himself, he always fished the opener alone. The solitude, the needed separation, the feeling of being disconnected, the weightless feeling of being out *there*. This is what awaited him on Sunday.

Junior was needed inside and Jud got on his bike and headed for the Boat Works thinking about *there*.

There: the angler's noun. *There*, every fisherman has one. Someplace on a river or stream. *There* is seldom a generality, but a precise footing on a bend somewhere, a place where every riffle, every willow, every cloud is in place. You can be near *there*, or around *there*, or by *there*, but there is no place like *there*. Easily dreamed, *there*. You can get *there* from an easy chair or on a downtown bus. *There* is an exact passage from a fisherman's back pages, virtual reality without the helmet. *There* is the reason for being here.

Jud was pedaling and grinning, because the only thing standing between him and *there* was Saturday.

Saturday and Michael seemed to arrive at the same time. But Michael had good reasons for rising early. Sure he wanted to get to work on time, but he was up before dawn, and he was excited. He had a new bike to ride. He and his sister had new clothes to wear, hand-me-downs, but new to them. The Chase family refrigerator was filled. Canned goods were in the cupboards. There were some used beds and furniture arriving this afternoon.

Saint Sarah was in full swing. Dolores and the church were right behind.

That Saturday Michael worked as a boy possessed. He did the work of three boys twice his age. That kid was all over that yard, raking leaves, weeding, and sweeping. But, wherever he was working, he would take the time to move his bike so it was close by.

Michael wanted to do the best job he could for two reasons. He wanted to be hired again, and he wanted somehow to get even. Michael knew there was a connection between meeting Jud and his sudden good fortune. Sarah, Dolores, Henry, and Mr. McCracken, all of them were there to help his family. All of them were Jud's friends. Only yesterday Jud had predicted that his luck would change. Today he had a new bike, and this, through the eyes of a ten-year-old, was more than a change in his luck. It was some kind of miracle.

"Hey, how about some lunch?" Jud shouted to him across the yard.

"Okay," and Michael came on the run.

"I was wondering, do you think we should walk down to the Tin Cup or take the bikes?"

"The bikes."

"Something told me that you might say that. All right, come on," Jud smiled and Michael laughed, realizing he had just been teased.

A boy on a new bike is like being one with the wind, Jud remembered as he watched Michael coast out in front of him and down the hill.

They ordered their sandwiches to go because it was just too nice outside to eat indoors. Anyway, the Tin Cup was packed, and all they saw of Sarah was just a wave from behind the grill. They rode over to the river and ate their lunch. Afterward, Jud suggested, "Let's bike on down to Miller's Bend. It's only a couple of miles."

"But what about the leaves?"

"The leaves, my boy," relapsing into W. C. Fields, "will be there waiting for us. There are only two things in life which are certain-n-n, my little tadpole, and that is death and ya-a-ardwork. Although, there are many among us who have trouble distinguishing between the two-o-o." Michael laughed.

"We'll take the old river road. See what that new bike of yours can do. C'mon I'll race you," and Jud stood on the pedals and gave a few hard pumps forcing Michael into the race. A contest Jud had no intention of continuing more than a hundred yards or so.

It took the two of them an hour before they managed to pedal back into Travers, as there was time spent at Miller's Bend skipping rocks across the Elkheart. Skipping rocks and a bike ride were a combination not found in one of Jud's days for many years. He was having fun. He pedaled over Town Bridge far behind Michael, who waited for him in front of McCracken's. He'd been there long enough to catch his breath and to grow a little impatient.

Fun, Jud ruminated coasting into Travers, *how many times as a grownup do you have fun?* And by that he meant the good ol' rock-skipping, daydreaming, bike-riding, wholesale, Huck Finn kind of fun. Maturity breaks down the good times into select behaviors and responses. For adults things can be enjoyable, amusing, entertaining. On certain nights mirth is still achieved. But, for the most part, adult fun is much more sedate, sophisticated, stuffy, practiced, and certainly much more expensive. Spontaneous childhood fun is an elixir of sorts, at least that's how Jud was viewing it, and it was free.

As they crossed Main and headed for the Boat Works, Jud looked over in the alley behind McCracken's. Junior, who was helping unload a shipment at the loading dock, spotted him and called out, "See ya tomorrow."

"See you out there," Jud waved.

"Where are you guys goin'?" Michael asked, pulling up next to Jud and riding without hands.

"Fishing."

"I'd like to go fishing," Michael said, and realizing that he had just invited himself along, he was embarrassed and grabbed the handlebars. "I've never done it before," he added, knowing that he had said it before, but there was no harm in a reminder.

"Well, we're going to do just that and one of these days soon."

But not tomorrow, for *there* is a place Jud went alone. When he thought of *there*, no one else was in the picture. *There* is a selfish moment, an afternoon stolen from the time continuum and stolen without an accomplice.

Michael worked until supper. The leaves were almost done, but there was yard work still ahead of him. Tired and sweaty, he picked up the rake and the hoe and leaned them back into their place beside the workshop. Inside, Jud was standing at the drill press when Michael came through the door. "I gotta go now," he said startling Jud from his calculations.

"Well, let's go out and see how you did." Turning Michael's shoulders around, Jud followed him outside.

"Wow! Look at this place. You've been busy. I am really very impressed. Well, I guess you've worked off that twenty-five dollars and then some."

"Ten hours and fifteen minutes at three twenty-five an hour is thirty-three, thirty-one. Subtract the sixteen dollars and seven cents I owe you, leaves seventeen dollars and twenty-four cents you owe me," Michael said.

Amazed once again and digging into his wallet to supply an already out-stretched palm, "I'll take your word for it. How do you do that?"

"I didn't finish that part over there by the picnic table, but I can do it tomorrow morning."

"Okay, whenever. I wasn't kidding you, Michael, you really did a great job and you should be proud of yourself." He pedaled away, heading for the trailers and home, without the smiles and laughter seen at lunch or on the ride to Miller's Bend, but with the same expression on his face as when Jud first saw him pulling laundry.

Sunday morning Jud was awakened to the sound of leaves being raked. This sound has the same effect as nails on a blackboard to a yardaphobic. It was seven o'clock. So much for the Sunday sleep-in.

From his window he could see Michael dragging the tarp closer to his work. "That kid's gonna be a CEO someday," he mumbled.

"Have you had any breakfast?" he shouted down from the second-story window, and Michael shouted back that he had. He had stopped by the Tin Cup for a doughnut, and ended up having biscuits and eggs with Sarah. In exchange he filled all the pepper- and saltshakers. He was ten, certainly not a man, but he had a very definite crush on Sarah.

Sunday morning. His season opener, and warm already. Jud was whistling. Not bothering to shave, he dressed and immediately began sorting through his tackle and gear. Though none of it had been used for the better part of six months, like most tackle and gear, it had somehow managed to move around. Things, not misplaced or forgotten, had at least been scattered. But nothing was lost.

Eventually the Willys was loaded, and with every trip from the house to the Jeep, Jud watched Michael's face growing longer. But, when he loaded up Annie the Wonderlab and slid the fly rods over the tailgate, Michael began to cry. Crying and raking, raking on blisters earned yesterday, Michael could barely see Jud coming through his tears.

"Hey, Michael, what's the matter?"

But he couldn't answer. His shoulders shook. The crying had taken his breath. It didn't take a degree in child psychology to realize that these weren't merely the tears of a child left out of a fishing trip, or even a boy working with blistered palms. These were deep-seated tears, flowing from a much sadder place, the tears of neglect and deprivation.

"Yard work affects me the same wa-a-y," Jud hoped a little W. C. could stop his crying. "Why the very thought of gardening makes me quive-e-r, covers me in go-o-osefle-e-sh." But there was no response, other than sobs. Jud was trapped. There was no way out. "Say, you know I think maybe you should go fishing with me today. In fact I could use the company. But, only if it's okay with your mother. You'll have to go on home and ask her."

When it came to children Jud was much closer to W. C. Fields than to Father Flanagan, but even the great W. C., who loved children,"pa-a-ar-boiled," could not have refused Michael.

"It's okay. My Uncle Jack is there."

"Well, you go home and ask anyway."

Michael pedaled home and back. He was right, she didn't care.

Michael, Annie the Wonderlab, and Jud were then southbound out of town. Things were just the way they were supposed to be, not a trace of cloud, not a hint of wind, save for the wind rushing through the windows. Michael had a Pepsi in one hand and a Snickers in the other and as they drove they talked about W. C. Fields, trout fishing, flies, rivers, Carrie Creek, trees, hawks, frogs, the many merits of not having any sisters, warts, math, *Star Wars* (the movie not the policy), Annie the Wonderlab, hunting, and the reasons why there were clouds. Michael had a curious and eclectic mind.

Normally the trip to *there* was reserved for time alone at the wheel, alone with his thoughts. Some great ideas have been born on a back road with a little Bob Dylan on the tape machine. Certainly being *there* is the best, but going *there* can be just as good. Instead, he was now playing Ask Me Another with a ten-year-old. But surprisingly, he was dealing with it. In fact, he was enjoying himself.

Rolling to a stop at streamside, Jud parked the Willys in his traditional spot, under the same old cottonwood, and at the same old angle to take advantage of the shade. This is where any similarities between his usual *there* and this one came to an end.

As he opened the door Annie bounded over the seat, somehow managing to squeeze her seventy pounds between Jud and the steering wheel before his left foot reached the ground. Then she was instantly thrashing through the willows and brush, securing the area against the possibility of any wildlife. She'd been here enough times to know the best places to look, and in moments a rabbit was chased out of the clump of sage.

"How come, if you don't like to hunt, that you have a Labrador retriever?"

"I need someone to take care of me."

Michael laughed.

"How come—"

Interrupting what had to be his fortieth question in a row, Jud said, "Okay, the first rule of fishing: you have to be quiet. You have to sneak up on them or they'll hear you, and that spooks them, and they never give you a second chance. Especially the big browns in this part of Carrie Creek."

"How come?"

"Well, once they get frightened they stop eating."

"What do they eat?"

"Bugs."

"Do trout have ears?"

So the questions flew as Jud rigged up. Questions on fly rods, reels, knots, leaders, floatant, and flies. They also had a rather lengthy discussion about catch-and-release as Michael wanted to keep some of the trout. The boy grasped everything he told him about the rods and reels, Jud could see it all registering in his eyes, but turning fish loose to a kid who knew hunger firsthand needed edification.

Finally, they were ready to fish. The questions put them twenty minutes behind schedule. "All right, here is how we are going to work it. Using one of these fly rods is kind of tricky if you've never done it before, so I'll do the casting. When I hook one, I'll get him on the reel, then you can take over. You will fight them and land them. Is that a deal?"

"It's a deal." Michael was excited, but he couldn't figure out why Jud was going to let him fight the fish. He'd never fished before, but he knew that had to be the best part. "Do fish sleep, and why—"

"Now, remember what I said about being quiet. We can make all the noise we want after we have hooked one." They moved closer to the edge of the creek and looked upstream.

"See, there are a couple of fish rising at the tail end of the current," he could see spinners and duns on the water. He whispered back to Michael and pointed, "That's what they are eating. They're called mayflies. I have imitation mayflies in my vest, so that's what we will put on first." He tied one on, and the fishing began.

That afternoon the trout were nosing in the current, next to the current, and nowhere near the current. Fish were up and feeding at every bend. Jud would hook them, and as agreed, Michael would land them. The first four got away. But the fifth one Michael, with a little help, landed, and he was thrilled. "A historic time in a man's life—his first trout," Jud said, and the boy swelled with pride. "And what a beauty. My first fish, and I remember it clearly, wasn't five inches long. But yours is fifteen inches and a fat one, and you played it just right, Mr. Michael. I think you have the makings of a fine fisherman."

They released the trout, which prompted a refresher course on catch-and-release. Michael didn't want to let it go. If he couldn't keep it, he wanted to at least hold on to it for a while. But the fish was released, as were the next five, and those came within an hour.

They worked out a system on wading as well. Michael would cross on his own where the stream was only knee-deep, and where the water was deeper, Jud would carry him piggyback. They stopped at a clearing in the willows for a quick lunch of granola bars and apples. From there they could see the roof racks of Junior's pickup through a clearing.

"Well, wonder how old Junior is faring?"

"Mr. McCracken?"

"Yeah."

"Is he a good fisherman?"

"He really loves fishing," Jud never disparaged another man's skill as an angler, but euphemisms aside, the answer would have to have been no. Although Junior is knowledgeable about fly fishing, buys all the books, buys the videos, ties his own flies, builds his own rods, fly fishing held the same unfortunate problem that he faced with tools. The hand-eye coordination just wasn't there. Jud laughed, as he grabbed his vest and his rod, remembering Junior in school. He had the biggest baseball card collection in the Elkheart Valley, knew all the players and their averages. He knew every rule and facet of baseball, but he couldn't throw the ball. He rarely caught the ball, and he almost never hit the ball.

"What are you laughing about?" Michael asked.

"Oh, I was just laughing 'cause I'm having a good time. How about you, are you having a good time?"

"Yeah, fishing is really fun."

"That's just what it is."

They fished on and the action remained a constant. By the middle of the afternoon, they had landed nineteen fish. It was just one of those days, and Jud had long switched to more durable flies: Renegades, Humpies, and the like. It made no difference what fly he threw out on the creek, the trout were going to eat it.

A little after three they finally had fished to within a bend of where Jud had parked the Willys. They had fished back to *there*. Jud always saved it for last. Clouds were building to the north, but there was still no wind. There soon would be.

"Michael," Jud introduced, "this is one of my favorite places on earth." He didn't bother going into the esoteric world of *there* with a ten-year-old. "There can be some big ones here. Really big ones. Great view of Mount D. Downey, huh?"

W. C. bubbled to the surface, not the voice but the attitude. "Michael, I know we have been fishing as a team all afternoon, but I was wondering if it would be all right if I fished this pool on my own? The fish here are very spooky and I just don't think it's a two-man job." Michael understood and agreed to stand by and watch. In fact he, with Annie, crossed in a riffle, and sneaked through the underbrush on the opposite bank. Then they inched their way, Michael on his belly, Annie on her belly right beside him, through the willows to a spot three feet higher than the creek, and with a perfect view of the pool. They were well hidden.

Checking his knots, Jud moved out into the riffle that he had fished so many times before. He felt his shoulders drop and a peaceful sigh rush from his lungs. Nothing feels quite so deep and easy as fishing a familiar haunt.

With Annie and Michael secured in the willows, he slipped into Carrie Creek. Above him the pale spring leaves of a cottonwood twisted in a wind no stronger than a sigh. He waded free of its shade and into the cool, clear water rushing against his legs, curling downstream in silver ribbons suspended in a watery breeze. The sunlight pierced the river and fragmented over its rocky bottom. He moved slowly and with each step the light and the colors of Carrie Creek would change. Each step a quarter turn on the kaleidoscope. Spotting a fairly large trout amid the ten or twelve actively feeding fish, browns and rainbows, he began to false-cast. It would be a very routine cast: short, straightforward, with a perfect angle to the trout.

From the corner of his eye there was at first movement. Then came a yelp from Annie. The bank had given way below their prime viewing spot, and seventy pounds of Labrador, seventy pounds of Michael, and about a ton of stream bank were suddenly in the creek. Annie was immediately swimming, Michael was instantly drowning. Throwing his rod up into the willows, Jud ran through the creek and grabbed Michael who was flailing in the current. The first cloud had reached the sun just as a cool gust of wind raced across the meadows.

"Are you all right?"

"Y-e-e-eah." Michael was soaked. The wind hit him and he was turning blue and shivering.

"C'mon, I got some dry clothes and a towel back in the Jeep. Man, that must have taken you by surprise."

Michael was so cold he couldn't speak. His troubled look had returned to his face, an expression that, until now, had been missing all afternoon.

Back at the Willys, Michael dried himself off and was slowly warming up inside the Jeep. Wearing one of Jud's sweaters, which fit him more like an overcoat, and a pair of Jud's socks, which went clear to his knees, his shivering subsided. His mood, however, remained the same. The wind arrived in a long, heavy gust.

"Hey, there is no reason for the long face. Everyone falls in the river now and then," Jud explained as he took off his vest and was loading it into the Jeep, "it's part of fishing."

"Well, I wrecked your chance for catchin' that big old fish."

A small fly box tumbled from an open vest pocket and landed beneath the truck. "Catching that fish didn't really matter that much," Jud said, lying through his teeth. "It's just fun being out here. That's what counts. There will be other days." The rationalizations rolled right off his tongue.

Through the open door Michael watched as Jud got down on his knees and then crawled halfway under the Jeep to retrieve his box of flies. Annie quickly moved into position. It was now time to perform her favorite of all Labrador tricks. The one where she waits until the least opportune moment to shake, to rid her coat of water, which, given its thickness, could easily measure in the gallons.

Jud backed out from behind the rear tire and looked up just as Annie gave it a good, full, hard shake. Cold, muddy creek water spiraled from her coat. He tried to block the spray by raising his arms, but it didn't work. He was drenched. Annie rolled in the grass, proud of her prank, and surely beside herself in dog laughter. Michael laughed. Jud, wiping the mud from his face tried to laugh, but couldn't until he saw Annie on her back, legs spread-eagled, and tail wagging. Even though her lips were curled upside down, nothing could hide her smile.

Standing up, he walked over to Annie and lapsed into W. C., "I think tonight I will have you in a stew. Retriever a la Fi-i-ields. Labrador pi-i-i-e."

Michael was legless against his giggles. Kids, Jud thought, one minute they're sad, the next minute they're laughing until their sides ache. Their feelings at the ready, their emotions so exposed, and all they have to protect them is their honesty. "I'm going back to get my fly rod. I threw it up on the bank when you and Annie decided to go swimming. I'll be right back. You better stay here and get warm."

The clouds were now threatening rain and the wind was a constant. He had crossed Carrie Creek, picked up his rod, and was now mid-riffle thinking of how this afternoon's *there* compared to those before. He glanced upstream. The water had cleared from the slide, but none of the fish had recovered from the spectacle of a flying Labrador and a falling human. Not a trout, rainbow or brown, was in sight.

Nearly across the creek, he paused and looked once more upstream. There in the deepest water heavy rings were forming, moving the water as only an eminent trout can. It was larger than the one he was going to try for earlier.

There is something completely irresistible about the ring of the rise; something so enticing, hypnotic, beckoning. The rings, the rises, the promise of trout—they hold the angler happy and powerless. Their wakes slap against his consciousness as surely and as rhythmically as the swings on Freud's pocket watch. The angler grows numb, inattentive, insensitive to all that surrounds him. His very being focused on a ring of water. Let no stone go unturned and let no ring go uncast.

The wind made the casting impossible, but still this angler had to try.

The trout was an indiscriminate diner, feeding on what appeared to be anything floating past, foraging on any and all insects caught in the wind. Jud made cast after cast trying to reach it but he needed to be closer. Ahead of him was deep water, deeper than his waders allowed. There was no way to get an angle on the fish either, as the banks were nothing but a tangle of willows and rose hips. Most of his casts fell short, crumpling against the wind. Overcompensating, other casts landed dangerously close to spooking the fish. Even his worst casts failed to put the fish down. It rose regularly. He did manage, in between the gusts, to put a few casts very close. Certainly close enough to earn the trout's interest, but none was taken. This was followed by the frustration of watching the fish come up for another morsel moments after his fly had completed a drift above it.

Over and over again, he sent his fly. Most fish would have long ago been spooked, but this was a fish that would not be put off its feed. He cast until his arm ached since the throw was a full-on effort; double-hauling while stretching, trying to get those last few feet. He was suddenly aware of someone watching him.

"Michael," he said, a little surprised. The fact that the boy had to come looking for him quickly told him perhaps he had been fishing a little longer than he thought. Jud hadn't forgotten about him, anymore than he had forgotten it was spring, that this was Carrie Creek, or that it was daytime. Michael was just sort of lost right along with everything else. Lost in that haze that lies beyond the rise.

"That's a really big fish over there," he explained, though he thought no explanation was necessary. After all, Michael had been fishing now. Surely he knew the meaning of the rise. But Michael had that sad look back on his face. Sad, not so much from being forgotten (with his mother he had grown accustomed to that), but sad because he felt like he was being left out. Left out of a rare moment, a good time—rare commodities in Michael's life.

Jud began to make the cast but the boy's face was imprinted over the rise. It was the rise of a grand trout, a trout that doesn't come along but once in a season, a trout most serious, but Michael's face finally got to him. "No matter how big it is, Michael, if I hook her I'm gonna let you land her. Okay?" He looked over his shoulder to see Michael, still with a sad face, his hand being nuzzled by Annie. "But I don't think we have a chance in this wind." He made several more casts, but couldn't get close. The rings continued.

The windstorm then died for a long moment, though not completely. There was still a breeze, but it had quieted to a wind he could deal with. He made the cast. The Renegade landed precisely where he wanted. He mended and mended again. The fly drifted along the lacy edges of the current and into the bulging water. The trout was right at the surface. She took it. She felt the prick of the barb, the tension of his line across her body, the sudden, unnatural, and frightening resistance to her movements, and she reacted accordingly. There was a midstream eruption of water and rainbow trout. Darting downstream, Jud gave her the lead. She jumped within fifteen feet of where Michael and Annie were standing. Michael was so astonished by her size his mouth dropped, and his knees buckled, and his breath was taken away. Annie became excited and began barking. She'd been fishing enough to know a big trout when she saw one.

Then the rainbow left the pool for the faster water downstream, jumping once above the riffle. It was a long run nearly taking Jud into his backing. He was now running through the shallows. "C'mon, Michael." he shouted. Michael had no shoes on, but he came on the run and jumped onto Jud piggyback. The trout shot straight down the current, then moved in behind a large, exposed rock. Hunched awkwardly under the added weight of the boy, Jud went after the fish. Michael was astride his back, but barely. He had one leg hanging free while the other was entangled with Jud's rod arm, making it nearly impossible to fight the heavy fish.

They traveled, in tandem, quickly over an uneven bottom. The rainbow was threatening another run downstream. Jud could feel it. Then it was no longer a threat. The trout took off.

Jud reeled in hot pursuit. Water sprayed all directions as he ran through the shallows. Michael, bouncing all over his back, was desperately searching for a better handhold. At first one hand was over Jud's left eye and the other grabbed his collar. But he just couldn't maintain a grip against Jud's running, that and the fact he was laughing so hard he could barely hang on. As they neared the big, exposed rock he had finally gained purchase. With both hands clasped tightly around Jud's neck, right on the windpipe in a near-perfect stranglehold, Michael was still hanging on. Jud reeled, splashing through the creek. He could feel the boy's laughter, Michael's ribs laughing against his backbone. Pure and infectious joy, and despite the fact that he was turning the first shades of choke-hold blue, he laughed as well.

"You get off here," Jud gasped, setting Michael on the boulder. "Rock-hop to that gravel bar," motioning with his head, "and wait for me." While he waded slowly, he reeled quickly.

The slack was in. He was straight to the fish—now in the thin water just above where Carrie Creek drops into another deep pool. Still winded, he waded out of the shallows up onto the sand. Making sure all the tackle was in order, Jud handed the boy the rod, but keeping one hand on the cork himself. Then he guided the boy's hand to the reel, but he kept Michael's small hand in his. They were set for whatever it was that was going to follow. "We'll play this one four-handed."

Though aware that he was being helped, Michael was lost in a world of his own. A boy against fish, a whale of a fish. His mouth was agape. His face contorted through all sort of wide-eyed, wondrous expressions, for he had no idea what was to happen next. Jud figured, "Just follow my lead, Michael. She's probably going to try another jump. She's tired. She won't have another long run in her." The line was taut to the fish. Michael played her, under Jud's hands, for quite a while. He helped Jud let line off the reel when the rainbow moved away. He helped Jud reel line in as she swam toward them.

They watched the trout slowly swim upstream into the shallow water. But just when she was dead opposite of where they were standing, she bolted; flying from the current, jumping high above Carrie Creek in a watery prism of spray and light. The hook broke loose. The rainbow was free, and now another memory from *there*.

"She's off, buddy. We lost her," Jud said sadly, looking over to Michael whose question was answered before he could ask it. He was speechless and a little in shock. Losing the fish had never entered his mind.

"How?"

"Just got off the hook."

"I really wanted to hold her. She was so big. I wish . . . I wish I didn't lose her."

"There's an old saying, 'if you caught everything you ever hooked, they wouldn't call it fishin', they'd just call it catchin'.' Anyway, it wasn't your fault. The fish just won, that's all. That happens more times than not some days, especially with the big fish like that one."

"How big was she?"

"About three pounds I'd wager."

"Wow."

"Wow is absolutely correct. I can tell you this much—it was one heck of a day of fishing. Believe me, most days are nowhere near this good. But for your *first* day of fishing, well, you just couldn't have had a better one."

They crossed the creek and walked through the meadows back to the Willys. Jud, with one hand on Michael's shoulder, fell back into his W. C., "Why I clearly remembe-e-er the first time I went fishing. I was a much younger fello-o-w then, no more than a bo-o-y. Took to the sport right away. I was a piscatorial prodigy-y-y. I could catch fish from a dry w-e-e-ell. I could pull leviathans from the deep at will. Immediately, I set about breaking most of the world reco-o-ords. Caught cod. Caught the mighty sturgeon-n-n. Marlin and swordfish were child's pla-a-ay, putty in my ha-a-nds. Caught a five-hundred-pound, man-eating, mackera-a-l with nothing but sewing thread, a safety pin, and a little tar-tar s-a-auce."

Michael laughed. "And you just caught a five-pound trout."

"Michael, my b-o-oy, as I said before, you have all the makings of a fine fisherma-a-an. With your mind and its math, exaggerations could prove to be-e-e positively logarithmic."

~

Well, as Jud predicted, Michael's future did improve. The county offices never did step in to help him or his sister. Of course, this was fortuitous. Instead of a bureaucracy of strangers taking over the children's lives, which surely would have separated the two and placed them in foster homes, they were sort of adopted—but not through the courts. Michael and Marcie were simply taken under the collective wings of the following flock: Dolores, Junior, Henry, Sal, Jud; under the leadership of Saint Sarah.

Seven years came and went. And in those seven years Michael and his sister excelled because of the fact that they were never at home. Marcie shared her time between Sarah and Dolores. Michael stayed mostly with Sarah for the school year then at Henry's during the summers where he earned his keep helping on the ranch.

This arrangement was perfect for Michael's mother. She had more time to have the men in for *company*. The company would express their gratitude for a good time by giving her money, more booze, and better pills. Welfare sent her a check and she nursed her phony back claim for all it was worth. Her illness gave new meaning to the term bedridden.

There was virtually no contact with her children, and she liked it that way.

Michael grew tall and rangy. Gone were the temper tantrums and fistfights in school. He began to make new friends, and he kept them. Jud and Henry were always around, so he learned how to ride and take care of Henry's horses. He learned quite a bit about woodworking hanging with Jud at the Boat Works and, of course, with Jud and Henry as his mentors, Michael learned how to row and fly-fish.

Schoolwork was never a problem for him. Absolute math wizard—in love with computers. Student body vice president. Played football all four years.

Marcie was fine as well, no longer shy, above average in her grades. She played the piano like a dream. She was funny and a little bit of an actress—and reminded Jud a little of Dolores. Marcie wants to be a schoolteacher.

Jud often recalls the summer Michael turned eighteen. He was working for McCracken's part-time. He'd graduated from high school. Full-ride scholarship in math to the University of Montana. He had grown too old for Little League many summers before, though he hadn't turned out to be the pitcher Sal had hoped for, and seems to hope for every season. But Michael was a darn good second baseman. In his final season he hit .352.

These days when Michael's name is mentioned, two images come together in Jud's mind: the first is Michael, ten years old, pulling his laundry wagons down the road, and the second is the picture of Michael in the doorway of his workshop, coming to ask a very large favor. He waited until the day of his eighteenth birthday.

He'd walked up to the Boat Works that afternoon knowing what he was about to ask was a lot. He certainly felt comfortable around Jud. He could ask almost any favor without trepidation. But, to ask Jud for the Jeep—well, that was another thing altogether. Jud had a thing about his Jeep. It was thirty years old then. He had it just the way he wanted it. He saw no reason, if it was well taken care of, that it wouldn't last him the rest of his life. He never let anyone drive his Jeep. Henry, maybe.

He could have borrowed Sarah's car, Dolores's car, Henry's truck, Junior's truck, and he borrowed Sal's car all the time, but he wanted to go back up to Carrie Creek in Jud's Willys. For only the Willys could truly transport him back to *there*.

"Er . . . I was wondering . . . if . . . er . . . umm . . . if I could, maybe . . . and I'll fill it with gas and everything and wash it and . . . mmm . . . wax it, well, maybe you would let me borrow the Willys?" he asked.

"What for?" Jud asked.

"I want to go fishing up on Carrie Creek."

"I see. And why do you need the Jeep?"

"Well, I know this is going to sound corny. But it's always been kind of a dream of mine to drive the Willys up to Carrie Creek. I suppose it's because that's the place you first took me fishing, remember?"

"Sure. If you can hold off until day after tomorrow, I could go up with you."

"Well, I . . . uuuh . . . really wanted to go up there . . . mmm . . . kind of by myself."

~

"Kind of out *there* on your own?"

"Yeah."

"Out *there* fishing and not a soul around?"

"Yeah."

"I understand," Jud smiled. "The keys are in it." Then he returned to his cedar work wondering what kind of world it could be if every child could have the chance to share in a *there*, to have the chance to realize his worth and his reason.

From The Journals of Traver C. Clark

October, 2 1873—

I gave my Leonard bamboo rod to D. Downey last night. I don't believe I have ever seen him or anyone else as happy. He then proceeded to tell me great whopping tales of the salmon in Scotland. "Fish as long as the length of ya. But this wee rod, the little bamboo darlin', it will be fine for the sea trout and those nights on the burns when it's just yerrself in the moonlight, you and yer dram, rod and line bringin' trout to hand." I think there is a poet lurking down deep in this giant man.

He talks of going back to Scotland soon, "Maybe as a visit, a wee while, maybe even more, depending on what my luck brings me, but goin' I am."

Albie says we will make Missoula in three or four days. Then it will be five days back to Denver. Five more days and I will see my Carrie. Wait until she hears about the creek I named after her and my plans for us to move. I know, as well as I know myself, which is a lot better after months in the wilderness, that she will love the idea. All she ever talks about is living in the country once more instead of the drudgery of

~

Denver. When I tell of Carrie Creek and my plans for a cattle ranch she will be packing her bags.

I knew that Carrie was the right woman for me, I knew as instantly as I realized a friend and a kindred spirit in D. Downey. Their being brother and sister came as a delight but no surprise.

No more crowded Boston. No more overbearing family. My life starts anew and my life will be Carrie.

~

Unbelievable

Winter had come to the Elkheart. The hard and cold truth of it hit the valley during the night, and Travers Corners had awakened to the first serious snowfall of the season. Though nearing midmorning, the town still lay in shadow, and it would be another half hour before dawn edged its way over the Elkheart Range. Daybreak in December is a long time coming, sunset comes at four.

But there wouldn't be much in the way of a sunrise, as the sky was dark, and the snow was once again falling. From the windows of his workshop, Jud could see as far as the river, and the beginnings of the West Bench, but the mountains were lost to the storm. He watched as a low-lying cloud began drifting in over Travers, rolling slowly for the Boat Works, and then the storm was around him. All he could see were the outlines of the cottonwoods and aspens—ghostly silhouettes behind the lacework of snow, now falling heavily and straight down. He could see a few of the lights from town. Giving Annie the Wonderlab a few scratches behind her ear, he threw two more logs on the fire, poured another cup of coffee, and waited for the stove to do its work. An arthritic finger would need to be warmer before he could start his work.

The panes of glass had warmed at their centers, leaving an oval of free glass within a frosted border in each of the squares and made the view a portrait of winter times six. "Sure does come quicker than it used to—one moment it's summer, and the rest of the time it's winter." There was no real sadness in his voice, but there was the hollow tone of resigned melancholy—the resolute acceptance of winter—an attitude all Montanans must have. "The way I figure it there's only a few things you can do about winter—accept it, bitch about it, or move on. Today I think I'm going to bitch about it." At the end of each sentence Annie's tail would rise and fall, a signal wag of understanding. She knew there was no one else in the workshop and all his conversation was directed at her. Though she might not comprehend all the words, Annie the Wonderlab recognized the mood. Making the supreme sacrifice for an old Labrador, she raised herself up with a moan, wobbled for a second, and once she got her stiff hips to stand, she hobbled around to where Jud was standing to nose at his pant leg, a conciliatory kindness he returned by stroking her forehead.

The phone rang. "Hello . . . oh . . . well . . . okay . . . okay . . . thanks, Pam . . ., I'll be right down."

"Just got some registered mail, girl," Jud said kneeling down and scratching her ears with both hands, "you expecting anything important?"

He slipped on his snow boots, and grabbed for his coat, hat, scarf, and gloves. He threw one more log on the fire. "By the time I get back, this place should be toasty. You stay here, girl," Jud said sympathetically. Though Annie had started to go through the motions of once again getting up, she dropped back down at his command with a great sigh—right back into her spot by the heat of the stove.

Stopping briefly outside the door to look at the thermometer, Jud read it aloud, "Seventeen degrees." The crunch of fresh snow under his footfall was the only sound he heard on the way down the hill to town. On his walk he thought about Annie and how if his wrist hurts him a little at fifty, what her old joints must feel like, doing his dog-years math, at ninety-one. He missed her on their walks. She just couldn't keep up anymore. The Boat Works, if lonely now, was going to be empty without her when she was gone.

The ritual of the morning mail in cities or suburbs is pretty much a faceless routine. Urbanites pick up their mail at a numbered P. O. box or else it is delivered by a postman they seldom see. In small towns like Travers, the distances between ranches are too great to have rural deliveries, and the town's population is too small for numbered P. O. boxes. The mail into Travers Corners comes general delivery and you pick it up at the rear of McCracken's General Store by asking Pam McCracken for it. Most of the town's mail gatherers were creatures of habit, picking up their post at the same time every day—as soon as Pam had finished sorting it—around 8:00. Jud usually got his mail after he had breakfast at the Tin Cup, but this morning he hadn't gone to the café and instead chose to have a bowl of stale cereal at home. He had made a pact not to go to town at all until Pam called.

Jud came through the front door of McCracken's, just as Etta Mae Harper was stepping up to the postmistress's window. She needed to pick up her mail, mail a package, and buy a new roll of stamps. Behind her stood Beverly and Lilly Jenkins. Looking over to see if Junior was in the pharmacy, which he wasn't, Jud joined them in line.

"Oh, good morning, Jud," Lilly smiled.

"Morning Beverly, morning Lilly. Cold morning."

"Yes, indeedy," was their answer in unison. Beverly and Lilly were twin sisters and solidly in their seventies. They answered most everything asked of them in unison. Jud, towering over the twins, could see Etta Mae pulling out her checkbook, and judging by the speed of that procedure, he thought, she should have her stamps bought, her post collected, and her parcel mailed sometime before the end of his fiftieth year. Etta Mae, hard of hearing, and a little bit blind, made the Jenkins girls look young. Etta Mae was ninety-two.

Pam, knowing why Jud was here, quickly opened the door by her window, and holding his registered letter as well as his regular mail, she motioned him over. "Jud, if you could just initial this." She smiled, knowing how slow it was to wait on Etta Mae, and waiting behind the Jenkins twins would be twice as slow.

Jud signed a form against the door and handed it back to her, "Where's Junior this morning?"

"Over at the bank."

Jud stepped around Etta Mae, who was blind and deaf to his presence. But, he tipped his hat to her anyway, then to the Jenkins girls. "Hope all you ladies have a good day."

"Bye-bye now, Judson, and you have a nice day, too," the Jenkinses chirped. In their small frail voices, "bye-bye, now," sounded like a bird call.

In Jud's usual morning mail there is a plethora of junk mail, an order now and then, and a check all too rarely. He wrote no letters but still wondered why he didn't receive any. He subscribed to a few magazines. In a post so prosaic, one might think that he would have been excited by a registered letter, but registered mail made him nervous. The IRS, the draft board, collection agencies, lawyers, and courts travel by registered mail. He looked at the return address—Sir Gordon Pendleton, Pendleton Castle, Glen Croick, Ross-shire, Scotland. "Penny," Jud muttered, then decided to wait until he was back home before he opened the letter. He wanted to be warm and by the woodstove, with Annie at his feet, a fresh cup of coffee in his hand when he read it.

The workshop was warm on his return and he added more wood to the fire as well as his junk mail. He glanced at but didn't open his telephone bill. He threw this week's *New Yorker* magazine on the workbench. Then, after taking a gulp of strong coffee and giving Annie a rub behind the ear, he opened the registered letter from Penny. It was handwritten on plain paper and it read:

> *Jud and Henry—*
>
> *Sorry for the hastiness of this note. No chance of coming this year as I had planned so a thought has occurred to me—why don't you, Henry, Doc, and Junior come to Scotland this summer and be my guests at the family estate? Please find enclosed, four tickets, round trip, from New York to Edinburgh. My friend, Richard Branson of Virgin Air, arranged them for me as our companies work together quite often. My suggestion is this: you four find your way to New York; hop*

on the jet; and come and stay as my guests for a week of Atlantic salmon fishing at Pendleton Castle. May would be best, really. You and Henry will surely enjoy the salmon fishing on the Carron, although there is nothing that could compare to your lovely Carrie Creek.

Give me a call and tell me what you all decide upon. If you cannot reach me, as I will be traveling a great deal this next month, you can call the castle and talk with Araminta—011-44-4989-876-490.

Hope this all can work out. Would love to have you.

All my best to all those wonderful people I met during my tragically short stay in Travers Corners.

Hope to hear from you soon—Penny.

This great, unexpected, from out of nowhere news stirred Jud's heart from its seemingly inert station just above his stomach. Suddenly buoyant and gorged, pumping hard and fast, it floated back to its rightful spot—next to the lungs that were gasping for air. The blood rush made him slightly dizzy, and he leaned back against the workbench. He took out his glasses and read the fine print: New York to London—London to Edinburgh and back again. First class.

He tried to call Henry, but there was no answer. He tried to call Doc, but he had gone to check on a patient and was due back shortly. He tried to call Junior, but he was still at the bank. He tried to call Sarah, but she had stepped out to the post office, and Jud smiled as he pictured her in line, stuck behind Etta Mae, who would probably be just about ready to sign her check by now. He had to tell someone the news. He paced. He tried Doc again.

"Hi, Kim, it's Jud again."

"Hi, Jud."

"Is Doc back yet?"

"Let me check. I thought I heard his car. Yep, he's coming through the door now. Aren't you feeling well, Jud?"

"I haven't felt so well in months."

Putting on his glasses while he waited on the line, Jud read the fine print once more on the tickets. It was all so unbelievable—Scotland, a castle, he, Henry and Doc and Junior and a week of salmon fishing—the thought of it made him laugh out loud. He'd been to Europe, backpacking around in the sixties but he never made it to Scotland though he'd always wanted to go. Henry had never been to Europe. Henry hadn't left the Elkheart in thirty years.

"Hello, Jud. What's up?"

"You're not going to believe this. I just got a registered letter from Penny. Inside, there's four free round-trip tickets to Scotland. First-class tickets. He's invited Henry and me and you and Junior for two weeks of Atlantic salmon fishing. He wants us to stay at Pendleton Castle."

"Well, bless my . . . count me in. Oh, that's the best news. I can't believe it. His castle. First-class tickets? I just can't believe it. Have you told Henry and Junior?"

"I'm trying but everybody is out and about."

"Listen, you get a hold of those two and let's all meet at the Tin Cup at noon."

"Okay."

Jud tried Henry once more. No answer. He tried Junior again.

"McCracken's Pharmacy," Junior answered.

"Junior you're not going to believe this." Then Jud filled him on the details of Penny's letter.

Jud was right, Junior didn't believe it. "First-class tickets to go and fish for Atlantic salmon. Naw . . . it can't be . . . I can . . . I don't . . . how could he . . . Atlantic salmon. Oh my. Somebody pinch me. I'll have to get all new tackle. I'll need a nine weight and a heavier reel and . . ."

"Junior," Jud interrupted, "meet Doc and me at the Tin Cup at noon. I'm driving out to tell Henry."

"He was going up to Helena today," Junior said.

"I wonder if he's gone yet."

"Dolores would know."

Dolores's phone was busy. He tried Henry again. Then it dawned on him. So caught up in the moment of travel, Scotland, Atlantic salmon, he had forgotten that it was Henry Albie he was trying to get in touch with. "What am I thinking about, Annie girl. Henry isn't going to want to go. I can just hear him. 'Scotland? What in the hell would I wanna go to Scotland for? I never lost anything over there. Whose gonna tend to the livestock? Whose gonna tend to Dolores?'"

He tried Dolores again. The phone in the beauty parlor rang, barely audible over the hair dryer. Dolores answered, she was at a critical part of baking someone's hair under the space helmet, "Beauty parlor."

"Dolores, is Henry at home? He isn't answering the phone."

"Should be at home. He was heading up to Helena but then Gypsy started to foal. So, he won't be far."

Sensing something was urgent, Dolores, in keeping with her job as investigative beautician, always on the lookout for news, or better yet, gossip, the salon sleuth had to ask, "What's so all-fired important? Yea—Wait a second, Jud." Dolores laid the phone and lifted the hood of the dryer to reveal Sue Cardinet in curlers. "Yeah, so you got a letter from Penny . . . okay . . . sure . . . yeah . . . okay . . . *What*? . . . *You're shitting me*? . . . What? . . . okay . . . you bet . . . I won't tell him until you tell him first . . . tell him to call me . . . that's what it is, Jud, it's unbelievable . . . bye-bye."

"Henry, Jud, and Doc jest got free first-class tickets to Scotland from Sir Gordon to stay free at his castle," Dolores explained to Sue while undoing her curler net. Then Dolores started shaking her head and laughing as she realized, "Hell, Henry won't want to go. I can't get him to take me as far as Reynolds for a dinner out or a movie. How is Jud going to git him to Scotland? Henry won't care if the tickets are free, if the castle is free. He'll say, 'even free ends up costin' you money.'" She shook her head. As she was starting to unwrap Sue's curlers, one eyebrow raised, and Dolores schemed aloud, "Now, I just gotta figure out a way to make Henry go and a way to make him take me along."

Jud tried Henry once more. No answer. "Going to have to go over there, Annie girl. You stay here and guard the woodstove." Annie would be happier by the fire, but when it's seventeen degrees who wouldn't be?

Within minutes Jud was pulling onto Henry's ranch. Down near the river there was a slight breeze, but it was enough breeze to gather the weightless flakes and send them gently over the snow-laden fields. The windblown snow traveled in waves of paper-thin mists, and where it sifted through the trees along the road it settled in long, narrow drifts.

Henry's lights came to Jud first. Then the ranch house and the corrals took form, appearing as shadows behind the storm. The lights were on in the barn as well, and smoke rolled down the sides of its chimney.

Jud laughed as he walked along the fences down to the barn thinking that any angler, given a chance to fly first class to Scotland, stay in a castle, and fish private waters, would leap, as an Atlantic salmon might leap, at the chance. But, this was Henry he was thinking about, and Henry held little interest in the outside world. He was, as Dolores is fond of saying, "Not a man to go places, or try something new and different, new being anything after 1956, different being anything you can't find in Travers Corners."

After sliding the large barn door open just wide enough to let himself in, he rolled it back to closed. He turned and saw Henry sitting on a bale of hay, rubbing his hands together, his hat tilted back on his head. There wasn't much light inside, but Jud felt in an instant and from forty feet away that something might be wrong. When Henry turned and looked at him, he knew something was wrong. How did Jud know Henry's feelings from the far side of a dark barn? The same way he knew what Henry was sure to say when he proposed the Scotland trip to him. He'd known Henry all his life. He was his best friend. "What's the trouble?" Jud asked walking around Henry's tractor.

"My foal just died, not an hour ago," Henry said.

"Oh, man. I am sorry," Jud felt the wind leave him as he saw the dead foal lying in the hay. The mare still licking it. "What happened?"

"I don't know. Don't reckon I'll ever know. I stayed up with Gypsy most the night. This was her third foal, and she's never had any trouble before. When the foal started to come I was right here. Everything went fine, and she dropped it without a hitch."

"In no time at all the colt was up and sucklin'. Wobblin' all over the place. Cutest damn thing. Everything was fine. I was just gettin' ready to head on in for a shower, when the foal just crumpled where she stood. Dead. Heart failure of some sort. There was nothin' I could do. Dammit. I am really hatin' this."

"That's the worst, Henry." Jud didn't know what to do or what to say. He'd come into the barn busting with good news: travel, Scotland, fishing, and free tickets. There was no way he could have known he was entering into a heart-wrenching death scene, and the bluest of all worlds, the death of an animal—Henry's long-awaited prize foal. He thought about Annie and how he was certain that soon he'd be feeling as Henry felt—only Annie the Wonderlab had led a good life, and a long one, and the foal never had the chance.

"What're you doing here?" Henry asked and lifted the lifeless long legged foal away from the mare, who was still trying to nose her dead child to its feet. He laid the foal gently in the back of the pickup.

"I got this registered letter this morn—"

"Hey, why don't we head over to the house, and you can tell me all about it over there," Henry interrupted. "I need some coffee—think I might jest give her a lick of J. D. It's been a tough mornin'." They had walked nearly to the house, the snow gathering on their hats and shoulders, when Henry abruptly turned and faced the barn, and in a voice both melancholy and mad he said, "Life sure is fickle sometimes, one minute you're the future champion cuttin' horse of Montana, and the next minute you're nothin' but coyote food." He swore and took a vicious kick at the snowfall.

Inside Jud started the coffee while Henry took a quick shower, and put on fresh clothes. He was back to the kitchen in the time it took the kettle water to boil. "So," Henry asked, through a thin-lipped smile of resolve, the life-keeps-on-going-and-all-you-can-do-is-hang-on grin, "What's all this about a letter?"

"Well, this morning I got a registered letter from Penny." He walked over to his coat hanging on the back of a kitchen chair, and slipped an envelope from its inside pocket. He thought about reading it aloud, but then thought the better of it, as the letter was addressed to Henry as well. He handed the mail, without the airline tickets (which were safely filed away back at the Boat Works) to Henry.

~

Unfolding the letter, Henry walked over to the window and held the letter up to the light. He needed glasses, but stubbornly had yet to buy a pair, so he held the page at arm's length. His face, naturally long and stoic, and not one to betray an emotion, remained unmoved as he read the mail, reading with the same calm detachment as if he were going over his electric bill. Then Jud noticed Henry's eyebrows raise slightly when he must have read about the fishing and the free tickets, but that's about as impassioned as he became.

He folded the letter slowly, carefully following its original creases, then looked out the window. He was silent for a moment. It was then Jud knew for sure that he wasn't going to take Penny up on his invitation. If only the news would have arrived on a different day, maybe . . . naw, Henry wouldn't have gone anyway.

"Next May he wants us to come . . . well, partner, that fits into my schedule jest fine. Call Penny and tell 'im I'm comin'. Always wondered what it would be like to catch me one of them Atlantic salmon."

"You mean—you want to go?" Jud was shocked at how quickly and how easily Henry had decided.

"Hell yes, I'm goin'. I ain't never been anywhere before, never had the fever to go, but right now jest feels like as good a time as any to give some travelin' a try."

"But, I thought for sure you would say—"

"I know. I know. But you wanna know somethin', Judson C., I had me some time to think out there in that barn this mornin'. There I was holdin' a new life, and in the snap of your fingers there I was holdin' a dead foal—a foal no more than hours old—and hell here I am—gonna be fifty-one *years* old soon," Henry said staring out into the snow. "Once yer past fifty you ain't got *that* much longer till you're coyote bait as well," he said forcing a grin through a grimace.

"God, that's great, Henry," Jud still had surprise in his voice about Henry's epiphany and would for months to come. "Doc, Junior, and me are meeting at the Tin Cup at noon to talk about it. If you want to join us."

"I'll be there."

"Oh," Jud said, tossing back the last of his coffee and then slipping on his coat, "you better give Dolores a call. She was kind of worried about you not answering the phone."

"Does she know about the tickets?"

"Well, yeah, I told her."

"Well, now that Dolores knows, I'm satisfied that the whole of Travers will know by noon, if'n they don't already know by now." Henry smiled, but it wasn't his real smile. It would be a long time coming before he had his real smile back again. He had counted on that horse to be just as she was, just as she would have been. She was only a foal, but Henry knew from the moment he laid eyes on her that she was destined to be a looker—her conformation—her four matching socks. He felt a sickness in his gut.

"I sure am sorry about your foal, Henry," Jud said heading for the door.

"Me, too," Henry nodded.

After Jud had left, Henry faced the most loathsome chore he'd had to do in a long time. He ached with the pain of it, and he hadn't laced his coffee yet with the Jack like he thought he would. In one motion, he put on his coat, slipping his right hand into the sleeve, working his way out the cuff, and kept right on going to open the cupboard next to the refrigerator. He pulled down a bottle of Jack and took a long pull from the bottle. Starting to put the bottle back in the cupboard, he hesitated, took another swallow, then set the bottle back on its shelf. He was out the kitchen door and just as quickly back in again. He grabbed the bourbon and stuck it in his coat pocket. Henry was far from a daytime drinker, usually never touched a drop before five, but he knew he was going to need another bracer and soon.

If it was summer he would certainly have buried Gypsy's foal, but the frozen ground made that impossible. All he could do was take her to a secluded place down by the river, down where the eagles hunted, down where the coyotes scavenged, down to a place where the ranch's carrion was always taken, down to where the worms do their work. The whiskey was softening his rage. The snow was slowing down, and it was getting colder. The wind stiffened. It was a perfect day for a funeral.

~

Word, as Henry predicted, did spread quickly around Travers Corners about Jud, Doc, Junior, and Henry's good fortune, and by the time they met at the Tin Cup for lunch it was doubtful if there wasn't a soul up and down the length of the Elkheart who hadn't heard the news in some form or another. Sarah was so happy for the four of them she actually had tears in her eyes as she looked up from the grill to see them, sitting at the back table, planning their trip. Doc and Junior never stopped smiling and both were making notes.

What a perfect foursome, old friends, best friends, lifelong friends all heading for Scotland. Sarah loved to travel and she longed for it. But there she was behind her grill and happy as she flipped the burgers, happy for her friends, and happy that her grill was in Montana. She wanted to sit down and have a beer with them but she would get the details tonight from Jud on their nightly call.

What surprised the folks around Travers the most was not so much the news of the trip itself, but the fact that Henry Albie had agreed to go. Granted it was a trip of a lifetime, and it was free, but even with that, Henry's acceptance was unexpected. To Dolores, who knew him better than anyone, it was a shocker. It was a trip she would try and finagle her way into for the next several months. It would be a conversation heard over and over again.

"You're stuck in the mud all your life, you don't go nowhere, you don't take me anywhere, we don't do nothin', and then whammo, Henry the Hermit gits himself a free ticket and yer off halfway around the world—and you're not takin' me?"

"Can't afford it."

"But yer ticket was free."

"Even free is gonna cost me money, Dolores," which was true, because a week after Jud had read him Penny's letter, Henry bought a brand new salmon rod and reel—top of the line.

"Well, look at it like this," she would counter, "if'n you're travelin' for free, with me goin' along it would like both of us travelin' for half."

"You've got a keen sense of economics. Maybe you should go to work for the government."

Dolores even used seduction to augment her plea to go, cuddling up to Henry and biting him on the ear, purring, "And jest think how much fun we could have—making love in a castle."

"Dolores, I ain't gonna take you, I'm sorry, but I jest can't afford it."

"You can't afford it because you bought a thousand dollars worth of fishin' stuff?"

"That's right."

"Well, you got fish right here in the Elkheart. You can go fishin' any ol' time, you got a dozen or more fishin' poles. I mean I don't understand." This is when Dolores, after trying sound economic principles, sensuous ploys, would reach for the tear tactics.

Henry tried to explain by elevating his Scottish quest to a higher order. "Dolores, like I've told you, this is *not* jest some kind of regular ol' fishin' trip, this here is fly fishin' for the greatest fish swimmin'—the Atlantic salmon."

"But I talked to Doc and he said you would be lucky to catch even one. He told me that you had every chance in the world of goin' over there and not catchin' nothin'."

"That's what I mean by a *fishin'* trip. When you go fishin' for salmon, you have to fish for salmon, ya can't be gawkin' at castles or wanderin' around in the museums. Salmon are damn near impossible to catch, so you have to fish for them long and hard. Have to have your fly in the water. There won't be much time for anything else."

"Yeah, well the next time your fly gits long and hard I ain't gonna have time for you, either."

"Dolores for the last time, this ain't no sightseein' trip. I'm goin' to catch an Atlantic salmon."

"Maybe," Dolores would always get in the last word.

This dialogue, or one similar, would surface on and off for another two months. It was then that Dolores's youngest sister announced her engagement. She wanted to be married at the family home, Dolores's home, in Travers. She wanted Dolores to be the maid of honor. She would marry, and the date was set, May 29. A date sent from heaven straight to Henry since his bickering with Dolores would end there and he would miss the wedding. He had little space for Dolores's sister and even less for her soon-to-be no-account husband.

During that same two months, Jud, Doc, Junior, and Henry had secured their flights. They were leaving for Scotland on the twenty-seventh of May and wouldn't be back home until the fourth of June. Winter, the longest one in twenty years, crept past; slowed not only by the length and cold of it, but also by the fact that Scotland was there waiting at the other end of it.

One the twentieth of May Sarah drove to Missoula. She generally left early in the morning, but this morning she had been delayed and didn't get back to the Tin Cup until dark, bone tired but with a pickup laden with supplies, bulk wholesale crates, and cartons. The café, save for one table, was empty, but the bar was busy for a Monday night in May—busy enough that Sal couldn't come to help her carry in her shopping. The grill was shut down and Sally had gone home. All who was left to help was Bonnie, who waitressed only on those days when Sarah went to the city, and at age sixty-two, the boxes of canned goods, the five-gallon buckets of cooking oils, vinegars, salad dressings, and the like, were just too heavy for her. Sarah did what she always did when she needed help—she called Jud.

The unpacking went swiftly once Jud arrived. He carried in the boxes, and Bonnie and Sarah quickly sorted everything into their rightful spots in the kitchen and the pantries. Other items could wait until tomorrow.

"Why don't you go on home, Bonnie," Sarah said closing the tailgate door. "Is there any one left in there?"

"It's just the Jenkins sisters in after Bible study. They have their niece with them who's visiting from Spokane. They're all done. They've paid for everything and they are just finishing up their dessert."

"Okay, thanks for coming down, Bonnie. I'll be going to Helena on the eighth. Could you help me out again then?"

"You bet," said Bonnie, taking off her apron and going back. "I'll see you two later." She went back by way of the front entrance in hopes the Jenkinses had left. They hadn't. In fact, their niece asked for more coffee.

She poured her another cup and left through the front door turning the open sign to read closed.

Switching off the light in the alley, the sky flashed on above them, starlight and a half-moon. "Quite a night," Jud said looking up to the Milky Way, bordered by the rooftops. They both paused to enjoy the infinite, and the shared silence. Just the barking of a distant dog. A truck was then heard gearing down for the crossroads. "I'll bet it just drives you pretty near crazy to be out here under all these romantic stars with me?" he said with a grin.

Sarah laughed, "You drive me crazy, indoors or out. You know I haven't stopped going all day, not even to grab a bite to eat. I'm going inside to make something up. I'm feeling a little light-headed."

"I'm sorry about that, Sarah, but I just can't help it. I just have that effect on women," Jud said. "They get outside with me in the moonlight and they *all* get lightheaded," he said rolling his eyes.

"I think you're confusing romance with nausea," Sarah said. "Come on, you hungry?"

"Well, I ate supper, but it was my cooking. So maybe, I'll just take a slice of your lemon meringue pie. Maybe your good cooking will counteract any poisoning I might have done to myself."

Sarah had a sandwich made and was back from the storeroom in the time it took for Jud to slice a piece from the pie. They sat at the back table putting a full restaurant between them and the Jenkins twins who were busy filling in their niece about Jud and Sarah. The Jenkins girls loved to talk about people. It was how they spent their day, when not napping or watching Oprah.

"You know Sarah is from New York City," Lilly Jenkins said. "The man with her is Jud Clark."

"He builds river boats; owns the Boat Works up on the hill above town," Lilly's sister, Beverly, added, "we always have thought they would make a lovely couple."

"They're both so nice," Lilly said nodding. The Jenkins twins, when telling a story, had a habit of trading back and forth the narrative, and while one was speaking, the other one was nodding at everything the other was saying. Of course, neither of the Jenkinses was above gossip.

"They always say they are just good friends," Beverly started.

"But they spend an awful lot of time together for just good friends," finished Lilly nearly tittering, while Beverly gleefully nodded.

Once the Jenkins twins and their niece had left the Tin Cup, after waving and saying their good nights to both Sarah and Jud, Sarah quickly left the table and locked the front door. She then switched off all the lights, but those over the grill, closed the door separating the bar from the restaurant, and threw the latch.

Noise from the bar side came through the walls, a muted jukebox, and the murmur of the bar crowd, the remains of a countywide meeting of the Rotary Club held earlier in the town library. Bright light streamed in from the kitchen, through the pickup window, past the empty order wheel, over the counter, and around its stools, but by the time it reached the back table it lit no more than a candle's worth.

Jud and Sarah sitting at the back table in low light, sipping late-night wine, talking and laughing—it was sightings like these that caused the Jenkins and the other rumormongers in Travers to have their suspicions.

They sat and talked about Scotland, things accomplished in Missoula, the fact that the herons had returned to the valley, and Sarah seeing her first pair of sandhill cranes yesterday. So the chatter was their usual blend of things: the interesting, the benign, and of course, the silly.

"There's a combination seldom seen," Sarah said, watching Jud take a bite, "lemon meringue pie and wine—sounds like a country and western song."

I woke up on the street in front of the bakery,
hung over and waiting for the sun to shine,

Jud sang as if his voice were a twangy guitar, then paused long enough for the second stanza to come to him.

All I had was what she left of me—
and lemon meringue pie and wine.

Sarah got the giggles. He loved to make her laugh. "Oh, listen everybody, it's Conway Witty," Sarah snorted as she started Jud laughing, and the laughter and the merlot felt good.

Reaching to pour Sarah then himself another glass of wine, his eyes, betraying his mind, held the distant look of someone lost in another place and a thousand miles away, in this case five thousand miles away and Scotland. "What are you thinking about?" Sarah asked.

"Huh, oh . . . ah . . . I was thinking about you and the first time I saw you and how I thought you were so beautiful, and I was thinking about how pretty you still are."

"You are the most chronic bullshitter I have ever met in my life, Judson C. Clark."

"You tell a woman the truth, and . . ." he finished his sentence not with words, but with a shrug of shoulders and a puzzled look, almost dazed.

"I remember that day," Sarah said, "and I'd say we both look every day of the added years."

"But," Jud added, unconsciously dragging his sleeve through the last few bites of meringue in order to set the empty wine bottle down, "we're doing it gracefully."

With three days left until departure, Jud headed to town for a cup of Tin Cup coffee and the last needed items at McCracken's. Annie came along for the walk since the day was unseasonably warm and her legs and hips, though not moving well, were moving easier. They stalled on the bridge as they always did, long enough to spot a few small brown trout darting about. "Going fishing in Scotland in a few days, Annie. I mean it's all so unbelievable." Jud stared into the creek, slightly muddy by the first of the runoff, and sort of lost in his imaginings of how it was all going to be: Scotland, the heather, bagpipes and tartans, salmon on the end of his line, staying in a castle.

Annie, whose attention had been undivided since Jud had mentioned fishing, sat down, her stiff leg straight out and beneath her. But her ears were perked, and her eyes, though a little cloudy, were looking down on Carrie Creek—looking for rises—fishing being her favorite pastime. Though her body was giving out, her mind was keen. Dolores would take good care of her while he was gone.

"Hi ya, Sarah," Jud greeted her as he took his usual stool. It was midmorning and there wasn't a soul in the café but Sal and Sarah. She poured a cup of coffee for him, one for herself, and sat down beside him. "Man, you must be *really* getting excited."

"Well, you are a good-looking woman but it's going to take more than watching you drink coffee to get me really aroused."

"I am talking about Scotland," she said rolling her eyes.

"I know. I know. Yeah, I have to admit I am getting pretty excited," Jud said and shifted around on his counter stool like a young boy waiting for a chocolate shake or a grown man awaiting an Atlantic salmon.

"God, I wish I were going. This place can be such a grind some days."

"Well, come on. Is your passport current?"

"My passport is current, but it has never been stamped. In fact, I think that this is the year it runs out."

Sal came into the kitchen for a bottle of Tabasco for the bar side, "Hey, Jud, how ya doin?"

"Just trying to get Sarah to go to Scotland with me."

"Le'me tell you somethin'. She should go. Scotland, I don't know. What do I know from Scotland? But she should get the hell outa here now and then, and I don't mean to Missoula. More like Mexico. Go somewhere and do somethin' while you're still young enough. Me and Jenny could run dis place fine.

"Le'me tell da bot' a youse somethin' else. The time between fifty and seventy is nothin' more than a snap of yer fingers," and with that and a snap of his fingers, Sal then went back to the bar mumbling out of earshot, "Why don't you dummies go to Mexico together? When are those two ever going to figure it out?"

"He's right you know," Jud said.

"Yeah, but the nature of *this* beast," Sarah replied, waving her hand around the restaurant, "You can *never* leave."

"But Jenny and Sal could run it."

"Yeah, right. I can't imagine what would happen then."

"You should get out of here now and then. How about San Francisco? No, New Orleans, you and me, great food, the French Quarter, blues bands, your treat." Sarah threw her towel at him, and they settled into conversation about the trip until Jud felt the need to leave. He was leaving in three days and there was a list of things for him to do, a list that Sarah could handle in two hours but was going to take him, Jud figured if he hurried, the next two days.

That evening just as Jud was slipping off his shoes, ready for bed, and about to make his nightly call to Sarah, the phone rang. It was Junior. "Hey Jud. Got some bad news. Kim just called. Doc ran into a deer tonight."

"Jeeez, is he okay?"

"He's all right. He's at home. But he did break his thumb and two fingers. Casting hand. Kim said that Doc, with a little of the Jack, set the bones himself. Messed his new Jeep up pretty good, too. But one thing for sure, he won't be going to Scotland."

"We have a free first-class ticket to Scotland to anybody who can leave day after tomorrow?"

"Well, we talked about that and Doc said if it's okay with you and me and Henry he'd like to see the ticket go to Sarah. It's okay by me and I've talked to Henry and it's okay by him. Doc said if there is one person in Travers who needs a vacation and deserves a vacation, it's Sarah."

There was no argument with that and it was agreed that it was Jud who needed to ask her. "I'll call her right now but I can tell you her answer. It'll be no. Told me today that she could never leave the Cup. Maybe for an afternoon. But nine days—it's not going to happen."

He called Sarah deciding that this was the kind of news best delivered in person, and said only, "I'm coming over. I got news. It's important good news."

~

He put his shoes back on, left Annie on her bed, and drove to Sarah's. She greeted him at the door in her robe with her hair tussled and her face freshly scrubbed, ready for sleep and not company. "What's up?" she yawned.

"Well, here it is: Doc hit a deer tonight. Broke a couple of fingers, casting hand, and he is not going to Scotland."

"Oh, my."

"That leaves Doc holding a first-class ticket to Scotland, leaving day after tomorrow, and he wanted you to have first crack at his ticket. Said if anyone in Travers deserves a vacation it's you."

"Oh, my."

Jud went to the refrigerator for a cold beer. "If you take the tickets, take this trip, New York, London, Edinburgh, Penny's castle for a week, and back again it's going to cost you zip, nada, goose egg, nothing, other than your ticket to New York."

Sarah sort of stood there a moment and then went to the fridge and took a beer for herself. She wandered down the hall and into the living room and sat down on the couch. Following her down the hall but saying nothing came Jud waiting for her answer, and already knowing what it would be, he was prepared to counter. Sarah made her decision. "I can't go. I would love to go, but I just can't go. I have the teachers' banquet next Thursday and Saturday is Chic Webb's retirement party. A sit-down dinner for forty. Jenny and Sal can't do it."

"If you don't do this it will be the dumbest decision you'll ever make," Jud said flushed by disbelief and just a hint of anger. "I mean do something, change, delegate, hire, close, lease, or sell. Do whatever it takes but do not miss this trip. This is a ten-thousand-dollar free vacation you're trading for Chic Webb's retirement party?"

"I can't go. The teachers' banquet is way too big a deal to mess up. The money I make on that banquet takes me through the spring. And, I have a very important city council meeting. Going to vote on the new wing at the rest home."

"If you broke your leg the restaurant would somehow get by, wouldn't it?"

"That's different."

"It's not different."

"You can stall the vote by a week, vote by proxy."

"Can't do it."

"You are the most stubborn, pigheaded woman I have ever known. All the things you have done for everyone in this town and now you have a chance to do something for yourself. Scotland and for free. C'mon." Jud was incredulous.

"Well, I know that this is the ant arguing with the grasshopper over work ethic and responsibility, but some of us have commitments."

"Dammit, Sarah. This is life—have some."

They were mad at one another, and this was nothing new. It happened from time to time, but Jud paused at the door as he started to leave. "I'll call you in the morning. Think about it. If you don't go we have to do something about that ticket." His voice had softened and his words came with a smile that asked forgiveness while his furrowed brow beseeched her to reconsider.

"Okay," was all that she answered as she brushed her hair from her eyes, eyes that told him he was forgiven.

At four in the morning the phone jangled Jud from his sleep. "He-hello?"

"I'm going."

"Huh?" Jud asked still in sleep and not sure who was going where.

"I'm coming with you guys to Scotland."

"You, you are? That's amazing."

"I'm going to Missoula this morning, leaving in about an hour, and I'm going to buy some new clothes, dresses. I haven't bought a dress in ten years. I'll call you tonight when I get back. I'm really excited."

"Wait a minute. Wait a minute," Jud yawned. "What changed your mind?"

"I dug out my passport and it expires, without it ever taking me anywhere, in two weeks, two days after we get back. Can you believe it? I took this as an omen. And there was another thing that helped me to change my mind and that was the 'This is life—have some' comment."

"You mean I was right about something?"

"Yeah, hard to imagine, isn't it?"

And that was that. Two days later the four flew out of Missoula. Junior left Pam in charge of McCracken's, Sarah left Sal and Jenny in charge of the Tin Cup, Jud left Dolores in charge of Annie the Wonderlab, while Henry was left wondering who would be in charge of Dolores.

The flight to New York was uneventful other than when Henry flew over Montana's eastern boundary, that being the farthest east Henry had ever been. It was his second trip on an airplane. He hated that one and he was hating this one so far.

It was when the four arrived in the First-Class Lounge at JFK that the trip really began. First class, starting with champagne, smoked salmon, access to everything, moist towelettes, fresh flowers at their table. Jud smiled over at Henry, "We're in foreign territory here and we haven't even left the ground."

Henry, who was beginning to like flying more and more with every glass of champagne served, was dressed in his ranch coat, cowboy hat, and boots. Jud wore a sport coat, brought only from his closet to this point in its twenty-five-year history for funerals and first-class flights. Junior was in the blue sport coat that he wore to Rotary, church, and events pertaining to his mayoral capacities.

But Sarah was looking first class. New clothes from head to toe. Her hair was done. She was wearing makeup. She was dressed down only slightly by the proximity of her traveling companions.

In flight from his first-class recliner, replete from an entrée of duck and an after-dinner J. D., while strawberries and Belgian chocolates were being served by beautiful women, Henry grinned, "You know Judson C., Montana and the Elkheart are nice and all, but I think I might wanna live right here."

Touch down London. Connecting flight to Edinburgh and there at the baggage claim, displaying a sign with their names, as promised, stood Penny's man, Driver Mac, who led the four of them to a Land Rover. Then it was out of Edinburgh, over the Firth of Forth Bridge and on to the A9 North to the Highlands quicker than one could say the Firth of Forth. But time was flying now as time does when all around you is new.

Junior, Sarah, and Jud were in the backseat of the Rover while Henry sat up front with Driver Mac. Though conversation between the two had been attempted a few times, little was being said. Henry in the passenger seat, which of course was on the wrong side of the car, had been distracted by the seemingly wrong-way traffic ever since their first roundabout leaving the city. But distractions aside, he couldn't understand a word Driver Mac was saying, and he wasn't going to crack the code of Driver Mac's thick Glaswegian any sooner than Driver Mac was going to decipher anything Henry, with his Rocky Mountain twangs and contractions, was trying to express from their common language. Adding to Driver Mac's burden was the fact that Henry hardly moved his mouth when he spoke, and Montanan coming to a Glaswegian through a mumble might as well have been Portuguese.

Motoring through a heavy rain, Driver Mac turned to Henry and said, "Aye, it's bucketin' dune noo," Mac was a smallish man, in his sixties, with sharp features and long, red eyebrows and a wicked grin that would flash every time Henry made another attempt at conversation.

"Jest like a cow pissin' on a flat rock," Henry smiled back. Then both nodded not knowing that he had just said the same thing.

Through Perth, over the Grampian Mountains to Inverness and on to Kincardine and the Dornoch Firth, the Highlands were coming to them through rain-streaked windows. Every so often patches of clear sky directed the sunlight in bands and breaths across the villages, the lochs, and the hardwood glens. Everything, save the purple heather, was green, a deep verdant green, a green millions of years deep. Planted fields of wheat and barley, land worked forever, stone houses, distant castles rolled past.

Driver Mac wheeled off the dual carriageway onto a one-track road and the rain stopped in favor of a rolling mist. Jud had a sudden and inexplicable feeling that something good was going to happen—something above and beyond a free first-class fishing trip to Scotland. Then Mac slowed, pulled off the one-track road onto a lane, passed the gate lodge down a corridor of rhododendron that opened suddenly onto a stone bridge. Below them the river rolled in and out of the mists.

"There she is—Pendleton Castle," Driver Mac pointed out.

Jud leaned forward for a better view through the Rover's windshield. There above them, above the mist, above the forest, and far and away above anything he'd ever seen before, towered the castle, originally the complete fortress: towers and turrets, tall stone walls, and, while it was missing the moat, it had the river.

The Rover came to a stop at the steps leading to a large, wooden door under a stone archway where a woman stood holding a red umbrella. All around her vines and flowers blossomed and beyond her the castle, clouded forests, the river flowing. Far from their usual views around Travers, Henry turned his interests to the one commonality—the river, the Carron, curving and disappearing into the hardwoods at the bottom of a giant lawn; darker, a tea color, and deeper than the Elkheart certainly, but it was no more than eighty feet wide.

"Welcome to Pendleton Castle," the lady greeted them and stepped from the doorway. And, while the door looked quite normal, considering the walls, five stories high, built from stones as large as a man, the scale snapped into perspective as the woman walked down the first few steps and was dwarfed by the grandeur. "My name is Araminta," she said extending her hand to them. "Dreadful weather in which to meet you, I'm afraid. Penny wanted to be here to meet you, but he is on his way and should be here soon.

"Mac, take them to their rooms, won't you? And after you have had time to freshen up, please come down for drinks." To Jud, towering over the lady, Araminta was first a shadow, then just a voice beneath an umbrella. Then the umbrella turned and was gone, heading for a large greenhouse at the side of the castle.

Grabbing their bags, Mac led them through an anteroom and into a great hall past suits of armor, shields, tartans, and tapestries, up two flights of stairs and down a hallway. "This'll be your r-ro-o-om 'ere, Henry," Mac said opening a door to a large suite complete with a small library, canopy bed, a fireplace with the fire lit.

"An' this is your r-ro-o-om, Jud," Mac added, swinging open a door across the hall, "you being the Pendleton relation, by way of the Downeys, and all, you get the River Room." Jud looked through his doorway to see a room with all the same amenities as Henry's, complete with a fire, but Jud's room had a glassed-in balcony and a full view of the Carron. Junior and Sarah's rooms were the next two down.

"This storm is the best possible news. We been dry for two weeks and the wee burns will turn to full spate and the fish will come, aye," Driver Mac said to Junior, who by appearances was the keenest of the three fisherman with his luggage obviously consumed by tackle. "Now once yer settled, ya coom down to the drawin' room for a dram of whisky to warm yer wet bones."

Driver Mac gone, the four, after unpacking and washing the travel away, eventually gathered in Jud's room to view the castle and their kingdom, for the seven days at any rate. "This place is unbelievable," Jud said to Henry as he came through his door.

"I gotta tell ya, I caught about one word in a hunnert of that feller's palaver on the way up here," Henry said walking to the window. "Can you imagine standing out there in that crick tomorrow, standin' where all them knights and earls fished, and hookin' into a twenty-pound salmon, the king of fish. I mean I can't wait. I mean look at this place. It's like living in a movie."

"It's gonna be interesting, but I am not setting any high expectations. Salmon are tricky business."

"You have dialed into some kind of kin, here, cousin Jud. I mean did you get a scope on this place? Big bucks. Megabucks. And, according to Driver Mac, the family owns fourteen miles of the river. *Owns*. Too bad all this descendant dinero don't make it out as far as yer limb on the family tree."

"Driver Mac said the salmon will be coming in with this rain and that we couldn't have timed it better," Junior said, entering the room only to be instantly distracted by the nearness of the river. He wanted to be fishing right now, but that would come tomorrow. "This could be great. I mean Atlantic salmon. I read in this book once that . . ."

When Sarah entered the room in a new, black dress, a string of pearls, lipstick and other forms of makeup, new shoes, her hair fashioned, all conversation stopped. "Whoa and howdy, look at you," Henry said.

"Sarah, you know me well enough to know there ain't a stick of bullshit in it when I tell ya that you are about the prettiest thing I have ever seen."

Jud said nothing. He just stood there stunned. Now he had to fall in love with Sarah for probably the hundredth time. He had fallen in love with Sarah at least once a month since she came to Travers Corners. It was easy to do. But he usually fell for the woman in her behind-the-grill attire, Hawaiian shirt and Yankees cap. Now, she was Grace Kelly beautiful and looked like she belonged here.

Junior looked up from the river for a glance in her direction, "Yeah, er, you look real nice," and then turned back to Henry, "anyway, in this book I read it said that Atlantic salmon—"

"Can you believe this place? I've never been anywhere like this, except maybe museums, in my life. My room is beautiful," Sarah said blushingly, changing the subject but liking the attention.

"Anyway in this book I read about salmon it had three chapters on—"

"Let's take 'er downstairs so we can sample a dram or two," Henry interrupted, turning Junior toward the door while he rolled his eyes at the other two. All of them knew it was necessary to stop Junior whenever he turned the conversation toward fishing because if they didn't stop him, there was every reason to believe that Junior might never stop talking about fishing.

"You really look great, Sarah," Jud said in a voice she had never heard before. She batted her eyes in a comical fashion.

At the bottom of the stairs the foursome turned down a hall filled with oil paintings, portraits mostly mixed with fishing and hunting scenes. Unsure as to where they should be going but following the sounds of laughter until they saw Araminta crossing a room, a room filled with wealthy and well-dressed people. Henry was in a clean shirt and a string tie, his goat ropers had a high shine. Jud had on his same sport coat and vest. Junior looked as if he were ready for Wednesday night Rotary, but Sarah was dressed to fit right in.

Jud looked at his pocket watch, at best an errant timepiece that favored no particular time zone, and though it was still set on Montanan time, it read six o'clock straight up, which was close to right according to the clock back in his room. But it made no matter where the time was read. Jud was feeling the first tremors of jet lag.

They entered the room quietly, almost timidly. None of them had ever been in such a room, a great hall with three fireplaces and tapestries hanging from its walls. The four were instantly greeted by Penny coming from the far corner of the room. "Jud, Henry, and Junior." The large reddish mane of a man, built like a hydrant, Sir Gordon to many, Penny to those who fish with him, shook their hands vigorously, "So good to see you all. Oh, my and Sarah how lovely you look. And I do so want to apologize for not being here to greet you but business called. Flight all right? Does Araminta have you settled into your rooms?"

"Penny, everything couldn't be better," Jud spoke for them all.

"First, let me extend my apologies for my wife, Gwendolyn. She is in Paris for the next two weeks. She did so want to meet you after my stories of Montana and all. But she will be gone the length of your stay. She sends her apologies.

"Now, without further delay I want you to meet some of your relations, Pendletons all, but favoring the D. Downey side of the family." The names came at the four of them quickly, eighteen people were too many to remember so Henry just smiled and nodded, "Hammish and Ann Pendleton, John and Mary Pendleton, Harold and . . ." The names were rolling over Jud and Henry who were slightly lost in all the tweeds and champagne being served. "Sir Nigel Pendleton . . ." "Roger and Beth Pendleton . . ."

When all the introductions had been made, Penny toasted, "Welcome to Scotland. This is a grand moment for the Clan Pendleton," and with that all glasses were raised.

"It was Roger here," Penny recalled, "who first brought the old bamboo rod to my attention. He was the one who found it and all the letters from Traver to D. Downey."

"Well, a small correction there, Penny, it was *actually* Araminta who found it and brought it to me," said Roger.

"Araminta, won't you join us for a moment?" Then the Clan Pendleton moved as a museum tour might move, past tapestries, elephant tusks, bells, mementos from a well-traveled, five-hundred-year-old family, until

Penny had situated Jud and Henry and the others in front of a display housing the bamboo rod that started this whole amazing story.

"Araminta, it was you who first found the fishing rod? All this time I have been crediting Roger with the discovery."

"Aye. I found it rolled under one of the old trunks back in the archives. When I saw it was an old fishing rod I thought it would interest you, Penny. But, Roger, being the clan historian, well, I showed it to him first." Henry was standing in between her and Jud, but Jud could in a glance, his first glimpse, see that Araminta was a woman of seventy with the movements of a twenty-year-old. But a glimpse would be all that he would get because she was gone again. Watching her walk across the room and disappear in what looked to be the kitchen, he noted that for an old woman she could cover ground.

The party then broke down into smaller groups, but it was the Elkheart foursome garnering most of the attention. For Henry the conversation centered around answering questions about Montana and home, while at the same time presenting a challenge to all those listening, answering in his mumbled Rocky Moutainese. "Well, it's a life sorta like this one. Got me a crick and fishin' out my back door, too, got me suitable acreage to prevent myself from bein' neighborly, and I got me a parlor sorta reminds me of this one . . . both being indoors and all." Henry was an immediate hit.

Junior found Hammish to be his Scottish equivalent, a man who could talk fishing until the wee hours. They teamed up that first hour and were hardly apart for the rest of the week, and when anyone listened in or passed by one of their conversations he could be assured that the topic was fishing.

Araminta, learning that Sarah was a cook, took her into the castle's kitchen, a kitchen that could easily house the entire Tin Cup Cafe. Jud could watch the two chattering away about cooking through the kitchen's constantly swinging door.

But for Jud this was much more than conversations. This was a family reunion and for the first time in his life, being the only child from parents with estranged families, he was suddenly part of a clan. Everyone gathered was either a cousin or married to one, and though someone was the third-cousin-once-removed-on-the-mother's-side-by-marriage kind of shirttail cousin, he was a blood relation, nonetheless. Nearly all of them were anglers, including several of the women, and would be spending the night, fishing with Jud, Henry, and Junior in the morning.

The dialogues during the cocktail hour centered around the fishing and family folklore from the Clan Pendleton, a clan with a castle traceable to the fifteen hundreds, and there was no shortage of stories on the bamboo rod that started it all.

Throughout dinner Araminta was in charge of the servants and was on top of every possible detail. Great candles were lit, which they were to find out was something that was only done for family weddings and New Year's, but tonight was such a celebration. Araminta tended to every detail. She missed nothing. During one brief encounter and the first time Jud was close enough to see Araminta's eyes, he found himself staring into an old soul, wise yet dancing eyes, knowing eyes. But most of the time Jud found himself staring at Sarah although she was at the very end of a table seating twenty-four. Even from that distance she was beautiful. Of course, she had been beautiful at every distance because Jud could hardly take his eyes off her.

With dinner over and everyone back in the parlor for tea, coffee, or single malt, it was Penny who assigned the beats, ". . . and Roger, you and Beth will be on beat six, Hammish and Junior will be on beat seven, and I'll fish with Jud and Henry on beat eight with Gillie Mac."

The party carried on and the single malt from the local distillery flowed. But when midnight came with some of the partiers just hitting their stride, jet lag had landed on the Montanans, and though they wanted to stay they instead said their good nights. At the top of the stairs, the four branching off into their rooms, Jud said it once more wishing he could say it in another way, "Sarah, you were the prettiest girl in the room."

"Thanks, Judson C.," she said as she stepped down the hall to her room.

The next morning on the group's way down to breakfast, Henry explained what he had learned from Hammish the night before about fishing the Carron. "Well, here's the deal," Henry explained, "this salmon fishing is a bit of a crap shoot. Nobody is fer sure why salmon do anything, specially when it gits around to swollerin' a fly. The pluses we have in our favor is that it's raining and that brings the fish into the rivers, and, by the way, a salmon is the only fish that can be referred to as a *fish*. All other fish, including trout, are carp by comparison.

"According to cousin Hammish, there's no other way but to keep your fly in the crick and hope that perhaps a salmon will swim past it and, for whatever reason, and no one knows why 'cause they certainly ain't eating, comes over and grabs your fly.

"Hammish took me down into the angler's room. There must be twenty-five rods down there strung up and ready to go and there ain't a one of them shorter than twelve feet."

Retracing their steps up the stone stairs, Jud turning to Henry said, "I keep expecting the tall shadow of Errol Flynn to come backing out of an archway, sword in hand, about to skewer a Norman or two."

After breakfast, which Sarah helped Araminta prepare, all adjourned to the anglers' rooms, the ladies to theirs, and the men to theirs, a walnut-paneled locker room with closets for one and all where Pendletons put on their Barbours and waders while remaining in their tweeds and ties. Jud and Henry were in fleece and Gore-Tex. Junior missed breakfast because of his hangover and was readying himself slowly for the fishing. On the rarest of occasions Junior has a drink, but last night caught up in the excitement of castles and salmon he tried to keep up with Hammish, a man who single-handedly supports the nearby distillery.

They went out into a courtyard where men and women gathered into Land Rovers, past a small room at the rear of the castle where Araminta and Sarah were. A break in the clouds allowed the light to briefly come through the sheets of rain on the leaded window and reflect broken rivulets of a muted sun through Sarah's hair. The light came softly to her face while her eyes caught the light and held it there. Hers was a beauty of the quietest kind, subtle, the kind of beauty that sneaks up on you and leaves you light-headed because you forget to breathe.

Jud stopped without realizing he had done so, causing Araminta eventually to look up. She and Sarah came to an open window. "Well now, I hear that you and Henry are the favored sons this morning, going to beat eight and all," Araminta said.

"Oh, and why's that?" Jud questioned.

"Well, as anyone will tell you, beat eight is the best beat on the Carron. Nobody knows why, it just is."

"Not knowing why seems to be the cornerstone to this thing called salmon fishing."

Araminta laughed. "Now you have that right. Is this your first chance at the salmon then?" Jud nodded. "Well, your chances of landing a salmon are thin, but they really aren't diminished by much just because of your not having done it before. But it looks as though you are trying to make the odds even worse if that half a rod you're holding is what you are intending on using. But you will end up being fine because you're going with Gillie Mac and I ought to know, been married to him for forty-two years."

Jud smiled and turned to see Hammish and Junior already gone and Henry and Penny standing by the Rover waiting. "Better go. Hey, Sarah what are you going to do today?"

"I'm going to help Araminta in the kitchen. I have a feeling I might learn something."

"Yeah, well, I think Araminta might pick up a pointer or two herself. She's the best cook in Montana, Araminta, and I ain't a whiffin' with ya."

"Good luck. Catch a bunch," Sarah waved.

Araminta looked at Sarah with a questioning, confused look. "I ain't a whiffing with you, ya?"

"Means he wasn't kidding," explained Sarah, who thought it was wonderful for Jud to say and was outwardly flattered by it.

Sitting at the wheel of the Rover was Gillie Mac who coincidently was Driver Mac from yesterday. "I thought you said your name was Driver Mac," Jud asked climbing into his seat.

"Well, when I'm drivin', I'm Driver Mac, and when I'm fishin', then I'm Gillie Mac. It's how Araminta keeps track of me whereaboots."

The weather was miserable, and for the whole day Henry fished one pool, Penny another, and Jud was on the first pool of the beat where he could see the next angler, Hammish, fishing beat seven. Junior would have been fishing, but he'd put a tangle in his line, a tangle visible from one hundred yards. The surroundings, while muted by the low-lying mist and rain, were beautiful, but he longed to see Scotland in the sunlight. They fished hard all morning in a cold, driving rain. Lunch was served in a small cabin by the river, then it was fishing again until five. Cocktails commenced in the parlor at five thirty where the twelve fishermen and fisher women, counted their fish, which was easy. It was zero, not a strike, not a sighting. Salmon fishing, at least on the first day, was living up to salmon fishing.

The room filled with conjecture as to why no one took a fish. The conversations surrounding Jud and those he was even engaged in would grow dim, almost inaudible as Sarah entered the room. At the bar Penny was pouring drams. Hammish had a stiff pour while Junior had a Pepsi. Henry and Jud had just joined them.

"Aye, the salmon will come, tomorrow or the next day, certain. There is more rain on the way," Gillie Mac explained to Henry.

Hammish began to recall the salmon season of 1964, "Oh, that was a banner year that one . . ."

Araminta crossed the room to tell Penny, "Dinner can be served in the next five minutes, Penny." Then she smiled at Jud and asked, "And how many salmon did you land on that child-sized rod of yours?"

"Tied for first place," Jud answered through a grin.

The next morning the clan's anglers were up early and out on the water fishing until noon in a cold drizzle. After lunch it would be fishing until five under lifting clouds. The rain had stopped for the first time since Jud, Henry, and Junior stepped from the plane. Now the three were stationed on beat one, Gillie Mac at the ready and Penny much farther upstream opposite him and fishing the last large pool before the Carron emptied into the Dornoch Firth. At midday blue sky appeared, scattered in the mist, and then Scotland for the first time appeared in all its past and present. The castle's tower was visible above the rhododendron, alder, and oak, its long banners flying lazily on the breeze. The highlands were a green Henry had never seen before, and he turned to Gillie Mac, saying "Well there's a howdy fer ya."

"Aye, Scotland's coming aboot now."

On the hill behind Jud small stone cottages appeared for the first time. Laying his rod down he began taking pictures in every direction starting with the firth. Then he took some photos of Henry and Mac on the opposite shore, an upstream shot of the Carron with rocky shores, a hardwood forest picture, the castle, the hills of rolling heather. He thought about the gang at home, about, Doc, Sal, and Dolores and Annie, wishing they could be here to see all of this, but photographs would have to do. Slipping his camera into his pack, he picked up his rod and waded back into the river. It had been a full, hard, cold day of fishing and he'd caught as many salmon as he had the day before.

Mac, whose brogue up until this moment had been doing to the English language what the clouds had been doing to the sun all day, said quite clearly, "That would be Araminta and Sarah walkin' doon from our cottage on her way back to the castle." Mac explained, nodding in the direction he wanted Henry to look, "Aye, she's right on schedule, always coomes by this way aboot four. Those two have formed a friendship, haven't they?"

"It'd be damned hard not to form a friendship with Sarah. She's the best."

With his back to the hillside, Jud had no way of seeing them until they were standing on the river's bank. He caught them in a glimpse just as Araminta shouted, "Have you caught anything on that child's rod of yours?" Jud answered by winding up and with five false casts he let out a crisp cast traveling the better part of seventy feet. His fly completed its swing, he then reeled in while walking back to the shore.

"Well, that was a long cast for a man with half a rod," Araminta said as Jud stepped from the river.

Jud laughed sloshing free of the river and on to the shore, "Well it wouldn't be the first time someone called me half-cast."

"Here the salmon travel closest to the shore but the fish have got to see it coming and have to see it going as well. You have to play all the water you can when you're up against the Atlantic salmon."

"Do you fish, Araminta?"

"No, not anymore. I did as a girl. My father, grandfather, and great-grandfather were all gillies for the castle. In fact, our family has worked for the Pendletons for seven generations, crofters, scullery maids, cooks, what have you. Anyway, I have lived on this river all my life."

~

"And it might be the most beautiful place on Earth," Sarah said.

"Tell me, Jud, do you and Sarah like music?"

"Sure."

"Then would you like to go to down to the local pub tonight with Mac and myself—get a bit of the local flavor—listen to our friends and two of our children play music?"

"Sure," Sarah answered for the both of them, then without realizing it she stuck her arm through Jud's.

"Good. Henry and Junior are invited as well, of course. We'll head out after supper. And making supper is what I better be doing. I'll see you tonight." And with that she and Sarah were heading upstream to the castle with Sarah looking back over her shoulder now and then to watch Jud casting in that slow and easy manner of his as if his long and lean frame had been born to do it. Though she had no desire to ever try fly fishing she appreciated its beauty.

Stopping on the trail just before it veered back into the woods Araminta tuned and stopped Sarah, "So, how much love does a man have to show ya?"

"Pardon me?" Sarah asked not sure of the reference.

"If Jud were any more in love with you he would surely burst. The love light is burning within him and it's shining only on you."

Sarah blushed but said nothing.

"There's another thing about that man. There's not a bad bone in his body," Araminta said, then added with a devilish certainty and the wink of a matchmaker, "I know these things." And with that Araminta walked ahead. Sarah turned to see Henry, Junior, and Jud spread out down the Carron. She had to laugh because even from way up here, Junior seemed awkward. She had no way of knowing that he had just fallen in.

That evening over cocktails Jud watched Sarah across the room. She was looking, if possible, even prettier than she had the nights before, while Henry laid out his plans for the night, "Hammish, Roger, Junior, and me are goin' after them salmon again this evening. Hammish and Roger both are sure the first wave of salmon will be coming in tonight. Wanna go?"

"Not going to make it tonight. I'm going to go listen to some music with Sarah, Gillie Mac, and Araminta," Jud answered.

It wasn't until eleven o'clock that the four finally left the castle. Jud, always in bed and asleep by ten, thought it an odd time to start an evening. He asked Gillie Mac, "Do you think the band will still be playing?"

"In all likelihood most of them haven't even showed up yet. Things don't really happen 'til around midnight." They pulled up in front of an unlikely but very large tavern. Then he learned as he read the sign, it was also a hotel. Coming through the door the place was deserted, only a bellman at the front desk. Walking in the bar Jud was surprised to see only a few people. Then he saw a man with a fiddle and another carrying a guitar go into a backdoor across the room.

"Oh, that is good news. Timmy and Sean are here. Great musicians and a good sign there will be some very good music tonight," said Araminta, raised up on her toes with excitement.

They followed the fiddle and guitar players entering a room that had a makeshift bar and tables all around a stage in the middle. At least that is how it looked since it was difficult to see through all the smoke. Inside the door Araminta and Mac knew everyone. And they couldn't pass a table without some small round of conversation, brief introductions, but Araminta was more concerned about a good place to sit and found a table close to the right-hand side of the stage. Sitting down they ordered four pints. Three more musicians came through the door.

"Oh, my. Look. Look. It's Davy Spillane," Araminta said shouting in a whisper. "I don't believe it. What a treat this evening is going to be." Jud let the rise of his eyebrows do the questioning. "Have you not heard of Davy Spillane?" Jud could only shake his head. "Only the greatest Irish pipes player in the world. He hasn't been here in years; used to play here often before he was famous."

"Aye, we're lucky," added Gillie Mac. "Last Saturday night we had two toothless old farts playin' their fife and fiddle." Jud laughed and looked around the room listening to the conversations, soaking every drop of Scotland he could hold. All of this and Sarah, too.

The musicians gathered on the stage. Two fiddlers, two guitars, a boran player, one whistle, and someone on the clarsach. And, of course, Davy Spillane. One of the fiddlers came to the front of the stage, "If you don't know or if you are fr-r-rom a different planet, sitting in with the regulars tonight is Davy Spillane himself."

The regulars counted the beat, a traditional Scottish reel. "It's one of my favorites," Araminta said. Jud looked under the table to see her feet dancing in her chair, her feet hopping over one another in time. She was spry and nimble for a woman of her age. But who could blame her since there was hardly anyone in the bar who wasn't at the very least tapping his toe. The music, the crowd, and a good time so infectious, Jud began feeling his Scottish blood pulsing, chromosomes and genes *reeling with the feeling*. One reel after another then Davy sat in and did what he and few others can do with Irish pipes. The music from the pipes flowed over a quiet room, not a word was spoken, not a glass was clinked.

Davy finished playing and Gillie Mac ordered four more Guinnesses. This was followed by other soloists, and when one of the guitar players stepped forward and played a little James Taylor, Jud began feeling closer to home, if not, Guinness being Guinness, a little closer to the floor.

The night went on. Reels were spun, flings were flung, and Sarah danced. Opting not to attempt any flings or fancy steps Jud was happy to watch Sarah having the time of her life. Davy did a few more solos as well as sitting in two sets. They played on until three in the morning with Davy winding up with a solo and sitting in for the last number. Gillie Mac just sat in his chair, not saying much, and never stopped grinning.

"What beat are you fishing tomorrow?" Araminta asked.

"Beat two with Hammish and Roger."

"Absolutely the worst beat on the Carron. You won't catch a thing. Isn't that right, Mac?" Mac, smiling into his pint, only nodded.

"Yeah, well I'm kind of getting used to that."

"Would you and Sarah like to go to Ullapool with me instead? It's a wee fishing village on the west coast. I'm going to visit my sister. You'll see some wonderful sights."

"I'd love to go," Sarah jumped at the invitation.

"Sure, that sounds great," Jud concurred.

The following day on the way downstairs to breakfast Henry informed Jud that there was one salmon taken last night around midnight, but it was Hammish who landed it. "Not a big salmon, nine pounds. And I had a strike. We're gonna catch ourselves one of them salmon. Fish will be caught on all the beats today. Hammish pert near guaranteed it."

"I'm going to Ullapool with Sarah and Araminta."

"*Yer what*?" Henry exclaimed, stopping on the next step, almost tumbling at the news. He said it in a voice louder than he wanted and *yer what* echoed off the giant stone walls down many of the hallways.

"Araminta is taking Sarah and me to the west coast of Scotland to Ullapool—stopping to see some of the sights along the way."

"Ya travel six thousand miles to catch a salmon and now on what Hammish says will be the best day of the season you're going sightseein'?"

"Well, there's more to Scotland than watching the end of your line."

Then Henry thought a moment about how beautiful Sarah was looking lately and how a blind man would have noticed the looks being exchanged between her and Jud. "Well, you might be on to something after all, buddy. I guess I can see why yer off to what-a-pool?"

"Ullapool."

Jud wasn't very surprised by Henry's reaction, because here on the fourth day of a possible seven he wouldn't be fishing, lessening his chances by Junior's instant calculations by 14 percent, and no matter how many times Henry tried to explain it to him, Junior just couldn't grasp Jud's reasoning. Of course, Junior being Junior was oblivious to everything around him but the fishing and the meals.

Oykell Bridge, Elphin, Strathkanaird, these were just some of the stops as they made toward Ullapool. Through rich farmland, heather, over the spine of Scotland and down to the west coast. "You like fish and chips?" Araminta asked.

"I guess they're all right, only had 'em once when I was in Oregon," Jud answered.

"I think they're okay I guess," Sarah said with reservation in her voice, having had a bad fish-and-chips experience as a child and having never tried it again.

"Oh, the Yanks don't know anything about making fish and chips. Fish and chips in Ullapool are the best. No comparison. Fresh oil and fresh fish is the secret."

Jud was slightly amazed, if not concerned, bordering on frightened as Araminta flew along a one-track road, nearly achieving two-tire corners. He could swear from his side of the Fiat that he could feel a certain lifting. Through the bends of heather, then along the ocean, Ullapool came to them first as a line of white along the shoreline, then a row of shops and homes, all painted white. And as they slowed into town Jud commented, "Now this is just what a town should look like." Of course, Jud had been loving nearly every building and farmhouse he'd seen. "It's so . . . I guess the word I want is tasteful, classy in a wonderfully rural way. If this town were in America we'd be passing a peewee golf course right now at the end of a row of fast-food clones across the road from something neoned and ugly."

After visiting the shops of Ullapool and a lunch of fish and chips, a lunch that lived up to its billing, Araminta was off to visit her sister while Sarah and Jud walked along the shoreline just south of town. The clouds came and went and when the sun was allowed to hit Ullapool, the small fishing village became a blaze of white. The rocky shore was receiving the smallest of waves, the ocean was nearly flat except for a light chop, while the gulls patrolled the shallows. Fishing boats bobbed at their moorings. Somehow Sarah's hand had slipped into his, which was a good thing in Jud's mind, because when he first touched her hand and found it reaching for his, he became buoyant, a little dizzy. He would have surely caught the wind and floated out to sea if she hadn't have anchored him.

Jud looked down on her with his silly toothy grin. Then Sarah surprised him by standing on her toes and kissing him lovingly, bordering on the passionate. He started to speak, but Sarah put her fingers to his lips. "Just leave it alone, Judson C., I don't want to talk about anything right now, at least anything that's going to get deep or meaningful. Not a word." She put her arm through his. "I'm a child again and I love Scotland. Araminta is wonderful. Gillie Mac, Penny, everyone is wonderful and everywhere I look lies something beautiful and new." Jud, as told, could only nod as she looked away but he never stopped holding her hand.

Late to the river because of business, e-mails, and faxes, Penny arrived on beat three after passing beat two being fished by Hammish and Roger, the clan's two best fisherman. He put on his waders and assembled his rod and walked upstream. Henry, concentrating hard on his fishing, only saw Penny coming when he was nearly on top of him. "Any luck?" Penny asked as Henry slogged free of the water and into a heavy rain.

"Nope," Henry answered shaking his head.

"Where's Jud?"

"Ullapool."

"What in the world is Jud doing in Ullapool?"

"He's with Sarah and Araminta."

Penny, puzzled and confused as to how anyone would leave the Carron on what *could* be the best day of the year and go to *Ullapool*, simply nodded.

A salmon rolled.

On the Ullapool side of Scotland it was sunny with a slight breeze, but on the return home to Glen Croick they were met with rain once again. They made a brief stop at Araminta's. Surrounded by flowers, roses, vegetable gardens, and vines covering most of its stone walls, Gillie Mac and Araminta's house was beautiful.

"Your home is wonderful, and what a view," Sarah said. "I would love to live here."

"This is a typical crofter's house, two up, two down," she explained turning on the lights, "it's three hundred years old. I'll give you the tour and it won't take long." Paintings hung from the limited wall space allowed by a small kitchen, a living room of about the same dimensions, and two dinky bedrooms upstairs made smaller by the pitch of the roof were connected by a narrow hall. In a word Araminta's house was small, but it was warm and wonderful. "My father, and back to my great,

great," she said counting on her fingers as she traced her lineage, "great-grandfather have worked and gillied on the river. My mother, who'll be one hundred and one this year, lives about a half a mile away in the house I was raised in, which looks exactly like this one."

"Well, it's a great spot and a great view. And you got it fixed up nice, cozy is what it is. Overlooking the Carron. It's a great place," Jud said standing at the window, looking down on the river and a lone fisherman and wondering how the day's fishing had gone for everyone.

"Aye, it is bonny. Mac and I have had a good life here."

"Araminta, if you don't mind my asking, why is it if you and Mac were both born and raised here on the river, that Mac has a heavy brogue and you don't?"

"The Pendletons sent me to a private school in Wales. We were taught to speak properly. But I love to hear my Mac talk." Araminta grabbed whatever it was she needed from a cabinet in the garage and they were back in the car and soon to the castle where in the great hall the mood was celebratory and had been since the fishermen returned from the river an hour before. Seventeen salmon had been caught in all. Henry had caught three. Junior had even caught one with the help of Gillie Mac, and several others from the Pendleton clan claimed a couple of fish a piece. Salmon were caught at every beat but beat two.

With over an hour behind them at the bar, Gillie Mac, Henry, and Junior were aglow with single malt and salmon and were reliving each catch of the day telling their tales and hearing the stories from all the other anglers in return, all but from Hammish and Roger, the best fisherman of them all, who had caught nothing. Sarah reached down and squeezed Jud's hand then went to her room, and Araminta went to the kitchen to see how everything was progressing for dinner, and Jud aimed for the bar to hear the stories. By the roar coming from the bar it sounded like he had missed some good fishing, but at the same time Jud wouldn't trade this day with Sarah for any other day so far in his life. There was something happening between them. There was that certain kind of heat generated by blushes, flushes, and lust. Slightly dizzy from that fleeting, if ever felt, moment when your mind and soul share the same page, when longitude and latitude run parallel, when your entire infrastructure—joints, bones, and organs—turns to quicksilver and your heart beats hard enough to know that your heart hasn't beat like that for a *lo-o-ong* time.

Junior crossed the room in his usual ungainly walk and headed up the stairs to ready himself for dinner. Henry poured himself another, as well as one for Jud and Gillie Mac. A bourbon drinker all his life, Henry was toying with making the switch because whether it was the single malt or the salmon or a combination of both, he couldn't remember, not counting sex with Dolores, when he had ever felt happier.

Gillie Mac was telling Henry about Junior and his salmon just as Jud joined them, "In all me born days, seventy-two years man and boy, and me whole life spent on the river, have I ever seen a more ungainly man. I think back on him landin' that salmon, and it was a bloody miracle he landed it at all. The man canna walk and talk at the same time."

"Been that way his whole life," Henry confirmed, "and sometimes it's positively scary to watch him."

"Hey, Mac, how did Araminta know that fish would be taken today, but not on beat two?" Jud asked.

"Well, the truth of it is," Gillie Mac answered leaning a little closer to Jud and Henry, "Araminta knows the river as well as I do, and bein' a woman, maybe better," he grinned. "That and she has the magic in her. She knows things that the wee mortals will never know. She's a bit of a seer that one, and the people up and down Glen Croick know it."

By the time Araminta called the Pendleton clan and their four guests, a happier gathering could not be found—salmon fishing and scotch being key ingredients to their heritage, and it had been a splendid day on the Carron. Everyone was greeted at the door by Araminta, and Jud following after Sarah were the last ones to the table. Jud stopped, "You know you were right about beat two. Roger and Hammish got skunked."

Araminta only smiled up at him and said, "Did you know that all the Scottish salmon records are held by women? I have lived every day of my life on the Carron and I have a knowledge of the river second to none. Not *my* knowledge, but the knowledge, the secrets really, that my father passed on to me from his forefathers—gillies and fishermen all. So, with all due respect, because I love them both dearly, Hammish and Roger don't know the river and its fishing like I do.

"My grandfather, a bit of a poet, and he knew salmon like no other man before him or since, made up rhymes and we learned them as children.

When the first rains come and you want to catch less
than a few
you could find no better beat than beat number two.

"And here's another little rhyme you should be aware of," Araminta added.

There will be no salmon caught after June's first rain
not until the full moon is on the wane.
And on that day every Scotsman alive,
would trade his wife gladly for beat number five.

Jud laughed, "That must have been a hit with your grandmother."

"Full moon last night. On the wane now. Five is a favorable beat for you. The river narrows there giving you a better advantage with your child-sized rod. I already had Gillie Mac sign you and Henry up for it."

"Oh, and one other thing you should do," Araminta added. "Tell her that you love her. Tell her now, tell her tenderly and be happy for the rest of your life."

The dinner progressed as all their dinners had, too much food followed by more food: duck, pheasant, salmon, everything on the table was shot, caught, raised, or farmed on Pendleton soil. Every meal had been served with a wine and followed by brandy. But tonight was different in one way—Sarah, who usually was seated at the table where Jud could only stare at her from a distance, was now sitting next to him. Araminta, in charge of the seating arrangements, which until this evening had the four Montanans evenly spaced around the table for all to share, had effected some last-minute changes.

After dessert, all fishermen were back to the bar. The beats were assigned and Henry, Jud, Penny, with Gillie Mac, were on beat five. Jud, privy to the beat five rhyme looked across the room to Araminta, who was smiling knowingly as a member of the staff came up to Henry and informed him that he had a phone call. "That'll have to be Dolores callin' to torment me. She ain't been able to do that for near a week so she'll have some stored up," Henry said and headed down the hall resigned to the fact that he would now have to listen to the latest gossip at a dollar a minute, and hear once again about how she was left behind while he was first-classing it around Europe.

Sarah, in the meantime, had made plans for tomorrow. She was going into Inverness with Cyril and Iris Pendleton for a day of shopping and stopping to see Culloden Battlefield, Cawdor Castle. But before retiring and saying all of her good nights she leaned in and whispered in Jud's ear, "Why don't you get a couple of cognacs and come up to my room. I have something I want to give you."

"Oh, and what's that?" Jud asked.

"Me." That was all that she said and then she was gone, but in that one short word she changed their lives forever.

At the bar Jud poured two cognacs then turned to see Sarah leaving with a long green-eyed come-hither stare. A moment later Henry came back into the room with a sad look on his face. There had been bad news from Travers Jud thought, probably about their old friend Red Peterson who was not supposed to last another day longer, but he was eighty-four. With a drink in each hand, love and lust in heart changing on the beat, Jud needed only to ask, "Red Peterson?"

"Yeah, ol' Red died yesterday, but he did good, lived a long life," Henry said. But there was more news from Dolores, bad news, but he didn't want to break it without a bracer. Changing and avoiding the subject at hand, he asked, "What're you, a two-fisted drinker or is one of those mine?"

~

"One's for Sarah," Jud said sheepishly, trying to look innocent, a gentleman's disguise.

"But I just saw Sarah headin' up the stairs. Said nothin' but good night and that she was headin' to bed," Henry leered. All Jud could do was to say nothing.

Henry grew a grin from ear to ear. "Yeah?"

Jud might not have said anything, but after a lifelong friendship his face betrayed him and he told Henry everything he wanted to know. "I been awatchin' you two all week, but then I been awatchin' you two for years, and partner, this night has been a long time comin'."

Jud, uneasy, changed the subject back, "What else did Dolores have to say?"

"All the other news can keep, Judson C. I'll tell you tomorrow. Right now you have a lady waitin'."

Taking the stairs Jud could never have believed what was happening anymore than he could have ever imagined where it was happening. He and Sarah—making love. All these years of being close friends and they were about to get a lot closer. A great friendship *without* making love, but sex, as everyone who's tried it knows, is the ultimate test, the last and first trial at once, a clarification to the greatest puzzle in life by making sure that the final pieces fit; a night filled with pleasure, where all the years and memories of enduring life alone disappear as easily as all things forgotten.

And as they finally lay sleeping, sleep coming just before the dawn, arms and legs intertwined, Jud's face in Sarah's long hair, her face smiling, that love, the full, warm, nurturing love that flirted and encircled them all these years, had finally arrived. At first light Jud sneaked back to his room for discretionary reasons while Sarah lay sleeping.

Sarah missed breakfast, missing purposefully the departure of all anglers, ensuring she would not see Jud. Anxiety attack would be much too strong a description of what she was going through, but her mind was frenzied about last night. Questioning everything from the night before, its propriety, its timing, and most of all the uncertainty of its long-term effects, Sarah paced around and asked an empty room, "I mean what was that all about, Easterly? You let the Italian take over, didn't you? Shit, why Jud?" To Sarah, to this point, Jud had always been that irresponsible, lackadaisical, ever insouciant man on the one hand, and on the other hand he weighed in with his kindness, his warmth, his friendship. The scale for their relationship had always been in balance when it had only these things to weigh, but last night physical love tipped the scale. "And, damn it," she said throwing her shoe across the room, "why did he have to be such a good lover?"

The reasons for her being in Scotland with Jud were accidental, Doc's breaking his fingers and all, but being in bed with Jud was intentional, thought out, planned, and though it seemed natural enough last night while she was the seductress, it seemed irrational now. "It was wrong. Oh, man was it wrong, but it felt so right. Shit." She threw the other shoe.

The rest of the morning passed as planned. Sarah was off to Inverness with Cyril and Iris, and the fishermen were off to their designated beats, Penny, Henry, Jud, and Gillie Mac to beat five. The salmon were uninterested, *dour*, according to Mac, but when the rains came the gillie knew, "Aye, they'll coom now and then the sport will be on."

They fished for another hour without bending a rod. Penny was at the top of the run, Henry at the bottom, and Jud was in the middle fishing with Gillie Mac. But, while Jud might have been wading up to his butt in the cold, dark Carron, casting his rod and sending his fly after salmon, he wasn't fishing. He wasn't even near the river. He was still back in Sarah's room, still in her arms, and he hadn't left there all morning. And now he worried if he would be able to leave there for his lifetime. Last night's pleasures had him spinning. But he couldn't be falling in love with Sarah, not stubborn, mule-headed, Saint Sarah. No thank you. He had always loved her but things had changed. "It wouldn't work," he mumbled and knew that living with her could only spell trouble. Loving with her, however, could only spell easy.

"Noo, accordin' to legend, Araminta's grandfather being the legend himself," Mac explained,

On Beat Number Five you'll do well if you place,
a Silver Doctor under the nose on the old woman's face.

~

"What?"

"Look upstream. Do you see those black rocks above the river, then?" Jud nodded. "Do you see a woman's face?"

Jud studied the cliff, but other than some rocks that stuck out a little farther than the rest he could see no nose or anything remotely resembling a woman's face. "No," he answered.

"You don't?" Mac said incredulously.

Jud looked again, harder this time, and still couldn't see anything human about the outcropping. "Sorry, but I don't see it, but then it's pretty hard sometimes to interpret another man's imaginations."

Mac laughed, "Well, I can't see it either, nor can anyone else, but Araminta's grandfather could."

Jud tied on the Silver Doctor. Then they walked to the limestone overhang, a place where the Carron swirled against the cliff, narrowing there to carve at the rock for a million years. Hollows above the river showed the high-water marks from an ancient age with moss covering it all. Wading back into the water he began to cast the good Doctor under the old woman's nose, a cast of no more than forty feet, then let the fly swing into the dark, tea-colored water. The wind kicked up and the clouds were coming. Casting over and over again, while Araminta's grandfather's rhymes repeated itself in his mind.

He looked downriver to Henry, who had worked his way upstream, and the mere sight of him caused Jud to laugh out loud as a thousand images from a lifelong friendship filled his head. And, now this adventure—the two of them in Scotland fishing; fishing the same riffles and pools as his forefathers had fished. The hills, the heather, the Carron, the distant bens beckoned Jud's Celtic ancestry. His bagpipes blew, his tartans flew, and he had a sudden yearning to own sporran, dagger, and kilt. He also wanted to have an Atlantic salmon strike his fly. He wanted Sarah to leave his mind for a while but there was no chance of it. The clouds darkened the sky. The wind hit. A salmon ate the Silver Doctor beneath the old woman's nose.

Out of the copper-colored reaches sprang the salmon, king of fish, the river his kingdom, three times as large as anything Jud had ever had on his line and ten times stronger. A giant salmon, fresh from the sea, as bright as light itself, and radiating silver, landed in the heavy current and headed upstream into a wide shallow, taking her fight out into the open.

Henry looked upstream to see the bend in Jud's rod, his arms held high above his head, and Gillie Mac running alongside him, net in hand. Scrambling up the bank to the path, Henry was coming on the run as was Penny.

The great salmon took flight again and in the darkness of the day her leap was arched and as silvered as winter's quarter moon. Her third jump, and her finest, was a spiraling, twisting, almost flying effort followed by a long run trying to make it to the next narrows and current. Jud, following the fish over an uneven shore of rocks, mosses, and brush, shouted over his shoulder to Gillie Mac, "This is a bigger fish than I have ever even seen, let alone tried to land."

"Twenty-five pounds plus would be a fair guess," Mac yelled for no other reason other than the excitement since he was running right beside him.

The salmon buried herself at the bottom of a deep hole where the current played heavy on Jud's line. Down deep behind a giant boulder, the fish tried to regain its strength while Jud tried to catch his breath. Leaning back on this rod, applying pressure then easing off, the salmon barely budged. The tug of war ended when Jud succeeded in turning the fish's head. The salmon shot downstream into the shallows, taking her fight back into the open. A long fight, and Jud's arm was growing tired.

"Now you've got her," Mac said with certainty.

Henry and Penny caught up to them to see the salmon going back and forth in the shallows searching for a way free. Jumping often but barely clearing the river, she finally began rolling on the line in one last effort to free herself.

The salmon was now at Jud's feet, "God, what a beauty. A big hen." Mac eased it into the net and lifted it for Penny and Henry to see. "Bloody well done," Penny exclaimed.

"Nice goin', Judson C.," Henry said, stepping into the river and patting his shoulder.

Gillie Mac killed the fish, then produced a flask from his pocket and passed it around. "Not for certain, now, but I think that this fish might well be some kind of record. I'll take it to some proper scales before it loses any of its weight." Then Mac was off to the castle.

"Jud, that is the grandest fish I have seen caught here in many, many years," Penny said excitedly, "I think I will just tag along with Mac to see what it weighs. I'll be back shortly."

This left Henry alone with Jud for the first time that day, and alone is how a man should be when he gets the kind of news Henry was about to deliver. It was good that Jud was fishing, Henry thought, bad news during good times goes down easier. Jud having just landed the fish of his lifetime might help soften the blow, but Henry doubted it. "Judson C., I didn't tell you this last night 'cause you were just heading up the stairs, but Dolores was callin' with bad news of the worst kind." He put one hand on Jud's shoulder. "So here it is straight, Annie died yesterday. Dolores said she went in her sleep, layin' in her spot on the porch. Sorry, buddy. She was one great dog—smartest one I ever saw." Jud just stood there for a moment, saying nothing, then turned and walked downstream.

Penny wasn't gone five minutes when he was back with Gillie Mac. They came to give Jud the news, but ran into Henry on the trail first. "Jud's fish weighed in at twenty-nine pounds, seventeen-ounces," Penny said beaming. "You've broken Hammish's standing record of forty-four years, by four pounds ten."

"Listen, I just had to give Jud some real bad news. Ya might want to leave him be for right now. His dog, Annie, died yesterday, and I jest now told him about it."

"I remember Annie. Lovely dog. Mac, in my locker, there is a bottle of very old scotch, would you mind?" And while Mac drove back to the castle, the two talked about dogs. "I lost my pointer last year. Best hunting dog I ever owned."

"Well, Annie, Annie the Wonderlab, Jud called her and she was just that, a wonder. Anyway she wasn't normal. I'd say she was about fifty percent smarter than most people, and Jud and her were inseparable. I had me a cow dog like that once named Maxie. Damn, he was a smart one, too. Used to beat me in cribbage all the time," Henry winked. "I remember this one time . . ."

Mac, bottle in hand, stopped by the kitchen to tell Araminta about the fish, the record, the Silver Doctor below the old woman's nose, and he explained in his rush to get back that the bottle was for Jud, about how Jud had just been told of the dog's death. "That's a weird one, eh," Mac said on his way back to the Rover, "One minute yer on top of the bloomin' world, a salmon of record class tucked freshly under yer belt, and the next minute you hear about yer dog. No bloody sense to this world."

Araminta understood one thing, that whatever complications Jud had in his life had been muddled even further by last night, because last night there was love made in the castle. She knew it, and there is nothing more complicated than love. She was smiling back at life and all of its trials when Sarah came into the kitchen, fresh from shopping, elated from her day but still worried about the night before, only to hear the news about Jud's fish and Annie.

Rain dripping from his hat, Jud sat on the river's bank staring into the river, but he didn't see the tea-colored Carron. He saw the crystal waters of Carrie Creek and Annie the Wonderlab joyously swimming its currents. He didn't see the old arthritic girl, the nearly deaf but with one good eye Annie. He saw her the day he first picked her up, a puppy riding home in her pasteboard box lined with towels. He saw her riding shotgun in the Willys, snapping at whitefish rises on the Elkheart, with a face full of porcupine needles, barking at the UPS man, and floating down the river in the stern of the SS *Lucky Me.* He saw her asleep on the front porch, but he could not picture her dead.

Gillie Mac was back with the scotch, but was stopped short of delivering it to Jud right away by Henry. "Maybe give him a few more minutes alone. So, Penny, what's a fifty-year-old scotch like?"

"I don't think a description will do justice. This is a question to be answered only by application," Penny answered at which point Mac produced three folding silver cups and poured each of them a dram and three toasts were made. One to Jud's Atlantic salmon, one to Annie, and one to Jud himself who sat miserably in the rain. Annie's death had brought Jud to tears, naturally, but at the same time he realized she had lived a long, trouble-free, outdoor Montana life, and what more could a Labrador ask for?

Suddenly, Sarah was sitting down beside him. Saint Sarah, always there to comfort those in need, especially her Jud, but she took one look at Jud's face and started to cry. "Oh, I can't bear it. She was the most wonderful dog I ever knew." Jud slipped his arm around her.

Henry, Gillie Mac, and Penny decided to return to the fishing. "You know, Henry, when I was in Montana I remember Sarah, certainly, but I also remember that she and Jud were very good friends. But here in Scotland they seem to be much more than that," Penny observed.

"Yeah, seems that way fer certain. Course it's been comin' for years. Everybody in Travers knows how Jud and Sarah feel about each other, 'ceptin Jud and Sarah. Yep, it's been a long time gettin' here, but if I know anything at all, I'm bettin' it's here to stay."

"Aye, it's goin' to happen. Araminta said so," said Gillie Mac.

Penny, who was partly raised by Araminta, tilted his head, wrinkled his brow, and said with certainty, "Well, then that is how it will be. Araminta is a bit of seer, you know?"

The fisherman returned to their beats. Jud and Sarah continued to sit in the rain, heading back to the castle shortly before the anglers called it a day. Henry caught one more fish in his last minutes of fishing for Atlantic salmon, which set his mood for the night.

For their last night in Scotland, the Montanans were treated to another Araminta feast. In the dining hall the ever-revolving members of the Pendleton clan had swollen to a crowd of thirty, nearly doubling the attendance gathered on the night the four first arrived. The only one still remaining from their first evening besides Penny was Hammish, whom Henry and Jud looked on as a godsend, a godsend because in Hammish, Junior had met his piscatorial match. If the two hadn't occupied each other for the week talking about the esoteric and abstruse aspects of angling for hours on end, Junior would have turned his fish talk on Jud and Henry, and they might have missed most of Scotland.

Unbelievable

~

Late that evening Henry was still at the bar where he had been joined by Junior, Hammish, Gillie Mac, and Penny. Sarah and Jud had made their excuses hours before, citing the early flight and long day ahead. They left the party a half an hour apart for discretionary purposes.

"I cannot believe that fish of Jud's. Never in my life have I seen a more magnificent fish, on the Carron or elsewhere, and Jud played him so brilliantly," Penny said.

"Aye," Gillie Mac substantiated, "finest fish I've seen since I watched Hammish land his, and he was no more than a lad of sixteen."

Hammish smiled from his end of the bar. He wanted to say something, but he couldn't. Hammish had been at the bar too long. The castle record, belonging to him for forty-four years had been broken, a painful enough experience in and of itself, but to have it broken by a trout fisherman, from Montana, on his fifth day of salmon fishing after Hammish fished the river for a lifetime was excruciating. So, anglers being an empathetic group, Hammish's obvious sorrow was excused, understood, and even toasted to.

At two o'clock the only two men sitting at the bar were Junior and Henry. Mac had gone home. Penny had helped Hammish to bed. "Sheee-it, Junior, we gotta git up in a coupl'a hours and I ain't even begun to pack yet. I'm headin for the barn," Henry said, seemingly unaffected by the scotch, but Henry was amazing that way. He could drink a fifth of whisky and outside of his eyes glazing slightly, the alcohol had little effect. His speech didn't slur, his thoughts remained fairly coherent. It would be the walking that gave his inebriation away.

Junior, who had developed quite a taste for the single malt in his brief sojourn to Scotland, was quite the opposite. He had drunk half of what Henry had and was twice as drunk and apparently so. "Yeah, we s-s-should go to bed. Hashn't thish been the besht week ever in your life? And wasshn't it wonderful about ol' Jud's fis-s-sh. Twenty nine pound shsevehenteen ounches. Thatch shumptin."

"That's somethin' all right, but tonight he landed one about a hunnert and thirty pounds, I'd guess."

Junior would have been confused without the drink, but with the drink he looked suddenly lost, "Jud we . . . we . . . went fissshin' tonight?

~

A hundred and how many pounds? Hey, wait jushht a minute. Whaddaya talkin' about?"

"Sarah and Jud are in love."

"I know that," Junior said. "Everybody knowsh that. Been in love for yearsh."

"Yeah, I know. But this time it's serious, Junior."

"Oh, that'sh nice," Junior agreed without actually understanding and then spooled onto the floor in a boneless mass. Henry, barely able to walk himself, had to then carry the unconscious Junior to a couch where he deposited him for the night. With that Henry went up the stairs, stumbling past Jud's door where all was quiet.

Inside Sarah slept in Jud's arms while he stared out into the night, the Carron shining only where the castle's lights hit its currents. They cried about Annie. They laughed about life and made some unexpected short-range decisions. Jud caught his salmon once more, in detail, and they made love twice.

Early morning found Henry and Driver Mac, replacing his Gillie Mac persona for the day, waiting by the Rover. In the backseat of the Rover and holding his head was Junior promising never to drink again, a promise he would keep until Thanksgiving.

Jud and Sarah were late, and when they finally did make it down the stairs, it was very evident they were going to be even later since neither of them was dressed for the flight and they had no luggage. "So, what the hell are ya doing? We gotta flight to git to and we gotta git goin'," said Henry.

"Well, uh . . . we're not coming," Jud answered.

"*What*?" Henry was incredulous.

"Yeah, we've decided to stay another week. Rent a car see some more of Scotland. Sort of play each day as it comes."

Junior stuck his head out the window, "What's going on?"

"We're going to stay another week, Junior," Jud explained once more.

"Oh, okay," Junior said and rolled his window back up. He was instantly aware with that sentence that he didn't want to talk or hear. Thinking was painful but bits of last night's conversation were coming back to him through the fog, something about Jud catching a hundred-plus-pounder, and when the realization that Sarah was the hundred-plus-pounder collided with the unexpected news of their staying, the impact made him wince. This romance came as more of a shock to Junior than to nearly everyone else in the castle. He, with the rest of Travers Corners, had long been waiting for this moment to arrive, and when it did he had missed it. Oblivious to all the signals and flirtations during the week between the two, Junior had spent his entire stay with Hammish in the world of salmon, angling, and its lore. But, even if it had happened back home on Main Street and right before his eyes, Junior would have a good chance of missing it if there was fishing to talk about.

"Henry, we really best be goin'," Driver Mac said.

Nothing more could have been said. Now there was no time. But nothing more needed to be said. So Henry just shook Jud's hand and gave Sarah a hug. "You two have a good time. Anything ya need me to take care of?"

"Would you mind calling Sal when you get home and tell him he's in charge for another week?" Sarah asked.

"You got it. See ya back in Travers." The Rover pulled away. Junior's arm appeared briefly out the window. He waved twice, but the motion nauseated him.

Penny appeared in the doorway behind them. Perplexed he asked, "I say, wasn't that the Rover and your ride to the airport pulling away?"

"Yep," Jud answered, "Sarah and I have decided to stay in Scotland for another week. Rent a car. See some of the sights."

"Nonsense, you won't rent a car. You will borrow the Rover for the week. And know you are welcome to stay any night you want here, all of the nights if you wish. I'll see that Mac can be your gillie, if you care to fish, and I'll have Araminta take some of the . . ." Penny's voice trailed off as he led the two of them back into Pendleton Castle.

When Henry and Junior arrived home they naturally told their respective women, Dolores and Pam, the news, the lead story from Scotland. Dolores cried first. Then she needed to tell someone, actually anyone until she had told everyone the news. It wasn't Junior's lead story. What had happened between Jud and Sarah came only after he had told Pam, in detail, about his Atlantic salmon.

~

Quicker than you can say Internet, faster than a fax, Dolores working the switchboard down at the parlor, and Pam covering her end from the post office side, the two spread the headlines of the Scottish romance, and by the middle of the same day the story, still pretty much intact, had reached nearly every man, woman, and child in Travers Corners, the outlying ranches, and certain sectors of Missoula.

There were a few glitches in the gossip pipeline, but not until the news had reached the farthest ranches on Carrie Creek. There the news had turned to rumor, but only slightly. The Schrupps, the Hjersmans, and the Colwells, the last three on an eight-party line, heard that what had happened between Jud and Sarah was more than a long overdue romance. They heard they had been married and were now honeymooning all over Europe.

When Doc got the news, a wizened smile crossed his face. Breaking a few fingers had an unforeseen reason, and all that he said was, "It's about time." He would think of himself from that day on as the unintentional matchmaker to a match made long ago.

Uncle Sal, being Italian, Sarah being his niece and only relation, naturally got emotional with the news concerning the two. Big tears formed in his overly large brown eyes. But the heartfelt emotion was twofold. Mostly he was ecstatic. "Da bot'a dem are gonna be happy from here on out. Done deal. I know dis wit'out any doubts whatsoever. Dey were made for each other. I knew it from da first day we came to Travers, only the timin' was all wrong." But beneath his elation there was also concern about Jud. Not about him becoming a son-in-law, but because his staying in Scotland the extra week would be conflicting the other loves in Sal's life—baseball, Little League, and his team, the T. C. Yankees. Jud wouldn't be there to help him with a week of practice, and worst of all he wouldn't be there for the season opener against Reynolds.

Four days later, it was Sal who got the call. Sarah and Jud had been married in Inverness. There was more good news. They were coming home two days earlier than expected. Jud would be there to help him coach the team for the opener.

The news of Jud and Sarah's marriage traveled like light itself, ignited by Dolores on the parlor network. Pam was all over it at the post office.

People gathered in the streets with the news, and the good Reverend Kilbourne down at the D. Downey Baptist Church pulled on the bell as if St. Peter himself was coming to meeting.

Down at the Tin Cup Bar and Cafe, the bar side was open and packed and Sal was buying the rounds.

Over at McCracken's, the cultural hub of Travers, everyone, shoppers and clerks alike, came to a halt, everyone of course but Junior, who only hesitated slightly when the news reached him because he was in the middle of telling Lee Wright about his Atlantic salmon. Lee, who had come into the general store that morning for nothing more than a can of Copenhagen, hoped to be back at the ranch in time for supper.

Henry only nodded when he heard the news. He was glad for his friends.

Now, in the history of Travers, as in the history of all small towns, there is news, good and bad, and there is gossip, true or false. The news, the truth, comes in the past tense, verified events. Things that have certifiably happened. Gossip, perhaps the truth, forms in the present tense. Things that could be happening. It is usually centered around who is doing what to whom, who is saying what about whom, and who is sneaking out on whom. And with any luck at all for Dolores and the ladies down at the parlor, all those involved in the latter will make the gossip scandalous.

But, this was one of the rare times when the news had arrived, at least to those ranches at the upper reaches of Carrie Creek, the Schrupps, the Hjersmans, and the Colwells, in the future tense—a strong form of gossip. Up there the wedding news had already fallen into the history pages. They'd known about it for days.

It was a great day for Travers Corners, and a better day for Jud and Sarah, with better days ahead. But it would still have to take a backseat to the town's most memorable day—June 12, 1932, when Herbert Hoover stopped for gas.

~

Afterword

It took a couple of months for the buzz about Jud and Sarah's marriage to finally die down around Travers Corners. But there were other decisions facing the pair, which kept them the focus of the town's collective eye.

The first two big changes came right away. Sarah kept her last name, but sold her home. With the revenue from her house she introduced taste and features to Jud's—features found in most houses, a working stove and a refrigerator built after 1955, things like that. Jud's decor had devolved into a kind of plain, but at the same time, ugly motif, where everything was earth tones, but that was only because of the dust, an indoor camping approach to domesticity. The only thing saving his Spartan interior was his craftsmanship throughout: the cabinets, the doors, and stairway all made from wagon parts befitting a carriage house. All of the handcrafted belongings were saved intact. Everything else was changed.

The introduction of Sarah and her tasteful belongings, her furniture, curtains, and paintings turned the old carriage house into a home, and throughout all the disruption, chaos, and complications of remodeling, Jud, contrary to all the predictions, didn't seem to mind. Usually, Jud was a man who disliked change. He was a man who had been on a schedule of his own design that followed a timetable set by an errant pocket watch, for many years. About the only things you could predict about Jud were the times when he did very certain things: the time he got up, the time he ate breakfast at the Tin Cup, and the time he picked up his mail at McCracken's. Everything in between in his usual day centered around the building of boats, unless the work ethic was interrupted by an important hatch, a daydream, or the formulation of a theory involving one of life's many mysteries.

The next big change came on an afternoon in October, Jud's birthday. With all the redecorating done, when life was settling in, Henry and Dolores pulled into the yard to change all of that. In a plan developed by Sarah and Sal, the two had just returned from Big Timber with Jud's present. A present that first wiggled, then peed, then ran to Jud, tripping twice. A yellow Labrador puppy ran around the yard receiving everyone's attention until exhaustion set in causing the pup to collapse, falling precisely on Annie's old spot on the porch. The name for the pup was, of that moment, no longer a problem. She was Annie the Wonderlab Two.

After that, there were adjustments, corrections, modifications, demands, negotiations, conditions, and concessions, but there were no big changes to be made for the two of them. They knew each other well. There were no surprises. It was Jud's lackadaisical insouciance balanced nicely against Sarah's ordered responsibility. It made for a comfortable compromise on most things and, consequently, there would be more dories built at the Boat Works, and more hours away from the Tin Cup for Sarah.

Winter and spring came and went. The following July found Henry and Jud sharing an afternoon on the upper meadows of Carrie Creek. The fishing wasn't very good, but the theorizing was fantastic.

Sitting on the bank with Annie nosing his neck, Jud watched Henry fish, his bamboo rod bending back and forth, back and forth. Henry was measuring his cast for a feeding trout, back and forth, but it was a tricky lie and the breeze wasn't helping. Back and forth. When all things seemed right Henry set his fly down only to have a gust of wind at the last second blow it into the brush. Jud laughed and Annie found a stick for him to throw. The clouds encircled the Elkheart leaving a great ragged hole of blue sky over the heart of the valley.

Jud gave thought, the foundation to hypotheses, to the back and forth of another bamboo rod that added a chapter to Montana's storied past—the old Leonard bamboo rod his great-grandfather brought forth from Boston to Denver where it caught the eye of D. Downey, whose sister, Carrie, caught Traver's eye. Gifting the rod to D. Downey, his new brother-in-law took it back to Scotland.

A century and more goes past, and from out of nowhere, cousin Penny comes forth to Travers Corners with the bamboo rod in hand. A few years later Jud goes back to Pendleton castle to visit his past, the cast of distant cousins, and, of course, the bamboo rod. Henceforth, on loan for one year, one hundred and twenty years later, the Leonard rod is back in the Elkheart displayed in its case down at the town's library.

How strange it was, if not a little bit mystic, Jud wondered, wonder being the springboard to theory, that romance came twice as the direct result of the old cane rod. Had D. Downey not commented on the rod, a friendship might never have formed. Traver then certainly would not have met Carrie. And without the fly rod and the four first-class tickets coming forth because of Araminta's finding the rod, Jud and Sarah, with a little help from Doc's hand, would have never gone back to Scotland. Back and forth, back and forth.

Jud's thoughts were now spinning. Wonderments and speculations were flying easily through his mind. Proof of theory within the concrete confines of science is difficult, but when trying to establish laws in the metaphysical, where all of Jud's best theories lie, it is a real tough sell. But there was something mythical if not magical about that cane wand, the back and forth bamboo. Jud knew it. What the connection was he would have to work on later because right now Annie was pestering him with a stick that needed tossing.

Throwing the stick a few times, Jud waded back into Carrie Creek. He looked up to see Henry casting again, back and forth, back and forth. But upon examination, Jud knew the line, while going back and forth, was doing so in elliptical arcs, especially if those casts are being thrown by a slow-moving bamboo—the line goes up on the backcast, then the line drops slightly as the loop is formed. It is then sent forward on an upward plane to unfurl, fly last, where it drops again only to be sent to the backcast. The line formed by casting, the elliptical arcs, the lazy, the lying-on-its-side elongated eight, Jud realized and for the first time, was the mathematical sign for infinity.

Within a few minutes there had been the metaphysical connection between romance and the old fly rod, followed by the realization that casting was a slow-moving rhythmic sign for the infinite. Because the incidents happened within moments of one another, Jud, in his never-ending search for unexplored theories pertaining to things that will never be understood (let alone proven), tried to see if there was some correlation. Jud's head drifted back for a look at the clouds as he entered briefly that whimsical branch of science where magic meets math, where proven theorems come together with daydreams, and where reality blends with imagination. "Fishing, romance, and infinity," Jud said to Annie, "Now there is a wondrous thought. I mean could there be a better way to spend forever than trout fishing and having romance?" Annie Two cocked her head. She rarely understood his theorems the way her namesake did, but she was still a pup, and Jud had great hopes for her.

He looked down to watch the water of Carrie Creek curl around his legs. A trout rose. Then another. Jud would have to put hypothesizing on hold until tonight when he would pursue his theories, usually conceived somewhere between the Elkheart Valley and the ethereal plane, with Sarah in the kitchen as they love and laugh their way around the Boat Works.

But for right now there were trout rising on the meadows of Carrie Creek where all the beauty ever dreamed of flows into the reasons for it all.

~

About the Author

Scott Waldie lives in Sheridan, Montana, with his wife Jane. He is the author of *Travers Corners* and *Return to Travers Corners*. A fly-fishing guide for twenty years, a travel writer for ten, Waldie has fished all over the world, but now favors the home waters. His fiction and travelogues have appeared in *Gray's Sporting Journal*, *Fly Fisherman*, *Sporting Classics*, *Big Sky Journal*, and *Rod and Reel*.